THE TENTH MAN

OTHER BOOKS BY

GRAHAM GREENE

NOVELS

The Man Within · Stamboul Train
It's a Battlefield · England Made Me · A Gun for Sale
Brighton Rock · The Confidential Agent
The Power and the Glory · The Ministry of Fear
The Heart of the Matter · The Third Man
The End of the Affair · Loser Takes All
The Quiet American · Our Man in Havana
A Burnt-out Case · Travels with my Aunt · The Comedians
The Honorary Consul · The Human Factor
Doctor Fischer of Geneva or The Bomb Party
Monsignor Quixote

SHORT STORIES

Collected Stories
(including *Twenty-one Stories, A Sense of Reality*
and *May We Borrow Your Husband?*)

TRAVEL

Journey Without Maps · The Lawless Roads
In Search of a Character

ESSAYS

Collected Essays · The Pleasure Dome
British Dramatists

PLAYS

The Living Room · The Potting Shed
The Complaisant Lover · Carving a Statue
The Return of A. J. Raffles · The Great Jowett
For Whom the Bell Chimes
Yes and No

AUTOBIOGRAPHY

A Sort of Life · Ways of Escape
Getting to Know the General

BIOGRAPHY

Lord Rochester's Monkey

CHILDREN'S BOOKS

The Little Train · The Little Steamroller
The Little Horse Bus · The Little Fire Engine

Graham Greene

THE TENTH MAN

The Bodley Head and
Anthony Blond
London

British Library Cataloguing
in Publication Data
Greene, Graham
The Tenth Man
I. Title
823'.912 [F]PR6013.R44
ISBN 0 370 30831 X

All rights reserved
MGM/UA Home Entertainment Group
© Introduction and revised text
Graham Greene 1985
Printed in Great Britain for
The Bodley Head Ltd
9 Bow Street, London WC2E 7AL
and Anthony Blond
by William Clowes Ltd, Beccles
First published 1985

CONTENTS

INTRODUCTION

I

In 1948 when I was working on *The Third Man* I seem to have completely forgotten a story called *The Tenth Man* which was ticking away like a time-bomb somewhere in the archives of Metro-Goldwyn-Mayer in America.

In 1983 a stranger wrote to me from the United States telling me that a story of mine called *The Tenth Man* was being offered for sale by MGM to an American publisher. I didn't take the matter seriously. I thought that I remembered—incorrectly, as it proved—an outline which I had written towards the end of the war under a contract with my friend Ben Goetz, the representative of MGM in London. Perhaps the outline had covered two pages of typescript—there seemed, therefore, no danger of publication, especially as the story had never been filmed.

The reason I had signed the contract was that I feared when the war came to an end and I left government service that my family would be in danger from the precarious nature of my finances. I had not before the war been able to support them from writing novels alone. I had indeed been in debt to my publishers until 1938, when *Brighton Rock* sold eight thousand copies and squared our accounts temporarily. *The Power and the Glory*, appearing more or less at the same time as the invasion of the West in an edition of about three thousand five hundred copies, hardly improved the situation. I had no confidence in my future as a novelist and I welcomed in 1944 what proved to be an almost slave contract with MGM which at least assured us all enough to live on for a couple of years in return for the idea of *The Tenth Man*.

Then recently came the astonishing and disquieting news that Mr Anthony Blond had bought all the book and serial rights on the mysterious story for a quite large sum, the author's royalties of course to be paid to MGM. He courteously sent me the typescript for any revision I might wish to make and it proved to be not two pages of outline but a complete short novel of about thirty thousand words. What surprised and aggravated me most of all was that I found this forgotten story very readable—indeed I prefer it in many ways to *The Third Man*, so that I had no longer any personal excuse for opposing publication even if I had the legal power, which was highly doubtful. All the same Mr Blond very generously agreed to publish the story jointly with my regular publishers, The Bodley Head.

After this had been amicably arranged mystery was added to mystery. I found by accident in a cupboard in Paris an old cardboard box containing two manuscripts, one being a diary and commonplace-book which I had apparently kept during 1937 and 1938. Under the date 26 December 1937 I came on this passage: 'Discussed film with Menzies [an American film director]. Two notions for future films. One: a political situation like that in Spain. A decimation order. Ten men in prison draw lots with matches. A rich man draws the longest match. Offers all his money to anyone who will take his place. One, for the sake of his family, agrees. Later, when he is released, the former rich man visits anonymously the family who possess his money, he himself now with nothing but his life. . . .'

The bare bones of a story indeed. The four dots with which the entry closes seem now to represent the years of war that followed during which all memory of the slender idea was lost in the unconscious. When in 1944 I picked up the tale of Chavel and Janvier I must have thought it an idea which had just come to my mind, and yet I can only now suppose that those two characters had been working away far down in the dark cave of the unconscious while the world burnt.

The unexpected return of *The Tenth Man* from the archives of MGM led also to a search in my own archives where I discovered copies of two more ideas for films, and these may amuse readers of this book. The first idea (not a bad one it seems to me now, though nothing came of it) was called 'Jim Braddon and the War Criminal'.

Here is how the outline went—a not untimely story even today, with Barbie awaiting trial.

There is an old legend that somewhere in the world every man has his double. This is the strange story of Jim Braddon.

Jim Braddon was a high-grade salesman employed by a breakfast cereal company in Philadelphia: a placid honest man who would never have injured anything larger than a fly. He had a wife and two children whom he spoilt. The 1941 war had affected him little for he was over forty and his employers claimed that he was indispensable. But he took up German—he had a German grandmother—because he thought that one day this might prove useful, and that was the only new thing that happened to him between 1941 and 1945. Sometimes he saw in the paper the picture of Schreiber, the Nazi Inspector-General of the concentration camps, but except that one of his children pretended to see a likeness to this Nazi, nobody else even commented on the fact.

In the autumn of 1945 a captured U-boat commander confessed that he had landed Schreiber on the coast of Mexico, and the film opens on a Mexican beach with a rubber dinghy upturned by the breakers and Schreiber's body visible through the thin rim of water. The tide recedes and the land crabs come out of their holes. But the hunt for Schreiber is on, for the crabs will soon eliminate all evidence of his death.

The push for post-war trade is also on, and Braddon

is despatched by his firm for a tour of Central and South America. In the plane he looks at *Life*, which carries the story of the hunt for Schreiber. His neighbour, a small, earnest, bespectacled man full of pseudo-scientific theories, points out the likeness to him. 'You don't see it,' he says. 'I doubt whether one person in ten thousand would see it because what we mean by likeness as a rule is not the shape of the face and skull but the veil a man's experience and character throw over the features. You are like Schreiber, but no one would notice it because you have led a very different life. That can't alter the shape of the ears, but it's the expression of the eyes people look at.' Apart from the joking child he is the only person who has noticed the likeness. Luckily for Braddon—and for himself—the stranger leaves the plane at the next halt. Half-way to Mexico City the plane crashes and all lives but Braddon's are lost.

Braddon has been flung clear. His left arm is broken, he is cut about the face, and he has lost his memory from the concussion. The accident has happened at night and he has cautiously—for he is a very careful man—emptied his pockets and locked his papers in his brief-case which of course is lost. When he comes to, he has no identity but his features, and those he shares with a dead man. He searches his pockets for a clue, but finds them empty of anything that will help him: only some small change, and in each pocket of the jacket a book. One is a paper-covered

Heine: the other an American paperback. He finds that he can read both languages. Searching his jacket more carefully, he discovers a wad of ten-dollar notes, clean ones, sewn into the lining.

It is unnecessary in this short summary to work out his next adventures in detail: somehow he makes his way to a railroad and gets on a train to Mexico City. His idea is to find a hospital as quickly as he can, but in the wash room at the station he sees hanging by the mirror a photograph of Schreiber and a police description in Spanish and English. Perhaps the experiences of the last few days have hardened his expression, for now he can recognize the likeness. He believes he has found his name. His face takes on another expression now—that of the hunted man.

He does not know where to go or what to do: he is afraid of every policeman; he attracts attention by his furtiveness, and soon the papers bear the news that Schreiber has been seen in Mexico City. He lets his beard grow, and with the growth of the beard he loses his last likeness to the old Jim Braddon.

He is temporarily saved by Schreiber's friends, a group of Fascists to whom Schreiber had borne introductions and who are expecting him. Among these are a brother and sister—a little, sadistic, pop-eyed Mexican whom we will call Peter for his likeness to Peter Lorre and his shifty, beautiful sister whom we will call Laureen for obvious reasons of casting. Laureen sets herself the task of restoring Jim's memory—the memory which she considers Schreiber *should* possess. They fall in love: in her case without reserve, believing that she knows the worst about this man: in his with a reserve which he doesn't himself understand.

Peter, however, is incurably careless. His love of pain and violence get in the way of caution, and as a result of some incident yet to be worked out, Jim is caught by the Mexican police, while the others escape.

Schreiber could hardly have complained of rough treatment. Nor does Jim complain. He has no memory of his crimes, but he accepts the fact that he has committed them. The police force him to sit through a film of Buchenwald, and he watches with horror and shame the lean naked victims of Schreiber. He has no longer any wish to escape. He is content to die.

He is sent north to the American authorities, and the preliminary proceedings against him start. The new bearded Schreiber face becomes a feature of the Press. His family among others see the picture, but never for a moment does it occur to any of them that this is Jim.

Among the spectators at the trial, however, is the little spectacled pseudo-psychologist who was on the plane with Jim. He doesn't recognize Jim, but he is puzzled by Schreiber (Schreiber is not acting true to character), and he remembers what he said to the man in the plane, that likeness is not a matter of skull measurements but of expression. The expression of horror and remorse is not one he would have expected to see in Schreiber's eyes. This man claims to have lost his memory, and yet he denies nothing. Suppose after all they have got a man who is simply similar in bone structure . . .

Meanwhile Peter and Laureen, who escaped from the police trap which had closed on Jim, travel north. They plan a rescue. What their plan is I don't know myself yet. Violent and desperate, it offers one chance in a hundred. But it comes off. Jim is whipped away from the court itself, and the hunt is on again. But this is not Mexico, and the hunt is a very short one. They are trapped in a suburban villa.

But Peter has taken hostages: a woman and her child who were in the house when they broke in. Jim has been obeying his companions like an automaton: there hasn't even been time to take off his handcuffs, but at this last example of Fascist mentality his mind seems to wake. He turns on his friends and the woman he has loved. He knocks out Peter with the handcuffs and gets his gun. The woman too has a gun. They face each other across the length of the room like duellists. She says, 'My dear, you won't shoot me.' But he shoots and her shot comes a second after his, but it isn't aimed at him: it hits her brother who has regained his feet and is on the point of attacking. Her last words are, 'You aren't Schreiber. You can't be. You're decent. Who the hell are you?'

Braddon gives himself up, and the truth of the

psychologist's theory is glaringly exhibited. The likeness to Schreiber has proved to be physical only. I imagine the little man remembers at this point the man he talked to on the plane, he gives evidence, produces Braddon's family. The happy ending needs to be worked out, but the strange case of Jim Braddon really comes to an end with the shots in the suburban villa. After that there's just the reaching for the coats under the seats. Anyone in the stalls could tell you what happens now.

3

The second sketch for a film, entitled *Nobody to Blame*, was written about the same time for my friend Cavalcanti. He liked the idea, but our work on it never began, for when he submitted it to the Board of Film Censors, he was told that they could not grant a certificate to a film making fun of the Secret Service. So this story too joined the others for a while in the unconscious, to emerge some ten years later as a novel—simplified but not, I think, necessarily improved—called *Our Man in Havana*.

There is no censorship for novels, but I learnt later that MI5 suggested to MI6 that they should bring an action against the book for a breach of official secrets. What secret had I betrayed? Was it the possibility of using bird shit as a secret ink? But luckily C, the head

of MI6, had a better sense of humour than his colleague in MI5, and he discouraged him from taking
action.

Nobody to Blame

I

Richard Tripp is the agent of Singer Sewing Machines
in some Baltic capital similar to Tallinn. He is a small
inoffensive man of a rather timid disposition with a
passionate love for postage stamps, Gilbert and Sullivan's music and his wife, and a passionate loyalty to
Singer Sewing Machines. Unofficially he is Agent
B.720 of the British Secret Service. The year is
1938/39.

Mrs Tripp—Gloria—is much younger than Tripp
and it is to give her a good life that he has allowed
himself to be enlisted in the Secret Service. He feels
he must spend more money on her than Singer
provide in order to keep her, although she has a
genuine fondness for her dim husband. She knows
nothing, of course, of his activities.

At HQ in London Tripp is regarded as one of their
soundest agents—unimaginative, accurate, not easily

ruffled. He is believed to have a network of sub-agents throughout Germany and he keeps in touch with HQ through the medium of his business reports written to his firm. What HQ does not know is that in fact Tripp has no agents at all. He invents all his reports and when London expresses dissatisfaction with an agent he simply dismisses one notional source and engages another equally notional. Naturally he draws salaries and expenses for all the imaginary agents.

His active imagination, from which he has drawn the details of a large underground factory near Leipzig for the construction of a secret explosive, does on one occasion lead to a little trouble with the local police. From an independent source London learns that B.720 is being shadowed, and they send him an urgent warning, but the warning arrives too late.

At the end of a programme of Gilbert and Sullivan opera by the Anglo-Latesthian Society in which Tripp takes a leading part the Chief of Police, who is sitting in the front row, hands up a bouquet with a card attached and the request that he may have a drink with Tripp immediately in his dressing-room. There he tells Tripp that the German Embassy have complained of his activities. Tripp confesses to his deception.

The Chief of Police is amused and pleased that Tripp's presence will keep out any serious agents, and he accepts the gift of a sewing machine for his wife. He will ensure that Tripp's messages go safely out of the country—and to keep the German Embassy quiet, he decides, they can have a look at them on the way. London's warning comes on the heels of the interview, and Tripp sends back a message announcing that he has appointed the Chief of Police himself as one of his agents, enclosing that officer's first report on the chief political characters of Latesthia and requesting that as first payment and bonus the Chief, who he says is an ardent stamp collector, should receive a rare Triangular Cape, and when the stamp arrives of course he sticks it in his own album. This gives him an idea, and soon the Chief of the Secret Service is commenting to the HQ officer in charge of Tripp's station, 'What a lot of stamp collectors he has among his agents.'

'It might be worse. Do you remember old Stott's agents? They all wanted art photos from Paris.'

'Stott's at a loose end, isn't he?'

'Yes.'

'Send him over to take a look at Tripp's station. He may be able to give Tripp some advice. I always believe in letting two sound men get together.'

2

Stott is a much older man than Tripp. He is bottle-nosed and mottled with a little round stomach and a roving eye. Tripp is naturally apprehensive of his visit and expects to be unmasked at any moment, but to his relief he finds that Stott is much more interested in the foods and wines of Latesthia, and in the night life, than in the details of Tripp's organization. There are even fleeting moments when Tripp wonders whether it could possibly be that Stott also had run his station on notional lines, but such a thought of course can hardly be held for long.

The first evening together Stott remarks, 'Now, the brothels, old man. You've got good contacts there, I suppose?'

Tripp has never been in a brothel in his life. He has to own that he has overlooked brothels.

'Most important, old man. Every visiting business-man goes to the brothels. Got to have them covered.'

He has a night round the town with Stott and gets into trouble with his wife for returning at two in the morning. Stott moves on to Berlin, but he has sown seeds in Tripp's mind. His notional agents in future follow a Stott line. London is asked to approve in rapid succession the madame of a high class 'house', a café singer, and, his most imaginative effort to date, a well-known Latesthian cinema actress who is described as Agent B.720's (i.e. Tripp's) mistress. Of course he has never spoken to her in his life, and he has no idea that she is in fact a German agent.

3

A second crisis—needing more delicate handling than Stott's—blows up. The threat of European war is deepening and London considers that Tripp's position in Latesthia is a key one. He must have a proper staff: Singer Sewing Machines are persuaded in the interests of the nation to build up their agency in Latesthia and they inform Tripp that they are sending out to him a secretary-typist and a clerk. Tripp is innocently delighted that his work for Singer has borne such fruit and that sewing machines are booming. He is less pleased, however, when the clerk and typist arrive and prove to be members of the Secret Service sent to assist him in handling his now complicated network of agents.

The clerk is a young man with a penetrating cockney accent and an enormous capacity for hero-worship —and heroine-worship. His devotion is equally aroused by what he considers the experience and daring of Tripp and by the legs and breasts of Tripp's wife. His name is Cobb, and he has an annoying habit of asking questions. He says himself, 'You don't have to bother to explain things, Chief. Just let me dig in and ask questions, and I'll get the hang of things for myself.'

The typist—Miss Jixon—is a withered spinster of forty-four who regards everyone and everything with suspicion. She believes that even the most innocent labourer is in the pay of the secret police, and she is shocked by the inadequacy of the security arrangements in the office. She insists on all blotting paper being locked in the safe and all typewriting ribbons being removed at night. This is highly inconvenient as no one is very good at fixing typewriter ribbons. Once she finds a used ribbon thrown in the wastepaper basket instead of being burnt in the incinerator and she begins to demonstrate the danger of the practice by deciphering the impress on the ribbon. All she can make out is 'Red lips were ne'er so red nor eyes so pure', which turns out to be a line of a sonnet written by Cobb—obviously with Mrs Tripp in mind.

'He's really rather sweet,' Mrs Tripp says.

The chief problem that Tripp has to solve is how to disguise the fact that he has no sources for his reports. He finds this unexpectedly easy. He goes shopping and returns with envelopes that have been handed to him, he says, from under the counter: he makes a great show of testing perfectly innocent letters about sewing machines for secret inks: he takes Cobb for a round of the town and now and then in the restaurants points out his agents.

'A very discreet man. You'll see he won't show the least flicker of recognition.'

The monthly payments to agents present a difficulty: Miss Jixon objects strongly to the payments being made by himself.

'It's irregular, insecure: HQ would never countenance it.'

By this time, for the sake of his assistants, he has drawn up an impressive chart of his sources: with the immediate head agents who control each gang. Miss Jixon insists that from now on he shall cut off his personal contacts with all but his head agents (of whom the cinema actress is one) and that he should meet them on every occasion in a different disguise.

Disguises become the bane of Tripp's life. What makes it worse, of course, is that his wife knows nothing. Miss Jixon shows a horrible ingenuity: Tripp's make-up box for the operatic productions of the Anglo-Latesthian Society is requisitioned. He finds himself being forced to slip out of back doors in red wigs and return by front doors in black wigs. She makes him carry at least two soft hats of varying colours in his overcoat pockets, so that he can change hats. Spectacles, horn-rimmed and steel-rimmed, bulge his breast pockets.

The strain tells. He becomes irritable and Mrs Tripp is reduced to tears. Cobb is torn between hero-worship and heroine-worship.

Next crisis: the enemy begins to take Tripp seriously. He becomes aware that he is followed everywhere—even to the Anglo-Latesthian musical *soirée*—'an evening with Edward German and Vaughan Williams'. Miss Jixon's security arrangements have been a little too good and the Germans are no longer able to keep an eye on the reports he sends.

She has objected to the use of the Chief of Police as transmitter and has evolved an elaborate method of sending secret ink messages on postage stamps. (There is a moment when Miss Jixon skirts shyly round the possibility of bird shit as a secret ink.) Unfortunately the ink never develops properly—single words will appear and disappear with disconcerting rapidity.

Tripp, in order to be able to fake his expenses sheet and show the expenditure of huge sums for entertainment, is forced to dine out at least three times a week. He hates restaurant meals—and in any case it would be fatal if one of his assistants saw him dining alone. He therefore rents a room in the suburbs and retires there for a quiet read (his favourite authors are Charles Lamb and Newbolt) or the writing of a bogus report, taking a little food out of the larder with him. (In his account book this appears as 'Dinner for three (political sources) with wines, cigars, etc., £5.10s.0d'.) This constant dining out had never been necessary in the old days before his assistants came, and Mrs Tripp resents it.

The domestic crisis reaches its culmination when on pay day Tripp has to pretend to visit the home of the cinema actress with pay for her sub-sources. Cobb keeps guard in the street outside and Tripp, wearing a false moustache, proceeds up to the actress's flat, rings the bell and enquires for an imaginary person. He turns away from the closing door just as Mrs Tripp comes down from visiting a friend in the flat above. His excuse that he was trying to sell a sewing machine seems weak to Mrs Tripp in view of his false moustache.

Domestic harmony is further shattered when Cobb, anxious to make peace between his hero and his heroine, tells Mrs Tripp everything—or what he thinks is everything. 'It's for his country, Mrs Tripp,' he says.

Mrs Tripp decides that she too will go in for patriotism. She begins to dine out too, and Tripp, not unduly disturbed, takes the opportunity of appointing her as agent with a notional lover in the Foreign Ministry.

'That fellow Tripp,' they say in London, 'deserves a decoration. The Service comes even before his wife. Good show.'

His notional mistress and his wife's notional lover are among his most interesting sources. Unfortunately, of course, his wife does not believe that his mistress is notional and her dinner companion, unlike the notional member of the Foreign Ministry, is a very real young man attached to Agriculture and Fisheries.

Mrs Tripp gets news of Tripp's hide-out and decides to track him down. She is certain she will find him in the company of the actress and that he will not be engaged in work of national importance.

The enemy are aware of his hide-out.

5

Tripp has got his legs up on the stove, some sausage rolls in his pocket, and he is reading his favourite poet Newbolt aloud, in a kind of sub-human drone which is his method with poetry. 'Play up, play up and play the game . . . the dons on the dais serene . . .' He is surprised by a knock at the door. He opens it and is still more surprised by the sight of his notional sub-agent, the cinema actress. Her car has broken down outside: can she have his help? Outside in the car two thugs crouch ready to knock Tripp on the head. A third—a tall stupid sentimental-looking German of immense physique—keeps watch at the end of the street. Tripp says he knows nothing about cars: now if it had been a sewing machine . . .

Mrs Tripp is coming up the road. She has obviously lost her way. Tripp by this time is demonstrating the special points of the Singer sewing machine . . . Mrs Tripp is cold and miserable. She leans against a fence and cries. A little further down the road the sentimental German watches her. He is torn between pity and duty. He edges nearer.

Mr Tripp is talking about poetry to the cinema actress . . .

Mrs Tripp weeps on the German's shoulder and tells him how her husband is betraying her at this moment, but she can't remember the number of the house . . .

The Germans in the car are getting very cold. They get out and begin to walk up and down . . . Tripp is reading Newbolt to the actress . . . 'His captain's hand on his shoulder smote . . .' Mrs Tripp and the German peer in at the window. He hasn't realized that this treacherous husband has anything to do with him. Mrs Tripp moans, 'Take me away,' and he obeys at once—in his comrades' car. Somebody—he is too sentimentally wrought up to care who—tries to stop him and he knocks him down. He deposits Mrs Tripp at her own door.

Tripp is still reading poetry when there is another knock at the door. One German pulls in the other German who is still unconscious. There is a babble of German explanations. 'He was trying to mend the car,' the actress explains, 'and it ran away from him.'

'I'll ring up the garage,' Tripp says. He goes in an alcove, where nobody has seen the telephone.

They prepare to knock him out. 'Wrong number,' he says furiously. 'It's the police.'

When he puts down the receiver again they knock him out.

6

Mr Tripp has not returned home for some days. Cobb and Miss Jixon are worried. Mrs Tripp is furious but finds consolation.

Tripp comes to himself inside the German Embassy. Enormous pressure is put on him to betray his organization, but he has no organization to betray. The threat forcibly resolves itself into this: either he will remain a prisoner in the Embassy until war starts, when he will be handed to the Gestapo as a spy, or he will send a message for them—containing false information carefully devised to discredit him—to London and then in due course he will be released. They show him films of concentration camps, they keep him from sleeping: he is shut up in a cell with the sentimental German, now disgraced, who wakes him whenever he tries to sleep and reproves him for betraying his wife.

The German Ambassador, in collaboration with the Military Attaché, plans out the message for him to send. On one sheet the Military Attaché notes the facts to be concealed: the date of invasion; number of divisions etc. On the other they note the lies to be revealed. A breeze from the open window whips the papers around. The wrong notes (that is to say the true notes) are handed to Tripp to write in secret ink. Tripp gives way. To send one more message of false information seems a small price to pay.

To make all secure and ensure that no Tripp message will ever be believed again, the Germans instruct the Chief of Police to go to the British Ambassador and expose Tripp's dealings with him —the invented messages which he used to show to the Germans before transmitting them. He gives the impression that Tripp knew that the Germans saw them.

Tripp is arrested by the police immediately he leaves the German Embassy. He is escorted home where he is allowed to pack a bag. Mrs Tripp is not there. Cobb shows him a decoded cable from London: 'Dismiss Agent XY.27 [his wife]. Intercepted correspondence to school friend shows she is carrying on intrigue with . . . of Agriculture and Fisheries Ministry instead of . . . of Foreign Ministry. Unreliable.'

Tripp says goodbye to his home, to Cobb and Miss Jixon, to his make-up box, presented to him by the Anglo-Latesthian Society, to his collected works of Gilbert and Sullivan. He empties his pockets of the false moustache, soft hats, spectacles. 'These were the trouble,' he says sadly to Miss Jixon.

He is put on board a plane to England.

An official enquiry awaits him at HQ. His Ambassador's report has been received, but opinion among his judges before he comes is divided. The trouble is that his reports have been welcomed by the armed forces. The whole Secret Service will look foolish if they have to recall hundreds of reports over the last two years—ones which have been acclaimed as 'most valuable'. The head of the enquiry points out that it will discredit the whole Service. Any of their agents could have done the same. None of them will be believed in future.

A message arrives that Tripp is in the outer office, and the youngest member of the enquiry—a dapper, earnest FO type—goes out to see him. He whispers to him urgently, 'Everything will be all right. Deny everything.'

'If only,' the chairman is saying, 'he hadn't sent that last message. All his other messages are matters of opinion. You remember the underground works at Leipzig. After all, they are underground—we can't be *sure* he invented them. General Hays particularly liked that report. He said it was a model report. We've used it in our training courses. But this one—it gives a time and date for zero hour, and the source claimed—the German Military Attaché himself—you can't get round that. Such and such divisions will cross the frontiers at ten o'clock today. If we hadn't been warned by the Ambassador we'd have had the whole Army, Navy and Air Force ringing us up to know who the devil had sent such nonsense. Come in, Tripp. Sit down. This is a very serious matter. You know the charges against you.'

'I admit everything.'

The dapper young man whispers excitedly, 'No, no, I said deny.'

'You can't possibly admit everything,' the chairman interrupts with equal excitement, 'it's for us to tell you what you admit and what you don't admit. Of course this last message—' The telephone rings: he raises the receiver: 'Yes, yes. Good God!'

He puts the receiver down and addresses the enquiry board. 'The Germans crossed the Polish frontier this morning. Under the circumstances, gentlemen, I think we should congratulate Mr Tripp on his last message from Latesthia. It is unfortunate that bungling in the British Embassy resulted in no use being made of it—but those after all are the chances of the Service. We can say with confidence among ourselves that the Secret Service was informed of the date and time of war breaking out.'

Tripp is given the OBE. He is also appointed chief lecturer at the course for recruits to the Secret Service. We see him last as he comes forward to the blackboard, cue in hand, after being introduced to the recruits as 'one of our oldest and soundest officers —the man who obtained advance news of the exact date and even the hour of the German attack —Richard Tripp will lecture on "How to Run a Station Abroad".'

THE TENTH MAN

PART

I

I

Most of them told the time very roughly by their meals, which were unpunctual and irregular: they amused themselves with the most childish games all through the day, and when it was dark they fell asleep by tacit consent—not waiting for a particular hour of darkness for they had no means of telling the time exactly: in fact there were as many times as there were prisoners. When their imprisonment started they had three good watches among thirty-two men, and a second-hand and unreliable—or so the watch-owners claimed —alarm clock. The two wrist-watches were the first to go: their owners left the cell at seven o'clock one morning—or seven-ten the alarm clock said—and presently, some hours later, the watches reappeared on the wrists of two of the guards.

That left the alarm clock and a large old-fashioned silver watch on a chain belonging to the Mayor of Bourge. The alarm clock belonged to an engine driver called Pierre, and a sense of competition grew between the two men. Time, they considered, belonged to them and not to the twenty-eight other men. But there were two times, and each man defended his own with a terrible passion. It was a passion which separated them from their comrades, so that at any hour of the day they could be found in the same corner of the great concrete shed: they even took their meals together.

Once the mayor forgot to wind his watch: it had been a day of rumour, for during the night they had heard shooting from the direction of the city, just as they had heard it before the two men with wrist-watches were taken away, and the word 'hostage' grew in each brain like a heavy cloud which takes by a caprice of wind and density the shape of letters. Strange ideas grow in prison and the mayor and the engine driver drew together yet more intimately: it was as though they feared that the Germans chose deliberately the men with watches to rob them of time: the mayor even began to suggest to his fellow prisoners that the two remaining timepieces should be kept hidden rather than that all should lose their services, but when he began to put this idea into words the notion suddenly seemed to resemble cowardice and he broke off in mid-sentence.

Whatever the cause that night, the mayor forgot to wind his watch. When he woke in the morning, as soon as it was light enough to see he looked at his watch. 'Well,' Pierre said, 'what is the time? What does the antique say?' The hands stood like black neglected ruins at a quarter to one. It seemed to the mayor the most terrible moment of his life: worse, far worse, than the day the Germans fetched him. Prison leaves no sense unimpaired, and the sense of proportion is the first to go. He looked from face to face as though he had committed an act of treachery: he had surrendered the only true time. He thanked God that there was no one there from Bourge. There was a barber from Etain: three clerks: a lorry-driver: a greengrocer: a tobacconist—every man in the prison but one was of a lower social plane than himself, and while he felt all the greater responsibility towards them, he also felt they were easy to deceive, and he told himself that after all it was better so: better that they should believe they still had the true time with them than trust to their unguided guesses and the second-hand alarm clock.

He made a rapid calculation by the grey light through the bars. 'It's twenty-five minutes past five,' he said firmly and met the gaze of the one whom he was afraid might see through his deceit: a Paris lawyer called Chavel, a lonely fellow who made awkward attempts from time to time to prove himself human. Most of the other prisoners regarded him as an oddity, even a joke: a lawyer was not somebody with whom one lived: he was a grand doll who was taken out on particular occasions, and now he had lost his black robe.

'Nonsense,' Pierre said. 'What's come over the antique? It's just a quarter to six.'

'A cheap alarm like that always goes fast.'

The lawyer said sharply as though from habit, 'Yesterday you said it was slow.' From that moment the mayor hated Chavel: Chavel and he were the only men of position in the prison: he told himself that never would he have let Chavel down in that way, and immediately began tortuously to seek for an explanation—some underground and disgraceful motive. Although the lawyer seldom spoke and had no friends, the mayor said to himself, 'Currying popularity. He thinks he'll rule this prison. He wants to be a dictator.'

'Let's have a look at the antique,' Pierre said, but the watch was safely tethered by its silver chain weighted with seals and coins to the mayor's waistcoat. It couldn't be snatched. He could safely sneer at the demand.

But that day was marked permanently in the mayor's mind as one of those black days of terrible anxiety which form a private calendar: the day of his marriage: the day when his first child was born: the day of the council election: the day when his wife died. Somehow he had to set his watch going and adjust the hands to a plausible figure without anyone spotting him—and he felt the Paris lawyer's eyes on him the whole day. To wind the watch was fairly simple: even an active watch must be wound, and he had only to wind it to half its capacity, and then at some later hour of the day give it absent-mindedly another turn or two.

Even that did not pass unnoticed by Pierre. 'What are you at?' he asked suspiciously. 'You've wound it once. Is the antique breaking down?'

'I wasn't thinking,' the mayor said, but his mind had never been more active. It was much harder to find a chance to adjust the hands which for more than half the day pursued Pierre's time at a distance of five hours. Even nature could not here provide an opportunity. The lavatories were a row of buckets in the yard and for the convenience of the guards no man was allowed to go alone to a bucket: they went in parties of at least six men. Nor could the mayor wait till night, for no light was allowed in the cell and it would be too dark to see the hands. And all the time he had to keep a mental record of how time passed: when a chance occurred he must seize it, without hesitating over the correct quartering of an hour.

At last towards evening a quarrel broke out over the primitive card game—a kind of 'snap' with home-made cards—that some of the men spent most of their time playing. For a moment eyes were fixed on the players and the mayor took out his watch and quickly shifted the hands.

'What is the time?' the lawyer asked. The mayor started as if he had been caught in the witness-box by a sudden question: the lawyer was watching him with the strained unhappy look that was habitual to him, the look of a man who has carried nothing over from his past to buttress him in the tragic present.

'Twenty-five minutes past five.'

'I had imagined it was later.'

'That is my time,' the mayor said sharply. It was indeed *his* time: from now on he couldn't recognize even the faintest possibility of error: his time could not be wrong because he had invented it.

Louis Chavel never understood why the mayor hated him. He couldn't mistake the hatred: he had seen that look too often in court on the faces of witnesses or prisoners. Now that he was himself a prisoner he found it impossible to adjust himself to the new point of view, and his tentative approaches to his fellows failed because he always thought of them as natural prisoners, who would have found themselves prisoners in any case sooner or later because of a theft, a default or a crime of sex—while he himself was a prisoner by mistake. The mayor under these circumstances was his obvious companion: he recognized that the mayor was not a natural prisoner, although he remembered clearly a case of embezzlement in the provinces in which a mayor had been concerned: he made awkward advances and he was surprised and mystified by the mayor's dislike.

The others were kind to him and friendly: they answered when he spoke to them, but the nearest they ever came to starting a conversation with him was to wish him the time of day. It seemed to him after a while terrible that he should be wished the time of day even in a prison. 'Good day,' they would say to him and 'Good night,' as though they were calling out to him in a street as he passed along towards the courts. But they were all shut together in a concrete shed thirty-five feet long by seventeen wide.

For more than a week he had tried his best to behave like a natural prisoner, he had even forced his way into the card parties, but he had found the stakes beyond him. He would not have grudged losing money to them, but his resources—the few notes he had brought into the prison and had been allowed to keep—were beyond his companions' means, and he found the stakes for which they wished to play beyond his own. They would play for such things as a pair of socks, and the loser would thrust his naked feet into his shoes and wait for his revenge, but the lawyer was afraid to lose anything which stamped him as a gentleman, a man of position and property. He gave up playing, although in fact he had been successful and won a waistcoat with several buttons missing. Later in the dusk he gave it back to its owner, and that stamped him for ever in all their eyes—he was no sportsman. They did not condemn him for that. What else could you expect of a lawyer?

No city was more crowded than their cell, and week by week Chavel learned the lesson that one can be unbearably lonely in a city. He would tell himself that every day brought the war nearer to an end— somebody must sometime be victorious and he ceased to care much who the victor was so long as an end came. He was a hostage, but it seldom occurred to him that hostages were sometimes shot. The death of his two companions only momentarily shook him: he felt too lost and abandoned to recognize the likelihood that he might himself be picked out from the crowded cell. There was safety as well as loneliness in numbers.

Once the wish to remember, to convince himself that there was an old life from which he had come and to which he would one day return, became too acute for silence. He shifted his place in the cell alongside one of the clerks, a thin silent youth who was known for some reason to his companions by the odd soubriquet of Janvier. Was it an unexpected touch of imagination in one of his fellow prisoners that saw him as something young, undeveloped and nipped by the frost?

'Janvier,' Chavel asked, 'have you ever travelled—in France, I mean?' It was typical of the lawyer that even when he tried to make a human contact he did so by a question as though he were addressing a witness.

'Never been far out of Paris,' Janvier said, and then by a stretch of imagination he added, 'Fontainebleau. I went there one summer.'

'You don't know Brinac? It's on the main line from the Gare de l'Ouest.'

'Never heard of it,' the young man said sullenly, as though he was being accused of something, and he gave a long dry cough which sounded as though dry peas were being turned in a pan.

'Then you wouldn't know my village, St Jean de Brinac? It's about two miles out of the town to the east. That's where my house is.'

'I thought you came from Paris.'

'I work in Paris,' the lawyer said. 'When I retire I shall retire to St Jean. My father left me the house. And his father left it to him.'

'What was your father?' Janvier asked with faint curiosity.

'A lawyer.'

'And his father?'

'A lawyer too.'

'I suppose it suits some people,' the clerk said. 'It seems a bit dusty to me.'

'If you had a bit of paper,' Chavel went on, 'I could draw you a plan of the house and garden.'

'I haven't,' Janvier said. 'Don't trouble anyway. It's your house. Not mine.' He coughed again, pressing his bony hands down upon his knees. He seemed to be putting an end to an interview with a caller for whom he could do nothing. Nothing at all.

Chavel moved away. He came to Pierre and stopped. 'Could you tell me the time?' he said.

'It's five to twelve.' From close by the mayor grunted malevolently, 'Slow again.'

'In your profession,' Chavel said, 'I expect you see the world?' It sounded like the false bonhomie of a cross-examiner who wishes to catch the witness in a falsehood.

'Yes and no,' Pierre said.

'You wouldn't know by any chance a station called Brinac? About an hour's run from the Gare de l'Ouest.'

'Never been on that run,' Pierre said. 'The Gare du Nord is my station.'

'Oh, yes. Then you wouldn't know St Jean . . .' He gave it up hopelessly, and sat down again far from anyone against the cold cement wall.

It was that night that the shooting was heard for the third time: a short burst of machine-gun fire, some stray rifle shots and once what sounded like the explosion of a grenade. The prisoners lay stretched upon the ground, making no comment to each other: they waited, not sleeping. You couldn't have told in most cases whether they felt the apprehension of men in danger or the exhilaration of people waiting beside a sick-bed, listening to the first sounds of health returning to a too quiet body. Chavel lay as still as the rest: he had no fear: he was buried in this place too deeply for discovery. The mayor wrapped his arms around his watch and tried in vain to deaden the steady old-fashioned stroke: tick tock tick.

3

It was at three the next afternoon (alarm clock time) that an officer entered the cell: the first officer they had seen for weeks, and this one was very young, with inexperience even in the shape of his moustache which he had shaved too much on the left side. He was as embarrassed as a schoolboy making his first entry on a stage at a prize-giving, and he spoke abruptly so as to give the impression of a strength he did not possess. He said, 'There were murders last night in the town. The aide-de-camp of the military governor, a sergeant and a girl on a bicycle.' He added, 'We don't complain about the girl. Frenchmen have our permission to kill Frenchwomen.' He had obviously thought up his speech carefully beforehand, but the irony was over-done and the delivery that of an amateur actor: the whole scene was as unreal as a charade. He said, 'You know what you are here for, living comfortably, on fine rations, while our men work and fight. Well, now you've got to pay the hotel bill. Don't blame us. Blame your own murderers. My orders are that one man in every ten shall be shot in this camp. How many of you are there?' He shouted sharply, 'Number off,' and sullenly they obeyed, '. . . twenty-eight, twenty-nine, thirty.' They knew he knew without counting. This was just a line in his charade he couldn't sacrifice. He said, 'Your allotment then is three. We are quite indifferent as to which three. You can choose for yourselves. The funeral rites will begin at seven tomorrow morning.'

The charade was over: they could hear his feet striking sharply on the asphalt going away: Chavel wondered for a moment what syllable had been acted — 'night', 'girl', 'aside', or perhaps 'thirty', but it was of course the whole world — 'hostage'.

The silence went on a long time, and then a man

called Krogh, an Alsatian, said, 'Well, do we have to volunteer?'

'Rubbish,' said one of the clerks, a thin elderly man in pince-nez, 'nobody will volunteer. We must draw lots.' He added, 'Unless it is thought that we should go by ages — the oldest first.'

'No, no,' one of the others said, 'that would be unjust.'

'It's the way of nature.'

'Not even the way of nature,' another said. 'I had a child who died when she was five . . .'

'We must draw lots,' the mayor said firmly. 'It is the only fair thing.' He sat with his hands still pressed over his stomach, hiding his watch, but all through the cell you could hear its blunt tick tock tick. He added, 'On the unmarried. The married should not be included. They have responsibilities . . .'

'Ha, ha,' Pierre said, 'we see through that. Why should the married get off? Their work's finished. You, of course, are married?'

'I have lost my wife,' the mayor said, 'I am not married now. And you . . .'

'Married,' Pierre said.

The mayor began to undo his watch: the discovery that his rival was safe seemed to confirm his belief that as the owner of time he was bound to be the next victim. He looked from face to face and chose Chavel — perhaps because he was the only man with a waistcoat fit to take the chain. He said, 'Monsieur

Chavel, I want you to hold this watch for me in case . . .'

'You had better choose someone else,' Chavel said. 'I am not married.'

The elderly clerk spoke again. He said, 'I'm married. I've got the right to speak. We are going the wrong way about all this. Everyone must draw lots. This isn't the last draw we shall have, and picture to yourselves what it will be like in this cell if we have a privileged class—the ones who are left to the end. The rest of you will soon begin to hate us. We shall be left out of your fear . . .'

'He's right,' Pierre said.

The mayor refastened his watch. 'Have it your own way,' he said. 'But if the taxes were levied like this . . .' He gave a gesture of despair.

'How do we draw?' Krogh asked.

Chavel said, 'The quickest way would be to draw marked papers out of a shoe . . .'

Krogh said contemptuously, 'Why the quickest way? This is the last gamble some of us will have. We may as well enjoy it. I say a coin.'

'It won't work,' the clerk said, 'You can't get an even chance with a coin.'

'The only way is to draw,' the mayor said.

The clerk prepared the draw, sacrificing for it one of his letters from home. He read it rapidly for the last time, then tore it into thirty pieces. On three pieces he made a cross in pencil, and then folded each piece.

'Krogh's got the biggest shoe,' he said. They shuffled the pieces on the floor and then dropped them into the shoe.

'We'll draw in alphabetical order,' the mayor said.

'Z first,' Chavel said. His feeling of security was shaken. He wanted a drink badly. He picked at a dry piece of skin on his lip.

'As you wish,' the lorry-driver said. 'Anybody beat Voisin? Here goes.' He thrust his hand into the shoe and made careful excavations as though he had one particular scrap of paper in mind. He drew one out, opened it, and gazed at it with astonishment. He said, 'This is it.' He sat down and felt for a cigarette, but when he got it between his lips he forgot to light it.

Chavel was filled with a huge and shameful joy. It seemed to him that already he was saved—twenty-nine men to draw and only two marked papers left. The chances had suddenly grown in his favour from ten to one to—fourteen to one: the greengrocer had drawn a slip and indicated carelessly and without pleasure that he was safe. Indeed from the first draw any mark of pleasure was taboo: one couldn't mock the condemned man by any sign of relief.

Again a dull disquiet—it couldn't yet be described as a fear—extended its empire over Chavel's chest. It was like a constriction: he found himself yawning as the sixth man drew a blank slip, and a sense of grievance nagged at his mind when the tenth man had drawn—it was the one they called Janvier—and the chances were once again the same as when the draw started. Some men drew the first slip which touched their fingers: others seemed to suspect that fate was trying to force on them a particular slip and when they had drawn one a little way from the shoe would let it drop again and choose another. Time passed with incredible slowness, and the man called Voisin sat against the wall with the unlighted cigarette in his mouth paying them no attention at all.

The chances had narrowed to one in eight when the elderly clerk—his name was Lenôtre—drew the second slip. He cleared his throat and put on his pince-nez as though he had to make sure he was not mistaken. 'Ah, Monsieur Voisin,' he said with a thin undecided smile, 'may I join you?' This time Chavel felt no joy even though the elusive odds were back again overwhelmingly in his favour at fifteen to one: he was daunted by the courage of common men. He wanted the whole thing to be over as quickly as possible: like a game of cards which has gone on too long, he only wanted someone to make a move and break up the table. Lenôtre, sitting down against the wall next to Voisin, turned the slip over: on the back was a scrap of writing.

'Your wife?' Voisin said.

'My daughter,' Lenôtre said. 'Excuse me.' He went over to his roll of bedding and drew out a writing pad. Then he sat down next to Voisin and began to write, carefully, without hurry, a thin legible hand. The odds were back to ten to one.

From that point the odds seemed to move towards Chavel with a dreadful inevitability: nine to one, eight to one: they were like a pointing finger. The men who were left drew more quickly and more carelessly: they seemed to Chavel to have some inner information—to know that he was the one. When his time came to draw there were only three slips left, and it appeared to Chavel a monstrous injustice that there were so few choices left for him. He drew one out of the shoe and then feeling certain that this one had been willed on him by his companions and contained the pencilled cross he threw it back and snatched another.

'You looked, lawyer,' one of the two men exclaimed, but the other quieted him.

'He didn't look. He's got the marked one now.'

4

Lenôtre said, 'Come over here, Monsieur Chavel, and sit down with us.' It was as if he were inviting Chavel to come up higher, to the best table at a public dinner.

'No,' Chavel said, 'no.' He threw the slip upon the ground and cried, 'I never consented to the draw. You can't *make* me die for the rest of you . . .'

They watched him with astonishment but without enmity. He was a gentleman. They didn't judge him by their own standards: he belonged to an unaccountable class and they didn't at first even attach the idea of cowardice to his actions.

Krogh said, 'Sit down and rest. There's nothing to worry about any more.'

'You can't,' Chavel said. 'It's nonsense. The Germans won't accept me. I'm a man of property.'

Lenôtre said, 'Don't take on now, Monsieur Chavel. If it's not this time it's another . . .'

'You can't make me,' Chavel repeated.

'It's not we who'll make you,' Krogh said.

'Listen,' Chavel implored them. He held out the slip of paper and they all watched him with compassionate curiosity. 'I'll give a hundred thousand francs to anyone who'll take this.'

He was beside himself: almost literally beside himself. It was as if some hidden calmness in him stood apart and heard his absurd proposition and watched his body take up shameful attitudes of fear and pleading. It was as if the calm Chavel whispered with ironic amusement, 'A grand show. Lay it on a bit thicker. You ought to have been an actor, old man. You never know. It's a chance.'

He took little rapid steps from one man to another, showing each man the bit of paper as if he were an attendant at an auction. 'A hundred thousand francs,' he implored, and they watched him with a kind of shocked pity: he was the only rich man among them and this was a unique situation. They had no means of comparison and assumed that this was a characteristic of his class, just as a traveller stepping off the liner at a foreign port for luncheon sums up a nation's character for ever in the wily businessman who happens to share the table with him.

'A hundred thousand francs,' he pleaded, and the calm shameless Chavel at his side whispered, 'You are getting monotonous. Why haggle? Why not offer them everything you possess?'

'Calm yourself, Monsieur Chavel,' Lenôtre said. 'Just think a moment—no one is going to give his life for money he'll never enjoy.'

'I'll give you everything I've got,' Chavel said, his voice breaking with despair, 'money, land, everything, St Jean de Brinac . . .'

Voisin said impatiently, 'None of us want to die, Monsieur Chavel,' and Lenôtre repeated with what seemed to the hysterical Chavel shocking self-righteousness, 'Calm yourself, Monsieur Chavel.'

Chavel's voice suddenly gave out. 'Everything,' he said.

They were becoming impatient with him at last. Tolerance is a question of patience, and patience is a question of nerves and their nerves were strained. 'Sit down,' Krogh rapped at him, 'and shut your mouth.' Even then Lenôtre made a friendly space for him, patting the floor at his side.

'Over,' the calm Chavel whispered, 'over. You weren't good enough. You've got to think up something else . . .'

A voice said, 'Tell me more. Maybe I'll buy.' It was Janvier.

5

He never really expected an offer: hysteria and not hope had dictated his behaviour, and now it took him a long moment to realize that he was not being mocked. He repeated, 'Everything I've got.' The hysteria peeled off like a scab and left the sense of shame.

'Don't laugh at him,' Lenôtre said.

'I'm not laughing. I tell you I'll buy.'

There was a long pause as though no one knew what to do next. How does one hand over everything one possesses? They watched him as though they expected him to empty his pockets. Chavel said, 'You'll take my place?'

'I'll take your place.'

Krogh said impatiently, 'What'll be the good of his money then?'

'I can make a will, can't I?'

Voisin suddenly took the unlighted cigarette out of his mouth and dashed it to the floor. He exclaimed, 'I don't like all this fuss. Why can't things go natural? We can't buy *our* lives, Lenôtre and me. Why should he?'

Lenôtre said, 'Calm yourself, Monsieur Voisin.'

'It's not fair,' Voisin said.

Voisin's feeling was obviously shared by most of the men in the cell: they had been patient with Chavel's hysteria—after all it's no joke to be a dying man and you couldn't expect a gentleman to behave quite like other people: that class were all, when you came down to it, a bit soft perhaps: but this that was happening now was different. As Voisin said, it wasn't fair. Only Lenôtre took it calmly: he had spent a lifetime in business and he had watched from his stool many a business deal concluded in which the best man did not win.

Janvier interrupted, 'Fair?' he said. 'Why isn't it fair to let me do what I want? You'd all be rich men if you could, but you haven't the spunk. I see my chance and I take it. Fair, of course it's fair. I'm going to die a rich man and anyone who thinks it isn't fair can rot.' The peas rolled again on the pan as he coughed. He quelled all opposition: already he had the manner of one who owned half the world: their standards were shifting like great weights—the man who had been rich was already halfway to being one of themselves and Janvier's head was already lost in the mists and obscurity of wealth. He commanded sharply, 'Come here. Sit down here.' And Chavel obeyed, moving a little bent under the shame of his success.

'Now,' Janvier said, 'you're a lawyer. You've got to draw things up in their proper form. How much money is there?'

'Three hundred thousand francs. I can't tell you exactly.'

'And this place you were talking about? St Jean.'

'Six acres and a house.'

'Freehold?'

'Yes.'

'And where do you live in Paris? Have you got a house there?'

'Only a flat. I don't own that.'

'The furniture?'

'No—books only.'

'Sit down,' Janvier said. 'You make me out—what's it called?—a deed of gift.'

'Yes. But I want paper.'

'You can have my pad,' Lenôtre said.

Chavel sat beside Janvier and began to write: 'I Jean-Louis Chavel, lawyer, of Rue Miromesnil 119, Paris, and St Jean de Brinac ... all stocks and shares, money to my account at ... all furniture, movables ... the freehold property at St Jean de Brinac ...' He said, 'It will need two witnesses,' and Lenôtre immediately from force of habit offered himself, coming forward as it were from the outer office just as though his employer had rung a bell and called him in.

'Not you,' Janvier said rudely. 'I want living men as witnesses.'

'Would you perhaps?' Chavel asked the mayor as humbly as if it were he who were the clerk.

'This is a very odd document,' the mayor said. 'I don't know that a man in my position ought to sign . . .'

'Then I will,' Pierre said and splashed his signature below Chavel's.

The mayor said, 'Better have someone reliable. That man would say anything for a drink,' and he squeezed his own signature in the space above Pierre's. As he bent they could hear the great watch in his pocket ticking out the short time left before dark.

'And now, the will,' Janvier said. 'You put it down —everything I've got to my mother and sister in equal shares.'

Chavel said, 'That's simple: it only needs a few lines.'

'No, no,' Janvier said, 'put it down again there . . . the stocks and shares and money in the bank, the freehold property . . . they'll want something to show the neighbours at home what sort of a man I am.' When it was finished Krogh and the greengrocer signed. 'You keep the documents,' Janvier told the mayor. 'The Germans may let you send them off when they've finished with me. Otherwise you've got to keep them till the war ends . . .' He coughed, leaning back with an air of exhaustion against the wall. He said, 'I'm a rich man. I always knew I'd be rich.'

The light moved steadily away from the cell; it rolled up like a carpet from one end to the other. The dusk eliminated Janvier while the clerk sitting by Voisin could still find light enough to write by. A grim peace descended, the hysteria was over and there was no more to be said. The watch and the alarm clock marched out of step towards night, and sometimes Janvier coughed. When it was quite dark Janvier said, 'Chavel.' It was as if he was calling a servant and Chavel obeyed. Janvier said, 'Tell me about my house.'

'It's about two miles out of the village.'

'How many rooms?'

'There is the living-room, my study, the drawing-room, five bedrooms, the office where I interview people on business, of course bathroom, kitchen . . . the servants' room.'

'Tell me about the kitchen.'

'I don't know much about the kitchen. It's a large one, stone paved. My housekeeper was always satisfied.'

'Where's she?'

'There's no one there. When the war came I shut the house up. I was lucky. The Germans never hit on it.'

'And the garden?'

'There's a little terrace above a lawn: the grounds slope and you can see all the way to the river, and beyond that St Jean . . .'

'Did you grow plenty of vegetables?'

'Yes, and fruit trees: apple, plum, walnut. And a glass-house.' He continued as much to himself as to Janvier: 'You don't see the house when you enter the garden. There's a wooden gate and a long curving gravel drive with trees and shrubs. Suddenly it comes right out in front of the terrace, and then divides: the left-hand path leads off to the servants' quarters, and the right round to the front door. My mother used to keep a look out for visitors she didn't want to meet. Nobody could call without her seeing him arrive. My grandfather, when he was young, used to watch in just the same way as my mother . . .'

'How old's the house?' Janvier interrupted.

'Two hundred and twenty-three years old,' Chavel said.

'Too old,' Janvier said. 'I'd have liked something modern. The old woman has rheumatics.'

The darkness had long enclosed them both and now the last light slid off the ceiling of the cell. Men automatically turned to sleep. Pillows like children were shaken and slapped and embraced. Philosophers say that past, present and future exist simultaneously, and certainly in this heavy darkness many pasts came to life: a lorry drove up the Boulevard Montparnasse, a girl held out her mouth to be kissed, and a town council elected a mayor: and in the minds of three men the future stood as inalterably as birth—fifty yards of cinder track and a brick wall chipped and pitted.

It seemed to Chavel now his hysteria was over that that simple track was infinitely more desirable after all than the long obscure route on which his own feet were planted.

THE TENTH MAN

PART

II

6

A man calling himself Jean-Louis Charlot came up the drive of the house at St Jean de Brinac.

Everything was the same as he had remembered it and yet very slightly changed, as if the place and he had grown older at different rates. Four years ago he had shut the house up, and while for him time had almost stood still, here time had raced ahead. For several hundred years the house had grown older almost imperceptibly: years were little more than a changed shadow on the brickwork. Like an elderly woman the house had been kept in flower—the face lifted at the right moment: now in four years all that work had been undone: the lines broke through the enamel which had not been renewed.

In the drive the gravel was obscured by weeds: a tree had fallen right across the way, and though somebody had lopped the branches for firewood, the trunk still lay there to prove that for many seasons no car had driven up to the house. Every step was familiar to the bearded man who came cautiously round every bend like a stranger. He had been born here: as a child he had played games of hide and seek in the bushes: as a boy he had carried the melancholy and sweetness of first love up and down the shaded drive. Ten yards further on there would be a small gate on to the path which led between heavy laurels to the kitchen garden.

The gate had gone: only the posts showed that memory hadn't failed him. Even the nails which had held the hinges had been carefully extracted to be used elsewhere for some more urgent purpose. He turned off the drive: he didn't want to face the house yet: like a criminal who returns to the scene of his crime or a lover who returns to haunt the place of farewell he moved in intersecting circles: he didn't dare to move in a straight line and finish his pilgrimage prematurely, with nothing more to do for ever after.

The glass-house had obviously been unused for years, though he remembered telling the old man who worked in the garden that he was to keep the garden stocked, and sell the vegetables for what he could get in Brinac. Perhaps the old man had died and no one in the village had the initiative to appoint himself his successor. Perhaps there was no one left in the village. From the trampled unsown earth beside the glass-house he could see the ugly red-brick church pointing like an exclamation mark at the sky, closing a sentence he couldn't read from here.

Then he saw that something after all had been planted: a patch had been cleared of weeds for the sake of some potatoes, cabbages, savoys. It was like the garden you give to children to cultivate: a space little larger than a carpet. All around the desolation lapped. He remembered what had been here in the old days —the strawberry beds, the bushes of currants and raspberries, the sweet and bitter smell of herbs. The wall which separated this garden from the fields had tumbled in one place, or else some looter had picked his way through the old stonework to get into the garden: it had all happened a long time ago, for nettles had grown up over the fallen stones. From the gap he stood and looked a long time at something which had been beyond the power of time to change, the long slope of grass towards the elms and the river. He had thought that home was something one possessed, but the things one had possessed were cursed with change; it was what one didn't possess that remained the same and welcomed him. This landscape was not *his*, not anybody's home: it was simply home.

Now there was nothing more for him to do except go away. If he went away, what could he do but drown himself in the river? His money was nearly gone: already after less than a week of liberty he had learned how impossible it was for him to find work.

At seven o'clock in the morning (five minutes past by the mayor's watch and two minutes to by Pierre's alarm clock) the Germans had come for Voisin, Lenôtre and Janvier. That had been his worst shame up to date, sitting against the wall, watching his companions' faces, waiting for the crack of the shots. He was one of them now, a man without money or position, and unconsciously they had accepted him, and begun to judge him by their own standards, and to condemn him. The shame he felt now shuffling like a beggar up to the door of the house went nearly as deep. He had realized reluctantly that Janvier could still be used for his benefit even after his death.

The empty windows watched him come like the eyes of men sitting round the wall of a cell. He looked up once and took it all in: the unpainted frames, the broken glass in what had been his study, the balustrade of the terrace broken in two places. Then his eyes fell to his feet again, scuffling up the gravel. It occurred to him that the house might still be empty, but when he turned the corner of the terrace and came slowly up the steps to the door, he saw the same diminutive signs of occupation as he had noticed in the kitchen garden. The steps were spotless. When he put out his hand and pulled the bell it was like a gesture of despair. He had tried his best not to return but here he was.

7

The flags of rejoicing had been months old when Jean-Louis Charlot had come back to Paris. The uppers of his shoes were still good, but the soles were nearly paper thin, and his dark lawyer's suit bore the marks of many months' imprisonment. He had thought of himself in the cells as a man who kept up appearances, but now the cruel sun fingered his clothes like a second-hand dealer, pointing out the rubbed cloth, the missing buttons, the general dinginess. It was some comfort that Paris itself was dingy too.

In his pocket Charlot had a razor wrapped in a bit of newspaper with what was left of a tablet of soap, and he had three hundred francs: he had no papers, but he had something which was better than papers—the slip from the prison officer in which the Germans had carefully recorded a year before the incorrect details he had given them—including the name Charlot. In France at this moment such a document was of more value than legal papers, for no collaborator possessed a German prison dossier authenticated with most efficient photographs, full face and profile. The face had altered somewhat, since Charlot had grown his beard, but it was still, if carefully examined, the same face. The Germans were thoroughly up-to-date archivists: photographs can be easily substituted on documents: plastic surgery can add or eliminate scars, but it is not so simple to alter the actual measurements of the skull and these the Germans had documented with great thoroughness.

Nevertheless no collaborator felt a more hunted man than Charlot, for his past was equally shameful: he could explain to no one how he had lost his money—if indeed it was not already known. He was haunted at street corners by the gaze from faintly familiar faces and driven out of buses by backs he imagined he knew: deliberately he moved into a Paris that was strange to him. His Paris had always been a small Paris: its arc had been drawn to include his flat, the law courts, the Opéra, the Gare de l'Ouest and one or two restaurants: between these points he knew only the shortest route. Now he had but to sidestep and he was in unknown territory: the Metro lay like a jungle below him: Combat and the outer districts were deserts through which he could wander in safety.

But he had to do more than wander: he had to get a job. There were moments—after his first glass of wine in freedom—when he felt quite capable of beginning over again: of re-amassing the money he had signed away, and finally in a burst of day-dream he had bought back his home at St Jean de Brinac and was wandering happily from room to room when he saw the reflection of his face—Charlot's bearded face—in the water decanter. It was the face of failure. It was odd, he thought, that one failure of nerve had ingrained the face as deeply as a tramp's, but, of course, he had the objectivity to tell himself, it wasn't one failure, it was a whole lifetime of preparation for the event. An artist paints his picture not in a few hours but in all the years of experience before he takes up the brush, and it is the same with failure. It was his good fortune to have been a fashionable lawyer: he had inherited more money than he had ever earned: if it had depended upon himself he would never, he believed now, have reached the heights he had.

All the same, he now made several attempts to earn his living in a reasonable way. He applied for the post of a teacher at one of the innumerable language institutes in the city. Although the war still muttered outside the borders of France, the Berlitzes and kindred organizations were already doing a thriving trade: there were plenty of foreign soldiers anxious to learn French to take the place of peacetime tourists.

He was interviewed by a dapper thin man in a frock coat, which smelled very faintly of moth balls. 'I'm afraid,' he said at length, 'your accent is not good enough.'

'Not good enough!' Charlot exclaimed.

'Not good enough for this institute. We exact a very high standard. Our teachers must have the best, the very best, of Parisian accents. I am sorry, monsieur.' He enunciated himself with terrible clarity, as though he was used to speaking only to foreigners, and he used only the simplest phrases—he was trained in the direct method. His eyes dwelt ruminatively on Charlot's battered shoes. Charlot went.

Perhaps something about the man reminded him of Lenôtre. It occurred to him immediately he had left the institute that he might earn a reasonably good living as a clerk: his knowledge of law would be useful, and he could explain it by saying that at one time he had hoped to be called to the Bar, but his money had given out . . .

He answered an advertisement in *Figaro*: the address was on the third floor of a high grey building off the Boulevard Haussmann. The office into which he found his way gave the impression of having been just cleaned up after enemy occupation: dust and straw had been swept against the walls and the furniture looked as though it had been recently uncrated from the boxes in which it had been stored away ages ago. When a war ends one forgets how much older oneself and the world have become: it needs something like a piece of furniture or a woman's hat to waken the sense of time. This furniture was all of tubular steel, giving the room the appearance of an engine room in a ship, but this was a ship which had been beached for years—the tubes were tarnished. Out of fashion in 1939, in 1944 they had the air of period pieces. An old man greeted Charlot: when the furniture was new he must have been young enough to have an eye for the fashionable, the chic, for appearances. He sat down among the steel chairs at random as though he was in a public waiting room and said sadly, 'I suppose like everyone else you have forgotten everything?'

'Oh,' Charlot said, 'I remember enough.'

'We can't pay much here at present,' the old man said, 'but when things get back to normal . . . there was always a great demand for our product . . .'

'I would begin,' Charlot said, 'at a low salary . . .'

'The great thing,' the old man said, 'is enthusiasm, to believe in what we are selling. After all, our product has proved itself. Before the war our figures were very good, very good indeed. Of course, there was a season, but in Paris there are always foreign visitors. And even the provinces bought our product. I'd show you our

(68)

figures only our books are lost.' From his manner you would have thought he was attracting an investor rather than interviewing a would-be employee.

'Yes,' Charlot said, 'yes.'

'We've got to make our product known again. When once it's known, it can't fail to be as popular as before. Craftsmanship tells.'

'I expect you are right.'

'So you see,' the old man said, 'we've all got to put our backs into it . . . a co-operative enterprise . . . the sense of loyalty . . . your savings will be quite safe.' He waved his hand above the wilderness of tubular chairs. 'I promise you that.'

Charlot never learned what the product was, but on the landing below a wooden crate had been opened and standing in the straw was a table-lamp about three feet high built hideously in steel in the shape of the Eiffel Tower. The flex ran down the lift shaft like the rope of an ancient hotel lift, and the bulb screwed in on the top floor. Perhaps it was the only desk lamp the old man had been able to obtain in Paris: perhaps—who knows?—it may have been the product itself . . .

Three hundred francs wouldn't last long in Paris. Charlot answered one more advertisement, but the employer demanded proper papers. He was not impressed by the prison dossier. 'You can buy any number of those,' he said, 'for a hundred francs,' and he refused to be persuaded by the elaborate measurements of the German authorities. 'It's not my job to measure your skull,' he said, 'or feel your bumps. Go off to the city hall and get proper papers. You seem a capable fellow. I'll keep the job open until noon tomorrow . . .' But Charlot did not return.

He hadn't eaten more than a couple of rolls for thirty-six hours: it suddenly occurred to him that he was back exactly where he had started. He leaned against a wall in the late afternoon sun and imagined that he heard the ticking of the mayor's watch. He had come a long way and taken a deal of trouble and was back at the end of the cinder track with his back against the wall. He was going to die and he might just as well have died rich and saved everybody trouble. He began to walk towards the Seine.

Presently he couldn't hear the mayor's watch any more: instead there was a shuffle and pad whichever way he turned. He heard it just as he had heard the mayor's watch and he half realized that both were delusions. At the end of a long empty street the river shone. He found that he was out of breath and he leaned against a urinal and waited for a while with his head hanging down because the river dazzled his eyes. The shuffle and pad came softly up behind him and stopped. Well, the watch had stopped too. He refused to pay attention to delusion.

'Pidot,' a voice said, 'Pidot.' He looked sharply up, but there was no one there.

'It is Pidot, surely?' the voice said.

'Where are you?' Charlot asked.

'Here, of course.' There was a pause and then the voice said like conscience almost in his ear, 'You look all in, finished. I hardly recognized you. Tell me, is anyone coming?'

'No.' In childhood, in the country, in the woods behind Brinac one had believed that voices might suddenly speak out of the horns of flowers or from the roots of trees, but in the city when one had reached the age of death one couldn't believe in voices from paving stones. He asked again, 'Where are you?' and then realized his own dull-wittedness—he could see the legs from the shins downwards under the green cape of the urinal. They were black pin-striped trousers, the trousers of a lawyer or a doctor or even a deputy, but the shoes hadn't been cleaned for some days.

'It's Monsieur Carosse, Pidot.'

'Yes?'

'You know how it is. One's misunderstood.'

'Yes.'

'What could I have done? After all, I had to keep the show going. My behaviour was strictly correct—and distant. No one knows better than you, poor Pidot. I suppose they are holding things against you too?'

'I'm finished.'

'Courage, Pidot. Never say die. A second cousin of mine who was in London is doing his best to put things right. Surely you know one of them?'

'Why don't you come out from there and let me see you?'

'Better not, Pidot. Separately we might pass muster, but together ... it's too risky.' The pin-striped trousers moved uneasily. 'Anyone coming, Pidot?'

'No one.'

'Listen, Pidot. I want you to take a message to Madame Carosse. Tell her I'm well: I've gone south. I shall try to get into Switzerland till it all blows over. Poor Pidot, you could do with a couple of hundred francs, couldn't you?'

'Yes.'

'I'll leave them on a ledge in here. You'll take the message, won't you, Pidot?'

'Where to?'

'Oh, the same old place. You know—on the third floor. I hope the old lady's still got her hair. The old bitch was proud of it. Well, goodbye and good luck, Pidot.' There was a scuffle in the urinal, and then the shuffle and pad went off in the other direction. Charlot watched the stranger go: tall and stout and black-clothed, with a limp and the kind of hat Charlot himself would have worn—so many years ago—between the Rue Miromesnil and the law courts.

On a shelf of the urinal there was a screw of paper—three hundred francs. Whoever Monsieur Carosse was, he had the rare virtue of being better than his word. Charlot laughed: the sound was hollow among the metal alcoves. A week had gone by and he was back exactly where he had started with three hundred francs. It was as if all that time he had lived upon air — or rather as if some outwardly friendly but inwardly malign witch had granted him the boon of an inexhaustible purse, but a purse from which he could never draw more than three hundred francs. Was it perhaps that the dead man had allocated him this allowance out of his three hundred thousand?

We'll soon test that out, Charlot thought; what's the good of making this last a week and be only a week older and a week shabbier at the end of it? It was the hour of apéritifs and for the first time since he had entered Paris, he deliberately stepped into his own territory, the territory of which he knew every yard.

He had not until then properly appreciated the strangeness of Paris: an unfamiliar street might always have been an unfrequented one, but now he noticed the emptiness, the silent little bicycle taxis gliding by, the shabbiness of awnings and the strange faces. Only here and there he saw the familiar face of the customary stranger sitting where he had sat for years, sipping the same drink. They were like the remains of an old flower garden sticking up in a wilderness of weeds after a careless tenant's departure.

I am going to die tonight, Charlot thought: what does it matter if someone does recognize me, and he pushed through the glass door of his accustomed café and made for the very corner — the right-hand end of the long sofa under the gilt mirror — in which he had always sat as a kind of right. It was occupied.

An American soldier sat there: a young man with

high cheekbones and a rough puppy innocence: and the waiter bowed and smiled and exchanged words with him as though he were the oldest customer in the place. Charlot sat and watched: it was like an act of adultery. The head waiter, who had always stopped for a word, went past him as though he did not exist, and he too paused by the American's table. The explanation soon came—the big bundle of notes the Yankee produced to pay with—and suddenly it occurred to Charlot that he too formerly had possessed a big bundle of notes, had been a payer; it wasn't that he was a ghost now: he was merely a man without much money. He drank his brandy and called for another: the slowness of the service angered him. He called the head waiter. The man tried to avoid him but at last he had to come.

'Well, Jules,' Charlot said.

The shallow eyes flickered disapproval: the man only liked his intimates—the payers, Charlot thought—to call him by his name.

'You don't remember me, Jules,' Charlot said.

The man became uneasy: perhaps some tone of voice echoed in his ear. The times were confusing: some customers had disappeared altogether, others who had been in hiding had returned changed by imprisonment, and others who had not been in hiding it was now in the interests of his business to discourage. 'Well, monsieur, you have not been here for some time . . .'

The American began to hit loudly on the table with a coin. 'Excuse me,' the waiter said.

'No, no, Jules, you can't leave an old customer like that. Leave out the beard.' He laid his hand across his chin. 'Can't you see a fellow called Chavel, Jules?'

The American beat again with his coin, but this time Jules paid him no attention, simply signalled another waiter across to take the man's order. 'Why, Monsieur Chavel,' he said, 'you are so much changed. I'm astonished . . . I heard . . .' But it was obvious that he couldn't remember what he had heard. It was difficult to remember which of his customers were heroes and which traitors and which simply customers.

'The Germans locked me up,' Chavel said.

'Ah, that must have been it,' Jules said with relief. 'Paris is nearly itself again now, Monsieur Chavel.'

'Not quite, Jules.' He nodded at his old place.

'Ah, I'll see that seat is kept for you tomorrow, Monsieur Chavel. How is your house—where was it?'

'Brinac. There are tenants there now.'

'It hasn't suffered?'

'I don't think so. I haven't visited it yet. To tell you the truth, Jules, I only arrived in Paris today. I've barely enough money for a bed.'

'I can accommodate you a little, Monsieur Chavel?'

'No, no. I shall manage somehow.'

'At least you must be our guest this evening. Another cognac, Monsieur Chavel?'

'Thank you, Jules.' The test, he thought, has

worked: the pocket book is inexhaustible. I still have my three hundred francs.

'Do you believe in the Devil, Jules?'

'Naturally, Monsieur Chavel.'

He was moved to recklessness. 'You hadn't heard, Jules, that I am selling Brinac?'

'Are you getting a good price, Monsieur Chavel?'

Suddenly Charlot felt a great distaste for Jules: it seemed to him incredible that a man could be so crass. Had he no possession in the world for which a good price was an insufficient inducement? He was a man who would sell his life . . . He said, 'I'm sorry.'

'What for, Monsieur Chavel?'

'After these years haven't we all reason to be sorry for a hundred things?'

'We have no reason to be sorry here, Monsieur Chavel. I assure you our attitude has always been strictly correct. I have always made a point of serving Frenchmen first—yes, even if the German was a general.'

He envied Jules: to have been able to remain 'correct': to have saved his self-respect by small doses of rudeness or inattention. But for him—to have remained correct would have meant death. He said suddenly, 'Do you know if any trains are running yet from the Gare de l'Ouest?'

'A few and they are very slow. They haven't got the fuel. They stop at every station. Sometimes they stop all night. You wouldn't get to Brinac before morning.'

'There's no hurry.'

'Are they expecting you, Monsieur Chavel?'

'Who?'

'Your tenants.'

'No.' The unaccustomed brandy was running along the dry subterranean channels of his mind: sitting there in the familiar café, where even the mirrors and cornices were chipped in the places he remembered them, he felt an enormous longing just to be able to get up and catch a train and go home as he had often done in past years. Suddenly and unexpectedly to give way to a whim and find a welcome at the other end. He thought: After all, there is always time to die in.

8

The bell like most things about the place was old-fashioned. His father had disliked electricity, and though he could well have afforded to bring it to Brinac, he had preferred lamps almost until his death (saying they were better for the eyes) and ancient bells which dangled on long fronds of metal. Himself he had loved the place too much to change things: when he came down to Brinac it was to a quiet cave of dusk and silence—no telephone could petulantly pursue him there. So now he could hear the long twanging wire before the bell began to swing at the back of the house, in the room next to the kitchen. Surely if he had been in the house that bell would have had a different tone: one less hollow, more friendly: less sporadic like a cough in a worn-out breast . . . A cold early-morning breeze blew through the bushes and stirred at ankle level the weeds in the drive: somewhere—perhaps in the potting shed—a loose board flapped. Without warning the door opened.

This was Janvier's sister. He recognized the type and in a flash built her up on the lines of her brother. Fair and thin and very young she had still had time to develop what must have been the family trait of recklessness. Now that he was here and she was there, he found he had no words of explanation: he stood like a page of type waiting to be read.

'You want a meal,' she said. She had read the whole page like so many women do at a glance, even to the footnote of his thin shoes. He made a gesture which might have been deprecation or acceptance. She said, 'We haven't much in the house. You know how things are. It would be easier to give you money.'

He said, 'I've got money . . . three hundred francs.'

She said, 'You'd better come in. Make as little dirt as you can. I've been scrubbing these steps.'

'I'll take off my shoes,' he said humbly, and he followed her in, feeling the parquet floor cold under his socks. Everything had changed a little for the worse: there was no question but that the house had been surrendered to strangers: the big mirror had been taken down and left an ugly patch on the wall: the

(78)

tallboy had been shifted, a chair had gone: the steel engraving of a naval engagement off Brest had been hung in a new place—tastelessly he thought. He looked in vain for a photograph of his father, and exclaimed suddenly, furiously, 'Where's . . . ?'

'Where's what?'

He checked himself. 'Your mother,' he said.

She turned round and looked at him as though she had missed something on the first reading. 'How do you know about my mother?'

'Janvier told me.'

'Who's Janvier? I don't know any Janvier.'

'Your brother,' he said. 'We used to call your brother that in the prison.'

'You were with him there?'

'Yes.'

He was to learn in time that she never quite did the expected thing: he had imagined that now she would call her mother, but instead she laid her hand on his arm and said, 'Don't speak so loud.' She explained, 'My mother doesn't know.'

'About his death?'

'About anything. She thinks he's made a fortune—somewhere. Sometimes it's England, sometimes South America. She says she always knew he was a clever son. What's your name?'

'Charlot. Jean-Louis Charlot.'

'Did you know the other one too?'

'You mean . . . Yes, I knew him. I think I'd better go

before your mother comes.'

A high old voice cried from the stairs, 'Thérèse, who's that you've got?'

'Somebody,' the girl said, 'who knows Michel.'

An old woman heaved herself down the last stairs into the hall, a huge old woman draped in shawl after shawl until she appeared like an unturned bed: even the feet were swathed, they padded and slopped towards him. It was difficult to see pathos in this mountain or appreciate the need to shelter her. Surely these huge maternal breasts were there to comfort, not to require comfort. 'Well,' she said, 'how's Michel?'

'He's well,' the girl said.

'I didn't ask you. You. How did you leave my son?'

'He was well,' Charlot repeated. 'He asked me to look you up and see how you were.'

'He did, did he? He might have given you a pair of shoes to come in,' she said sharply. 'He hasn't done anything foolish, has he, lost his money again?'

'No. No.'

'He bought all this for his old mother,' she went on with fond fanaticism. 'He's a foolish boy. I was all right where I was. We had three rooms in Menilmontant. Manageable they were, but here you can't get help. It's too much for an old woman and a girl. He sent us money too, of course, but he doesn't realize there's things nowadays money won't buy.'

'He's hungry,' the girl interrupted.

'All right, then,' the old woman said. 'Give him

food. You'd think he was a beggar the way he stands there. If he wants food why doesn't he ask for food?' she went on just as though he were out of earshot.

'I'll pay,' Charlot snapped at her.

'Oh, you'll pay, will you? You're too ready with your money. You won't get anywhere that way. You don't want to offer money till you're asked for it.' She was like an old weather-worn emblem of wisdom—something you find in desert places, like the Sphinx—and yet inside her was that enormous vacancy of ignorance which cast a doubt on all her wisdom.

One turned out of the hall on the left, through a door with a chipped handle: this led to a long stone passage leading halfway round the house: he remembered in winter how the food was never quite hot after its journey from the kitchen and how his father had always planned alterations, but in the end the house had won. Now without thinking he took a step towards the door as though he would find his own way there: then stopped and thought, I must be careful, so careful. He followed silently behind Thérèse and thought how odd it was to see someone young in that house where he only remembered old, trustworthy, crusty servants. Only in portraits were people young: the photograph in the best bedroom of his mother on her wedding day, of his father when he had taken his degree in law: his grandmother with her first child. Following the girl he thought with melancholy that it was as if he had brought a bride to the old house.

She gave him bread and cheese and a glass of wine and sat down opposite to him at the kitchen table. He was silent because of his hunger and because of his thoughts. He had hardly been in the kitchen since he was a child: then he would come in from the garden about eleven and see what he could scrounge: there was an old cook—old again—who loved him and fed him and gave him odd toys to play with—he could remember only a potato forked like a man, a merry-thought dressed carefully up as an old woman in a bonnet, and a mutton-bone which he believed then was like an assegai.

The girl said, 'Tell me about him.' It was what he had dreaded, arming himself with suitable false phrases. He said, 'He was the life and soul of the prison—even the guards liked him.'

She interrupted him: 'I didn't mean Michel . . . I mean the other one.'

'The man who . . .'

'I mean Chavel,' she said. 'You don't think I'd forget his name, do you? I can see it just as he wrote it on the documents. Jean-Louis Chavel. Do you know what I tell myself? I tell myself that one day he will come back here because he won't be able to resist seeing what's happened to his beautiful house. We have lots of strangers passing through here like yourself, hungry, but every time that bell starts swinging, I think to myself, "Maybe it's him."'

'And then?' Charlot said.

'I'd spit in his face,' she said and for the first time he noticed the shape of her mouth: a beautiful mouth as he remembered Janvier's had been. 'That's the first thing I'd do . . .'

He watched it when he said, 'All the same, it's a lovely house.'

'Sometimes,' she said, 'if it wasn't for the old woman I think I'd set it alight. What a fool he was,' she cried out at Charlot as though this was the first time she had had a chance of saying what she thought aloud. 'Did he really think I'd rather have this than him?'

'You were twins, weren't you?' Charlot said, watching her.

'Do you know the night they shot him? I felt the pain. I sat up in bed crying . . .'

'It wasn't at night,' Charlot said, 'it was in the morning.'

'Not in the night?'

'No.'

'What did it mean then?'

'Just nothing,' Charlot said. He began to cut a bit of cheese into tiny squares. 'That's often the way. We think there's a meaning but then we find the facts are wrong—there just isn't one. You wake with a pain and afterwards you think that was love—but the facts don't fit.'

She said, 'We loved each other so much. I feel dead too.'

He cut the cheese and cut the cheese. He said

(83)

gently, 'The facts are wrong. You'll see.' He wanted to convince himself that he wasn't responsible for two deaths. He felt thankful that it was in the night that she had woken and not in the morning, at seven o'clock.

'You haven't told me,' she said, 'what *he* looks like.'

He chose his words with great care. 'He's a little taller than I am—perhaps an inch, or not so much. He's a clean shaven . . .'

'That doesn't mean a thing,' she said. 'You can grow a beard in a week. What colour eyes?'

'Blue. They looked grey in some lights, though.'

'Can't you think of a single thing you can tell him by for certain? Hasn't he got a scar somewhere?'

He was tempted to lie but resisted: 'No,' he said. 'I can't remember anything like that about him. He was just a man like the rest of us.'

'I thought once,' the girl said, 'that I'd have someone from the village here to help us and to keep an eye out for him. But I wouldn't trust one of them. He was popular there. I suppose because they'd known him from when he was a kid. You don't trouble about a kid's meanness, and by the time he's grown up, you're so used to it, you don't notice.' She had her wise sayings as her mother had, but hers had not been inherited: they had been learned in the street with her brother: they had an odd masculine tinge.

'Do they know down there,' he asked, 'what he's done?'

'It wouldn't make any difference if they did. He'd

have just put a smart one over on a Parisian. They'd sit back and wait to see him do it again. That's what I'm waiting for too. He was a lawyer, wasn't he? You don't tell me he hasn't managed somehow to make those papers just rubbish.'

'I think,' Charlot said, 'he was too frightened to think as clearly as that. If he'd thought all that clearly, he'd have died, wouldn't he?'

'When he dies,' the girl said, 'you can take your oath it will be in a state of grace with the sacrament in his mouth, forgiving all his enemies. He won't die before he can cheat the Devil.'

'How you hate him.'

'I'll be the one who's damned. Because I shan't forgive. I shan't die in a state of grace.' She said, 'I thought you were hungry. You don't eat much of that cheese. It's good cheese.'

'It's time I got along,' he said.

'You don't have to hurry. Did they let him have a priest?'

'Oh, yes, I think so. They had a priest in one of the other cells who used to do that sort of job.'

'Where are you going from here?'

'I don't know.'

'Looking for a job?'

'I've given up looking.'

She said, 'We could do with a man here. A couple of women can't keep a place like this clean. And there's the garden.'

'It wouldn't do.'

'It's as you like. Wages wouldn't be a difficulty,' she said bitterly. 'We're rich.'

He thought, If only for a week . . . to be quiet . . . at home.

She said, 'But your chief job, what I'd be paying you for, is just to keep on looking out—for him.'

9

For twenty-four hours it was strange and bitter to be living in his own house as an odd-job man, but after another twenty-four it was familiar and peaceful. If a man loves a place enough he doesn't need to possess it: it's enough for him to know that it is safe and unaltered—or only altered in the natural way by time and circumstance. Madame Mangeot and her daughter were like temporary lodgers: if they took a picture down it was only for some practical purpose—to save dusting, not because they wished to put another in its place: they would never have cut down a tree for the sake of a new view, or refurbished a room according to some craze of the moment. It was exaggeration even to regard them as legal lodgers: they were more like gypsies who had found the house empty and now lived in a few rooms, cultivated a corner of the garden well away from the road, and were careful to make no smoke by which they could be detected.

This was not entirely fanciful: he found they were in fact afraid of the village. Once a week the girl went into Brinac to the market, walking both ways though Charlot knew there was a cart they could have hired in St Jean, and once a week the old woman went to Mass, her daughter taking her to the door of the church and meeting her there afterwards. The old woman never entered until a few moments before the Gospel was read, and at the very first moment, when the priest had pronounced the *Ita Missa*, she was on her feet. Thus she avoided all contact outside the church with the congregation. This suited Charlot well. It never occurred to either of them as strange that he too should avoid the village.

It was he who now went into Brinac on market day. The first time that he went he felt betrayed at every step by familiar things: it was as though even if no human spoke his name the signpost at the crossroads would betray him: the soles of his shoes signed his name along the margin of the road, and the slats of the bridge across the river sounded a personal note under his tread which seemed to him as unmistakable as an accent. Once on the road a cart passed him from St Jean and he recognized the driver—a local farmer who had been crippled as a boy, losing his right arm in an accident with a tractor. As children they had played together in the fields round St Jean, but after the boy's accident and the long weeks in hospital obscure emotions of jealousy and pride kept them apart, and when they met at last it was as enemies. They couldn't like duellists use the same weapons: his own strength was matched against the crippled boy's wounding tongue which bore the bedsores of a long sickness.

Charlot stepped back into the ditch as the cart went by and put up his hand to shield his face, but Roche paid him no attention; the dark fanatical eyes watched the road in front, the great lopped torso stood like a ruined buttress between him and the world. In any case, as Charlot soon realized, there were too many on the roads to attract attention. All over France men were picking their way home, from prison camps, from hiding places, from foreign parts. If one had possessed a God's eye view of France, one would have detected a constant movement of tiny grains moving like dust across a floor shaped like a map.

He felt an enormous sense of relief when he returned to the house: it was really as if he had emerged from a savage and unaccountable country. He came in at the front door and trod the long passage to the kitchen as though he were retreating into the interstices of a cave. Thérèse Mangeot looked up from the pot she was stirring and said, 'It's odd the way you always come in at the front. Why don't you use the back door like we do? It saves a lot of cleaning.'

'I'm sorry, mademoiselle,' he said. 'I suppose it's because I came that way first.'

She didn't treat him like a servant: it was as if in her eyes he was just another gypsy camping there until the

(88)

police turned them out. Only the old woman sometimes fell into an odd apoplectic rage at nothing at all and swore that when her son returned, they would live properly, like the rich people they were, with servants who were really servants, and not tramps taken off the road ... On these occasions Thérèse Mangeot would turn away as if she didn't hear, but afterwards she would fling some rough inapposite remark to Charlot—the kind of remark you only make to an equal, giving him as it were the freedom of the street.

He said, 'There wasn't much to be got in the market. It seemed absurd to be buying so many vegetables with this big garden here. Next year you won't have to ...' He counted out the money. He said, 'I got some horse-meat. There wasn't even a rabbit there. I think the change is right. You'd better check it.'

'I'll trust you,' she said.

'Your mother won't. Here's my account.' He held out to her the list of things he had bought and watched her over her shoulder as she checked. 'Jean-Louis Charlot ...' She stopped reading. 'It's strange,' she said, and suddenly looking over her shoulder he realized what he had done—he had as near as made no difference signed his name as he had signed it on the deed of gift.

'What's strange?' he asked.

'I could almost swear,' she said, 'that I knew your

(89)

writing, that I'd seen it somewhere . . .'

'I suppose you've seen it on a letter I've written.'

'You haven't written any letters.'

'No. That's true.' His lips were dry. He said, 'Where do you think you've seen it . . . ?' and waited an age for her answer.

She stared at it and stared at it. 'I don't know,' she said. 'It's like those times when you think you've been in a place before. I don't suppose it means a thing.'

10

Nearly every day someone came to the door to beg or to ask for work. The vagrants flowed aimlessly west and south, towards the sun and the sea, as if they believed that on the warm wet margin of France anyone could live. The girl gave them money rather than food (it was less scarce), and they drifted on down the weedy path to the river. There was no stability anywhere, least of all in the big house. And yet the Mangeots had a great sense of property. In Paris Madame Mangeot had owned a small general shop—or rather she had owned the goods in the general shop. Year after year, since her husband had died, she had traded carefully—never giving credit and never accepting credit, and never making more than a bare livelihood. Her husband had had ambitions for his children: he had sent his daughter to a secretarial school to learn typewriting and his son to a technical college, but Janvier had run away, and Thérèse had been withdrawn soon after he died. It was all nonsense, that, in Madame Mangeot's eyes, and the sole result of the few months' training was a second-hand typewriter in the back of the shop on which she typed letters—very badly—to wholesalers. There was no future for the store, but Madame Mangeot didn't worry about that. When you reach a certain age you don't care about the future: it is success enough to be alive: every morning you wake with triumph. And there was always Michel. Madame Mangeot believed implicitly in Michel. Who knows what fairy stories of her infancy gathered about the enigmatic absent figure? He was the prince searching the world with a glass slipper; he was the cowherd who won the King's daughter; he was an old woman's youngest son who killed the giant. She was never allowed to know that he was after all just dead. Charlot learned this story slowly, from half-sentences, outbreaks of temper on the part of Madame Mangeot, even from the dreams the two women recounted at breakfast. It wasn't quite the truth, of course—nothing is ever that, and Madame Mangeot's neighbours in Menilmontant would never have recognized this coloured version of her commonplace story. Now suddenly she had come into a fortune. It was the complete justification of Madame Mangeot's daydreams, but the stories of her childhood had also warned her that there was such a thing as fairy gold. Without knowing why, she never felt sure of anything in this house; even of the kitchen table or the chair she sat in, as she had felt sure of everything in Menilmontant, where she knew exactly what had been paid for and what hadn't: here nothing, as far as she knew, had been paid for: she wasn't to realize that the payment had been made elsewhere.

Charlot slept at the top of the house in what had once been the best servant's bedroom—a little room under a sloping roof with an iron bedstead and a flimsy bamboo chest of drawers, the flimsiest thing in the house where every piece of furniture was heavy and dark and built to last generations. This was the only part of the house he hadn't known: as a child he was forbidden the top floor for some obscure maternal reason that seemed vaguely to be based on morality and hygiene. Up there, where the carpet stopped, beyond the region of bathroom and lavatory, the physical facts of life seemed to lurk with a peculiar menace. Once and once only had he penetrated into the forbidden territory: on tiptoe, under the light weight of six years, he had approached the bedroom he now slept in and peeked round the door. The old servant, whom his parents had inherited and whom they called with rather terrified respect Madame Warnier, was doing her hair—or rather she was taking off her hair: great strands of pale brown hair like dry seaweed were unpicked and laid on the dressing table.

All over the region lay a sour miasma. For more than a year after Charlot believed that all long hair was like that—detachable.

One night he couldn't sleep: he followed that clandestine track of his childhood the opposite way in search of water. The servants' stairs creaked under his tread, but unlike his footsteps on the way to Brinac they meant nothing: they were new hieroglyphs nobody had learned to read. On the floor below was his own old room: nobody slept in it now, perhaps because it bore too clearly the marks of his occupancy. He went in. It was exactly as he had left it four years before. He pulled open a drawer and there was a ring of stiff collars turning a little yellow like papyrus with disuse. A photograph of his mother stood in a silver frame on his wardrobe. She wore a high whalebone collar and stared out with an expression of complete calm on a scene that never changed: death and torture and loss had no effect on the small patch of wall that met her gaze—the old wallpaper with sprigs of flowers that *her* mother-in-law had ordered. Above one sprig was a small pencilled face: at fourteen it had meant someone and something he had forgotten: some vague romantic passion of adolescence, perhaps a love and a pain he had believed would last as long as his life. He turned and saw Thérèse Mangeot watching him from the doorway. Seeing her was like remembering. It was as if he had connected a broken wire and the forgotten voice spoke to him out of thirty years ago.

'What are you doing?' she asked roughly. She wore a thick corded dressing-gown like a man's.

'I couldn't sleep, so I came down for water. And then I thought I heard a rat in this room.'

'Oh, no, there hasn't been a rat here for four years.'

'Why don't you clear out all these things?'

Her dressing-gown cord trailed wearily across the floor. 'It would almost make one sick, wouldn't it,' she said, 'to touch them? But I would all the same. Even the collars.' She sat down on the bed: it seemed to Charlot inexpressibly sad that anyone so young should be so tired—and yet awake. 'Poor thing,' she said.

'Wouldn't it be better if she knew?'

'I didn't mean my mother. I mean her—in the photograph. It can't have been much to boast about, can it, being his mother?'

For the first time since his arrival he found himself stung into protest. 'I think you're wrong. I knew him, after all, and you didn't. Believe me—he wasn't such a bad chap.'

'Good God,' she said.

'He acted like a coward, of course, but, after all, anybody's liable to play the coward once. Most of us do and forget about it. It was just that the once in his case proved—well, so spectacular.'

She said, 'You can't tell me he was unlucky. It's as you say. That thing happens to everyone once. All one's life one has to think: Today it may happen.' It was obvious that she had brooded and brooded on this subject, and now at last she brought out the result aloud for anyone's hearing. 'When it happens you know what you've been all your life.'

He had no answer: it seemed to him quite true. He asked her sourly, 'Has it happened to you yet?'

'Not yet. But it will.'

'So you don't know what you are. Perhaps you are no better than he is.' He picked up a yellow collar and twirled it angrily and trivially round his wrist.

'That doesn't make him any better,' she said, 'does it? If I'm a murderer, must I pretend that other murderers . . . ?'

He interrupted her, 'You've got an answer, haven't you, to everything? If you were a man you'd make a good lawyer. Only you'd be a better counsel for the prosecution than for the defence.'

'I wouldn't want to be a lawyer,' she told him seriously. 'He was one.'

'How you hate him.'

'I've got such hate,' she said, 'it goes on and on all day and all night. It's like a smell you can't get rid of when something's died under the floorboards. You know that I don't go to Mass now. I just leave my mother there and come back. She wanted to know why, so I told her I'd lost my faith. That's a little thing that can happen to anyone, can't it? God wouldn't pay much account to anyone losing faith. That's just stupidity and stupidity's good.' She was crying but from her eyes only: it was as if she had everything under control except the mere mechanism of the ducts. 'I wouldn't mind a thing like that. But it's the hate that keeps me away. Some people can drop their hate for an hour and pick it up again at the church door. I can't. I wish I could.' She put her hands over her eyes as if she was ashamed of this physical display of grief. He thought, This is all my work.

'You're one of the unlucky ones who believe,' he said gloomily.

She got up from the bed. 'What's the good of talking? I'd like him here in front of me and me with a gun.'

'Have you got a gun?'

'Yes.'

'And afterwards I suppose you'd go to confession and be happy again.'

'Perhaps. I don't know. I can't think so far.'

He said, 'You good ones are so horrifying. You get rid of your hate like a man gets rid of his lust.'

'I wish I could. I'd sleep better. I wouldn't be so tired and old.' She added in a serious voice, 'People would like me. I wouldn't be afraid of them any more.'

He felt he was in front of a ruin: not an old ruin which has gained the patina and grace of age, but a new ruin where the wallpaper crudely hangs and the wound lies rawly open to show a fireplace and a chair. He thought to himself: It isn't fair. This isn't my fault. I didn't ask for two lives—only Janvier's.

'You can have those collars,' she said, 'if they are any

good to you. Only don't let Mother know. Do they fit you?'

He replied with habitual caution, 'Near enough.'

'I'll get you a glass of water.'

'Why should you get me the water? I'm the servant here.'

'The Mangeots,' she said, 'don't run to servants. Anyway I want to walk about a bit. I can't sleep.'

She went away and came back holding the glass. As she stood there in the rough dressing-gown holding the glass out to him he instinctively recognized the meaning of her action. She had told him all about her hate and now she wanted to indicate by a small gesture of service that she had other capacities. She could be a friend, she seemed to indicate, and she could be gentle. That night, lying in bed, he felt a different quality in his despair. He no longer despaired of a livelihood: he despaired of life.

I I

When he woke the details of the scene, even the details of his emotions, had blurred. Everything for a while might have been the same as before, but when he put his hand on the knob of the kitchen door and heard her stirring within, his troubled heart beat out an unmistakable message under his ribs. He walked straight out of the house to try to clear his thoughts, and over the small patch of cultivated garden he spoke aloud the fact, 'I love her,' across the cabbages as if it were the first statement of a complicated case. But this was a case of which he couldn't see the end.

He thought, Where do we go from here? And his lawyer's mind began to unpick the threads of the case, and to feel some encouragement. In all his legal experience there had never been a case which didn't contain an element of hope. After all, he argued, only Janvier is responsible for Janvier's death: no guilt attaches to me whatever I may feel—one mustn't go by feelings or many an innocent man would be guillotined. There was no reason in law, he told himself, why he should not love her: no reason except her hate why she should not love him. If he could substitute love for hate, he told himself with exquisite casuistry, he would be doing her a service which would compensate for anything. In her naïve belief, after all, he would be giving her back the possibility of salvation. He picked up a pebble and aimed it at a distant cabbage: it swerved unerringly to its mark, and he gave a little satisfied sigh. Already the charge against himself had been reduced to a civil case in which he could argue the terms of compensation. He wondered why last night he had despaired—this was no occasion for despair, he told himself, but for hope. He had something to live for, but somewhere at the back of his mind the shadow remained, like a piece of evidence he had deliberately not confided to the court.

With their coffee and bread, which they took early because of the market at Brinac, Madame Mangeot was more difficult than usual: she had now accepted his presence in the house, but she had begun to treat him as she imagined a great lady would treat a servant and she resented his presence at their meals. She had got it firmly into her head that he had been a manservant to Michel, and that one day her son would return and be ashamed of her for failing to adapt herself to riches. Charlot didn't care: he and Thérèse Mangeot shared a secret: when he caught her eyes he believed that they were recalling to each other a secret intimacy.

But when they were alone he only said, 'Can I find you anything at the market? For yourself, I mean?'

'No,' she said. 'There's nothing I want. Anyway, what would there be at Brinac?'

'Why don't you come yourself?' he said. 'The walk would do you good . . . a bit of air? You never get out.'

'Somebody might come when I was away.'

'Tell your mother not to open the door. Nobody's going to break in.'

'He might come.'

'Listen,' Charlot earnestly implored her, 'you're driving yourself crazy. You're imagining things. Why, in heaven's name, should he come *here* to be tormented by the sight of everything he's signed away? You're making yourself ill with a dream.'

Reluctantly she lifted up one corner of her fear like a

child exposing the broken crinkled edge of a transfer. 'They don't like me in the village,' she said. 'They like him.'

'We aren't going to the village.'

She took him by surprise at the suddenness and completeness of her capitulation. 'Oh,' she said, 'all right. Have it your own way. I'll come.'

An autumn mist moved slowly upwards from the river: the slats of the bridge were damp beneath their feet, and brown leaves lay in drifts across the road. Shapes faded out a hundred yards ahead. For all the two of them knew they were one part of a long scattered procession on the way to Brinac market, but they were as alone on this strip of road between the two mists as in a room. For a long while they didn't speak: only their feet moving in and out of step indulged in a kind of broken colloquy. His feet moved steadily towards their end like a lawyer's argument: hers were uneven like a succession of interjections. It occurred to him how closely life was imitating the kind of future he had once the right to expect, and yet how distantly. If he had married and brought his wife to St Jean, they too might in just this way have been walking silently together in to the market on a fine autumn day. The road rose a few feet and carried them momentarily out of the mist: a long grey field stretched on either side of them, flints gleaming like particles of ice, and a bird rose and flapped away: then again they moved down-hill between their damp insubstantial walls, and his footsteps continued the steady unanswerable argument.

'Tired?' he asked.

'No.'

'It's still strange for me to be walking on and on in a straight line, instead of up and down.'

She made no reply and her silence pleased him: nothing was more intimate than silence, and he had the feeling that if they remained quiet long enough everything would be settled between them.

They didn't speak again until they were nearly in Brinac. 'Let's rest a little,' he said 'before we go in.' Leaning against a gate they took the weight off their legs and heard the clip clop of a cart coming down the road from the direction of St Jean.

It was Roche. He checked his pony and the cart drew slowly up beside them.

'Want a lift?' he asked. He had developed a habit of keeping himself in profile, so as to hide his right side and it gave him an air of arrogance, a 'take it or leave it' manner. Thérèse Mangeot shook her head.

'You're Mademoiselle Mangeot, aren't you?' he asked. 'You don't need to walk into Brinac.'

'I wanted to walk.'

'Who's this?' Roche said. 'Your man-of-all-work? We've heard about him in St Jean.'

'He's a friend of mine.'

'You Parisians ought to be careful,' Roche said. 'You don't know the country. There are a lot of beggars about now who are better left begging.'

'How you gossip in the country,' Thérèse Mangeot said sullenly.

'And you,' Roche addressed Charlot, 'you are very quiet? Haven't you anything to say for yourself? Are you a Parisian too?'

'One would think,' Thérèse Mangeot said, 'that you were a policeman.'

'I'm of the Resistance,' Roche replied. 'It's my business to keep an eye on things.'

'The war's over for us, isn't it? You haven't any more to do.'

'Don't you believe it. It's just beginning down here. You'd better show me your papers,' he said to Charlot.

'And if I don't?'

'Some of us will call on you at the house.'

'Show them to him,' Thérèse Mangeot said.

Roche had to drop the reins to take them and the pony, released, moved a little way down the road: suddenly he looked odd and powerless like a boy who has been left in charge of a horse he can't control. 'Here,' he said, 'take them back,' and snatched the reins.

'I'll hold the pony for you if you like,' Charlot offered with studied insulting kindness.

'You'd better get proper papers. These aren't legal.' He turned his face to Thérèse Mangeot. 'You want to be careful. There are a lot of queer fish about these days, hiding, most of them. I've seen this fellow somewhere before, I'll swear to that.'

'He markets every week. You've probably seen him there.'

'I don't know.'

Thérèse Mangeot said, 'You don't want to raise trouble. The man's all right. I know he's been in a German prison. He knew Michel.'

'Then he knew Chavel too?'

'Yes.'

Roche peered at him again. 'It's odd,' he said. 'That's why I thought I knew him. He's a bit like Chavel himself. It's the voice: the face of course is quite different.'

Charlot said slowly, wondering which syllable betrayed him: 'You wouldn't think my voice was like his if you could hear him now. He's like an old man. He took prison hard.'

'He would. He'd lived soft.'

'I suppose you were his friend,' Thérèse Mangeot said. 'They all are in St Jean.'

'You suppose wrong. You couldn't know him well and be his friend. Even when he was a boy he was a mean little squit. No courage. Afraid of the girls.' He laughed. 'He used to confide in me. He thought I was his friend until I had this accident. He couldn't stand me after that because I'd grown as wise as he thought he was. If you are in bed for months you grow wise or die. But the things he used to tell me. I can remember some of them now. There was a girl at Brinac mill he was sweet on . . .'

It was extraordinary what things one could forget. Was that the face, he wondered, that he had drawn so inexpertly on the wallpaper? He could remember nothing, and yet once—'Oh, she was everything to him,' Roche said, 'but he never dared speak to her. He was fourteen or fifteen then. A coward if ever there was one.'

'Why do they like him there in the village?'

'Oh, they don't like him,' Roche said. 'It's just they didn't believe your story. They couldn't believe anyone would die for money like your brother did. They thought the Germans must be mixed up in it somehow.' His dark fanatic eyes brooded on her. 'I believe it all right. It was you he was thinking about.'

'I wish you'd convince them.'

'Have they troubled you?' Roche asked.

'I don't suppose it's a case of what you call trouble. I tried to be friendly, but I didn't like being shouted at. They were afraid to do it themselves, but they taught their children . . .'

'People are suspicious round here.'

'Just because one comes from Paris one isn't a collaborator.'

'You ought to have come to me,' Roche said.

She turned to Charlot and said, 'We didn't know the great man existed, did we?'

Roche laid his whip to the pony's flank and the cart moved away: as it receded the lopped arm came into view—the sleeve sewn up above the elbow, the stump like a bludgeon of wood.

Charlot rebuked her gently: 'Now you've made another enemy.'

'He's not so bad,' she said looking after the cart for so long a time that Charlot felt the first septic prick of jealousy.

'You'd better be careful of him.'

'You say that just as if you knew him. You don't know him, do you? He seemed to think he'd seen you . . .'

He interrupted her: 'I know his type, that's all.'

12

That night, after they had returned from Brinac, Thérèse Mangeot behaved in an unaccustomed way —she insisted that they should eat in future in the dining-room instead of in the kitchen where previously they had taken all their meals, hurriedly as if they were prepared at any moment for the real owner of the house to appear and claim his rights again. What made the change Charlot had no means of knowing, but his thoughts connected the change with the meeting on the Brinac road. Perhaps the farmer's attack on Chavel had given her confidence, the idea that one man at any rate in St Jean was prepared to play her friend against him.

Charlot said, 'It'll need sweeping out,' and took a broom. He was making for the stairs when the girl stopped him.

She said, 'We've never used the room before.'

'No?'

'I've kept it locked. It's the kind of room he'd have swaggered in. It's smart. Can't you imagine him drinking his wine and ringing for his servants . . .'

'You sound like a romantic novel,' he said and moved to the foot of the stairs.

'Where are you going?'

'To give the room the once-over of course.'

'But how do you know where it is?' It was like putting his foot on a step that didn't exist: he felt his heart lurching with the shock: for days he had been so careful, pretending ignorance of every detail, the position of every room or cupboard.

'What am I thinking of?' he said. 'Of course. I was listening to you.'

But she wasn't satisfied: she watched him closely. She said, 'I sometimes think you know this house far better than I do.'

'I've been in this sort of house before. They follow a pattern.'

'Do you know what I've been thinking? That perhaps Chavel used to boast about his house in prison, draw pictures of it even, until you got to know . . .'

'He talked a lot,' he said.

She opened the door of the dining-room and they went in together: the room was shuttered and in darkness: but he knew where to turn on the light. He was cautious now and shuffled a long time before he found the switch. It was the biggest room in the house with a long table under a dust sheet standing like a catafalque in the centre, and portraits of dead Chavels hanging a little askew. The Chavels had been lawyers since the seventeenth century with the exception of a few younger sons in the church; a bishop with a long twisted nose hung between the windows, and the long nose followed them round from wall to wall, portrait to portrait.

'What a set,' she commented. 'Maybe he hardly had a chance to turn out differently.'

He turned his own long nose up to the face of his grandfather and the man in robes stared down at the man in the green baize apron. He looked away from the supercilious accusing eyes.

'What a set,' the girl said again. 'And yet they married and had children. Can you imagine them in love?'

'That happens to anyone.'

She laughed. It was the first time he had heard her laugh. He watched her avidly, just as a murderer might wait with desperate hope for a sign of life to return and prove him not after all guilty.

She asked, 'How do you think they'd show a thing like that? Would they blow those long noses? Do you think they could weep out of those lawyers' eyes?'

He put out a hand and touched her arm. He said, 'I expect they'd show it in this way . . .' and at that moment the front door bell began to clatter and clang on its long metal stalk.

'Roche?' he wondered.

'What would he want?'

'It's too late for beggars, surely?'

'Perhaps,' she said breathlessly, 'it's him at last.'

Again they could hear the long steel tendril quiver before the bell shook. 'Open it,' she said, 'or my mother will come.'

He was gripped by the apprehension anyone feels at any time hearing a bell ring at night. He moved uneasily down the stairs with his eyes on the door. So much experience and so much history had contributed to that ancestral fear: murders a hundred years old, stories of revolution and war . . . Again the bell rang as if the man outside were desperately anxious to enter, or else had a right to demand admittance. The fugitive and the pursuer give the same ring.

Charlot put up the chain and opened the door a few inches only. He could see nothing in the dark outside except the faint glimmer of a collarband. A foot stirred on the gravel and he felt the door strain under a steady pressure against the chain. He asked, 'Who's that?' and the stranger replied in accents inexplicably familiar, 'Jean-Louis Chavel.'

THE TENTH MAN

PART

III

13

'Who?'

'Chavel.' The voice gained confidence and command. 'Would you mind opening the door, my good fellow, and letting me in?'

'Who is it?' the girl said: she had paused half way down the stairs. A wild hope beat in Charlot's breast, and he called to her in fearful hilarity and relief, 'Chavel. He says he's Chavel.' Now, he thought, at last I am really Charlot. Somebody else can bear all the hate . . .

'Let him in,' she said, and he unchained the door.

The man who came in was as familiar as the voice, but Charlot couldn't place him. He was tall and well made with an odd effect of vulgarity that came from a certain flashiness, something almost jaunty in his walk . . . His skin was very white and looked powdered, and when he spoke his voice was like that of a singer: he seemed too aware of its intonations. You felt he could play any tune on it he pleased.

'My dear lady,' he said, 'you must excuse my breaking in like this.' His gaze passed to Charlot and he suddenly paused: it was as though he too recognized . . . or thought he recognized . . .

'What do you want?' Thérèse said.

He dragged his eyes reluctantly from Charlot and

said, 'Shelter—and a bit of food.'

Thérèse said, 'And you are really Chavel?'

He said uncertainly, 'Yes, yes, I am Chavel.'

She came down the stairs and across the hall to him. She said, 'I thought you'd come . . . one day.' He put his hand out as though his mind couldn't grasp the possibility of anything beyond the conventional. 'Dear lady,' he said, and she spat full in his face. This was what she had looked forward to all these months, and now it was over, like a child at the end of a party, she began to cry.

'Why don't you go?' Charlot said.

The man who called himself Chavel was wiping his face with his sleeve. He said, 'I can't. They are looking for me.'

'Why?'

He said, 'Anybody who has an enemy anywhere is a collaborationist.'

'But you were in a German prison.'

'They say I was put there as an informer,' the man said quietly. The promptitude of the retort seemed to give him back his self-respect and confidence. He said to the girl slowly, 'Of course. You are Mademoiselle Mangeot. It was wrong of me to come here, I know, but any hunted animal makes for the earth it knows. You must forgive my want of tact, mademoiselle. I'll go at once.'

She sat on the bottom step of the stairs with her face covered by her hands.

'Yes, you'd better go quickly,' Charlot said. The man swivelled his white powdery face round on Charlot: his lips were dry and he moistened them with a tiny bit of tongue: the only genuine thing about him was his fear. But the fear was under control: like a vicious horse beneath a good rider it showed only in the mouth and the eyeball. He said, 'My only excuse is that I had a message for mademoiselle from her brother.' Charlot's unremitting, curious gaze seemed to disconcert him. He said, 'I seem to know you.'

The girl looked quickly up. 'You ought to know him. He was in the same prison.'

Again Charlot had to admire the man's control.

'Ah, I think it comes back,' the man said, 'there were a great many of us.'

'Is he really Chavel?' the girl asked.

The fear was still there, but it was hidden firmly and Charlot was amazed at the man's effrontery. The white face turned like a naked globe towards him prepared to outglance him, and it was Charlot who looked away. 'Yes,' he said, 'it's Chavel. But he's changed.' An expression of glee crinkled the man's face and then all was smooth again.

'Well,' the girl asked, 'what's your message?'

'It was just that he loved you and this was the best thing he could do for you.'

It was bitterly cold in the big hall, and the man suddenly shivered. He said, 'Goodnight, mademoiselle. Forgive my intrusion. I should have

(113)

known that the earth is closed.' He bowed with stagy grace, but the gesture was lost on her. She had turned her back on him and was already passing out of sight round a turn of the stairs.

'The door, Monsieur Chavel,' Charlot mocked him.

But the man had one shot left. 'You are an impostor,' he said, 'you were not in the prison, you did not recognize me. Do you think I would have forgotten any face there? I think I ought to expose you to your mistress. You are obviously preying on her good nature.'

Charlot let him ramble on, plunging deeper. Then he said, 'I was in the prison and I did recognize you, Monsieur Carosse.'

'Good God,' he said, taking the longest look he had yet. 'Not Pidot? It can't be Pidot with that voice.'

'No, you mistook me for Pidot once before. My name is Charlot. This is the second time you've done me a service, Monsieur Carosse.'

'You give me a poor return then, don't you, pushing me out into the night like this? The wind's east, and I'm damned if it hasn't begun to rain.' The more afraid he was, the more jaunty he became: jauntiness was like a medicine he took for the nerves. He turned up the collar of his overcoat. 'To be given the bird in the provinces,' he said, 'a poor end to a distinguished career. Good night, my ungrateful Charlot. How did I ever mistake you for poor Pidot?'

'You'll freeze.'

'Only too probable. So did Edgar Allan Poe.'

'Listen,' Charlot said, 'I'm not as ungrateful as that. You can stay one night. Take off your shoes while I slam the door.' He closed the door loudly. 'Follow me.' But he had only taken two steps when the girl called from the landing, 'Charlot, has he gone?'

'Yes, he's gone.' He waited a moment and then called up, 'I'll make sure the back door is closed,' and then he led the man in his stockinged feet down the passage leading to the kitchen quarters, up the back stairs, to his own room.

'You can sleep here,' he said, 'and I'll let you out early tomorrow. Nobody must see you go, or I shall have to go with you.' The man sat comfortably on the bed and stretched his legs. 'Are you *the* Carosse?' Charlot asked curiously.

'I know no other Carosse but myself,' the man said. 'I have no brothers, no sisters, and no parents. I wouldn't know if somewhere in the wastes of the provinces live a few obscure Carosses: there may be a second cousin in Limoges. Of course,' he winced slightly, 'there is still my first wife, the old bitch.'

'And now they are after you?'

'There is an absurd puritanical conception abroad in this country,' Monsieur Carosse said, 'that man can live by bread alone. A most un-Catholic idea. I suppose I could have lived on bread—black bread—during the occupation, but the spirit requires its luxuries.' He smiled confidently. 'One could only obtain luxuries from one source.'

'But what induced you to come here?'

'The police, my dear fellow, and these ardent young men with guns who call themselves the Resistance. I was aiming south, but unfortunately my features are too well-known, except,' he said with a touch of bitterness, 'in this house.'

'But how did you know . . . what made you think . . . ?'

'Even in classical comedy, my friend, one becomes accustomed to gag.' He smoothed his trousers. 'This was a gag, but not, you will say, my most successful. And yet, you know, had I been given time I would have played her in,' he said with relish.

'I still don't know how you came here.'

'Just an impromptu. I was in an inn about sixty miles from here, a place beginning, I think, with B. I can't remember its name. A funny old boy who had been released from prison was drinking there with his cronies. He was quite a person in the place, the mayor, I gathered—you know the sort, with a paunch and a fob and a big watch the size of a cheese and enormous pomposity. He was telling them the whole story of this man who bought his life, the tenth man he called him: quite a good title, that. He had some grudge against him, I couldn't understand what. Well, it seemed to me unlikely that this Chavel would ever have had the nerve to go home—so I decided to go home for him. I could play the part much better than he could—a dull lawyer type, but of course *you* know the man.'

'Yes, you hadn't counted on that.'

'Who would? The coincidence is really too great. You *were* in the prison, I suppose? You aren't playing the provinces too?'

'No, I was there.'

'Then why did you pretend to recognize me?'

Charlot said, 'She's always had the idea that Chavel would turn up one day. It's been an obsession. I thought you might cure that obsession. Perhaps you have. I'll have to go now. Unless you want to be turned out into the rain, don't move from here.'

He found Thérèse back in the dining-room. She was staring at the portrait of his grandfather. 'There's no likeness,' she said, 'no likeness at all.'

'Don't you think perhaps in the eyes . . .'

'No, I can't see any. You're more like that painting than he is.'

He said, 'Shall I lay the table now?'

'Oh, no,' she said, 'we can't have it in here now that he's around.'

'There's nothing to be afraid of. You see, the transfer's genuine. He'll never trouble you any more.' He said, 'You can forget all about him now.'

'That's just what I can't do. Oh,' she broke out passionately, 'you can see what a coward I am. I said the other day that everyone's tested once and after-wards you know what you are. Well, I know now all right. I ought to shake him by the hand and say

"Welcome, brother: we're both of the same blood." '

'I don't understand,' Charlot said. 'You turned him out. What more could you have done?'

'I could have shot him. I always told myself I'd shoot him.'

'You can't walk away and fetch a gun and come back and shoot a man in cold blood.'

'Why not? He had my brother shot in cold blood. There must have been plenty of cold blood, mustn't there, all through the night? You told me they shot him in the morning.'

Again he was stung into defence. 'There was one thing I didn't tell you. Once during the night he tried to call the deal off. And your brother would have none of it.'

'Once,' she said, 'once. Fancy that. He tried once. I bet he tried hard.'

They had supper as usual in the kitchen. Madame Mangeot asked peevishly what the noise had been in the hall. 'It was like a public meeting,' she said.

'Only a beggar,' Charlot said, 'who wanted to stay the night.'

'Why did you let him into the house? Such riffraff we get here when my back's turned. I don't know what Michel would say.'

'He didn't get beyond the hall, Mother,' Thérèse said.

'But I heard two of them go along the passage towards the kitchen. It wasn't you. You were upstairs.'

Charlot said quickly, 'I couldn't turn him out without so much as a piece of bread. That wouldn't have been human. I let him out the back way.' Thérèse sombrely looked away from him, watching the wet world outside. They could hear the rain coming up in gusts against the house, beating against the windows and dripping from the eaves. It wasn't a night for any human being to be abroad in, and he thought, how she must hate Chavel. He thought of Chavel detachedly as another man: he had been enabled to lose his identity, he thought, for ever.

It was a silent meal. When it was over Madame Mangeot lumbered straight off to bed. She never helped in the house now, nor would she wait to see her daughter working. What she didn't see she didn't know. The Mangeots were landowners: they didn't work: they hired others . . .

'He didn't look a coward,' Thérèse said.

'You can forget him now.'

'That rain's following him,' Thérèse said. 'All the way from this house it's followed him. That particular rain. It's like a link.'

'You needn't think about him any more.'

'And Michel's dead. He's really dead now.' She passed her palm across the window to wipe away the steam. 'Now he's come and he's gone again, and Michel's dead. Nobody else knew him.'

'I knew him.'

'Oh yes,' she said vaguely: it seemed to be a knowledge that didn't count.

'Thérèse,' he said. It was the first time he had called her by that name.

'Yes?' she asked.

He was a conventional man: nothing affected that. His life provided models for behaviour in any likely circumstance: they stood around him like tailor's dummies. There had been no model for a man condemned to death, but he had not grown to middle age without making more than one proposal of marriage. The circumstances, however, had been easier. He had been able to state in fairly exact figures the annual amount of his income and the condition of his property. He had been able before that to establish an atmosphere of the right intimacy, and he had been fairly certain that he and the young woman thought alike on such things as politics, religion and family life. Now he saw himself reflected in a canister carrying a dishcloth; he was without money, property or possessions, and he knew nothing of the woman—except this blind desire of heart and body, this extra-ordinary tenderness, a longing he had never experienced before to protect . . .

'What is it?' she said. She was still turned to the window as though she couldn't dissociate herself from the long, wet tramp of the pseudo-Chavel.

He said stiffly, 'I've been here more than two weeks. You don't know anything about me.'

'That's all right,' she said.

'Have you thought what you'll do when she dies?'

'I don't know. There's time enough to think.' She took her eyes reluctantly away from the streaming pane. 'Maybe I'll marry,' she said and smiled at him.

A feeling of sickness and despair took him. There was no reason after all for him to assume that she had not left a man behind her in Paris, some stupid boy probably of her own class who shared her *gamin* knowledge of the streets round Menilmontant.

'Who?'

'How do I know?' she said lightly. 'There aren't many round here, are there? Roche, the one-armed hero: I don't much fancy marrying a piece of a man. There's you, of course . . .'

He found his mouth was dry: it was absurd to experience this excitement before asking a trades-woman's daughter . . . but he had missed the opportunity before he could get his tongue to move. 'Maybe,' she said, 'I'll have to go to Brinac market for one. I always heard that when you were rich, there were lots of fortune hunters around. I can't see any about here.'

He began formally again, 'Thérèse.' He paused, 'Who's that?'

'Only my mother,' she said, 'who else could it be?'

'Thérèse,' a voice called from the stairs. 'Thérèse.'

'You'll have to finish washing-up without me,' Thérèse said. 'I know that voice. It's her praying voice. She won't sleep now till we've done a rosary at least.

Goodnight, Monsieur Charlot.' That was what she always formally called him at the day's end to heal any wound to his pride the day might have brought. The moment had gone, and he knew it might be weeks before it returned. Tonight he had felt certain she was in the giving mood. Tomorrow . . .

When he opened the door of his room Carosse was stretched on the bed with his coat draped over him for warmth: his mouth was open a crack and he snored irregularly. The click of the latch woke him: he didn't move, he simply opened his eyes and watched Charlot with a faint and patronizing smile. 'Well,' he asked, 'have you all talked me over?'

'For an experienced actor you certainly chose the wrong part this time.'

'I'm not so sure,' Carosse said. He sat up in bed and stroked his broad plump actor's chin. 'You know, I think I was too hasty. I shouldn't have gone away like that. After all, you can't deny that I had aroused interest. That's half the battle, my dear fellow.'

'She hates Chavel.'

'But then I'm not the real Chavel. You must remember that. I am the idealized Chavel—a Chavel re-created by art. Don't you see what I gain by being untrammelled by the dull and undoubtedly sordid truth? Give me time, my dear chap, and I'd make her love Chavel. You never by any chance saw my Pierre Louchard?'

'No.'

'A grand part. I was a drunken worthless *roué*—a seducer of the worst type. But how the women loved me. I had more invitations from that part alone . . .'

'She spat in your face.'

'My dear fellow, don't I know it? It was superb. It was one of the grandest moments I have ever experienced. You can never get quite that realism on the stage. And I think I did pretty well too. The sleeve: what dignity! I bet you she's thinking in her bed tonight of that gesture.'

'Certainly,' Charlot said, 'Chavel can't compete with you.'

'I'm always forgetting you knew the man. Can you give me any wrinkle for the part?'

'There's no point in that. You're going before it's light. The curtain's down. May I have my bed, please?'

'There's room enough for two,' the actor said shifting a few inches towards the wall. In tribulation he seemed to be reverting, with hilarity and relief, to the squalor, the vulgarity of his youth. He was no longer the great and middle-aged Carosse. You could almost see youth creep into the veins under the layers of fat. He hitched himself up on an elbow and said slyly, 'You mustn't mind what I say.'

'What do you mean?'

'Why, my dear fellow, I can see with half an eye that you are in the throes of the tender passion.' He belched slightly, grinning across the bed.

'You are talking nonsense,' Charlot said.

'It's only reasonable. Here you are, a man at the sexual age when the emotions are most easily stirred by the sight of youth, living alone in the house with a quite attractive young girl—though perhaps a little coarse. Add to that you have been a long time in prison—and knew her brother. It's just a chemical formula, my dear fellow.' He belched again. 'Food always does this to me,' he explained, 'when I eat late. I have to be careful about supper if I am entertaining a little friend. Thank God, that sort of romance dies in a few years, and with older women one can be oneself.'

'You'd better go to sleep. I'm waking you early tomorrow.'

'I suppose you're planning to marry her?'

Charlot, leaning against the washstand, watched Carosse with dull distaste—watched not only Carosse: a mirror on the wardrobe door reflected both of their images: two middle-aged ruined men discussing a young girl. Never before had he been so aware of his age.

'Do you know,' Carosse said, 'I'm half regretting that I'm leaving here. I believe I could compete with you—even as Jean-Louis Chavel. You haven't any dash, my dear fellow. You ought to have gone in and won tonight when emotion was in the air—thanks to me.'

'I wouldn't want to owe you thanks.'

'Why ever not? You've nothing against me. You're forgetting I'm not Chavel.' He yawned and stretched.

(124)

'Oh well, never mind.' He settled himself comfortably against the wall. 'Turn out the light, there's a good fellow,' he said and almost immediately he was asleep.

Charlot sat down on the hard kitchen chair, the only other perch. Wherever he looked there were signs of how completely at home the pseudo-Chavel had made himself. His overcoat hung on the door, and a little pool had collected on the linoleum beneath it; on the chair he had hung his jacket. When Charlot shifted he could feel the sagging weight of the other's pocket against his thigh. The bed creaked as the actor rolled comfortably towards the centre. Charlot turned off the light and again felt the heavily weighted pocket beat against his leg. The rain washed against the window regularly like surf. The exhilaration and the hope died out of the day, he saw his own desires sprawl upon the bed, ugly and middle-aged. We had better both move on, he thought.

He shifted and felt the heavy pocket beside him. The actor rolled onto his back and began to snore softly and persistently. Charlot could just make out his shape like a couple of meal sacks flung down at random. He put his hand into Carosse's pocket and touched the cold butt of a revolver. It wasn't surprising: we had returned to the day of the armed citizen; it was as normal as a sword would have been three hundred years before. Nevertheless, he thought, it would be better in my pocket than his. It was a small old-fashioned revolver; he rotated the chamber with his finger and found five of the six compartments full. The sixth was empty, but when he held it to his nose he smelt the unmistakable odour of a recent discharge. Something like a rat moved on the bed among the meal sacks: it was the actor's arm. He muttered a phrase Charlot couldn't catch, a word like '*destin*'; he was probably, even in his sleep, playing a part.

Charlot put the revolver in his own pocket. Then again he felt Carosse's jacket: he drew out a small bundle of papers, fastened with a rubber ring. It was too dark to examine them: carefully he opened the door and went into the passage. He left the door ajar for fear of noise and switched on a light. Then he examined the nature of his lucky dip.

It was obvious at once that these were not Carosse's papers. There was a bill made out to a man called Toupard, a bill dated and receipted in Dijon on 30 March 1939 for a set of fish knives: a long time, he thought, to keep a receipt unless one were very careful, but careful Toupard undoubtedly was—there was his photograph on his identity card to prove it: a timid man afraid of being done, scenting a trap on every path. You could see him—Charlot had known dozens like him in the courts—making endless detours throughout his life with the idea of avoiding danger. How was it that now his papers had come into the possession of Carosse? Charlot thought of the empty chamber in the actor's revolver. Papers nowadays were more valuable than money. The actor had been ready to play impromptu the part of Chavel for the sake of a night's lodging, but could he have hoped to get away with *this* identity? The answer was, of course, that five years work many changes. At the end of a war all our portraits are out of date: the timid man had been given a gun to slay with, and the brave man had found his nerve fail him in the barrage.

He went back to his room and stowed the papers and the gun back in the actor's pocket. He no longer wished to keep the gun. The door behind him shut suddenly with a crack like a shot, and Carosse leapt upon the bed. His eyes opened on Charlot and he cried with anxiety, 'Who are you?' but before an answer came he was again as soundly asleep as a child. Why couldn't all those who have killed a man sleep as soundly, Charlot wondered?

14

'Where've you been?' Thérèse said.

He scraped the mud off his shoes with a knife and replied, 'In the night I thought I heard someone move by the garden shed. I wanted to make sure.'

'Were there any signs?'

'No.'

'It may have been Chavel,' she said. 'I lay awake for hours thinking. It was an awful night to turn a man out in. There we were, my mother and I, praying and praying. And he was outside walking. So many *Pater Nosters*,' she said. 'I couldn't leave out the bit about forgiveness every time or my mother would have spotted something.'

'Better to be walking in the rain than shot.'

'I don't know. Is it? It depends, doesn't it? When I spat in his face . . .' She paused, and he remembered very clearly the actor lying on the bed boasting of his gesture. She'll be thinking about it, he had said. It was horrifying to realize that a man as false as that could sum up so accurately the mind of someone so true. The other way round, he thought, it doesn't work. Truth doesn't teach you to know your fellow man.

He said, 'It's over now. Don't think about it.'

'Do you think he got some shelter? He'd have been afraid to ask for it in the village. It wouldn't have done any harm to have let him spend a night here,' she accused him. 'Why didn't you suggest that? You haven't any reason to hate him.'

'It's better just to put him out of mind. You weren't so anxious to forgive him before you'd seen him.'

'It's not so easy to hate a face you know,' she said, 'as a face you just imagine.'

He thought, If that's true what a fool I've been.

'After all,' she said, 'we are more alike than I thought, and when it came to the point I couldn't shoot him. The test floored me just as it floored him!'

'Oh, if you are looking for points like that,' he told

her, 'take me as an example. Aren't I failure enough for you?'

She looked up at him with a terrible lack of interest. 'Yes,' she said. 'Yes. I suppose you are. Michel sent a message by him.'

'So he said.'

'I don't see why he should have lied about that and not about the big thing. As a matter of fact,' she said with an awful simplicity, 'he didn't strike me like a man who told lies.'

During the night Madame Mangeot had been taken ill: those large maternal breasts were after all a disguise of weakness: behind them unnoticeably she had crumbled. It was no case for a doctor and in any event there were not enough doctors in these days to cover so obscure a provincial corner as Brinac. The priest was of more importance to the sick woman, and for the first time Charlot penetrated into the dangerous territory of St Jean. It was too early in the morning for people to be about and he passed nobody on his way to the presbytery. But there his heart drummed on his ribs as he rang. He had known the old man well: he had been used to dining at the big house whenever Chavel visited St Jean. He was not a man who could be put off by a beard and the changes a few years wrought on the face, and Charlot felt a mixture of anxiety and expectation. How strange it would feel to be himself again, if only to one man.

But it was a stranger who replied to his ring: a dark

youngish man with the brusque air of a competent and hardworked craftsman. He packed the sacrament in his bag as a plumber packs his tools. 'Is it wet across the fields?' he asked.

'Yes.'

'Then you must wait till I put on my galoshes.'

He walked quickly and Charlot had difficulty in maintaining the pace. Ahead of him the galoshes sucked and spat. Charlot said 'There used to be a Father Russe here?'

'He died,' the young priest said, striding on, 'last year.' He added sombrely, 'He got his feet wet.' He added, 'You would be surprised at the number of parish priests who die that way. You might call it a professional risk.'

'He was a good man, they say.'

'It isn't difficult,' Father Russe's successor said with asperity, 'to satisfy country people. Any priest who has been in a place forty years is a good old man.' He sounded as though he sucked his teeth between every word, but it was really his galoshes drawing at the ground.

Thérèse met them at the door. Carrying his little attaché case the priest followed her upstairs: a man with his tools. He could have wasted no time: ten minutes had not passed before he was back in the hall drawing on his galoshes again. Charlot watched from the passage his brisk and businesslike farewell. 'If you need me,' he said, 'send for me again but please remember, mademoiselle, that though I am at your service I am also at the service of everyone in St Jean.'

'Can I have your blessing, father?'

'Of course.' He rubber-stamped the air like a notary and was gone. They were alone together, and Charlot had never felt their loneliness so complete. It was as if the death had already occurred, and they were left face to face with the situation.

THE TENTH MAN

PART

IV

The great actor Carosse sat in the potting shed and considered his situation. He was not cast down by his somewhat humiliating circumstances. He had the democratic feeling of a duke who feels himself safely outside questions of class and convention. Carosse had acted before George V of Great Britain, King Carol of Rumania, the Archduke Otto, the special envoy of the President of the United States, Field-Marshal Goering, innumerable ambassadors, including the Italian, the Russian and Herr Abetz. They glittered in his memory like jewels: he felt that one or another of these great or royal men could always when necessary be pawned in return for 'the ready'. All the same he had been momentarily disquieted early that morning in St Jean, seeing side by side on the police station wall a poster that included his name in a list of collaborators at large and an announcement of a murder in a village more than fifty miles away. The details of the crime were, of course, unknown to the police, otherwise Carosse felt sure that the description would have read homicide. He had acted purely in self-defence to prevent the foolish little bourgeois from betraying him. He had left the body, he thought, safely concealed under the gorse-bushes on the common, and had borrowed the papers which might just get him past a formal cursory examination. Now that they could no longer be useful to him, and might prove dangerous, he had burnt them in the potting shed and buried the ashes in a flower pot.

When he saw the two notices he had realized it was no good going further. Not until those notices everywhere had become torn and wind-blown and discoloured by time. He had got to lie up and there was only one house where that was possible. The man Charlot had already lied to his mistress by supporting Carosse's imposture, and he had broken the law by harbouring a collaborator: there was evidently here a screw that could be turned sharply. But as he sat on a wheelbarrow and considered the situation further his imagination kindled with a more daring project. In his mind a curtain rose on a romantic situation that only an actor of the finest genius could make plausible, though it was perhaps not quite original: Shakespeare had thought of it first.

Watching through a knothole in the wall he saw Charlot cross the fields towards St Jean: it was too early for market and he was hurrying. Patiently Carosse waited, his plump backside grooved on the edge of the wheelbarrow, and he saw Charlot return with the priest. Some time later he saw the priest leave alone, carrying his attaché case. His visit could have only one meaning, and immediately the creative process absorbed the new fact and modified the scene he was going to play. But still he waited. If genius be indeed an infinite capacity for taking pains, Carosse was an actor of genius. Presently his patience was rewarded: he saw Charlot leave the house and make his way again towards St Jean. Brushing the leaf-mould off his overcoat Carosse stretched away the cramp like a large, lazy, neutered cat. The gun in his pocket thumped against his thigh.

No actor born has ever quite rid himself of stage fright and Carosse crossing in front of the house to the kitchen door was very frightened. The words of his part seemed to sink out of his mind: his throat dried and when he pulled the bell it was a short timid tiptoe clang that answered from the kitchen, unlike the peremptory summons of his previous visit. He kept his hand on the revolver in his pocket; it was like an assurance of manhood. When the door opened he stammered a little, saying, 'Excuse me.' But frightened as he was, he recognized that the involuntary stammer had been just right: it was pitiable, and pity had got to wedge the door open like a beggar's foot. The girl was in shadow and he couldn't see her face; he stumbled on, hearing his own voice, how it sounded, and gaining confidence. The door remained open: he didn't ask for anything better yet.

He said, 'I hadn't got beyond the village when I heard about your mother. Mademoiselle, I had to come back. I know you hate me but, believe me, I never intended this—to kill your mother too.'

'You needn't have come back. She knew nothing

about Michel.' It was promising: he longed to put his foot across the threshold, but he knew such a move would be fatal. He was a man of cities, unused to country isolation, and he wondered what tradesman might at any moment come up behind his back: or Charlot might return prematurely. He was listening all the time for the scrunch of gravel.

'Mademoiselle,' he pleaded, 'I had to come back. Last night you didn't let me speak. I didn't even finish the message from Michel.' (Damnation, he thought, that's not the part: what message?) He hedged: 'He gave it to me the night he died,' and was astonished by the success of his speech.

'The night he died? Did he die in the night?'

'Yes, of course. In the night.'

'But Charlot told me it was in the morning—the next morning.'

'Oh, what a liar that man has always been,' Carosse moaned.

'But why should he lie?'

'He wanted to make it worse for me,' Carosse improvised. He felt a wave of pride in his own astuteness that carried him over the threshold into the house: Thérèse Mangeot had stepped back to let him in. 'It's worse, isn't it, to let a man die after a whole night to think about it in? I wasn't villain enough for him.'

'He said you tried once to take the offer back.'

'Once,' Carosse exclaimed. 'Yes, once. That was all

(138)

the chance I had before they fetched him out.' The tears stood in his eyes as he pleaded, 'Mademoiselle, believe me. It was at night.'

'Yes,' she said, 'I know it was at night. I woke with the pain.'

'What time was that?'

'Just after midnight.'

'That was the time,' he said.

'How mean of him,' she said, 'how mean to lie about that.'

'You don't know that man Charlot, mademoiselle, as we knew him in prison. Mademoiselle, I know I'm beneath your contempt. I bought my life at the expense of your brother's, but at least I didn't cheat to save it.'

'What do you mean?'

He had remembered the mayor's description of how they all drew lots. He said, 'Mademoiselle, we drew in alphabetical order starting at the wrong end because this man Charlot pleaded that it should be that way. At the end there were only two slips left for him and me, and one of them was marked with the death token. There was a draught in the cell and it must have lifted the slips of paper and shown him which was marked. He took out of turn—Charlot should have come after Chavel—and he took the unmarked slip.'

She pointed out doubtfully the obvious flaw: 'You could have demanded the draw again.'

'Mademoiselle,' Carosse said, 'I thought at the time it was an honest mistake. Where a life depended on it, one couldn't penalize a man for an honest mistake.'

'And yet you bought your life?'

He was playing, he knew it, a flawed character: the inconsistencies didn't add up: the audience had to be stormed by romantic acting. He pleaded, 'Mademoiselle, there are so many things you don't know. That man has put the worst light on everything. Your brother was a very sick man.'

'I know.'

He caught his breath with relief: it was as if now he couldn't go wrong, and he became reckless. 'How he loved you and worried about what would happen to you when he died. He used to show me your photograph . . .'

'He had no photograph.'

'That astonishes me.' It was an understatement: momentarily it staggered him: he had been confident, but he recovered immediately. 'There was a photograph he always showed me; it was a street scene torn out of a newspaper: a beautiful girl half hidden in the crowd. I can guess now who it was: it wasn't you, but it seemed to him like you, and so he kept it and pretended . . . People behave strangely in prison, mademoiselle. When he asked me to sell him the slip . . .'

'Oh, no,' she said, 'no. You are too plausible. He asked *you* . . . That wasn't how it happened.'

He told her mournfully, 'You have been filled with lies, mademoiselle. I'm guilty enough, but would I have returned if I was as guilty as *he* makes out?'

'It wasn't Charlot. It was the man who sent me the will and the other papers. The Mayor of Bourge.'

'You don't have to tell me any more, mademoiselle. Those two men were as thick as thieves. I understand it all now.'

'I wish *I* did. I wish I did.'

'Between them they cooked it perfectly.' With his heart in his mouth, he said, 'I will say goodbye, mademoiselle—and God bless you.' *Dieu*—he dwelt on the word as though he loved it, and indeed it was a word he loved, perhaps the most effective single word on the romantic stage: 'God bless', 'I call God to my witness', 'God may forgive you'—all the grand hackneyed phrases hung around *Dieu* like drapery. He turned as slowly as he dared towards the door.

'But the message from Michel?'

16

Carosse leant on the fence gazing towards the small figure that approached across the fields from St Jean. He leant like a man taking his ease in his own garden: once he gave a small quiet giggle as a thought struck him, but this was succeeded, as the figure came closer and became recognizably Charlot, by a certain alertness, a tautening of the intelligence.

Charlot, who remembered the revolver in the

pocket, stood a little distance away and stared back at him. 'I thought you'd gone,' he said.

'I decided to stay.'

'Here?'

Carosse said gently, 'It's my own place, after all.'

'Carosse the collaborator?'

'No. Jean-Louis Chavel the coward.'

'You've forgotten two things,' Charlot said, 'if you are going to play Chavel.'

'I thought I'd rubbed up the part satisfactorily.'

'If you are going to be Chavel you won't be allowed to stay—unless you want more spittle in your face.'

'And the other thing?'

'None of this belongs to Chavel any more.'

Again Carosse giggled, leaning back from the fence with his hand on the revolver 'just in case'. He said, 'I've got two answers, my dear fellow.'

His confidence shook Charlot who cried angrily across the grass, 'Stop acting.'

'You see,' Carosse said gently, 'I've found it quite easy to talk the girl round to my version of things.'

'Version of what?'

'Of what happened in the prison. I wasn't there, you see, and that makes it so much easier to be vivid. I'm forgiven, my dear Charlot, but you on the contrary are branded—forgive my laughing, because, of course, I know how grossly unfair it is—as the liar.' He gave a happy peal of laughter: it was as if he expected the other to share altruistically his sense of the comedy of

(142)

things. 'You are to clear out, Charlot. Now, at once. She's very angry with you. But I've persuaded her to let you have three hundred francs for wages. That's six hundred you owe me, my dear fellow.' And he held out his left hand tentatively.

'And she's letting you stay?' Charlot asked, keeping his distance.

'She hasn't any choice, my dear. She hadn't heard of the Decree of the 17th—nor you either? You don't see the papers here, of course. The decree which makes illegal all change of property that took place during the German occupation if denounced by one party? Do you really mean to say you never thought of that? But there, I only thought of it myself this morning.'

Charlot stared back at him with horror. The fleshy and porky figure of the actor momentarily was transformed into its own ideal—the carnal and the proud, leaning negligently there on the axis of the globe offering him all the kingdoms of the world in the form of six freehold acres and a house. He could have everything—or his three hundred francs miraculously renewed. It was as if all that morning he had moved close to the supernatural: an old woman was dying and the supernatural closed in: God came into the house in an attaché case, and when God came the Enemy was always present. He was God's shadow: he was the bitter proof of God. The actor's silly laugh tinkled again, but he heard the ideal laughter swinging behind, a proud and comradely sound, welcoming him to the company of the Devil.

'I bet you Chavel thought of it when he signed the transfer. Oh, what a cunning devil,' Carosse giggled with relish. 'It's the nineteenth today. I bet he won't be far behind the decree.'

The actual trivial words made no impression on Charlot's mind: behind them he heard the Enemy greeting him like a company commander with approval—'Well done, Chavel,' and he felt a wave of happiness—this was home and he owned it. He said, 'What's the good of your pretending to be Chavel any longer, Carosse? It's as you say. Chavel will be on his way home.'

Carosse said, 'I like you, old man. You do remind me of good old Pidot. I'll tell you what—if I pull this thing off you need never want for a few thousand francs.'

The grass was his and he looked at it with love: he must have it scythed before winter, and next year he would take the garden properly in hand ... The indentation of footmarks ran up from the river: he could recognise his own narrow shoe-marks and the wide heavy galoshes of the priest. By this route God had moved into the house, where it was suddenly as if the visible world healed and misted and came back into focus, and he saw Carosse quite clearly again, porky and triumphant, and he knew exactly what he had to do. The Decree of the 17th—even the gifts of the

Enemy were gifts also of God. The Enemy was unable to offer any gift without God simultaneously offering the great chance of rejection. He asked again, 'But what's the good, Carosse?'

'Why,' Carosse said, 'even a day's shelter, you know, is a gain to a man like me. People will come to their senses soon, and the right ones will get on top. One just has to keep on hiding.' But he couldn't resist a boast. 'But that's not all, my dear man. What a triumph if I married her before Chavel came. I could do it. I'm Carosse, aren't I? You know your Richard III. "Was ever woman in this humour wooed?" And the answer of course is Yes. Yes, Charlot, yes.'

It is always necessary to know one's enemy through and through. Charlot asked a third time, 'Why? What's the good?'

'I need money, my dear. Chavel can't refuse a split. That would be too abominable after swindling the brother of his life.'

'And you think I won't interfere? You said last night that I loved the girl.'

'Oh, that!' Carosse breathed the objection away. 'You don't love her enough, my dear man, to injure your own chances. You and I are too old for that kind of love. After all, if Chavel comes back you get nothing, but if I win, well, you know I'm generous.' It was quite true: he was generous. His generosity was an integral part of his vulgarity. 'And anyway,' he added, 'what can I do? You've told her I'm Chavel.'

'You forget I know who you are: Carosse the collaborationist—and murderer.'

The right hand shifted in the pocket: a finger moved where the safety catch should be. 'You think I'm that dangerous?'

'Yes.' Charlot watched the hand. 'And there's another thing—I know where Chavel is.'

'Where?'

'He's nearly here. And there's another thing. Look down there across the fields. You see the church?'

'Of course.'

'You see the hill behind, a little to the right, divided into fields?'

'Yes.'

'In the top right-hand corner there's a man working.'

'What about it?'

'You can't tell who he is from this distance, but I know him. He's a farmer called Roche, and he's the Resistance leader in St Jean.'

'Well?'

'Suppose I went down there now and up the hill and told him he'd find Carosse at the big house—not only Carosse but the murderer of a man called Toupard.' For a moment he thought Carosse was going to fire: an act of recklessness and despair in this exposed place. The sound would carry right across the valley.

But instead he smiled. 'My friend,' he said, 'we

seem to be inextricably tied together.'

'You have no objection then if I return with you to the house.' Charlot approached slowly as one would to a chained dog.

'Ah, but the lady may.'

'The lady, I feel sure, will take your advice.'

The right hand came suddenly and cheerfully out of the pocket and beat twice on Charlot's back. 'Bravo, bravo,' Carosse said, 'I made a mistake. We'll work together. You're a man after my own heart. Why, with a little skill we'll both have a nibble at the girl as well as at the money.' He passed his arm through Charlot's and urged him gently homewards.

Once Charlot looked back at the tiny figure of Roche on the hillside: he remembered the period when they had not been enemies, before sickness had tipped Roche's tongue with venom . . . The little figure turned his back and marched up the field behind the plough.

Carosse squeezed his right arm. 'If this Chavel,' he said, 'is really on his way, we'll make a stand against him—you and I. And if the worst comes to the worst, you know I've got my gun.' He squeezed his arm again. 'You won't forget that, will you?'

'No.'

'You'll have to apologize for the lies you've told her. She feels badly about those.'

'The lies?'

'That her brother died in the morning.'

The sun flashed at him from the window of the house: he lowered his dazzled eyes and thought, What am I to do? What am I trying to do?

17

That night Madame Mangeot died. The priest had again been summoned, and from his room on the top floor Charlot heard the sounds of death going on—the footsteps to and fro: the clink of a glass: a tap running: two voices whispering. His door opened and Carosse looked in. He had moved into what he called his own bedroom, but now he was keeping out of the way of strangers.

He whispered, 'Thank God, that's nearly over. It gives me the creeps.'

Death is not private: the breath doesn't simply stop in the body and that's the end—whisper, clink, the creak of a board, the gush of water into a sink. Death was like an operation performed urgently without the proper attendants—or like a childbirth. One expected at any moment to hear the wail of the newborn, but what one heard at last was simply silence. The tap was stopped, the glass was quiet, the boards ceased to creak.

Carosse gave a contented sigh: 'It's happened.' They listened together like conspirators. He whispered, 'This brings it to a head. She'll be wondering what to do. She can't stay here alone.'

'I must go and see the priest home,' Charlot said.

The priest was pulling on his galoshes in the hall. On the way back through the fields he asked curtly, 'You'll be leaving now?'

'Perhaps.'

'Either you will have to go, or Mademoiselle Mangeot will have to find a companion from the village.'

Charlot was irritated by the man's assumption that human actions were governed incontestably by morality—not even by morality, but by the avoidance of scandal. He said, 'It's for Mademoiselle Mangeot to decide.'

They stopped at the outskirts of the village. The priest said, 'Mademoiselle Mangeot is a young woman very easily swayed. She is very ignorant of life, very simple.' He stood like a black exclamation mark against the grey early morning sky: he had an appearance of enormous arrogance and certainty.

'I wouldn't have said that. She has seen a good deal of life in Paris. She is not a country girl,' he added maliciously.

'You don't see more of life,' the priest said, 'in one place than another. One man in a desert is enough life if you are trained to observe or have a bent for observation. She has no bent.'

'She seemed to me to have a great deal of *gamin* wisdom.'

'You didn't bother, I imagine,' the priest said, 'to notice whether it was really wisdom?'

'No.'

'Shrewdness often sounds like wisdom, and ignorance often sounds like shrewdness.'

'What do you want to say—or do?'

'You are a man of education, monsieur, and you won't retort that this is none of my business. You know that it is my business. But you think because I say you must go or Mademoiselle Mangeot must find a companion that I'm prudish. It is not prudery, monsieur, but a knowledge of human nature which it is difficult to avoid if you sit like we do day after day, listening to men and women telling you what they have done and why. Mademoiselle Mangeot is in a condition now when any woman may do a foolish action. All the emotions have something in common. People are quite aware of the sorrow there always is in lust, but they are not so aware of the lust there is in sorrow. You don't want to take advantage of that, monsieur.'

The clock in the ugly church struck. It was half past six: the hour when in prison he had made his only attempt to go back on his bargain: the hour when it had first become possible to make out Janvier's unsleeping eyes. He said, 'Trust me, father. I want nothing but good for Mademoiselle Mangeot,' and turned and strode rapidly back towards the house. It was the hour when one saw clearly . . .

The lower rooms were in darkness, but there was a

light on the landing, and when he entered the hall, he entered so quietly that neither person heard him. They were poised like players before a camera waiting for the director's word to start. So much sorrow in lust and so much lust in sorrow, the priest had said—it was as if they were bent on exhibiting one half of the truth. He wondered what had just been said or done to slice the line of dissatisfaction on the man's cheek and make the girl lean forward with hunger and tears.

'Why don't you leave me alone?' she implored him.

'Mademoiselle,' he cried, 'you are alone now—so alone. But you need never be alone again. You've hated me, but that's all over. You needn't worry any more over this and that.' He knew the game so well, Charlot thought: the restless playboy knew how to offer what most people wanted more than love—peace. The words flowed like water—the water of Lethe.

'I'm so tired.'

'Thérèse,' he said, 'you can rest now.'

He advanced a hand along the banister and laid it on hers: she let it lie. She said, 'If I could trust anybody at all. I thought I could trust Charlot, but he lied to me about Michel.'

'You can trust me,' Carosse said, 'because I've told you the worst. I've told you who I am.'

'Yes,' she said, 'I suppose so.' He moved towards her beside the banister. It seemed incredible to Charlot that his falsity was not as obvious as a smell of sulphur, but she made no effort to avoid him. When he took her in his arms she let herself go with closed eyes like a suicide. Over her shoulder Carosse became suddenly aware of Charlot standing below. He smiled with triumph and winked a secret message.

'Mademoiselle Mangeot,' Charlot said. The girl detached herself and looked down at him with confusion and shame. He realized then how young she was, and how old they both were. He no longer felt the desire at all: only an immeasurable tenderness. The light on the landing was dimming as daylight advanced and she looked in the grey tide like a plain child who had been kept from bed by a party that has gone on too long.

'I didn't know you were here,' she said. 'How long . . .' Carosse watched him carefully: his right hand shifted from the girl's arm to his pocket. He called cheerily down, 'Well, Charlot, my dear fellow, did you see the priest safe home?'

'My name,' Charlot said, standing in the hall and addressing his words to Thérèse Mangeot, 'is not Charlot. I am Jean-Louis Chavel.'

18

Carosse called harshly down, 'You're mad,' but Chavel went on speaking quietly to the girl. 'That man is an actor called Carosse. You've probably heard of him. He's wanted by the police as a collaborationist and the murderer of a man called Toupard.'

'You're crazy.'

'I don't understand,' the girl said. She wiped a damp strand of hair from her forehead. She said, 'So many lies. I don't know who's lying. Why did you say you recognized him?'

'Yes, tell us that,' Carosse called triumphantly.

'I was afraid to tell you who I was because I knew how much you hated me. When he came I thought here was a chance of losing myself for ever. He could have all the hatred.'

'What a liar you are,' Carosse mocked him over the banister. They stood side by side above him and it occurred to Chavel with horror that perhaps he was too late: perhaps this was not simply the lust of grief that the priest had spoken of, but genuine love which would be as ready to accept Carosse the cheat as it had Chavel the coward. He no longer cared about anything in the world but building an indestructible bar-rier between them—at whatever risk, he thought, at whatever risk.

Carosse said, 'You'd better pick up your bed and walk. You're not wanted here any more.'

'This house is Mademoiselle Mangeot's. Let her speak.'

'What a cheat you are.' Carosse put his hand on the girl's arm and said, 'He came to me yesterday and told me that this house was really mine: that some decree or other, I don't know what, had made changes during the occupation illegal. As if I'd take advantage of a quibble like that.'

Chavel said, 'When I was a boy in this house I had a game. I used to play with a friend across the valley.'

'What on earth are you talking about now?'

'Be patient. You'll find the story interesting. I used to take a torch like this or a candle, or if it was a sunny day a mirror—and I used to flash a message like this through the door here. Sometimes it would be just "Nothing doing".'

Carosse said, with a note of anxiety, 'What are you doing now?'

'This message always meant: "Help, the Redskins are here".'

'Oh,' the girl said, 'I can't understand all this talk.'

'The friend still lives over the valley—even though he's not a friend any more. This is the time he'll be going out to the cows. He'll see this light on and off and he'll know Chavel's back. The Redskins are here, he'll read. No one else would know that message.' He saw Carosse's hand tighten in the pocket: it was not enough to prove the man a liar. He could turn even a lie to romantic purposes. There must be the inde-structible barrier.

Thérèse said, 'You mean that if he comes it will prove you are Chavel?'

'Yes.'

'He won't come,' Carosse said uneasily.

'If he doesn't come, there are other ways of proving it.'

'Who is your friend?' Thérèse said, and he noticed that she said 'your friend' as if she were already half convinced.

'The farmer Roche: the head of the Resistance here.'

The girl said, 'But he's seen you already—on the road to Brinac.'

'He didn't look very closely. I am much changed, mademoiselle.' He took the torch again and stood in the doorway. He said, 'He can't help seeing this. He'll be in the yard now—or the fields.'

'Put that torch down,' Carosse shrieked at him: it was his moment of triumph. The pretence was over: the actor was like a man under third degree: the sweat, even in the cold early air, stood on his forehead.

Chavel, watching the pocket, shook his head and his body stiffened against the coming pain.

'Put it down.'

'Why?'

'Mademoiselle,' Carosse implored, 'a man has the right to fight for his life. Tell him to put down the torch or I'll shoot.'

'You *are* a murderer then?'

'Mademoiselle,' he said with absurd sincerity, 'there's a war on.' He backed along the banister away from her and taking the revolver from the pocket swivelled it between them: they were joined by the punctuation of the muzzle. 'Put the torch down.'

In the village a clock began to strike seven: Chavel

with the torch depressed counted the hour: it was the hour of the cinder track and the blank wall and the other man's death. It seemed to him that he had taken a lot of trouble to delay a recurring occasion. Carosse mistook his hesitation: he became masterful. 'Now drop your torch and stand away from the door.' But Chavel raised it and flashed it again off and on and off and on again.

Carosse fired in quick succession. In his agitation the first bullet went wide, splitting the glass of a picture: at the second the torch fell and lay on the hall floor making a little bright path to the door. Chavel's face creased with pain. He was driven back as though by the buffet of a fist against the wall and then the acuteness of the pain passed: he had had far worse pain from an appendix. When he looked up Carosse was gone and the girl was in front of him.

'Are you hurt?'

'No,' he said, 'look at the picture. He missed.' The two shots had been too rapid for her to distinguish them. He wanted to get her out of the way before anything ugly happened. He moved a few feet gingerly towards a chair and sat down. In a few moments the stain would soak through. He said, 'That's over. He'll never dare come back.'

She said, 'And you really are Chavel?'

'Yes.'

'But that was another lie about the message, wasn't it? You never flashed the same way twice.'

'Another lie. Yes,' he said. 'I wanted him to shoot. He can't come back now. He thinks he's killed me like . . . like . . .' He couldn't remember the other man's name. The heat in the hall seemed to him extraordinary at that early hour; sweat ran like mercury beads across his forehead. He said, 'He'll have gone the opposite way to St Jean. Go down there quickly and get the priest to help you. Roche will be useful. Remember he's the actor Carosse.'

She said, 'You must be hurt.'

'Oh, no. I got a ricochet from the wall. That's all. It's shocked me a bit. Get me a pencil and paper. I'll be writing a report of this while you fetch the police.' She brought him what he wanted and stood puzzled and ill at ease before him. He was afraid he'd faint before she'd gone. He said gently, 'You're all right now, aren't you? All the hatred's gone?'

'Yes.'

'That's good,' he said, 'good.' There was nothing left of his love—desire had no importance: he felt simply a certain pity, gentleness, and the tenderness one can feel for a stranger's misfortune. 'You'll be all right now,' he told her. 'Just run along,' he said with slight impatience, as to a child.

'You're all right?' she asked anxiously.

'Yes. Yes.'

Immediately she had gone he began to write: he wanted to tie everything up: his lawyer's instinct wanted to make a neat end. He wished he knew the exact wording of the decree, but it was unlikely to affect the original transfer without a denunciation by one party. This note he was writing now: 'I leave everything of which I die possessed' was merely contributing evidence to prove that he had no intention of denouncing—it had no legal force in itself—he had no witness. The blood from his stomach was running now down his leg. It was as well that the girl was out of the way. The touch of blood cooled his fever like water. He took a quick look round: through the open door the light returned now across the fields: it was oddly satisfactory to die in his own home alone. It was as if one possessed at death only what the eyes took in. Poor Janvier, he thought—the cinder track. He began to sign his name, but before he had quite finished he felt the water of his wound flowing immeasurably: a river: a torrent: a tide of peace.

The paper lay on the floor beside him, scrawled over with almost illegible writing. He never knew that his signature read only Jean-Louis Ch . . . which stood of course as plainly for Charlot as for Chavel. A crowning justice saw to it that he was not troubled. Even a lawyer's meticulous conscience was allowed to rest in peace.

PENGUIN BOOKS

Second
Chance
Summer

Praise for Phillipa Ashley

'Escapism at its very best. What a book!'
Milly Johnson

'Filled with warm and likeable characters. Great fun!'
Jill Mansell

'Sheer joy!'
Katie Fforde

'Sunshine, secrets and a stunning setting
make this the perfect summer read!'
Heidi Swain

'Gloriously uplifting and unashamedly warm-hearted'
Faith Hogan

'Full of genuine warmth and quirky characters'
Woman's Own

'A lovely, summery read, full of secrets and hope'
Jo Thomas

'A blissful story, full of sunshine'
Cressida McLaughlin

About the Author

Phillipa Ashley is a *Sunday Times*, Amazon and Audible bestselling author of uplifting romantic fiction.

After studying English at Oxford University, she worked as a copywriter and journalist before turning her hand to writing. Since then, her novels have sold well over a million copies and have been translated into numerous languages.

Phillipa lives in an English village with her husband, has a grown-up daughter and loves nothing better than walking the Lake District hills and swimming in Cornish coves.

Phillipa Ashley

Second Chance Summer

PENGUIN BOOKS

PENGUIN BOOKS

UK | USA | Canada | Ireland | Australia
India | New Zealand | South Africa

Penguin Books is part of the Penguin Random House group
of companies whose addresses can be found at global.
penguinrandomhouse.com

Penguin
Random House
UK

Published in Penguin Books 2024
001

Set in 10.4/15 pt Palatino LT Pro
Typeset by Jouve (UK), Milton Keynes
Printed and bound in Great Britain by Clays Ltd, Elcograf S.p.A.

The authorised representative in the EEA is
Penguin Random House Ireland, Morrison Chambers,
32 Nassau Street, Dublin D02 YH68

A CIP catalogue record for this book is available from the British Library

ISBN: 978–1–804–94552–0

www.greenpenguin.co.uk

MIX
Paper | Supporting
responsible forestry
FSC® C018179

Penguin Random House is committed to a
sustainable future for our business, our readers
and our planet. This book is made from Forest
Stewardship Council® certified paper.

For Charlotte and James
With love
xx

Also by Phillipa Ashley

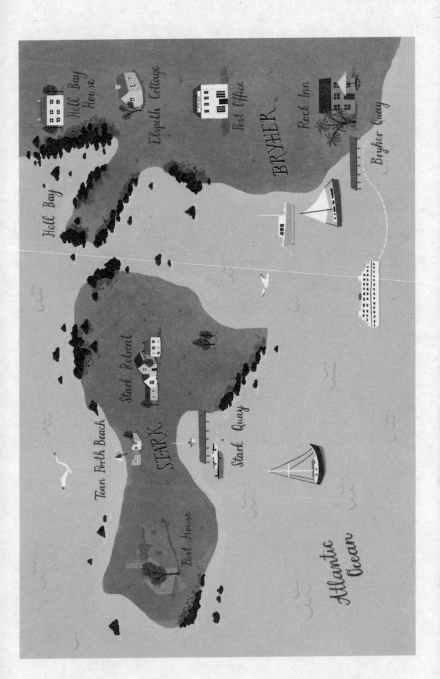

Chapter One

So, this was what it was like to be dead.

Lily had to admit, she thought there'd be lights and a tunnel in the afterlife, not this syrupy darkness. Even the Almighty must be struggling with their energy bills.

'Lily! Boss! Are you OK?' The voice penetrating the darkness was not that of a supreme being unless they had a strong Brummie accent. Richie's voice cut through the bizarre mixture of thoughts that had been swirling through Lily's semi-conscious mind. Why was her PA using his panicked tone as if she very much *wasn't* going to be OK?

She opened her eyes to find herself lying on the carpet in her office with her PA staring down at her. 'W–what happened?' she said, feeling very groggy.

'I don't know. You kind of just . . . crumpled.'

Crumpled? How was that possible? Lily didn't crumple. She wasn't a crumpler. Never had been. She was strong, resilient. She was the embodiment of the metal metaphor: Woman of Steel. That's what a journo had dubbed her a few years ago and it had stuck.

Richie's eyes seemed huge – wide with alarm behind his trademark red-framed glasses. 'Are you OK, hun?'

'Yes. I'm fine. I'm getting up.'

'Don't you dare move! I'm calling an ambulance.' Richie rested a hand on her shoulder. 'You might have hit your head. You probably did – you collapsed. Right in front of me.'

'I don't need an ambulance.'

Lily slowly sat up, wincing at the ache in one temple.

Richie was on his knees next to her, tutting. 'Go easy, hun.'

'Why do you keep calling me "hun"?' she murmured. 'You never call me that.'

'Because you said you'd sack me after the first time I tried it.'

'I was obviously joking.'

'Were you?' He raised an eyebrow. 'It's better than "bab", which my nanna calls everyone.'

'If you dare to call me "bab", I really will sack you,' Lily said, smiling as she spoke, even though it made her forehead throb.

He exhaled with relief. 'Sounds like you're feeling better.'

'I am.' Lily attempted another smile but it turned into a grimace. She'd either hit her head or she had the mother of all headaches. 'Thanks for helping me. I don't know what I'd do without you.'

'I know what I'd do without *you*: have a much easier time and be able to see my boyfriend occasionally.'

'I am very, very grateful,' Lily said, before fixing him with pleading eyes. 'Have you told anyone about – about *this*?' she asked.

'Not yet,' Richie said warily. 'I'd have called the company first-aider but she's gone home.'

'Good! I don't want anyone to know that I'm not . . . feeling one hundred percent.'

'Lily, you're not even ten percent. At least let me call Étienne.'

'No!' Lily said, horrified at the thought of her brother-in-law, an A&E consultant in a nearby hospital, being dragged into her office. 'I'm sure he's too busy saving genuinely sick people.'

She also didn't want anyone knowing she'd collapsed, particularly not with the deal that was sitting in her inbox – a deal that could, potentially, affect the future of everyone at this company, including Richie.

'And you're sure you're not sick?' he said. 'You can fire me if you like, but if you don't get checked out by a doctor, I might resign anyway.'

Richie stood and glared at her, hands on hips. It reminded Lily of the time her mum had come home to find she'd 'repurposed' the dining-room table by painting it purple and green. Well, how was ten-year-old Lily to know it had been a family heirloom?

Twenty-three years later, her parents would be equally horrified – and be on their way to London in a flash – if they knew she'd been taken ill. Since the loss of her sister, Cara, Lily daren't even admit to a sniffle or her mum had palpitations. Cara had died in a car accident two years before and losing her had turned the Harper family's lives upside down. They now knew all too well how fragile life was.

'Do *not* call *anyone* about this. I'll speak to Étienne myself . . . when I've got up off the floor. By the way, can you have a word with the cleaning team, please? There's a mouldy muffin under the desk and the skirting board is thick with dust.'

Richie rolled his eyes. 'Glad to see you're feeling more like yourself.'

He held out his hand to her, which Lily accepted. She still felt weak and woozy. Her blood sugar must be low. The last thing she'd eaten was a chocolate bar that she'd grabbed as she'd dashed out of her Shoreditch penthouse at six that morning. Since then, she'd been glued to her computer.

As she lowered herself gingerly into her chair, Lily spotted the empty mug on her desk: one thing she *had* had a lot of was espresso . . .

'I just need something to eat. Would you mind having a takeout sent in, please?'

'I've got some dried fruit and nuts in my drawer. I'll fetch them and a glass of water. As for a takeout, you're surely not thinking of carrying on working here after your funny turn?'

'I did *not* have a funny turn. I'm not ninety.'

'It looked like a funny turn – my nanna has them sometimes.'

I'm not your nanna, Lily was about to reply before guilt wormed its way in. Richie was only trying to help. He was a fusspot, a bit of a young fogey, but had a quality that Lily prized more than gold: fierce loyalty. She probably – certainly – didn't deserve it. Any CEO would kill to have him and she knew he'd had several approaches but had stayed with her. She needed to make sure it stayed that way.

Richie folded his arms defensively. 'I'm just looking

out for you and the company. I'm your PA – I'm paid to assist you personally, and if you won't look after yourself, I will!'

'Wow, who knew you could be so fierce?' Lily smiled. 'OK, I'll have the water and nuts, thank you, and then I'll *think* about going home.'

Richie went to fetch her supplies while she rested her head on the back of the chair, secretly grateful for the support. She blinked: the bookshelf opposite her desk still looked a little fuzzy but she wasn't going to let on to her PA. She'd hardly glanced up from her screen all day, she'd been so focused on weighing up the pros and cons of the business opportunity that had been presented to her.

A supermarket chain was interested in teaming up with the Lily Loves brand; it was the biggest thing yet to have happened to her precious business, which had grown in ways she could never have imagined when she'd first started selling her own handmade jewellery and accessories from a market stall as a teenager.

Soon, her arty friends were asking her to sell their products too because they didn't have the time, the confidence or the skills. Lily, however, loved talking to customers and helping her friends, and gained a small commission every time she sold an item.

Gradually, she'd realised that curating and selling other people's pieces was where her real strength lay so she'd moved her business online and sales had exploded. Now she had a London office, a team of staff and scores of talented craftspeople under her Lily Loves banner.

The business had grown steadily, but she was faced with a dilemma.

The supermarket chain that was interested in featuring her branded gifts in their stores wanted thousands of items, from mugs and placemats to tea towels and trinket boxes. There was no way the individual craftspeople she worked with could meet the demand, which meant the supermarket would have to stock mass-produced items.

On the other hand, they were offering a lot of money to use the Lily Loves brand on the products, with the promise of much more if the venture took off. Who knew? If it was a success, Lily Loves might be stocked in other retailers, increasing profits and enabling her to invest in and help the artisans who'd originally inspired her to set up the company.

It would mean Lily Loves could expand and secure its future. However, it also meant she'd have to make compromises on what the brand stood for: high quality gifts, individually made with love.

Lily was torn in two over whether to accept the offer – and she didn't have long to decide, as they wanted an answer soon. Whilst she deliberated, she was certain of one thing: the supermarket could not find out the CEO of Lily Loves was prone to fainting at inopportune moments. And after her recent TV fiasco, she couldn't afford any more negative PR.

'Here's your snack!'

Though she could feel the stress pulsing through her veins, Lily forced a smile as Richie put the glass of water and a bowl of trail mix in front of her. He insisted on watching over her like a mother hen.

'The colour's coming back into your cheeks,' he said with satisfaction a couple of minutes later, making Lily smile. She really *did* feel better. The earlier episode had only been a blip after all.

When he left the room to call his boyfriend and say he'd be late – again – Lily took her chance. She turned back to her desktop, determined to get a bit more work done before she finally went home.

'Oh, God . . . not again . . .'

What she hadn't admitted to Richie was that her memory of the minute or so before she'd fainted had been completely wiped out. She'd only recalled that something unpleasant had happened that had caused her to leap from her chair and shout out.

Now she knew exactly what it was. The social media site she'd been looking at was still open on her Windows tab and her name was fifth on the list of trending stories.

#LilyHarper

A news story about something completely unrelated had reignited an X thread about her. She'd thought it was old news and the harpies had moved on to trash someone else's reputation, but no, there she was again. Trending. Public Enemy number one. 'Ruthless bitch' and 'spiteful cow' were among the least awful phrases used to describe her. Some of the abuse was unprintable, including threats and language that made her feel physically sick again.

And all because of a momentary lapse of judgement six months previously.

The vicious comments seemed to leap out at her, bringing nausea to her throat and sweat trickling down her back. She mustn't look. If she fainted again, Richie would piggyback her to A&E himself. How could people be so vile, so vicious . . .

Sinking back in her chair, Lily moaned softly. Her head throbbed but she couldn't tear her eyes away.

The screen went blank.

'Oh, no!'

She thumped at the esc key. 'Richie! What's happened to the computer?'

'*Bonjour.*'

A very tall, stern-looking man stood behind the monitor, holding up a cable with a plug visible at one end of it.

'Étienne! I could have been halfway through a billion-pound deal.'

'Were you?'

'No, actually, I was—' Knowing her visitor wouldn't approve of her doom scrolling, Lily stopped herself. She massaged her temples. 'What are you doing here?' She arched an eyebrow, hopefully in an ironic way, then winced. 'As if I don't know. Did Richie call you? Oh, God, you weren't *at* work, were you?'

'No, I was on my way home.'

'I wish you hadn't come. I'm sorry you were called out . . .'

She glanced over to the door expecting to find her PA peering through the crack, but he'd made himself scarce.

Her brother-in-law, however, had dropped the cable on the floor and perched on her desk, staring at her.

Étienne could look spectacularly stern: anyone who didn't know him to be the kindest of men might be a little intimidated by his serious expression and the tribal tattoos adorning most of his visible skin.

'Someone needs to save you from yourself,' he said, his face softening into concern. 'What would Cara have said if she'd seen you like this?'

'I've no idea.'

'She'd have told you to stop working yourself into an early grave.'

'Pshh,' Lily snorted, then regretted it. 'I'm only thirty-four. I don't smoke, I have a couple of glasses of wine a week, and I exercise. Usually.'

Truth was, she hadn't troubled the gym for weeks and her exercise consisted of dashing between Tube stations. Lately she'd had to forgo even that activity as she'd spent several nights sleeping on her office couch.

'Cara would want you to be happy. To live well.' Étienne's eyebrows knitted together in the way her sister had always said made her want to drag him off to bed. Being honest, Lily only thought it made him look cross, not brooding, but then she wasn't the one who'd fallen for him hook, line and sinker while working in a nursing placement on a remote French Polynesian island.

'It's not fair to put words into Cara's mouth when she can't speak for herself. And you might be a doctor but you're not *my* doctor.'

He didn't smile. This was serious, thought Lily. 'Me being your doctor would certainly be unethical but that doesn't mean I can't give you my advice. I heard what happened – you passed out, didn't you?'

'I wouldn't say that . . .'

'Did you lose consciousness?'

'Not completely. Things went a bit woozy, I'll admit, like a veil had been drawn across my eyes.'

'So, you *did* lose consciousness?'

'No. I *crumpled* according to Richie, but he does have a sense of the dramatic.'

'I'd trust his account of what happened a lot more than I'd trust yours,' Étienne said tartly. 'Sounds like vasovagal syncope.'

'Vaso-syn-what?' Lily asked. 'Is it serious?'

'Vaso-vagal-syn-co-pe,' Étienne enunciated slowly. 'It means fainting.' He rolled his eyes. 'Look, if you've been hunched over the computer for hours without proper food, you probably fainted when you jumped up suddenly. Stress doesn't help. Added to which, you look pale and worn out.'

She rolled her eyes. 'Thanks, I love you too, Étienne.'

'You're welcome. You've told me often enough you're always busy, always "on" and always at the office. Richie says you've been sleeping here and you haven't been eating properly.'

Lily gasped. 'Richie said that? You do know he works for me? That he's signed an NDA?' She was joking but was still shocked that her PA had called Étienne. To be fair, he was her emergency contact, but she felt bad that he'd had to rush over to see her.

'He cares about you. We all do.'

'I'm fine,' Lily said, though Étienne's words were hitting home. She had been working round the clock, and she'd missed quite a few important family events in the past few weeks alone – something she wasn't proud of, but her business was all-consuming. People were counting on her. And yet, as hard as she worked, it was impossible not to let *other* people down.

'Lily?'

Étienne frowned down at her, his warm brown eyes full of concern. 'If you carry on like this, you'll get completely burned out and there may not be a way back.'

'Work has been busy. Challenging. I'll admit, I'm a bit knackered.'

He sighed deeply. 'For once in your life, listen. You can describe what happened – and is happening to you – any way you like. Lack of sleep, not looking after yourself, not eating properly, pressure of work, stress – unresolved grief . . .'

She snorted. 'Unresolved? It's been over two years.'

'That's not a long time and Cara's accident would have floored anyone. Losing a sister is a huge shock and you practically carried on as normal.'

Normal. Tears stung the back of her eyes. What was a normal way to react when your beloved sister was killed in a car accident at the age of thirty-seven?

'Don't give me any clichés about me blotting out the pain with work and not dealing with it adequately,' she said, painful memories giving her tone a sharp edge she hadn't intended.

'Dealing with it *adequately*?' The way he flinched made her instantly regret her words. ' "Adequately" is not a word I'd use to describe the way I felt about losing Cara.'

'Étienne, I'm sorry . . . I didn't mean to be insensitive. Maybe I am a bit tired . . .'

'It's up to you,' he said briskly, choosing not to answer her or let her off the hook. 'You're smart – or at least I thought you were. Work it out for yourself – you clearly don't need me or any medical professional. I have other patients who welcome my help. I came here on my way home from a particularly shitty shift in A&E.'

Lily noticed the slate-blue smudges under his eyes, the lines around his mouth, the exhaustion. 'Oh, God, I am so sorry. Look, let me give you a cliché that we can both agree on. We all deal with that stuff in our own way and – maybe you're right. I do need a break.'

He picked up his bag. 'You do what you want. I'm going to take the girls home, stuff my face with pizza and watch *Frozen*. Again.'

'The girls – the girls are *here*?'

'Yes. They're in the chill-out room downstairs watching your corporate video and eating their own weight in those mini biscuit packets you provide for the staff.'

'What? Why? I—' She let out a groan of horror. 'Oh My God. I was supposed to pick them up from *The Lion King*, wasn't I? And take them to meet the cast afterwards and for dinner?'

'Yes.'

'Oh, Étienne. I am so sorry. I must apologise to the girls. Oh, God. How did I forget?'

'Because you had more important things on your mind?'

'No. Yes. I am sorry.'

'It's an overused word.'

'I mean it. I'll make it up to them.'

'No need. Their nanny took them. They still met the cast and she brought them here in a cab after I'd heard you were taken ill. They can do without dinner, but they did miss *you*.'

'Please can I see them?'

'Richie's gone to fetch them.'

Before Lily could offer up another word, two six-year-olds hurtled into the office like an explosion in a Haribo factory. Amelie and Tania were dressed in frocks of pineapple yellow and peppermint green, their hair flying behind them. They were impossibly pretty, a combination of their father's French Polynesian heritage and Cara's English rose looks.

Amelie launched herself at Lily. 'Auntie Lily! We missed you but Daddy said you weren't feeling very well.'

Lily's head throbbed afresh but she pulled her nieces to her. 'All the better for seeing you. I'm so sorry I forgot to meet you.'

Tania looked at her solemnly. Lily swallowed a lump in her throat. She looked so much like Cara. 'You aren't going to die like Mummy, are you?'

Lily choked back tears. Her heart was so full, it felt as if it might burst. 'No, poppet, I'm not. I'm not going anywhere, I promise you.'

13

She gathered the girls against her, for her own sake as much as theirs, because the world was shifting beneath her. In this moment, the only thing holding it together was them; their warmth, their life force, and through them, the memory of her late sister. Étienne was right. Cara would have wanted her to stay well; to stay alive – for the twins.

Over their shoulders, she saw Étienne and Richie looking at her. Her brother-in-law was tight-lipped. Richie was dabbing his eyes with a tissue.

'I suppose a nice holiday would do me good,' she said.

Richie jumped in. 'Shall I book something?'

'Yes,' Lily said. 'I think you ought to. Somewhere quiet and peaceful and restful, away from all of this for a couple of weeks.'

Richie was already on his way out of the office. 'I'm on it now!'

'Make sure it's got decent WiFi though!' Lily called after him.

The girls released her. Tania sat in Lily's Herman Miller chair and started twirling round.

'Can I play with your toy?' Amelie said.

'Of course,' Lily said, smiling as her niece took the retro stress-relieving pendulum off the desk and started crashing the metal spheres into each other.

Étienne gave her a peck on the cheek. 'Well done,' he said. 'The first step is always the hardest.'

'Well, I'm not as stubborn as I look,' Lily said to a raised eyebrow from her brother-in-law. 'Shall we get out of here? I could join you for pizza at your place?'

'That sounds like a very good idea. You can watch *Frozen* again while I fall asleep.'

'I can't wait,' Lily said, adding earnestly, 'really. It will be wonderful to spend the whole evening with you all. It's been too long . . .'

Étienne touched her arm. 'I know. Come on, let's all go home.'

With a farewell to Richie, Lily shrugged on her suit jacket and, for the first time in months, left the office before it was dark. Today had been a wake-up call – one that she needed to heed for the sake of the company's future.

A week or two of pampering at a nice spa resort would soon set her to rights and then, refreshed and revived, she could get straight back to the office. Even better, she might be able to carry on catching up with emails and keeping her potential new client in the loop in between massages and cocktails.

It was such a brilliant idea, she was amazed she hadn't thought of it before.

Chapter Two

Three days later

This has got to be one of the worst decisions I've ever made in my entire life.

Lily didn't say the words out loud because there was no point. No one could hear her, and she couldn't even hear herself. Even though the helicopter crew had supplied ear defenders, the noise was like lying with your ear pressed to a washing machine.

So far, it had taken almost eleven hours to reach this point. A cab from her flat to Paddington, a train journey to Penzance during which she'd planned to do some work but felt too tired and travel sick, and a short taxi ride to the heli-port. Now she was on the flight to Tresco, one of the Isles of Scilly.

The helicopter crossing was only supposed to take fifteen minutes but Lily already felt as if she'd been on it for a lifetime – and she still had a short boat journey from Tresco to Bryher to contend with, followed by a speedboat to Stark. Several times, she reflected that she could have been enjoying a cocktail in a New York bar by now. New York, however, would not have been a restful break from the mayhem, whereas Stark definitely should be.

'The view will be amazing when we come in to land on the islands,' the woman in the seat beside her had said as they boarded. 'The colours look like the Caribbean.'

When Lily had first started her business, she couldn't have dreamed of visiting the Caribbean. Now she could afford it, she didn't have the time. She'd never been in a helicopter either, though she'd thought it looked glamorous in a James Bond kind of way.

It wasn't.

She'd had her eyes tightly closed since the moment the pilot had said they were ready for take-off, but she'd still felt the sickening feeling of the ground dropping away as the machine rose, improbably, into the sky. Only once had she glanced out of the window to find grey churning waves seemingly inches below.

'Quick, look!'

At a prod on her arm, Lily's eyes flew open. The woman beside her must literally be screaming because, by reading her lips and following her extravagant gestures, Lily could just about follow what she was saying. 'There's the Eastern Isles! And the trees in Tresco Abbey Gardens! I always know I'm here when I see those!'

She heaved a rapturous sigh as if she'd sighted the end of the rainbow. 'What a shame it's a grotty day. To be honest, I didn't think we'd even take off. I heard the check-in guys say we were at the absolute limit for safe travel.'

'They said *what*?' Lily shouted back, hoping she'd misheard the last part.

The woman laughed but her next words were inaudible. She poked a finger at the window. 'Oh, that's Stark.'

'Where? What? Which one?'

'You missed it,' she said, laughing again.

Five minutes later, a jolt signified that today, at least, Lily would spend another day on Planet Earth. The noise ended abruptly and she was climbing down the steps into a rough field with a shed at one side.

Her fellow passengers forged ahead like spaniels let off the lead, chattering excitedly. They all seemed to know exactly where they were heading. Dressed in walking gear and trainers, they made Lily feel slightly self-conscious in her blazer, skinny jeans and loafers. It was her weekend uniform in London, perfect for casual brunch in a café – not that she had time for many brunches, casual or otherwise – but much too smart for hanging around a wild and windy airfield.

Lily trudged behind them, taking in the grey sky and the shed that served as the heliport on Tresco Island, her 'gateway to Stark' according to the website.

Inside the shed, the other passengers were already collecting their bags and climbing into a fleet of green golf buggies. Richie had told her that the Stark Island Retreat reception team would be waiting for her at the heliport ready for her onward transfer to the resort.

One by one, the other passengers whizzed off in their electric buggies until only Lily stood in the shed, with her bag for company. She whipped out her compact mirror, a quirky hand-made one that had been produced by a talented Lily Loves client and was part of a new collection of make-up accessories recently added to the portfolio. Her face was shockingly pale but a quick application of a lip and cheek tint helped to make her look and feel more human and ready to meet the retreat welcome team who'd doubtless turn up at any moment with apologies and warm smiles.

Five minutes later a weather-beaten man carrying a spade strolled into the shack and stared at Lily as if she was an alien.

'Hello there. Are you all on your own? Where are you staying, love?'

'Stark Island,' Lily said tightly.

After a moment of incredulity, he threw back his head and roared with laughter. 'I don't think that's likely, m'dear. No one's stayed on Stark for nigh on two centuries.'

'Ah, but I'm at the brand-new retreat,' Lily said, trying not to let her exhaustion and travel sickness get the better of her politeness.

'New *retreat*?' The man scrunched up his face. 'I dunno—' Suddenly, he nodded and grinned. 'You must mean Sam Teague's place. Is that what he's calling it? Hmm. Last thing I heard, he was still trying to finish it. Well, I'm sure he'll be along in a minute. I must get on, I only came up here from the gardens to fill in some rabbit holes on the landing pad. Enjoy your stay. I hope you don't mind the odd ghost.'

He gazed up at the sky. 'Looks like the fog's on its way. Shame, you should have been here yesterday.'

With that, he sauntered off towards the helipad, whistling to himself.

Lily stared into the gloom of the airfield. Minutes before, she'd been able to make out the grey sea. Now, all that was visible was low cloud that seemed to be creeping towards her menacingly. Moisture was already clinging to her clothes and hair. How could it possibly be *June*?

Still trying to finish it . . . I hope you don't mind the odd ghost. Lily pushed aside a feeling of unease. This guy must be winding her up. She didn't believe in ghosts and, in fact, they were now the least of her concerns about Stark Island Retreat.

OK, Richie had admitted the retreat was having a 'soft opening' prior to its official launch later in the summer, but that had made it sound even more exclusive and quiet. The fact it wasn't officially open also meant they'd been able to fit her in at short notice – and at a price so low Richie found it hard to believe.

'The view looks incredible on the website,' he had enthused after he'd booked her a two-week stay in an ocean-view suite. 'Your cottage is called Cowrie. How cute is that?'

Lily had had to agree. Stark Island Retreat did indeed look beautiful, with its stone-and-wood cottages, a mix of Old and New England that seemed to blend in perfectly with the dunes and low grassy hills of the island. There were photos of shells and translucent water, of driftwood and footprints on bone-white sand.

It looked almost too good to be true.

And what was Lily's first rule of business success? If it looks too good to be true, it almost certainly is.

Fifteen minutes later, she checked her watch, standing in the porch of the helicopter hut. She was the only person left, fog had enveloped the whole field and she felt alone and abandoned. Several times, she'd seemed to be on the verge of tears, which was absolutely shameful.

She had to get a grip on herself. She'd had many setbacks in her life and she'd overcome those. The fact some resort manager wasn't ready with flower leis and hot towels at the airport was a minor glitch.

Still, leaving a client waiting for twenty-five minutes without a call wasn't a good start, especially when they'd – she'd – had such a long and tiring journey.

'Ah. There you are. I suppose you're the guest.'

Lily glanced up at the gruff voice.

Its owner was wearing cargo shorts, a Henri Lloyd waterproof and muddy construction boots.

Lily almost burst out laughing. If you could have conjured up a ruggedly handsome outdoorsy type, this man lived up to every expectation. He was tall, tanned and clearly hadn't had time for a shave that morning – or to change his clothes, judging by the splashes of cream paint on his shorts.

'Sorry I'm late,' he said. 'I was on my way but there was a rope caught around Rory's propellor. He asked me to help and I thought it'd be a five-minute job but it took longer. Hoped you'd be OK for a few minutes.'

'You must be Mr Teague,' Lily said coolly when he didn't introduce himself.

He laughed. 'Oh, call me Sam. Everyone's on first-name terms here. You must be Lily.'

21

'That's me,' she said, thinking he could at least have checked if she minded being addressed by her first name – especially as he was running a high-end resort.

'Well, I do apologise again for keeping you waiting,' he said, though the words came out tersely. 'I did message you.'

'Unfortunately, I didn't get it.'

'Bugger.' Sam raked his hands through curly black hair that had clearly fought a losing battle with the sea air and damp. 'No, well, the phone signal on the islands can be patchy to say the least.'

'I *do* understand,' Lily said, trying not to live up to the stereotypical image of a city grockle or emmet or whatever derogatory name tourists were probably known by in these parts. Then again, she was supposed to be a valued client. Perhaps Sam would benefit from some guest–relations tips. 'Let's just hope the signal will be better at the retreat!'

Sam rubbed his stubbled chin. 'To be honest, we tend to communicate by radio with the main island.'

'The *main* island?' she echoed.

He pointed into the mist where Lily could – if she tried very, very hard – make out the vague outline of twin low hills across sand flats. 'Bryher. That's the island just over the channel from here. There are five settled islands in Scilly and lots of little uninhabited ones, including Stark. There's a signal on Bryher, of course. Think of it as Australia to Stark's Tasmania.'

'Ha,' Lily muttered, unsure if he was being serious or not.

Sam led the way to a golf buggy parked by the shed. 'OK, time and tide wait for no one. Jump in and I'll take you to the Bryher quay, then it's a quick scoot over to Stark in the jetboat.'

Exhaustion washed over her. 'Can't we go straight to Stark? It's been a tiring journey and I can't wait for a nice bath and a chill out before dinner.'

'I need to collect supplies from Bryher first. I promise I won't be more than fifteen minutes, then we'll be on our way.' He picked up her suitcase and dumped it in the back of the buggy.

Lily couldn't resist. 'Are we likely to be there before darkness falls?'

'I should think we might just make it, if we're lucky,' he said, leaving her unsure if he was joking or not.

Ten minutes later, they were indeed in the jetboat – a speedboat called the *Hydra*, which at least had a cabin to huddle in away from the mizzle and sea spray.

She waited in there while Sam nipped onto the stone quay of Bryher. A few people waited, trussed up in Gore-tex from head to toe, yet seeming very happy about standing outside in the drizzle.

A weather-beaten man in yellow oilskins greeted Sam cheerfully. 'Hello! You picked your weather, mate!'

'Yeah. Everything OK with the boat now?'

'Fingers crossed. Thanks for helping me out. Hope it didn't make you late for anything important.'

'Naw, mate, it was fine.'

Lily shrank back inside the cabin, astonished to hear herself dismissed as not important. This must be Rory the fisherman whose propellor she'd been abandoned for earlier.

'Left you a thank you present in that cool box there,' Rory said. 'Need a hand? In this fog, you'll be wanting to get over to Stark before low tide.'

'Thanks. There's a couple of crates in the shed.'

Lily found a spot in the cabin where she could peer through the window without being seen. More people started to arrive on the quay.

A minute later, Rory returned with two more boxes, followed by Sam with two large cans of what Lily assumed to be fuel. One more trip for further open boxes of stuff and Sam jumped on board, poking his head into the cabin. 'Won't be long now.'

'Oh, I've got all day,' Lily muttered though her sarcasm was lost on her host, who was busy taking supplies from Rory and stowing them under the canopy.

She tucked her feet up on the bench seat to avoid anything dropping on her toes and tried to message Richie.

'Yes!' She almost punched the air when one bar of 3G flickered on her mobile. Thank God Richie was on speed dial. It was Saturday, his day off, and she vaguely remembered him saying he was taking his partner, Jakob, away to celebrate his birthday. Lily made a business decision. She might never have a signal again and, in the circumstances, he wouldn't mind, surely?

The call went straight to voicemail and Lily swore.

'Richie. Lily here. Almost at Stark. I do hope it's better than the nightmare journey I've had so far. Waiting for Mr Grumpy Local to take me over to the island now. I'll call when I get to the hotel and have WiFi. I've been making some notes about the new range of plant pots from that maker in Dartmouth – maybe we can speak on Monday about them or have a quick FaceTime? I do hope you got all that? Bye.'

Lily peered at the phone. There was now no signal at all and she'd forgotten to wish him a happy birthday and to have a good weekend with Jakob.

She waved the mobile in the air. *Nada*. She wanted to climb out onto the quay but her way was barred by crates and boxes. Jeez, they must have enough stuff here to last a fortnight. A chilling realisation dawned. She was due to stay two weeks . . . but surely she wouldn't be stuck on one tiny islet for the whole time? There had to be a boat service so she could go shopping and eat out on the other islands?

She didn't mind taking a break, but she couldn't be cut off from her business entirely – not with this deal looming. Plus, she'd promised to keep Étienne and her parents regularly updated on how she was.

Right. That was it. The signal would probably be much better if she got off the boat.

As she squeezed between the boxes, she stubbed her toe on a wooden crate and bit back an expletive, silently cursing the scuff on her loafers.

Ignoring the throbbing pain, she clambered off the boat and onto the quayside.

Some of the ferry passengers had decided to wait for the next service on the terrace of a building that displayed a bright blue sign reading *Quayside Café*. It also had an A-board outside with 'Closed' chalked on it.

Oblivious to her presence, Sam was almost hidden by a pile of lobster pots and, she assumed, deep in conversation with Rory.

Lily waved her phone in the air and a bar of signal flickered yet again. She had to be careful because the battery was low but, with a bit of luck, she might be able to call Richie back. She walked up and down the quayside, praying for the magical bars to appear. The drizzle was light but enough to wet her hair and blazer. She hadn't had time to unpack her waterproof from her case so she'd have to put up with it.

Seeing the people sitting on the café chairs, Lily had a stroke of genius: even though the café was shut, she might be able to piggyback its WiFi. She marched towards it, hoping to find a clue to the password.

The entrance was via a small stone porch, which gave her shelter from the rain and enabled her to read the notices in the doorway. They were mostly about local events; no hint as to the WiFi password.

Her heart sank and she was wondering whether to ask any of the waiting passengers if they knew the code when all of a sudden they rose as one and headed for the quay where a ferry had just pulled in.

Lily was left alone in the porch, peering through the window, in a final desperate bid to spot a WiFi sign inside. She was about to despair when a teenage girl hurtled from somewhere at the back of the café, purple hair flying behind her. She was followed by an older woman wearing a white kaftan.

Neither of them even noticed Lily lurking in the doorway.

'Sam!' the teenager shrieked. 'Wait!'

He emerged from behind the lobster pots and met the two women on the terrace a few feet away from where Lily was standing, unobserved.

'Don't go yet!' the teenager said. 'Auntie Elspeth says you've forgotten the chest!'

Sam heaved a sigh. 'Thank you, Morven. I hadn't forgotten.'

'Really?' she said sarcastically. 'Auntie Elspeth says you're not to leave without it under any circumstances. Oh—' Her voice rose with excitement. 'Is *she* on the actual boat now?'

'Yes, Morven,' Sam replied, his voice fraught with anxiety. 'My guest is waiting for me to take her to the retreat.' Lily would have laughed at his panicked tone if she hadn't been so alarmed to hear about his obvious inexperience at caring for guests.

'Oh my God!' Morven squealed. 'I wasn't sure if you'd picked her up yet. What is she like – horrible?'

'Morven . . .' Sam hissed.

'What? She can't possibly hear us from here,' the girl declared.

Er . . . *wrong*, thought Lily.

'It's not nice to be rude about people you haven't met,' the older woman said.

'Why not? I know she's that nasty cow from the TV.'

'Morven! That will do!' Sam said sharply.

Lily's stomach turned over. She'd come all this way to

27

escape from stress and here she was, being discussed and abused in public by a stranger.

The older woman tutted loudly. 'Morven, don't be so unkind. Sam, I'm glad I caught you.'

'In the nick of time, Auntie Elspeth, but I have to be going now or we'll be caught out by the spring low tide. This weather isn't doing us any favours either.'

'Well, be careful. The fog could last for days.' Elspeth shuddered. 'I don't like it.'

Lily broke out in a cold sweat at the thought of being trapped in the middle of nowhere for days. That made it more important than ever that she should get a message to Richie.

'Ooooh!' Morven cried. 'The fog . . . It must be a portent, signifying you oughtn't to be setting out on this venture. Stark belongs to its ancient guardians, your ancestors.'

'That isn't helpful, Morven,' Sam warned.

'It's not a very auspicious start, though,' Elspeth agreed gloomily.

'Auntie Elspeth,' Sam sounded very frustrated, 'we've had this conversation many times before. The only portents I pay any heed to are the ones telling me I need to make a living, to support my family. And as for our ancestors: a tranquil luxury retreat is the best way to honour the island's history.'

Morven sniggered. 'Luxury? Like, yeah! Last time I saw it, the paint in the cottages was still wet and the toilets didn't flush.'

Filled with dismay, Lily shrank further back into the porch. On top of being absolutely knackered and apprehensive about the boat transfer to Stark, the idea of coping with a blocked toilet for days was just too much.

'It's all fixed!' Sam said in exasperation. 'And I am about to take my *valued guest* to the island for a wonderful break. So, if you wouldn't mind untying the boat, I'm leaving now.'

'Don't forget this!' Elspeth thrust a small wooden chest into his arms. 'You might need it.'

'Thank you. Now, I *must* get back to my guest.'

Lily summoned up her courage: she was, after all, a confident businesswoman who could deal with anything.

'Actually, *she's* here.'

She stepped out of the porch and strode forward.

Three jaws dropped in horrified amazement.

'How nice to meet you,' she said sweetly to Elspeth alone. 'Apologies if I took you by surprise but I got off the boat to try and find a mobile signal.'

'I – er – didn't see you there,' Sam muttered. 'And I'm sorry but we have to go *now*,' he added.

'Because of the fog, so I heard,' she added smoothly. 'However, I'd like to call my family and was hoping to pick up some WiFi from this café. Does anyone know the code?'

'The signal's always crap in the fog,' Morven said.

'We don't have th—' Sam muttered, before Elspeth interjected.

'The code is quayside111, all lower-case,' she replied pleasantly. 'It's my café, you see, my dear.'

'Oh, thank you so much,' Lily said, Elspeth climbing even higher in her estimation. 'It does look lovely. I'll have to pop over while I'm here on holiday.'

Morven let out a kind of snort, which could have been of contempt or horror – or both.

'Absolutely, but there's no time for that now,' Sam said, suddenly firm again.

'Hold on!' Lily waved her mobile in the air as he marched off towards the boat. 'Can't you hang on for half a minute while I make a call?'

'Sorry. No. We might not be able to get to Stark at all if we wait any longer.'

Lily was wondering if that was such a bad thing, considering Bryher had a lovely café with WiFi and at least one civilised person in Elspeth.

'I should do as Sam says, dear,' his aunt said. 'And you can always come over tomorrow.'

'*If* the fog clears,' Morven said with some relish, leaving Lily wondering what she'd done to incite the teenager's wrath – unless Morven simply hated everyone by default.

'You'll be fine,' Elspeth said. 'If you go with Sam now.'

With difficulty, Lily wrenched herself away from the lifeline that had been briefly held out to her.

When she reached the boat, Sam put out his hand to help her on board. She had no choice but to accept it before squeezing back between the crates to huddle inside the cabin. Her toe had started to throb inside her scratched loafer.

Sam took the wheel and turned back to face her.

'Sorry about that,' he said. 'My aunt is into local folklore and rather superstitious, and Morven . . . well, she just likes to wind people up.' He attempted a smile that fizzled out as fast as a dud sparkler. 'We'll soon be at Stark.'

After a tentative pull away from the quay through waters that seemed barely deep enough to cover the propellor, he opened the throttle and Lily fell back against her seat, wondering how the hell they weren't going to end up impaled on the pillars of sharp rock emerging from the sea all around. She also kept wondering what on earth could be in that wooden chest . . . a Ouija board? Magic charms and potions? The mummified carcass of a toad?

Soon, two low hills, almost twins of each other, rose out of the mist, reminding Lily bizarrely of a pair of boobs. She couldn't help but snort.

'What's up now?' Sam twisted round again, making Lily wish he'd keep his eyes on the rocks.

'Nothing, only the shape of the island. It looks . . .' *Like a giant cleavage emerging from the sea*, she thought, but didn't dare say.

To her surprise, he nodded. 'Yeah, it does. Everyone thinks the same. Even back in the day, travellers wrote about it. Quite crudely, some of them.'

'Glad it's not just me . . .' Lily said as the busty outline loomed closer.

Finally, a brief smile lit his face. 'It's not just you, I promise. OK, brace yourself. We're here.'

Chapter Three

Now, Sam really *did* have to be kidding her. All Lily could see was a tangle of tooth-like rocks emerging from the gloom.

The engine note died to a whisper and the boat glided as if through a portal, stopping very precisely alongside a tiny stone jetty. Sam jumped onto the quay and coiled the rope around a mooring post, tying it off with a knot so complicated, it would surely be impossible ever to undo.

He jumped back on board. 'I'll just clear some of these out of your way,' he said, hurriedly landing the boxes and bags that covered the bottom of the boat.

While he nipped deftly from bobbing deck to jetty and back, Lily stared out at the quayside with a creeping sense of foreboding. The mist and the mysterious wooden chest all added to the eerie atmosphere and a feeling of gloom settled on her. Coming to this retreat now seemed like a very bad idea and she wished she could beam herself home.

Still, a nice hot soak and a decent dinner would surely do wonders for her mood. She might watch a new movie on Netflix. By Monday she'd be refreshed and might even touch base with Richie just to double-check that the team were totally happy about dealing with any issues that arose while she was away.

'OK. You can get off now,' Sam told her. 'Be careful, though.'

'I'll be fine,' Lily said, making her way to the bow, ready to step across. The boat rocked.

'No, wait! Let me give you a hand.' Without allowing a second for her to protest, Sam grasped her hand and helped her from the deck to the jetty.

'Thanks,' she muttered, relieved to be on solid ground again. After twelve hours of travelling, she also felt a little light-headed.

Sam plucked her bags from the cabin. 'I'll come back for the supplies after I've shown you to your cottage.'

Lily cast her eye over the pile of goods on the jetty. 'Is there anyone who can help you move that lot?'

He frowned. 'Only me – I run this place.'

Lily felt her jaw drop. '*Just* you? You mean, you run it on your *own*?'

'Well, no. That's not strictly true. My niece Morven – who you just met on Bryher – is going to lend a hand with the changeovers when she can and Auntie Elspeth will step in too, if I need her. At least, that's the plan.'

Lily was struck dumb for a few seconds as the pieces of the jigsaw slotted into place and formed an alarming picture. *Not finished . . . soft opening . . . amazingly cheap . . . available at short notice.*

'I'm your guinea pig, aren't I?' she said, her spirits plummeting towards rock bottom.

'Guinea pig? No, of course not. Please come this way. Your cottage is only a short walk from here.' He picked up her bags and set off up a path as rain began to fall heavily.

Determined not to be put off, Lily trotted behind. 'I'm your first guest, though?'

'One of the first, yes.'

'Who else is here, then?' she said, stopping halfway up the path.

Sam was forced to come to a halt. 'I can't tell you that. It's confidential.'

'Really? I don't think N. O. Body is going to complain about you telling me.'

'Reception is up here,' he said brightly, forging off towards a stone building, just visible through the drizzle. 'There's a spot of mizzle, so you might need this.' He offered her a green golf umbrella, bearing the logo of the retreat. 'Of course, it would have been a good idea to prepare yourself for the elements . . .'

'And if you'd come prepared to meet your first guest – it might have been an even better one!'

Judging by his open-mouthed expression, Lily's riposte had hit home.

'Yes, well, er— We'll be inside soon.'

He offered the umbrella again and she took it but didn't unfurl it. The mood she was in, she might have other ideas for it. Lily stomped after him, simmering with annoyance at his rudeness.

Ten seconds later he stopped outside a stone building with a wooden porch. Although plain, it did seem at least to have a roof, which was more than Lily had been expecting after the gardener's remarks. A wooden sign lay on the ground outside.

'This is it,' said Sam. 'Sorry I didn't have time to fix the sign. Welcome to the reception hub of Stark Island Retreat.'

'And *spa*,' Lily said, huffing. 'It did mention a spa on the website.'

'Did it?' He seemed puzzled. 'Morven must have added that. There *will* be a small spa at some point,' he elaborated, waving his hand airily towards the shrouded coastline. 'In the meantime, there's that big bubbly thing all around us.'

'You mean the sea?' Lily said, hoping he was joking. 'And what about the wellness retreat? My assistant definitely said there was a "wellness retreat".'

'Step out of your door and look up at the sky.'

'I am. It's chucking it down.' Exhaustion and disappointment finally overwhelmed her. 'So, let me get this straight. You've no spa, no staff and I'm the first and only guest.'

Sam looked at the ground because he could barely meet her eyes. 'Look, I made it clear to your PA that the retreat is on a soft opening. Actually, I wasn't going to accept any guests yet but Richie insisted you were desperate. He said you needed to get away from it all, and I quote: "no calls, no hassle, complete tranquillity and privacy". I felt sorry for you so – against my better judgement, if I'm honest – I agreed. I'm sorry if you were expecting Champneys.'

'Firstly, there's no need to feel sorry for me,' Lily said, hardly able to believe what she was seeing and hearing. 'Secondly, I wasn't expecting Champneys, but I was hoping for a boutique retreat in a stunning location with personal service. You do know you're breaking the Advertising Standards Code? And that you'll never recover from the crappy reviews on every travel site when visitors get here and find your website doesn't live up to the reality of HMP Back of Beyond!'

'Back of Beyond this may be, but a prison it is not!' Sam shot back. 'Maybe some aspects of the place don't live up to the website as yet, but as for a stunning location and personal service, you'll definitely get that.' His eyes held a fiery challenge.

Lily glanced around in despair. She was a whisker away from bursting into tears again. This so wasn't her. She was truly desperate for a break, but *here*? 'I suppose the next thing you're going to tell me is that there's no cottage?' she said. 'That I have to build my own from driftwood? Bathe in a rockpool to wash? Skin a rabbit with my bare hands for food?' She laughed but Sam wasn't smiling back. 'Frankly, I'd rather go camping on a traffic roundabout on the North Circular.'

Her mouth snapped shut. Sam said nothing. He seemed at a loss for words and Lily felt uncomfortable – and, suddenly, a bit guilty.

The cloud was now so thick and the rain so heavy that she couldn't even make out the other cottages. She and Sam might have been the only two people on the planet, might have been anywhere on the planet. Somewhere in the distance, a foghorn sounded.

Sam gazed through the mist towards the sea. 'That's the Bishop,' he said, almost reverently, before continuing in a more conciliatory tone: 'Look, I'm sorry – again – that you're so disappointed. I'm sure this weather isn't helping.

However, you are going to stay in one of the most exclusive locations in Britain – in the world, in fact. What's more, you're the first person to spend the night here in two hundred years.'

'Two hundred years? I'm not sure what you mean?'

'The island was inhabited once, centuries ago, but the islanders abandoned it.'

'Really?' With a glance around her, Lily murmured, 'I can't think why,' before giving a resigned sigh. 'OK, there's no point in us standing around like this. There's clearly a mismatch in expectations here so if you don't mind, please could you take me back to Tresco so I can get the next helicopter back to Penzance? I'll find a hotel there.'

'Sorry, but that won't be possible.'

'Why not?'

'There are no more flights because of the fog.'

Lily stiffened. 'OK. Then please be kind enough to take me to one of the other islands and I'll book myself into a hotel there and fly out tomorrow.'

'Tomorrow,' Sam stared at her as if she was mad, 'is Sunday.'

'That we agree on at least.' She smiled. 'Sunday is fine. First flight out of here? I'm not afraid of early mornings,' she added.

'We don't allow helicopter or fixed-wing flights or sailings on Sundays.'

'What? On cultural grounds?' Lily suppressed a sigh. She was much more in her comfort zone when she was finding solutions, taking control. 'OK, I can charter a private helicopter or plane then.' It would cost an arm and a leg, she thought, but would be worth it.

'It's not cultural so much as practical. There are no flights of any kind on a Sunday, on the grounds that everyone should have a day off: pilots, ferry workers, airport staff, ground crew.'

'A day *off*?'

'Yes. Everyone needs time to rest and recuperate,' he said pointedly. 'I suppose,' he added, forestalling her next question, 'that you *could* try and find a skipper who'd sail you back to Penzance, but in this weather, no one in their right mind would attempt it.'

'So,' Lily said, seeing every other option disappearing through the hourglass, 'you're saying that I'm trapped here until Monday?'

' "Trapped" is not the word I'd use.'

He shrugged. Had Richie known about the situation? Had he deliberately sent her to some form of bootcamp? Lily burst out laughing; a proper guffaw, the likes of which she hadn't heard for years. In this silence and mist, it had an edge of hysteria to it. Then she realised another thing. She was stuck with Sam Teague, a grumpy rural hunk whom she had no knowledge of other than that he ran a poor excuse for a wellness retreat on an island unfit to sustain life.

'Then I'll stay on one of the other islands. In . . . another hotel.' She'd almost said 'a proper hotel', but didn't want to fan the flames.

'Well, you could try if you want to. It's getting late in the day and they're probably all fully booked for the weekend, but you're welcome to use the radio in reception and maybe make alternative arrangements. Or one of the islanders might be able to put you up. I'm prepared to take you over the channel to Bryher or Tresco, but in this fog I daren't risk taking the boat to the other off islands.'

She was about to say, 'OK, let's go for it,' when he spoke again.

'Lily,' he said, in a voice that was suddenly gentle, 'your cottage is finished. It has a claw-foot tub and power shower, and a mini-kitchen – though you won't have to catch or cook your own dinner because among the boxes on the quay down there is fresh seafood, salad, home-baked bread, some island gin and a very nice bottle of wine from the St Martin's vineyard. Or you may, of course, go foraging for limpets as the islanders had to when they couldn't get off here for weeks and the potatoes had run out. It's your choice.'

'*My* choice?'

'Yes. And if you do stay, I promise I'll do my very best to find a flight for you on Monday morning, so you can be out of here as soon as possible.'

A wave of weariness washed over her but she pushed it aside and lifted her chin defiantly. 'I suppose I'll have to concede,' she said, her voice sounding lonely and small.

'Concede?' He shook his head. 'You haven't lost,' he said with perfect seriousness. 'It's just the situation.'

'OK,' she said, feeling as if she could lie down and sleep right here on the path. 'I think that's a good interim solution.'

'Good, because while I don't mind a bit of rain, we're

both getting bloody soaked out here. Why don't I show you your cottage so you can relax before dinner?' He picked up her bag without asking her. 'After you,' he said, holding open the door so she could walk into the reception hub.

Lily stepped out of the fog's chilly embrace and into the silence of the retreat. Well, it was definitely *new*, she'd give it that . . . fitted out with an oak bar and countertop, and a couple of small tables and chairs, one of which was still covered in plastic wrap. However, Lily was more concerned about communicating with the outside world than the fixtures and fittings.

'You said you could contact the other islands by radio . . . I don't suppose there's WiFi here?'

He stared at her as if she'd asked him to take her to the moon. 'I use a VHF radio for operational purposes but there's no Internet connection of any description and no TV. We'd rather keep Stark Retreat as a tech-free zone.'

'Tech-free?'

'Stark was conceived as a place where guests can get completely away from screens.' He produced a small wicker basket from behind the bar and lifted the lid. 'In fact, you might like to switch off your phone and leave it here during your stay?'

Lily bit back a gasp. Hand over her phone? Leave it in a basket?

'Of course, it's not compulsory, but we'd rather you bought into the spirit and ethos of the retreat. All you really need to bring to Stark is an open mind . . .'

So many responses crowded Lily's head that she didn't

dare pick one. In the end, she pulled her phone from her jeans pocket, switched it off and dropped it into the basket.

'As there's no connection, it won't be much use to me,' she said coolly, and had the satisfaction of seeing a flicker of surprise in Sam's eyes. Clearly he hadn't been expecting her to comply.

He put the lid on the basket. 'I'll keep this locked in the office and return it when we leave the island.'

'That's very big of you,' Lily said, already feeling twitchy and wondering what she was going to do with herself until then.

'Now for the good news,' he declared, clutching the basket. 'Your cottage has lots of books and we've provided artist's materials.' He smiled. 'Richie happened to mention that you're creative.'

'Creative?' she echoed. A profound sense of loss, for so many things, enveloped her. 'I used to be.'

Chapter Four

'What's she like then? She looked a total whinger from what I saw. Moaning about phone signal and WiFi when she'd only just got here.'

'Cardinal rule of hospitality: don't call the guests "total whingers".'

'I don't want to work in hospitality. I'm only doing it to help you and because Auntie Elspeth keeps going on and on at me that I ought to be more grateful to you and pull my weight. Whatever the feck that means.'

Sam sighed. 'Goodnight, Morven. Please be kind to Auntie Elspeth and I'll see you tomorrow.'

'If you last that long with Lily. She was evil to Tyrone on the *Great British Craft Show*.'

'From what I read, "evil" is a bit harsh for what she said to that bloke.' Sam checked himself before he ended up in a very heated debate with Morven whose opinions tended to be not simply polarised but sited at opposite ends of the universe to his. 'I think Lily's more worried about being stuck here with me than I am with her. Now, I have dinner to prepare so I suggest . . .' He stopped, hearing footsteps outside the reception hub.

'Is that her?' Morven shrieked down the radio.

'No,' Sam exhaled in relief. 'Now, I'll see you tomorrow on Bryher.'

He didn't tell Morven that Lily had demanded to be flown out of the place as soon as possible. After he'd shown her the cottage, he'd promised to take her over to Bryher in the morning, weather and tides permitting, so she could use the WiFi at his house and make some arrangements.

Before heading into the catering kitchen, he flicked the off switch and made sure the radio was set to send only. He couldn't risk Morven coming on the radio insulting his new – and only – guest again, even if he'd been sorely tempted to shout at her himself since he'd picked her up from the heliport. He'd lost count of the times he'd regretted opening up before the retreat was ready, especially to a demanding business mogul used to five-star cosseting.

Since Morven had given him a lurid account of Lily Harper's life to date, he'd wished he'd risked life and limb to ship her back to the mainland himself. When he'd agreed to the booking, her name hadn't rung any bells with him – hardly surprising when he rarely watched TV.

Richie hadn't mentioned anything beyond the fact Ms Harper was looking for an away from it all break at short notice, so Sam had expected a stressed-out exec – but not a 'Z- list celebrity' as Morven had put it.

He had to admit he'd checked out Lily's Wiki entry. It turned out she wasn't just any businessperson; she was a notorious businessperson who'd caused some kind of five-minute rumpus on a TV crafting competition.

But Sam didn't really care about that. What he did care

about was that his guest hated the retreat and thought he was an incompetent charlatan.

After the disastrous start, she would probably trash their reputation when she got home. He'd have to offer her a discount. In fact, he might offer her all her money back and hope she'd forget about him and move on to her next victim.

At least she'd seemed happy enough with Cowrie Cottage, which was just as well because the others weren't ready for receiving guests. Or perhaps she'd been too exhausted to complain after her long journey. Sam had pointed out the facilities and the coffee- and tea-making tray with its mini hamper of local goodies, which he'd brought over earlier.

Lily's relief at finding her accommodation was up to standard had both pleased and shamed him. The weather was shit, the journey had been horrible and her PA had said she'd been unwell. Added to which he'd found out that one of the Tresco gardeners had been talking to her at the heliport and God knows what he'd had to say. She hadn't chosen this break – it had clearly been thrust upon her.

Then there was Morven. She'd done a decent job of preparing the cottage, even if she'd moaned about having to help. He was paying her a generous rate and allowing her far more leeway in her hours than any island hotel would have. They'd never have put up with her truculent attitude either. As her uncle, he had no choice. Her father – Sam's older brother, Nathan – was living in the States, working as a games designer, and hadn't been back to the islands for six months. He'd left Morven with Elspeth and Sam, promising to send for her when he'd found his feet.

But even though Nate now had an apartment and a job, there was still no sign of an invitation to his daughter. He had, however, told Sam that his new girlfriend Grady wasn't super keen on the idea of having a 'hostile seventeen-year-old moving into the condo'.

Morven had declared she'd rather poke out her eyeballs than move in with 'The Gorgon' as she called Grady. Though they'd never met in person, two Zoom calls had been enough.

Morven's paternal grandparents – Sam and Nate's mum and dad – lived near Exeter and she hadn't wanted to up sticks and live with them either. She'd finished her A-level exams and hadn't as yet made plans for September – now it was probably too late and Morven still wouldn't discuss any options. Although she didn't seem to want to move away or go to college, she moaned constantly about Bryher being 'boring' and 'a dump'.

Sam had constantly to remind himself to cut her some slack. Nate had only been twenty-two – five years older than Sam – when Morven's mum, Holly, had handed over custody of the baby to him.

Holly and Nate had had a brief holiday fling. Holly was married and had two young children already. Her husband had refused to let another man's child live with them. She had been forced to make the very tough decision not to be involved in Morven's upbringing. The upshot was that Nate had brought his daughter up with the help of his brother.

Her grandparents had done what they could, though living on the mainland, they could only see her during the holidays. Without their aunt Elspeth, Sam didn't know how he and Nate would have coped at all.

Elspeth was like a surrogate grandmother while Nate was away and Morven did love her. However, the girl clearly sometimes felt she wasn't wanted and didn't fit in anywhere. If Sam was in her situation, he'd probably feel hurt and rejected too.

She'd been a big help to him when it had suited her, helping to paint and decorate the cottages, offering advice on the interiors with her flair for quirky design, yet he hated to see her wasting her talents and simply drifting around.

Sam was at a loss. He was trying to get his business off the ground. He was too old to be a friend to Morven and couldn't be a replacement father to her. Nate was her dad, even if he was five thousand miles away.

So, they existed in an uncomfortable limbo, with Morven living in the attic suite at the top of Hell Bay House, Sam's home. Elspeth was only a few hundred yards away in her own cottage. She and Morven made a formidable pair, with Morven rowing with her great-aunt one minute and then ganging up with her on Sam when it suited her.

At times, it was all too much for him and working on the retreat had provided a much-needed escape, from all kinds of issues he'd rather not confront.

On the downside, he'd practically had to abandon the building business he still owned with his mate Aaron, but there was no going back now. Too many locals had said he'd never finish the work.

Yet Sam had *needed* to throw himself into a project that

was almost too big for him. The challenge of building the retreat had consumed him at a time when he was desperate for something to help blot out the grief and despair he was feeling. Gradually, Stark had become a place of solace too; somewhere he could escape into hard physical labour with the wildness of nature to comfort him.

That had been the idea behind calling Stark a 'retreat', not a 'resort'. He'd always found it a place of sanctuary since he was a boy. If he and Nate had rowed, or if Sam just felt he needed space, he'd come over and lose himself amid the heather and ruins, or take his kayak and go fishing. Now, he hoped to share that with other people in need of peace and solace, who would surely benefit from the natural beauty of the island . . .

His heart sank. That didn't seem to be happening with Lily: in fact, his half-finished project had only caused her further stress. Though he did wonder if *any* place, however luxurious or beautiful, could ever work its magic on such a driven character.

With a sigh, he tried to focus on preparing the evening's meal. After checking the menu with Lily, he'd decided to make a lobster salad, followed by tarragon chicken. He'd eaten and cooked with Scilly seafood since he was young so the salad was a staple.

The leaves, like the tarragon, had been grown on the islands; only the chicken was brought in, chilled. Pudding wasn't his strong point but Bryher's café made wonderful cakes and desserts. He hoped Lily would enjoy the strawberry millefeuilles.

She'd seemed amazed that he was going to cook a three-course dinner, but of course was unaware he was used to cooking for himself and Morven.

He'd hastily unwrapped the plastic from the new chair in reception, added some coasters to the tables and lit the lamps. He then turned his attention to the small dining room, laying the table with the sea blue napkins and aqua glassware that Morven had chosen. The napkins were linen and, along with the top-notch cutlery, had cost more than he'd wanted to pay. However, with the addition of a tea-light, he had to admit the table looked good.

It was such a shame that there was only one guest.

With an inner sigh, he walked back into the bar.

'Hi there.'

Lily was shaking the drops off her umbrella in the entrance to the bar.

She was wearing spa slippers from her room, skinny jeans, and an oversize silky sweater that slipped off her slender frame. Her hair was still damp from the shower, fluffing round her head like a cherub's. Sam did a double take. She looked more angelic than Morven's description of 'evil', though he still braced himself for conflict.

'Is everything OK with the cottage?'

Her reply disarmed him.

'I wondered if –' she said politely '– there was any fresh milk available. For a cup of tea?'

'M–milk?' Sam stuttered. 'Ah, of course. Sorry, I meant to bring it round. I just popped the bottles in the fridge. I'll be along with some ASAP.'

'There's no rush.'

That was probably a tactic. Her mention of 'conceding' had troubled him. Did she view her relationships with the people around her as skirmishes to be won?

Perched on a stool, her wraith-like presence seemed to make the bare shelves and lack of guests seem even more jarring.

'I'm happy to wait here and collect it, to save you from having to come over. You must have a lot to do, being the only one here,' she said.

Sam was about to retort but caught a hint of amusement in her blue eyes and remembered he was supposed to be a host.

'If you wait here, I'll put some in a jug.'

'Thanks.'

He came back from the kitchen at the rear of the hub to find her still sitting on the stool and put the small jug of milk on the bar in front of her. 'There you go, I'll make sure it's replenished if you need any more.'

'Thank you. That should keep me going until Monday morning.' Her eyes travelled to the bare shelves that he'd been meaning to stock with local spirits yet, so far, only held a cocktail shaker and glasses. 'So, this is going to be your bar, is it?'

'Yes, though I need to stock it, of course. Why?'

'I was thinking that it could look really good,' she said, gazing around her with narrowed eyes. 'When it's finished,' she added with a mischievous glint in them.

Sam didn't rise to the bait. He was doing his very best as

it was but he hadn't had time to put the final touches to the bar before he'd had to dash off to collect her from the airport. 'It only needs a few bottles,' he said. 'And like I said, I brought over some gin, wine and some mixers earlier so there's enough for a pre-dinner drink. I'm sorry the choice will be limited, only everything has to come over by boat.'

'To be honest, before you mentioned the gin, I was half-expecting bread and water.'

This line was delivered with amusement so Sam decided to give her the benefit of the doubt and return the joke. 'You haven't tried my cooking yet.'

'Oh, I can't wait.'

Again, the teasing smile . . . And again, he was wrong-footed. He could see how she had got on in life. She was now an iron fist in a velvet glove, although earlier, he'd only experienced the iron fist.

'Is there anything else I can do for you?' he asked. 'Is your room comfortable?' he asked, unable to disguise the hopeful uplift in his voice.

'It's – yes. It's fine,' Lily said.

She slid off the stool and picked up the milk, and her eyes went to the treasure chest that Sam had dumped on the end of the bar on his way in. 'Don't forget what your aunt Elspeth said about that chest.'

Inwardly, he swore. She *had* heard every word of the exchange on the quayside then. How could she have failed to? No wonder she was pissed off on the way to the island. 'I won't,' he said, sounding gruffer than he'd meant to.

She seemed to be about to leave when she said, 'May I

ask what's inside it? Your aunt seemed very insistent you should bring it over. Is it something to ward off evil spirits?'

'You can take a look if you dare,' he said.

She arched an eyebrow. 'Oh, I always dare.'

He could well believe it and pushed the box towards her. 'Please feel free.'

Lily undid the catch and – perhaps a little nervously – lifted the lid. Her mouth opened in surprise and then she burst out laughing.

'Chocolate brownies. Highly significant.'

Sam wondered what on earth she'd expected. 'Elspeth made them at the café. She thought you might need a treat in this horrible weather. Would you like one with your tea?'

'Your aunt is a very perceptive woman,' Lily murmured. 'I'd love one.'

Having wrapped a brownie in a cocktail serviette, he handed it over, relieved he'd at least done something right with her room, the gin and the brownies – though he had to thank his aunt for the latter.

'Now,' he said lightly, 'I must get on with dinner. Is seven-thirty still OK? Come across for seven if you want a pre-dinner drink.'

'Oh, I do,' she said, clutching her brownie as if it was treasure. 'See you later.'

Chapter Five

Lily hadn't been quite straight with Sam when he'd asked if the cottage was OK. Her throwaway 'fine' didn't do justice to the beautifully finished interior.

While she lounged on the huge bed with her tea and brownie, she cast a business eye over it.

It was obvious the cottage had been renovated to a very high standard, with exquisite finishes and natural materials in keeping with its age – two hundred years old at least. There was also some interesting contemporary art on the walls. Mixed media, using sand and shells . . .

There was a coffee-maker but she'd already decided on the Cornish tea – who knew that was even a thing? While she made the drink, she investigated the mini-hamper of treats: shortbread, cheese nibbles, a local beer and a small bottle of Scilly gin. All of them nestled in a cute canvas mini-bucket that was obviously hand-sewn, and rather beautifully at that.

It was exactly the type of item she would have been proud to offer through Lily Loves. As were the mugs and crockery, obviously artisanal with the stamp of a Scilly Island pottery on them, and there was a pretty shell-decorated trinket box where Lily placed the dress ring and necklace she wore every day. The pendant had once been Cara's.

As a boutique hotel suite, she couldn't fault it – and it had the understated style and rustic character of any small luxury hotel she'd stayed in in the Cotswolds or rural France.

She'd almost nodded off in the copper claw-foot tub, situated in front of a window, which, if there hadn't been thick mist cloaking the landscape, might have had a lovely view. The toiletries were sourced locally and perfumed with extracts of Scilly flowers.

Wrapped in a fluffy robe, she'd lain on the bed and wished she could get her phone. She wanted to check in with her parents and Étienne, then have a quick scroll through her emails to ensure nothing urgent had come in from Lily Loves today. With a sigh, she sank back against the pillows.

No matter now gorgeous this place was, the difficult access and lack of connection to the outside world would drive her mad if she had to stay here long . . . and, she had to admit, the comments from the gardener and Elspeth had spooked her.

The idea that she and Sam were alone together on the island, trapped by the bad weather, was creepy.

Sam wasn't creepy, though; he was the opposite. Even scruffy and unshaven, he was handsomer than most men could manage with the benefit of a Savile Row suit and the services of a top men's salon. His physical attractiveness was enhanced by the fact he didn't seem to be aware of it or to give a toss how he looked.

Perhaps if he hadn't made such extravagant and spurious claims for the resort, she could warm to him more. Admittedly, he had a dry sense of humour, was clearly popular with the locals and he was trying hard with the food. Ah, food ... her mouth watered. Lily hadn't eaten properly since breakfast, being too scared to have lunch with the *Hell*-i-copter ride ahead.

Rain spattered the windows and she was sure she could hear the foghorn of the lighthouse calling and maybe even the waves breaking on the shore as she allowed herself, finally, to relax her exhausted body and mind ...

'Oh my God!' Lily's eyes flew open. Something was tapping on her window, over and over, like a ghostly finger ... like Cathy trying to get into Heathcliff's chamber.

She jumped off the bed and laughed in relief to see a branch blowing against the window.

On the bedside table stood a half-full cup of cold tea and the remains of the brownie. The clock by the bed told her she'd been asleep for almost an hour! It was unheard of for her to take a nap in the day. Even worse, it was now a minute after seven and she was late for dinner.

She was the only dinner guest, though, so it probably didn't matter what time she turned up.

As she made a quick check in the bathroom mirror, Lily thought that at least the woman staring back at her didn't look quite as exhausted and drawn as the one who'd arrived. The sleep had done her good. Even so, she was shocked by her pale face and the blue smudges under her eyes that she'd normally disguise with an expensive concealer.

Some sunshine and sleep would soon set that to rights. In the meantime, she dabbed under her eyes with the concealer wand, swiped blusher over her cheekbones and added a slick of lip gloss.

She might be the only guest, but she was still on show.

'Good evening. Welcome – again – to the Stark Retreat.'

'Er . . . hi,' Lily said, taken aback by the sight of Sam holding open the door of the reception hub as if it were the entry to the Ritz. Good grief, he was almost smiling.

'I thought we'd start again,' he said, taking her umbrella and stowing it in a stand. Cushions had appeared on the seating area, along with tealights flickering on the tables. Softly lit, it looked cosy and inviting, despite the rain drumming on the roof. A delicious aroma wafted through from a door next to the bar and Lily's mouth watered.

'Can I get you a drink? Wine? Beer? A cocktail?'

'Erm . . .' Lily floundered. She wasn't sure she could cope with this shiny new version of her host, partly because of the way her body was reacting to the sight of him, freshly shaved and rocking a crisp white shirt and black jeans.

'A G&T would be nice. Please.'

'Sit down and relax while I pour it.'

Lily was taken aback because he was clearly trying very hard to make an effort, even though she could still see he was tense and uncomfortable with playing the host. Deciding to give him the benefit of the doubt, she perched on a bar stool, watching him uncork the stopper from a green lighthouse-shaped gin bottle.

Lit by fairy lights, the bar was now more respectably stocked with a choice of drinks. He added tonic to the generous measure of gin and chunks of ice from the bucket.

'Enjoy!' Sam said, almost too chirpily, pushing a bowl of roasted nuts and olives towards Lily.

'Thanks.'

She didn't know what to make of this transformation from grumpy local to *maître d'*, and secretly thought it didn't quite suit him. Nonetheless, he *was* trying, even if a little too hard, so she'd better be grateful for that and not discourage him. Her earlier barbs must have hit home and her hopes lifted of spending her short stay on Stark a little more pleasantly than she'd expected.

'I'll be back in a moment,' he said.

Half-expecting him to give a little bow, Lily watched him disappear through the door, leaving her alone in the bar.

For a minute, the silence was broken only by the rain and the occasional muffled boom of 'the Bishop'.

Sam returned with a hastily handwritten card, which he placed in front of her.

'Would you care to choose from the wine list? I've red, white or fizz. The good news is the white hasn't travelled far, and even the red and fizz are from Cornwall.'

Pretending to deliberate carefully over the choice between three, Lily eventually plumped for a local white from the St Martin's Island vineyard.

'Good selection,' he said.

'I had an idea it would be. Thank you.'

Sam left her alone and music began to play from a

speaker on the bar: Nina Simone's smoky tones purred out, melancholy and rich. 'My Baby Just Cares for Me' . . .

A lump formed in Lily's throat. She wished he'd chosen anything but that; but how could he know it was the song Étienne had chosen to play at Cara's funeral?

Her vision went a little blurry as tears welled in her eyes.

She rubbed her face with the back of her hand, wishing she'd brought tissues. Where could she find one? As she was looking around for a guest bathroom, she remembered there were the cocktail serviettes behind the bar.

Fanning her face to fight back the tears, she went behind the bar, searching for anything to stem the flow. Yes! There was a roll of blue kitchen paper. That would do. Thank God she hadn't bothered with mascara.

'Is everything OK?'

Swivelling round, a wad of kitchen paper bunched in her fingers, she was confronted by Sam's anxious face. 'Yes. I – um . . .'

He looked as embarrassed as she felt. 'Are you alright?'

'Yes. I – I could smell you chopping onions in the kitchen.'

'There are no onions in the dinner tonight.'

Lily smiled weakly. 'It was a joke. I'm fine. Absolutely fine. It's the . . . er . . . song, you see.'

A deep frown. 'Jazz makes you sad?'

'No, I quite like it,' she said hastily. 'It's just that it has some bittersweet associations for me.' That was as far as she was prepared to go.

The song had ended and Nina had launched into 'Sinnerman'.

Lily could see Sam was thrown off kilter. 'I thought this would be soothing and, er, create the right ambience.' He reached for his phone. 'I'll change it.'

'You don't have to. Really, it's f—'

'Fine. You said. Even so, I'll play something else,' he said quickly, as if he was eager to get out of her sight. He clearly couldn't deal with emotion – not that Lily could either. 'By the way, your starter is ready, if you'd like to come through to the dining room.'

With relief, she followed him into the dining room to one side of reception. While not large, it had the same air of rustic sophistication as her room. There were six tables, and all were laid with cloth napkins and glasses as if expecting guests.

'I gave you a window seat,' Sam said, 'although there's not much of a view at the moment.'

She followed his apologetic gaze to the raindrops sliding down the glass. Beyond that was a wall of grey mist.

'It'll clear up tomorrow,' he said.

Sharing none of his confidence, Lily turned her attention to the interior to cheer herself up and keep the conversation neutral. 'Nice room. Lovely old beams,' she said, pointing to the gnarled oak trusses that were holding up the roof.

'Oh, yes. Apparently, the big one was salvaged by the islanders from the wreck of a ship.'

'You're kidding me?'

'It's well documented in the parish records. Elspeth will

know more about it.' He grimaced. 'Though maybe asking her about the history of the island isn't the best idea.'

'No, I've already been spooked once by a branch tapping at my window. Thought it was the shades come to wreak revenge.'

'Ouch! I am sorry you heard some of that conversation. Like I said, my aunt is very keen on the history of the islands. Our family go back generations and she's never left here. Any kind of change is hard for her to accept.'

'Change can be hard for all of us but sometimes you need to do something different,' Lily said, thinking of Lily Loves and the supermarket offer to stock her brand. Perhaps it was exactly the injection of fresh ideas and finance her business needed, even if it would take her away from the original idea behind Lily Loves.

'I do know what you mean,' he muttered. 'I'll get your starter.'

Thoughts of work took a back seat when Sam arrived at the table a few minutes later with a plate of pink lobster meat on fresh leaves, dressed with a citrus vinaigrette.

'Rory caught it this morning,' he said, with a hint of a twinkle in his eye. 'If I hadn't helped him untangle the propellor, we'd have had no fresh shellfish today.'

'I'll let you know if it was worth it,' Lily said, trying to sound jokey.

'I'll await your verdict.'

'Well?' he asked, returning a while later to clear her empty plate.

'Totally worth the wait. It was so sweet and delicate. I rarely eat seafood in London but that was a treat.'

'Tarragon chicken next?'

'Sounds good.'

While he was in the kitchen, Lily wandered around the room, noting the tealights on the tables in their teal ceramic holders glazed with an imprint of wavy fronds of seaweed. There were prints on the walls; more contemporary artwork interspersed with a few photographs of, she presumed, islanders of the past. They were standing next to small boats or hauling in nets, the hardship of their lives etched on strained faces.

'Here we go!'

Her spirits were lifted by the fragrant aroma of herbs that accompanied Sam when he re-entered the dining room with a plate of chicken in a creamy sauce, fresh new potatoes and cavolo nero.

'Enjoy!' he said in his best host fashion before he headed back to the kitchen.

'Wait,' Lily said. 'Aren't you going to eat?'

'I'll grab something in the kitchen.'

'Oh. OK. It's just that . . .' She glanced around the empty room. 'It feels a bit strange, sitting here, eating alone.'

'You're my guest. I can't sit down at your table and start tucking in. I'll fetch the wine.'

With that, he vanished again, leaving Lily alone with her tarragon chicken. She pictured him standing in the kitchen, eating scraps like a kitchen maid. The thought made her smile: he was about as far from a kitchen maid as you could get.

Music tinkled out of the speaker – some generic classical stuff that made her feel like she was a guest in Downton Abbey. It lent a rather stiff and formal air to the meal: like dining with the Beast in his castle, except Sam was the post-transformation version.

Perhaps on the journey here, when he was dishevelled and grumpy, he might have qualified for beastly status. Now, he was simply gorgeous and trying to be more pleasant, although Lily was convinced it didn't come naturally to him. He really wasn't the right type of person for front of house.

She was halfway through her main when he returned to top up her glass with wine from the ice bucket on her table.

'How's your chicken?' he asked, lingering.

'It's delicious. Really,' she said.

'And the music?' he asked, a hopeful lilt in his voice telling her that he really was trying to please his guest.

'It's – um – OK,' she said, popping a forkful of tender chicken in her mouth.

'I found a classical mix download on my phone,' he said, then frowned. 'But I'm sensing you're not impressed?'

Lily mused while she finished chewing. 'It's very nice.'

Sam eyed her sharply. '"Nice?" I'm sensing that's a loaded word.'

'No. Not really.'

'I'd rather you were honest with me.'

Lily wasn't too sure if he meant that, but he *had* asked. 'Maybe a classical mix is a little too . . . staid? You might be better to play stuff that's in line with your brand rather than

61

what you enjoy or even what you think your guests will enjoy.'

He frowned. 'How do I do that?'

'There are companies that specialise in music for businesses. They'll curate a playlist to suit your brand and sort out all the licensing rights. And I'm sure you won't have to stream it so don't worry about the WiFi,' she said. 'For a price, of course. You haven't looked into that?'

'Not yet.'

'OK. For now, let's just say you and I are simply listening to some music together but when you have guests – after you've opened properly – you'll have to think about it.'

'I'll add it to the list,' he said, his shoulders slumping in dejection. Lily suspected he'd probably bitten off more than he could chew with the retreat and needed all the professional help he could get.

She laid down her cutlery. 'What's your brand?' she asked. 'Is it modern and sophisticated? Or elegant and traditional?'

'Erm . . .'

She smiled. 'Don't tell me you haven't thought about your brand because I know you have. I've seen your guest welcome pack and website. You've done a great job with those.'

'I have?' He gave a wry smile. 'Actually, Morven and her friend designed the website. I was going for barefoot luxury like you get in exotic island hotels. We did some travelling after uni, working in a couple of resorts in the Seychelles. I worked in the kitchens briefly and then in maintenance. It gave me some ideas – and a pipe dream.'

She noted the 'we' followed by the hasty change to the first person.

'Barefoot luxury is very on trend, though I have to say that Stark is more at the barefoot end of the scale than the luxury one, at the moment.'

His lips parted in dismay.

'Don't worry, we can do something about that. First things first, back to the music: this is a retreat, so you want something that's chilled out but contemporary. Look, why don't you at least sit down at the table rather than hovering by it? I'm sure that doesn't count as fraternising with your guests.'

Her comment drew a smile that lit up Sam's eyes. Lily was struck by his handsome profile, tempered by the lines fanning out from beside his eyes. He could only be in his mid-thirties but the telltale marks of strain and responsibility were etched on his face.

'I don't want to interrupt your meal,' he said.

'You aren't.'

Reluctantly, he drew back a chair and sat down opposite her.

'We invested a lot of money on getting the Lily Loves branding spot on. We don't have our products in stores,' she said, careful not to add 'yet', 'but I learned a lot about the retail environment – and that includes all the strategies they use to maximise spend. One of those is sounds.'

'*Sounds?*' he echoed.

'Oh, yes. Guests linger longer and spend money if you can perfect your music branding,' she said, getting into her stride.

Sam's brow creased. 'I'd no idea. Here I was, thinking I could simply connect my iPhone to a speaker.'

'We could brainstorm some ideas after dinner if you like, or set up a time to do it tomorrow?'

'I'm sure you've plenty to do without being a mentor to me.'

'On the contrary. With no Internet or distractions, it's the perfect opportunity to do a deep dive into the whole ethos of the Stark Island Retreat. It's practically the only free time I'll ever have to do it. I'll be back in the thick of it once I can get back to civilisation.'

He nodded but pushed back his chair and got to his feet.

'Lily, this is all very kind of you, and I appreciate the offer, but I'm sure we'll both have plenty to do tomorrow. I'm flattered you're willing to spend your precious time helping me, but I'm also conscious you're here for a *rest* – even if only for two nights.'

'Okayyy . . .' she said, taken aback.

'My number one promise to guests is to offer them a relaxing escape away from everyday cares,' he went on, firmly. 'It's why I called Stark a *retreat*, not a resort. It's wild and remote – a prison to some, but hopefully, soon, it will also be a haven. Your PA said you'd try to resist taking a break and he begged me to resist *you*.'

'He said *what*?' Lily could hardly believe what she'd heard.

'He said you needed saving from yourself. And from what I've seen, you do need the rest.'

'Isn't that a bit paternalistic?' Lily said.

'Of Richie or me?' he asked.

'Both, actually.' Lily set her jaw.

Sam grinned. 'Maybe, but that's what I'm going to do: make sure you have a complete break. Now, please,' he said, 'relax and finish your meal.'

Lily arched an eyebrow, torn between annoyance at Richie and Sam – and being secretly touched that they cared.

'And if I'm good, I get pudding?' she joked.

'Something like that,' Sam said drily. 'If you're very good, I might even take you on a tour of the island tomorrow.'

Chapter Six

'Good morning.'

Sam was aware how the brief banter of the previous evening had turned to dwindling enthusiasm when Lily slouched into the dining room the next day. They hadn't spoken much after he rebuffed her offer of brainstorming branding and business ideas. She'd eaten half the dessert then disappeared off to her room with the rest of the bottle of wine. He could hardly blame her: he wasn't sure his comments had come across as he'd intended.

'Sleep well?' he asked, his jaw aching with putting on a cheery face when he felt so grim inside. Lily's comments had reminded him of how much he still had to do at the retreat and made him feel more than a little out of his depth.

'Surprisingly, yes,' she muttered, 'Even though it's still raining.'

'Only a bit and not for long.' He placed a platter of fresh fruit in front of her. 'The storm front's almost passed. We'll be the first in the country to see the sunshine.'

She raised her eyebrows, disbelief etched on her face. 'Can I get that in writing?'

'I've seen the forecast. It'll be better today. Would you like tea or coffee?'

'Coffee. Please.'

Sam filled a cafetière. It was for the second time that morning, the first having been for himself as he needed the caffeine. Unlike Lily, he hadn't slept well. He'd lain awake wondering if he'd gone too far in telling his guest she had to take a rest, and deciding that he had.

Not only had he turned down the invaluable advice of an expert, but he'd also made Lily think he was a chauvinistic pig. On the other hand, Richie had pleaded with him to 'make sure' she rested, and said that he'd 'have a nightmare' trying to stop her from working.

Sam had wondered if Lily's need for a break, and brittle mood, might have anything to do with the sad associations that had been triggered by the Nina Simone track.

God knows, he knew how difficult – impossible – it was to come to terms with sadness. Hadn't he also tried to blot out the pain of his own losses by throwing himself into work? Was creating Stark – trying to bring life back to a dead island – his way of clawing back what had slipped away from him so unexpectedly?

He'd no idea. He'd tried not to analyse his actions too deeply, until Lily had arrived.

Had last night been a cry for help – did she want to talk about what was upsetting her? Sam was no therapist; he'd barely got to grips with being a host. He'd also felt that interfering in Lily's life in this way was too much of a burden to bear, so he'd listened, been vague, and joked that Stark was a place where he could guarantee complete quiet if nothing else.

He would have many guests in need of recuperation, peace and quiet – so long as Lily didn't go home and spread the word that Stark was a dump and its owner a bully.

'Is the fruit OK? Would you like a cooked breakfast or continental?' he asked, trying to smile and be as helpful as possible. 'I have bacon, eggs, sausage – vegetarian alternatives . . . Or pastries, which I baked fresh this morning.'

'Continental is fine,' Lily said, adding archly, 'and stop trying too hard.'

Her amused tone took the sting out of her remark. She looked less exhausted this morning. He had to admit her eyes held a glint of mischief he found disturbingly attractive.

'OK, I'll fetch the croissants,' he said, back in host mode.

While he arranged pastries in a basket, he heard a yelp and dashed into reception. Lily was standing in the porch with the door wide open.

'What's the matter?' he said.

'The sun's out! And, oh my God, will you look at that *view*?'

Sam followed her outside, blinking in the dazzling light of a June morning like a creature emerging above ground after a long winter. The full panorama of dozens of low islands and rocky skerries unfolded ahead of them, floating in a sea of azure, turquoise and deepest blue. Even though he'd known they were there all along, hidden by the veil of fog, he was seeing them through Lily's eyes and experiencing the full impact on her.

She seemed to blossom under his eyes, holding her arms wide and saluting the dazzling orb in the sky.

Touched by her happiness, he stood by her side. 'You can have breakfast out here if you like.'

'Oh, I'd love to.'

He smiled, lifted by her lighter mood. 'I'll bring it outside with some fresh coffee.'

She switched her focus to him. 'You will join me though? I'm dying to find out what all these other islands are. I can't believe it's the same place as yesterday. It looks like the Greek islands or the Caribbean.'

Sam had heard his home described that way before and it always gave him a glow of pride, though Scilly was, in his eyes, even more beautiful than those other glamorous destinations. 'I'm glad it's cleared up for you.'

'I must have been very good.' Her blue eyes sparkled, like a kid let out of school to go to the seaside.

Sam went back into the kitchen, thinking of how Lily had reminded him of himself, a young boy at the end of term, arriving back on Bryher from the Island Comp, knowing there would be no more lessons or boarding for six weeks. He'd enjoyed school and staying in dorms had been fun up to a point. He'd settled well unlike some of the other islands children, who'd found it hard to get used to boarding during the week because the daily journey would have been too disruptive.

Yet nothing compared to home, to the freedom of running free on Bryher; sailing to Samson with his father and Nate and, later, with his friends Aaron and Ben. More recently, he'd loved exploring with someone else, sitting on deserted beaches or swimming together in the crystal waters. Once again, his desire to share that passion with others came back to him.

When he returned, Lily was pointing across the ocean under shaded eyes. 'What's that island there, with the square building and the waves breaking over it?'

'St Helen's.'

'And the lighthouse in the distance. That's the Bishop that we heard last night, I presume?'

'Yes.' He seemed surprised she knew.

'And beyond?'

'Nothing until Newfoundland.'

She swung round to look at him. 'Wow. I'd no idea that it would be like this.'

'Despite the website?'

'I had a quick look after Richie booked, but not in detail. I was too busy trying to tie up loose ends before I came away.'

He shook his head. 'I thought you were supposed to have a complete break.'

'I couldn't just *leave*. Not without letting key people know I'd be back.'

'Well, you'll be back with them tomorrow.'

'Yes, but I think I can allow myself today off. As I'm stuck here.'

Her eyes challenged him but he wasn't fazed. 'How long has it actually been since you took a proper holiday?'

'Oh . . . I'm not sure.' Lily appeared to be dredging a corner of her mind. 'I went on a hen weekend to Barcelona last May, though I flew back earlier than everyone else to prepare for the team's mid-year reviews. I was in France on business earlier this year.' She sighed. 'I missed my parents' Ruby Wedding party. I regret that.'

Sam's interest was piqued by this admission. 'What happened?'

'I *was* all set to go to the party. I even had my bags packed in the office – but a potential client asked me to fly urgently to Paris for a meeting.'

'Couldn't you have put them off?' Sam said.

'No.' She sighed. 'Well, I didn't think so at the time, but afterwards . . . I wish I'd gone to the party. My auntie Tina had flown over from Australia and I missed that. And my great-uncle Matthew was there. He was a hundred and two.' Her voice faltered. 'Unfortunately he passed away the week after.'

'That's such a shame. I am sorry,' Sam murmured, seeing the genuine regret in Lily's eyes.

'We all were, even though he'd had a wonderful life. He just keeled over while he was feeding the ducks in the grounds of his nursing home. I hadn't seen him for a long time and because I missed the party . . . well, I never got to talk to him again. To tell him how much he'd inspired me. He used to love making things. He did wood turning and carving.'

Sam listened, surprised and moved to see her lift the corner of this veil on her private life.

'Maybe that's where you got your creative side from.'

'Maybe.' She shrugged and then declared, 'So I'm going to make the most of this opportunity. Even though it will be short.'

'I'll try to make sure it's not too awful,' Sam said wryly, noting the reminder that she expected to leave the next morning. 'Would you like to see the island with me after breakfast or explore on your own?'

'Both, please. A tour and then a solo adventure.' She stopped and rolled her eyes. 'How embarrassing. Will you listen to me, sounding like a little kid?'

'We all need to be kids again from time to time,' he said, wondering when he'd last enjoyed a carefree day himself. 'Though it may surprise you, I do plan on offering activities to guests. Nature and history walks, beachcombing . . .'

'All of which sound great,' Lily said.

He smiled, feeling genuine pleasure. 'Before I leave you to enjoy the rest of your breakfast, I'd like to check this evening's menu with you.'

She seemed more than happy with most of it: goat's cheese salad, with a key lime cheesecake he'd brought over from the bakery. It was just as well, as the only dessert alternative he could have offered was cheese and biscuits.

However, she hesitated over the lamb shank he'd intended to braise for the main course.

'Do you have any more of Rory's fish?' she asked. 'It seems a shame not to eat more seafood when it's so delicious and fresh.'

'I could probably rustle up some sea bass,' Sam said, thinking that while she was off exploring he could take out the fishing kayak and catch some. Not that he would admit to Lily that he'd have to go out 'specially.

'Great.' She rewarded him with a smile that almost made the effort worthwhile. 'That's one of my favourites.'

Sam left her, basking in her approval of his ideas for activities – when he could get them sorted – and of his plans for the evening menu. Even though these small aspects had gone well, he needed to get his supplies and logistics sorted. There were two big freezers in the utility building behind the kitchen, but they were virtually empty. It was one more sign of how badly he'd underestimated the amount of work and staff needed to run the retreat. One guest and one night had made him feel completely exposed.

And it had to be *this* guest: a celebrity business owner with a big online presence. If she did choose to go public with her opinion of the retreat, any review could be shared far and wide. Perhaps he should thank Lily for shining a light on its – and his – failings so he could take steps to improve things.

At least the weather was on his side now and Lily looked happier than she had at any moment since he'd collected her from the heliport.

With the sun shining, and his guest warming to her island 'prison', today was his last chance to make a good impression before she flew home and offered her verdict.

Chapter Seven

Wow, wow and wow.

Lily was fully aware she'd uttered the words too often and they'd only left the retreat ten minutes previously. She'd become embarrassed by saying it again and again but there was no doubt that while the retreat had its shortcomings, the natural setting was simply out of this world.

They were climbing the gentle slope of what Sam called the South Hill and, with every step, the views became better and better.

Could she really be in England? she wondered for the umpteenth time, gazing around at isles sprinkled like jewels over a turquoise sea. Light bounced off the water, dazzling her; gulls wheeled overhead; foxgloves and daisies flourished in the shelter of ruined walls. Far below, great rounded boulders and jagged rocks sheltered pocket-sized coves with pale sand.

Automatically, she reached into her pocket to whip out her phone and take photos before realising her contraband tech had been handed over. 'I wish I could share these views with my family and Richie.'

Sam pushed his Ray-bans onto his head. 'You'll be able to tomorrow when we reach Bryher.'

'Now the weather's cleared, could we go over there today?' she offered.

'We could. If you *really* want to, we can . . . or you could enjoy the digital detox for one more day if you think you can cope?'

'Of course I can cope,' Lily retorted, refusing to admit she was twitchy without her phone. 'I should have brought a sketch pad. I left it in the cottage.'

'We can go back and fetch it?'

She softened. 'No, it's OK. I'll come out later once I've got my bearings around the island. Although,' she said, pausing again to shade her eyes and drink in the vista, 'I already know I'll be so frustrated when I can't capture this place as I'd like to.' She'd be leaving the island tomorrow and would do her best to create a lasting memory of how gorgeous it was in the summer light.

'I'm sure you won't.'

'I will. All artists are doomed to fail in their mission: it's the trying that counts. I've also seen the artwork on your walls. I couldn't produce anything of that quality.' She noticed his mouth curve as he listened to her. 'What's funny?'

'Nothing much – only I'm wondering if this is really Lily Harper talking? The uber-confident entrepreneur who made a man cry on TV?'

'That was a slip of the tongue! I let my mouth engage before my brain and the producers edited the clip to make me sound even worse,' she said, instantly on the defensive. 'I never called Tyrone "talentless". I actually gave him some positive feedback, despite my misgivings. It was what I said when I thought I was off air that caused all the trouble.'

Even telling Sam what had happened brought the tell-tale knot back to her stomach.

'If you've seen it, you'll know how it came out.'

'I don't watch much TV but after you booked, I'll admit I did watch the clip,' he said, rather sheepishly.

'Morven sent you the link, did she?'

Sam gave a wry smile. 'She suggested I watch it, yes, but I'm interested in *your* side of the story.'

Lily inhaled in surprise. 'Thank you, because no one usually cares. What actually happened,' she said, shuddering at the memory, 'was that I was talking to one of the other judges – who also hadn't been impressed by Tyrone – and made a comment: *"Tyrone just keeps ripping off another artist's work. His talent doesn't match the other contestants' here. How did he get through the selection process?"* '

Even repeating the words made her grow cold, but she wanted to be completely honest with Sam. 'I didn't know my mic was still on. I apologised to Tyrone at once. He was upset but he calmed down when I tried to explain he needed to have confidence in his own original creations – and I thought he'd accepted my apology and my feedback.' She let out a breath. 'I was wrong.'

Sam winced. 'Ouch.'

'I felt awful for treading on his dreams.'

'It was a competitive show, though,' Sam said. 'I can't imagine ever taking part in anything like that, but he must have known what he was letting himself in for?'

'Possibly, but I shouldn't have been so naive. Things were far worse when the show was aired. The editors cut all my positive feedback and only showed my off-mic – but *on-mic* – remark. There was also a scene where Tyrone ran off the set in tears. That definitely didn't happen!'

'Jeez. Are you saying they staged it?'

Lily gave a bitter laugh. 'Yes, but how could I accuse him and the show's producer of lying?' Tyrone had also made the most of the incident since, repeating the misquote and putting other words into her mouth, Lily might have added, but didn't.

'Can producers even do that?' Sam said, incredulous.

She groaned. 'Apparently, they can do anything. I was stupid not to realise what could happen and be more guarded. Nothing I say or do can change it. No one really cares what I actually said. I'm just the Wicked Witch of the Craft Show.'

Sam turned his blue gaze on her, and Lily felt a shiver – a pleasant shiver – run up her spine. 'If it's any consolation, you don't seem like the kind of person who would be deliberately cruel to anyone,' he said.

'Thank you.' She was amazed at the warmth in his voice and more touched than she dared admit. 'Unfortunately, my reputation always precedes me now.'

He screwed up his face in embarrassment. 'I shouldn't have Googled you. And I apologise for Morven, too. She almost never lets her brain engage before her mouth.'

Lily laughed. 'It's OK. I've heard far worse said about me than "horrible". You have no idea ...' She shuddered, recalling the vile online abuse and newspaper comments that had followed her ill-judged remark on the craft programme.

'You know the comments that hurt the most?' she said. 'The ones that said because I was successful, I should be championing people who were struggling to make it in the crafting world – not bringing them down. I set up Lily Loves to do just that: help makers gain a higher profile and proper reward for their work. I've always wanted to support my friends and fellow makers, right from the start. It's why I agreed to be a judge on the show. Now I wish I could turn back the clock.' She stopped, realising she was talking about work again, yet also that she'd never told anyone how deeply the trolling had hurt her.

'You don't have to worry about any of that today. I know you found the lack of connectivity here frustrating to begin with, but I hope it means that you can forget about the trolls – while you're on Stark at least – and just be present,' he said gently. 'I'm sorry for bringing it up.'

'It's OK,' she said airily. 'And I'm not so confident when I'm not "on show", of course I'm not. Who is? I also like to be honest. While I did do A-level Art and Textile Design at school, I've never really been good enough at one thing to make a living solely from that.'

'I thought you started off selling your own work on a market stall?'

'I did, and it took off in a way I'd never dreamed, but the real breakthrough came when I sold other people's creations as well as my own. I have an eye for the beautiful and unique, you see . . .'

Lily wished Sam hadn't been giving her his full attention at that precise moment. The light caught his profile, illuminating eyes the exact colour of deep ocean in the distance. His thick hair, almost black, stirred in the soft breeze. He lifted tanned, strong arms to push it off his face.

'Go on,' he encouraged her.

Lily forced her attention back to what she'd been saying.

'My work sold well, but other artists' sold even better, so I sought out more and more of it.' She gave a rueful sigh. 'I wouldn't have any old thing on the stall, only the pieces I loved and that complemented my vision. My artist friends didn't want to have the hassle of sales and admin. I did – I was naturally pretty good at it and taught myself to be even better.'

Still embarrassed about her reaction to him and having opened up a little too much, she pointed to the hill. 'Shall we get to the top or do you think I won't make it?'

He grinned. 'Let's see, shall we?'

He didn't try to lead the way, or follow, but walked beside her. Lily found herself caring what he thought, drawn by his interest in her background and what made her tick. He seemed to be genuinely interested in how the trolling had affected her, and it was cathartic to talk to a virtual stranger about how hurtful it had been.

She hoped he'd appreciate her honesty – she wanted him to like her, which surprised and disturbed her because it made her feel vulnerable.

She'd long ago got over the embarrassment of being proud of her achievements and frank about her strengths, while privately recognising her limitations and finding staff who could make up for them. It was essential in business and too many people – sadly too many women, even of her generation – still found it almost impossible to laud or even acknowledge their own achievements.

She'd lost count of the men who were not only unafraid to big themselves up, but also unaware of how very average they were.

Sam wasn't one of them. He could be a very good retreat proprietor if he played to his strengths but his discomfort front of house was all too obvious. Could he find and afford a manager who would be good at that role? He'd made it quite clear the previous evening that he thought she should take a complete break from all things business so she wouldn't offer her opinion again.

'Here we are.'

'Wow,' said Lily, forgetting her vow. 'Just amazing.'

'Not too shabby.' Sam stood, hands on hips. The three-sixty panorama enabled them to see all the other islands in the archipelago: St Mary's, Tresco, Bryher, St Agnes . . . 'And beyond St Martin's, that hazy cliff-shaped shadow is Land's End.'

'The metropolis,' Lily murmured.

'Feels like it after here. It's low tide so if you look over there, where the pest house is, you can just see some old wall systems running across the sand flats.'

Pest house. Lily didn't like the sound of that, but couldn't deny the history of the island intrigued her.

She looked hard and then saw the dark lines in the bay. 'I

see them. They almost reach Bryher. Who would build walls in the sea?'

'They weren't always under the sea. There was a low plain between Tresco, Bryher and Samson that was used by medieval farmers. Then sea levels rose and drowned the fields and separated the islands.'

Imagining the farmers' land and homes being flooded, year by year, Lily shivered. 'That is pretty eerie.'

'Some say that Scilly is the land of Lyonesse featured in the King Arthur myths,' Sam went on. 'And that once you could walk from Land's End to here.'

'Of course you believe that,' Lily said wickedly, secretly entranced by the idea of a mythical landscape.

Sam frowned. 'Of course. Doesn't everyone?'

She laughed.

'Let's head down the hill towards the pest house,' he said.

As they walked, Lily's curiosity was well and truly piqued. 'Have you lived on Bryher your entire life?' she asked.

'Apart from when I went to uni and a year of travelling around after.'

She noticed he didn't say 'we' again so if he'd had a companion on his gap year, that person had now been erased from the narrative.

'You said Elspeth has never left at all?'

'Only for holidays and not too many of those. Travel to and from here is expensive. Young people tend to go away and either don't come back or try to return a decade later,

81

but making a living and finding a home in any rural spot is hard.'

'Did you ever think of making the cottages into homes for the islanders?'

'I did but there are only six ruins left and I wouldn't want to build on the natural landscape. By developing the retreat, I can provide jobs and I've created two studio flats above the hub for my live-in staff. Who I will be recruiting very soon,' he added pointedly.

'I'm glad to hear it, otherwise you'd end up needing a retreat yourself. Now, can you show me this "pest house"? It sounds horrifying and fascinating at the same time.'

'It's both of those things. Come on, we need to go down and up again.'

Annoyingly, Lily was puffing a little by the time they'd trekked down one hill and up another. Sam stopped again so she could look down on the western end of the island where the pest house was situated well away from the cottages of the Island Retreat. There were also a couple of ruined buildings behind a beach on the northern coast.

'The retreat was one of two settlements with a handful of dwellings,' he explained. 'Each of its cottages originally housed a different family, though most of the inhabitants were related in some way. That was another reason for life on Stark being unsustainable. People tended to stay in one place their whole lives and it's obviously not great for people's health when generations keep on marrying their cousins.'

'Oh, dear,' she said, realising the implications.

'However, the main reason they eventually had to leave was that the well dried up. My first job here was to find a new water supply. Without that, there would be no retreat.'

'You said the well was the *main* reason people left?'

'There were others. Generally, the place was too tiny and too isolated to be viable. Stark is wild, windswept and not terribly fertile. For a few decades, the inhabitants made a living harvesting seaweed for fertiliser, and they had a rowing gig that was used to pilot visiting ships safely to the other islands. They lived on potatoes and limpets and kept a few sheep, cattle and goats.'

'It sounds a very hard life.'

'It was bad enough in summer but in the winter they could be cut off for weeks. The community only had one rowing gig between it and that was wrecked one winter. No one could afford to buy another. Food was in short supply, the well was running dry and the young people all left. Eventually in eighteen fifty-five, there were only two families clinging on and it was decided by the Cornish authorities that they should be evacuated to Bryher.'

'Surely that was better for them?' Lily said, finding it hard to imagine how any sane person would want to live in such harsh conditions, always on the brink of starvation.

'In one way it was, because life on Stark had become unbearable. However, one of the families still didn't want to leave, even though they were practically starving. There are documents about the mother, Mabel, having to be led away forcibly from her cottage, cursing the men sent to evict her. While being dragged from her home, she cursed anyone who ever set foot on Stark again.' He smiled. 'I didn't tell you that before.'

'Thanks!' Lily said, forming a picture of Mabel, screaming as she was carried away from her home in a tiny boat, with her few possessions, never to return. 'The poor woman. It must have been traumatic.'

'Apparently so. My aunt found an old newspaper cutting in the Scilly Library describing the scene. She was Elspeth's great-great-great-grandmother.'

Lily gave an audible gasp. 'Oh, my God. No wonder your aunt has such a strong connection to the place.'

'Yes, Stark – its inhabitants – are literally in her blood. Talking of which, shall we visit the pest house?'

They walked on, to a lower, flatter area of scrubland facing the Atlantic coast. The roofless stone building was situated at the edge of the island, well away from the cottages, and surrounded by gorse bushes and wildflowers. As they approached, Sam told her about its history.

'It was built in the mid-seventeenth century as an isolation hospital for sailors with the plague. They were dropped off here by ships sailing for Scilly.'

'That's awful,' Lily said, beginning to think that Stark had a very sad history, despite its idyllic location. 'I'm surprised you wanted to rebuild anything on here.'

'I had no choice,' he said, then quickly corrected himself. 'I mean, I needed to build the retreat, for all kinds of reasons,' he muttered. 'Let's go inside.'

Intrigued by his comment, Lily walked inside, staring up at the clear blue skies surrounded by granite walls. She imagined people – sick and perhaps dying – looking through the windows, wondering when – or if – they might ever escape these four walls. She shuddered and hugged herself.

'Those poor sailors. Imagine being abandoned here.'

'Yes, and some people want me to leave it as a memorial to them.'

'Will you?'

'I'd prefer to breathe new life into it, give it a purpose that benefits the living and future generations. If all goes well, this place would be further staff accommodation.'

'Won't the staff think it's creepy?'

'I'm hoping they'll be more relieved they have a decent place to live. I was planning to create four bedsits in it with a communal area. With the other studio above reception, that'll provide accommodation for me and five more people during the season.'

'You certainly have ambition,' Lily said, admiring his pragmatism.

'I've never thought I was ambitious. It's more of a passion – a compulsion. I've always wanted to resurrect the island but never dared to.'

'Until now. What made you decide to go for it?'

'I don't know . . .' He stopped. 'Let's just say that my life took an unexpected turn.'

'A good one?' Lily murmured.

'Not really. I didn't think so at the time.'

'And now?'

He kicked at a pebble. 'It was what it was. I simply came to accept I couldn't change what had happened. The old path was barred forever, and I had no choice but to walk down a new one – or stagnate. I decided that wasn't for me. It never has been.'

They both fell into silence. The lonely walls, the isolated yet beautiful spot ... the contrast of a dark past with the bright promise of a summer's day ... all of it threatened to overwhelm Lily. Sam seemed to be affected too, standing by the wall, gazing out at the vastness of the sea before snapping out of his trance-like state.

'Come on, I think we've had enough doom and gloom. The pest house can wait for now, let me show you something special.' He smiled. 'I think it will be exactly what you need.'

Chapter Eight

Sam's 'something special' was, indeed, exactly what she needed.

For an hour or so, Lily had been completely entranced by the sight of seals basking on the rocks and cute puffins flying in and out of their burrows in the cliffs with their beaks full of sand eels to feed their pufflings. The idea of new life being born around this rugged coast gave her a warm glow. She could see how the natural beauty of Stark would cast a healing spell on anyone.

Even its owner had smiled more in the past hour than he had in the rest of the time since she'd arrived on the island. By the time she'd returned to the retreat hub, she was feeling energised and buzzing with creative inspiration.

While Sam went to work on a nearby cottage, Lily collected her sketch pad and a sandwich and set off to explore on her own. Avoiding the pest house, she returned instead to the cliffs where they'd seen the puffins. The breeze had freshened but the sun was still dazzlingly bright.

She found a sheltered spot on a low grassy bluff out of the wind, kicked off her trainers and sat in the shelter of a large boulder. The granite warmed her back and the sun brought a pleasant glow to her bare legs. Waves rolled into the cove a few feet below, with soothing regularity. Who in the world had a whole island all to themself? Or almost totally to themself.

She started to sketch, absorbed in capturing the scene, yet after only a few minutes, she was muttering in frustration that she couldn't do it justice.

She tried again on a fresh sheet of paper . . . and again . . . until she was on her sixth attempt.

Flinging down the sketch pad, she let out a cry of frustration. 'Arghhhhh!'

No one could hear her. It had felt cathartic, so she shouted again. 'Arghhhh!'

Maybe she needed fresh inspiration. Ahead of her, she found it. Along the beach, beyond a headland, she came across a tiny cove with turquoise water glittering in a pool. The rocks surrounding it shimmered with bright green weed and cormorants perched offshore, drying their batlike wings in the sun.

Lily was seized by the urge to capture the scene. It only took a moment for her to scramble down the few feet to the beach, which was even more beautiful close up. The sand was strewn with tiny shells, in delicate shades of palest pink and cream. She hadn't beachcombed for years and couldn't resist popping a few shells into the pocket of her shorts. Soon, she'd abandoned her sketch pad and paints on a rock and given herself over to shell collecting.

She recognised limpets, cockles and periwinkles, and

even some of the cowries that had given her cottage its name. All were tiny and perfect. She would take some back to the retreat and draw a still life. Perhaps she might collect enough to make a bracelet.

With the sun warm on her back, she felt completely absorbed in her task and soon climbed off the beach and onto the rocky spit that separated the sand from the pool. Its blue-green depths looked so inviting, she was tempted to strip off and dive in, especially as there was a sea cave on the far side that just begged to be explored. Its mouth reminded her of a sea monster gaping wide.

She poked around in the rock pools for a while, marvelling at scuttling crabs, urchins and jewel-like sea anemones. There was so much inspiration here.

'Oh!'

She let out a cry as a wave rolled into the pool, crashed onto the rocks and wet her with its spray. That water was colder than she'd expected.

Lily decided she'd better go back and start sketching while all the marine life she'd seen was fresh in her mind. Bursting with ideas, she finally turned to head across the rocks to the beach again.

Only to find it had vanished.

It was now underwater, and waves were crashing onto the base of the bluff she'd climbed down. She couldn't see her sketch pad or the rock she'd left it on; it must have already been washed away.

The cliffs on the other side of the cove were too steep and jagged to climb and she could feel spray on her face as more waves rolled into the pool, turning its unruffled surface into a churning whirlpool and crashing into the cave.

A desperate glance out to sea showed a yacht and a fishing boat, both much too far out for anyone to be able to hear her if she called for help.

She was cut off and no one knew where she was.

Chapter Nine

An hour later, Lily was trapped on a small ledge of rock.

She'd grazed her hands trying to climb up the rough cliffs and waves were now breaking over her knees. No one was coming to her rescue and the tide could only recently have turned, which meant there were hours to go until it started to recede.

The fishing boat was at anchor further out. She could make out the man hauling in his pots. Was it Rory? The yacht had gone, although another had sailed past in the opposite direction.

Even though she was trying to stay calm, every moment brought fresh dread as the tide flooded in. The waves seemed to roll in in sets, with much larger ones every ninety seconds or so. She'd counted the interval: one elephant, two elephant.

She'd given up shouting. It was pointless and only made her throat raw, and besides, she needed to conserve her strength for what now seemed to be her only course of action: she must enter the water and try to swim back to the little cove. It was about two hundred metres away. She had a badge for a thousand metres. She would be OK.

Even as she told herself this, she knew she was being

ridiculous. Any serious swimming she'd done had been at school. Even if she'd kept up her visits to the pool at the health club, how could she battle the cold, churning water with rocks lying in wait under the treacherous Scilly surface? Sam had said that the jetty was the only safe passage to the shore, apart from risking holing a small boat by running it onto the beach.

Yet Lily had no other choice but to swim. She'd weighed up the risks, as she had many times in her business life, and calculated that this was the only course of action left open to her. The tide would carry on rolling in, the waves growing bigger and swamping the rocks on which she was now perilously perched.

She pulled off her trainers and stuffed them in a rough niche above her, though she may as well have flung them into the water. They were her favourite pair, bought the day that the new design had been released. They'd cost two hundred pounds. How ludicrous they seemed now.

She took a deep breath. Swim or die. Both, probably.

She turned towards the cliff face, lowering her foot until it felt a slender ledge. The sharp rocks hurt her feet, though a few grazed toes were the least of her worries. Slowly, she let herself down to a narrow platform six feet below, that would soon be buffeted by the waves.

She had sixty seconds left before the big set rolled in. A quick check for hidden rocks during a moment when the water receded, and . . . *jump*.

Instantly she regretted her leap. She was stunned by the icy cold and disorientated, but kicked her legs until she reached the surface, gasping for air and thrashing at the water in a parody of front crawl. The swell and cold were way worse than she'd anticipated: like being tumbled inside a washing machine. She continued to flounder, kicking as hard as she could in an attempt to move forward, but the little cove seemed to come no closer. Her limbs were growing heavier much quicker than she had expected.

She screamed 'Help!' and then heard the roar of water. The ninety seconds had ticked away, the next set of waves just a heartbeat away. Her last heartbeat.

She felt the swell lift her, closed her eyes and dived under before the wave engulfed her. She'd closed her lips tightly but water still entered her mouth. Everything was a churning mass of green; she didn't know which way was up or whether at any second she'd be pushed down onto rocks or hurled towards the cliffs.

She attempted to breathe but began to choke on the salty water.

This was the end, then.

Her parents' Ruby wedding party flashed into her mind. She would never have the chance to celebrate their next. She would never see her nieces again. All those missed occasions: the anniversary party, forgetting to pick the girls up from the theatre, neglecting her friends . . . what she would give for that time back.

Above all, when she reached the other side, would Cara forgive her for throwing her life away?

Chapter Ten

A hand plunged down through the water.

It grasped her arm, hauling her above the surface like a brutal rebirth. She spluttered as she gulped in air then coughed violently.

'Hang on to me! I'll pull you up.'

Sam's face was above her, leaning over the side of a fishing kayak. Lily's throat was on fire from the seawater and she felt like throwing up but he held on to her by the shoulders and the back of her T-shirt.

'Don't give in now!' he ordered. 'Come on, kick *hard*! Help me get you on board before the next wave comes.'

Lily thought she *was* kicking, though her legs were so cold and weak she could barely feel them.

'I – I'm try – ing.'

Somehow Sam dragged her half over the edge of the kayak, almost capsizing it as he did so. She kicked again and felt herself thrust upwards before his eyes widened in horror.

'Lily! Hold on! I—'

A deep roar drowned out the rest of his words, then a wave – bigger than any before – broke over the kayak and toppled it sideways, tossing Sam into the waves and Lily back into the maelstrom.

She went under again briefly but was flung upwards amid a whirlpool of foaming white water.

The kayak rolled past her, its sharp rudder just inches from her face, and she choked back a scream. Before she could think, another wave hurled the craft into a rock where it bounced off again, this time the right way up.

Eyes streaming from the salt, almost choking, she trod water desperately as she scanned the sea for Sam. What if he'd drowned trying to save her? She was still being tossed around like a cork. She had to reach the kayak before another set of massive breakers rolled in.

'Sam!' she screamed as loud as she could, even though her throat was raw. '*Help!*'

Everything was green and black and white, the roar of the surf deafening her and the salt stinging and blinding her.

'*Sam!*'

'Here!'

Gloriously, miraculously, he was swimming out of the gulley that separated the cave from the rocky ledge.

'Grab the kayak!' he shouted.

Lily struck out, her clothes weighing her down, her limbs cold and numb. The kayak seemed no closer until a wave lifted it and brought it towards her, almost on top of her. The wave set had passed – for now – but she had to get hold of the craft. She clung to the side while Sam swam over. Even from a few metres away, she could see the blood on his forehead.

A few strong strokes later, he was beside her in the water. 'Get in!' he shouted, shoving his hand under her bum so she could haul herself into the craft. With one last monumental kick, she scrambled into the base and held her hand down into the water for Sam, who was still clinging onto the kayak.

'Come on!' she said, desperately.

'No, I might capsize it.'

Fresh strength flooded her. She wasn't going to leave him now. 'Get in!' she said, reaching for his hand. After a moment's hesitation, he took it and her arm felt as if it was being ripped from its socket while he struggled aboard, the kayak rocking under his weight.

His forehead was gashed and he was breathing hard but he sat down on the seat and issued orders to Lily, who was half-lying in the stern.

'The rudder's probably done for, but we have to get away from the rocks. There's a paddle strapped to the side, grab it and use it.' His bent legs worked frantically to propel the kayak away from the jagged teeth of the rocks.

Fumbling with cold fingers, Lily unfastened the paddle from the inside of the kayak.

'Use it like an oar – both sides, as hard as you can,' he said.

She saved her breath for paddling. With Sam propelling them, the little craft began its agonising escape from the cliffs. Foamy crests of waves appeared ahead. Lily wanted to scream but she was too busy paddling. The waves broke over the kayak but it stayed upright.

'Keep going!' Sam shouted.

Even though her muscles screamed for mercy, Lily didn't give up. She remembered the moment when she'd gone under; all the opportunities to be with loved ones that she'd missed – and the second chance she'd been given now.

No, she wouldn't give up this close to safety.

Once the kayak was out of the breaking waves, Sam heaved a huge sigh of relief and turned back to her.

'You can ease up now,' he said.

'No, I have to keep going.' Lily kept paddling even though her arms were on fire.

'Lily, you can stop.' Sam let the craft drift for a few seconds to take the paddle from her hands. 'We're safe.'

Safe.

Twice in the past few minutes, Lily had thought that was impossible: had almost given up on the idea, had – in those few seconds when she was underwater – almost accepted that her end had come.

'Are you OK?' he asked, twisting to look at her while still piloting the kayak around the island.

She hugged herself to try and stop trembling. 'I th–think so.'

'I'll check you over when we get back. I lost the radio when the kayak capsized so I can't call the coastguard.'

'D–don't – please don't call the coastguard. There's no need. I'll be OK.'

He started paddling again. 'There's such a thing as secondary drowning, you know,' he said. 'You must have swallowed water.'

'Yes, but I'll take the risk.'

'We'll see when we get back. Now, rest, and for God's sake, try to stay awake.'

He said no more, clearly saving his energy to paddle back to the quay as soon as possible. Lily sank back in the now-empty rear of the kayak. It stank of fish but all the gear and tackle must have gone to the bottom of the sea.

They passed the pest house, its blank windows like accusing eyes.

Although physically exhausted, Lily didn't think she'd ever sleep again. Adrenaline surged through her, making her hyper aware of the landscape: the gulls shrieking, the waves breaking on the shore. She was shivering with cold and shock. All kinds of strange stuff must be happening to her body – none of it good – yet she felt euphoric, as if she could fly out of the kayak, above Stark, looking down on everything.

She'd come a whisker away from dying – not once but twice. She still didn't know how she'd made it out of the sea alive. If Sam hadn't been in the right place at the right time . . . if the kayak hadn't righted itself when it had bounced off the rocks . . . if Sam hadn't managed to swim out of the gulley . . . if he hadn't been able to push her into the boat or steer them away.

The moment when she'd gone under flashed back again: the moment when she'd half-accepted death.

'OK, we're almost here. Hold tight, the steering's shagged and we might bump into the jetty.'

She snapped to attention, clinging on while the little craft – their saviour – slipped through the rocky gap and bumped the stone wall gently.

She looked up at the walls of the haven, cradled in its shelter, hearing only the gulls crying.

Sam seized an old iron ring in the wall and tied the kayak to it. He climbed onto the steps and offered his hand to her. 'Careful, they're slippery.'

Only then did she notice his knuckles were grazed and bleeding before he grasped her hand and helped her stagger up to dry land.

Eyes closed, Sam lifted his face heavenwards and let out a sigh. 'Jesus, that was a close one.'

Though her legs felt wobbly Lily forced herself to stay upright, saw the pink stains on his T-shirt and what a mess his face was in. He was bleeding from above his temple and from cuts across his cheeks.

'Sam. You've cut yourself . . .'

'Have I?' He touched his head and looked at the blood in surprise. 'Must have been when the kayak fell on me. It pushed me into the gulley. It's only a scratch.' He stared at Lily. 'What happened? I was out fishing and rounded the rocks by the cove to see you jump into the water.'

'I got cut off by the tide and had no choice but to swim for it. I didn't know you'd be along at any moment.'

'No. It was – fortunate – I was.'

'Until that wave capsized the kayak,' she said, hearing the sea rolling in again and recalling her terror and exhaustion. The moment when Sam capsized and she went under for the second time, into the darkness, she really had thought her time was up.

He touched her arm gently. 'You're shivering. Are you sure you don't want me to call the coastguard or air ambulance? Or I could take you over to Bryher in the boat now if you like? Get you checked out by the island nurse?'

'No. Thanks. I don't want to get on a boat right now . . .' *Or ever*, thought Lily. She also didn't want her family to know anything about the incident. They'd freak out, especially her parents. 'I just need a shower, warm clothes, a hot drink.'

'We both do. Come on.'

As soon as they reached the hub, he found a blanket from the sofa and draped it around her without asking. 'I'll take you to your cottage and bring the first-aid kit.'

She tugged the blanket tighter, grateful for the warmth yet determined not to be fussed over. 'I'll be fine now. It looks like it's you who needs the first-aid kit. Why don't we both get dry and warmed up and meet back here? I've done first-aid courses for work. I can take a look at the cut on your head and those grazes on your cheek.'

He nodded and they parted, Lily to her cottage and Sam to his flat.

She'd said she was fine but the moment she shut the cottage door, her legs threatened to give way as the adrenaline ebbed. However, she also knew she needed to warm up. She drank most of a glass of water, showered and put on jeans and a sweater.

She'd stopped shivering. She'd be fine. *Fine.*

It was Sam who worried her. That cut on his head might not be the only injury he'd sustained. He really needed to be checked over, not her.

She slurped the rest of the water and was halfway out of

the door to go and join Sam when a flashback gripped her, causing her to lean against the door frame for support.

The shock of the cold water, the roar of the waves . . . the kayak overturning, just at the moment she'd thought she was safe . . . and Sam nowhere to be seen.

Slamming the door on the cottage and the memories, Lily hurried to the hub, hoping that she wouldn't find Sam passed out on the floor.

Chapter Eleven

'Sorry, I didn't expect you yet!'

'I can come back,' Lily said, confronted by Sam in the bar, a towel slung round his neck and another slipping low over his hips.

She let her gaze linger too long on his broad shoulders, toned stomach, and a trail of dark hair that vanished below the towel. Was that wrong after a near-death experience? She shivered again. Surely anything that took her mind off the moment when she'd sunk beneath those waves was a good thing . . .

'I was worried about you,' she said, trying to calm her racing pulse. 'Your head, I mean.'

Sam clutched the towel tightly to his waist. 'Yes. Thanks. No. I mean, hang on. Let me put some clothes on.'

Lily heard him thumping around in the upstairs flat then he was back, still barefoot but in jeans and a hoodie. He also carried two mugs of tea and handed one to her. 'I put sugar in it.'

'Thank you, just what I need.' She took the mug, hoping her fingers would stop trembling. She sipped the hot sweet tea. It was, without a doubt, the best drink she'd ever had in her life.

'Are you OK?' he asked, sitting down next to her.

'A few bumps and bruises. My shins are grazed and my elbow's a bit sore but other than that, I think I'll survive.' She stopped, recalling the moment she'd dived under to avoid the wave. She hadn't expected to surface and then Sam's hand had reached out to her. A shudder travelled through her.

His brow creased in concern. 'Are you cold? Shall I get a blanket? I could light the fire.'

'I'm fine,' she said, hastily. 'What about *you*?'

He shrugged. 'Grazed in places but otherwise I've been lucky – apart from this scratch above my eye. It won't stop bleeding. I've tried sticking a plaster on it but it didn't work and fell off.'

'I can see that.' She grimaced at the oozing cut in his hairline. 'Do you want me to take a look, pop a dressing on it?'

'Um. Well . . .'

'Otherwise, it *will* keep bleeding and make a mess in your lovely new reception area.'

'So you *do* think it's lovely, then?'

With an eye roll, she stood up. 'That's your first-aid kit on the bar?'

He put his mug down. 'Yes. I'll get it.'

'Sam, would you do something for me?'

He raised an eyebrow and winced.

'Stay there and let me deal with this?'

'I'll be as good as gold.'

He gazed up at her, a hint of mischief in his eyes that made her stomach flip. Now she'd offered to dress his wound, although it gave her something to focus on, it meant she'd have to touch his skin, the same skin she'd seen so much of when she'd walked into the bar.

She had, she'd admit, thought about his body quite a few times over the past twelve hours. And having seen it in all its strong, toned magnificence, wasn't going to help her think about it any less.

Opening the lid of the kit, she tried to remember what the course had recommended for minor cuts. She picked out a cotton pad and a bottle.

'Keep still,' she instructed. 'This might sting.'

She dabbed at the cut with the cotton pad soaked in alcohol.

'Ouch,' said Sam, with a grin.

Lily shook her head. 'There's no need to act all macho.'

'Macho?' he scoffed. 'Me?'

Her cheeks warmed up. She put more alcohol on the pad and pressed it firmly to the graze.

He flinched. 'Ow! That did hurt!'

Lily shrugged. 'I'm no nurse, as you've probably worked out.'

'And I'm no hotelier. You've probably worked that out too.'

'Hmm . . .'

After cleaning the wound, she stuck a small sterile dressing over it. 'That should stem the blood. I don't think it needs stitches but, like I said, I'm not a medic.'

'Thanks for the help and apologies for finding me – like you did – earlier.'

The ironic twist of his mouth made her stomach do a double back flip.

'Given we both narrowly escaped death, seeing you without your shirt is probably the least of my worries,' she said, trying to inject some humour into the situation.

Sam nodded. 'Actually, I'd rushed out of the shower because I heard a radio message come through.'

Her pulse jumped for a different reason. She didn't want news of the accident getting back to her family and Richie. 'You didn't tell anyone about this?'

'No, because you asked me not to. It was the heliport calling about your flight out of here. They might have a space tomorrow.'

'My flight . . .' She'd forgotten about it. 'Thank you.'

'There's a slim possibility you could leave on an earlier flight *if* someone can be persuaded to cancel. I won't know until later or even first thing. I bet you can't wait to get out of here as fast as you can now. I don't blame you. This has been even more of a disaster than I'd imagined in even my worst nightmares.'

'It wasn't your fault. I was distracted by the view and not paying attention to the tide.'

'I should have warned you about the tides. I should have given you a safety briefing or something. Or stayed with you.'

'Sam – are you going to nursemaid all your guests, all the time? It's not possible. The best you can do is issue a warning to them.'

'So you won't be suing me?'

She scratched her chin. 'Well, I *did* consider it . . .'

His face fell so she rolled her eyes.

'I'm joking! I don't want any more drama. I don't want anyone to know what happened. If my family found out, especially Étienne or my parents, they'd freak out.'

'Étienne?'

'My late sister's husband. He's a doctor and it was he who practically forced me to take a break. He and Richie. They bullied me into it. Frankly, I didn't want to come at all.'

'Really?' The dressing on Sam's brow twitched. 'I'd never have guessed. Why were – *are* – you so dead set against taking a break? Everyone needs downtime.'

If ever there was a time to be honest, this was it. She had to recognise that there was a new bond between them: that Sam had saved her life. That had brought them together and so it was probably unsurprising that she was temporarily attracted to her handsome rescuer.

'I suppose I see slowing down as a weakness,' she said.

'A weakness? How can taking care of yourself be weak?'

'When you put it like that, it does sound counter-productive, but I've never been afraid of hard work. I guess it started when I had my market stall. I absolutely loved running it and every sale gave me a buzz, whether it was for my own stuff or a friend's. The thought of how happy they'd be when I gave them their share of the takings . . . It made me happy and I became addicted.'

'Addicted?' Sam looked intrigued. 'That's a powerful word.'

'Accurate, though. Once I decided to expand, well,

establishing any new business is tough. You need to give it your all and, inevitably, other things in your life suffer. You must know that,' she said, looking around at the retreat. 'You did say you *needed* this project, remember?'

'Did I?' he said, with an air of surprise.

'Hmm.'

'Yes, I did. I suppose I've also become obsessed, staying here night after night. When the buck stops with you, you've no choice but to carry on. There's no safety net.'

'Exactly, and—' Lily hesitated, but realised that she wanted to be honest with him. Perhaps he would understand her need to keep moving, be in constant motion to save herself from dealing with her grief.

'I need to tell you something. That Nina Simone song. There's a reason I was so upset. It's the same reason I find it hard to take a break, the same reason I don't want my parents to find out how close we came to being in serious danger just now.' Lily took a pause before she could go on. She still found it difficult to talk about such a painful time in her life, but Sam's reassuring gaze encouraged her.

'Please, go on,' he said gently.

'My sister Cara – she died two years ago. That was the song her husband played at the funeral.'

Sam groaned softly. 'I am *so* sorry. I'd no idea.'

'How could you?' she said. 'Please don't feel bad. But, you see, since she died, I've thrown myself into the business even more. It was easier to keep running at a hundred miles an hour rather than dwell on what I'd – what we'd all – lost. Does that make sense?'

'Yes. It makes sense to me.' The timbre of his voice told her that he really did understand. But before she could ask him why, he went on.

'Do you mind me asking what did happen?'

Lily braced herself. Even now, she hated relaying the details but Sam deserved to know and perhaps it might be cathartic – after what they'd been through, was there any point holding back? Even though it was exhausting telling people what had happened, it was just as exhausting keeping it all inside.

'It was a car accident. She'd been out with some girl-friends and the road was icy and the car skidded on black ice and hit a tree. It was instant, apparently, which people kept saying was a blessing. I didn't think of it like that. I still can't. All I can think of is that I never got the chance to tell her what she meant to me, how much I loved her, how I looked up to her and how absolutely amazing she was . . .'

Lily looked up from her mug to find Sam listening intently: encouraging her with his steady gaze. 'She really was perfect. She worked in ICU as a paediatric nurse. She was wonderful with the children. She and Étienne were devoted to each other, yet she still found time to see Mum and Dad, do all the extended family stuff. Whereas I . . . had no partner, no kids, and only myself to look after yet I couldn't find the time to be there for an important landmark for my parents.'

Once again, the guilt assailed her. She felt that constant need – a compulsion – to be busy yet she was slowly accept-ing that there were boundaries between work and relaxation.

When she returned to London, she had to give herself permission to spend some time on herself – with herself.

'I always thought that Cara was the maternal, caring one. She was destined to be a mother and find a gorgeous, kind husband. Her work as a paediatric nurse was a huge part of her life and personality,' Lily went on. 'Whereas I've always been driven. Mum says that from a young age I'd get a bee in my bonnet about something and there was no stopping me. At first it was making clothes for my dolls. I once made a little boilersuit and welding mask for my Barbie.'

Sam smiled. 'I'd like to have seen that.'

'The twins – Cara's daughters – still have it, though it's tatty now. I also made a rainbow playsuit for Ken but I think that disintegrated.'

'Lucky Ken.' He laughed.

'Then it was sewing pouches and bags . . . I even had a go at pottery and the house was filled with wonky bowls and mugs. The handle fell off my dad's one morning while he was drinking hot coffee. I can still picture him hopping around the kitchen trying to rip off his boiling shorts.'

Sam's eyes shone with amusement. 'I'm guessing you gave up the pottery?'

'Mum and Dad gently suggested my talents lay in other areas. So, I went for the market stall and the online business. It grew and after Cara died, I went into overdrive. I blotted out my grief with work. I knew that and so did everyone around me, but I didn't care. While I was focused on the business, I couldn't think about her and dwell on the terrifying, sickening fact she was never coming back. While I worked, I couldn't cry or lose control – I hated feeling I might burst into tears at any second. Sorry,' she said, suddenly embarrassed at revealing too much. 'I can't expect you to understand.'

'Oh, I understand more than you think,' he murmured. 'So you were saying that you reacted by throwing yourself into work?' he added quickly.

'I suppose I realised the true meaning of "you only live once" and felt I needed to get everything done and achieved as fast as possible because it can all be snatched away in a heartbeat. And I also felt guilty.'

'Why?' Sam said with a puzzled frown. 'Cara's death wasn't your fault. It was an accident.'

'You're right, I had nothing to do with it, but I had – what's the phrase? – survivor's guilt. It felt wrong that I was alive, when I have so many faults, when I'm not always the nicest person to be around, yet my beautiful kind sister had died.'

'I'm so sorry for your loss, Lily. Cara sounds like she was an incredible woman. But, you know, no one's perfect,' he said, with a sadness and firmness that surprised her. He really did seem to understand – or perhaps he was merely being kind.

'Cara was as close to perfect as possible, and I say that without any envy or edge. Everyone adored her because she deserved to be adored. And that's why my family must never *ever* hear of this. No one can. They were devastated after losing her. If anything happened to me, I think it would finish off Mum and Dad.'

'I won't tell anyone . . . I promise. Though perhaps they'd want to know.'

'No. They're already worried about me passing out at work. I didn't want them to know but when they heard I was coming to this retreat, I had to tell them that I was worried about burnout . . . I can't possibly tell them I almost drowned on top of that!' Lily put her mug down. 'Anyway, I don't mind admitting, I feel pretty whacked. I'm not used to wild swimming and kayaking.' She laughed and got to her feet. 'I am sorry. It's all about me, me, me again, isn't it? You do realise you'll have to employ a professional counsellor for your guests to talk to? You're too good a listener.'

With old-fashioned chivalry, Sam rose to his feet too. 'Only because I don't have any answers. You came here to escape, and you've ended up running headlong into your trauma and having a very close call.'

'We both did. Doesn't that bother you?'

'Like you, I don't want to dwell on it. I can't look back.'

'I agree . . . you know, I think I'll go and have a lie down and see you later for dinner?'

'OK.' He gave an apologetic grimace. 'Though I'm afraid there won't be sea bass. The fish and the rest of the gear went to the bottom of the sea.'

'I'll forgive you. In the circumstances.'

'That's why I went out, you see. Rory was meant to put some bass in the order I collected but he must have forgotten.'

'So,' Lily said, her blood running cold once again, 'you're saying if I hadn't been such a demanding guest and asked for sea bass tonight, you might not have come out in the kayak at all?'

'Let's not think of it like that,' Sam said. 'I *was* there, and everything is OK.'

'Baked beans on toast would taste great after what I've been through.'

'I'll do better than that,' he said firmly.

'Great. Though, Sam, promise me one thing?'

He frowned, obviously unsure what she was going to throw at him next. 'What is it?'

'That you'll let me help make dinner and you'll join me from the start. I'm not used to sitting around being waited on, especially not by someone I've shared a near-death experience with. And besides, it's our last night. We can break the rules this one time, eh?'

Chapter Twelve

Lily prepared the goat's cheese salad while Sam whisked up eggs, spinach and potatoes for the Spanish tortilla that was to be their ad hoc main.

'This is fun,' she said, placing the rinsed leaves on a plate. Fun was something she hadn't had in a long time and, after their earlier experience, she desperately needed a distraction.

Sam handed her a glass of white wine. 'Chef's perks,' he said, his eyes crinkling at the corners.

'I'm not sure if making a salad counts as proper cooking, although I can't remember the last time I made one for myself.'

'It definitely counts. As you've probably gathered, I'm hardly a professional chef.'

'You've done all right so far.' Lily nodded at the new kitchen. Although bijou, its stainless-steel surfaces gleamed.

'When I'm catering for one, I enjoy cooking. I've looked after myself for years. I'm not sure Morven always appreciates my food, though.'

Lily placed sliced roundels of crumbly goat's cheese on the salad. Their shared experience made her feel more confident about asking him personal questions: 'Does she live with you?'

'Yes, since her dad left.' He sighed. 'My brother Nate got a job as a games designer in LA. It was meant to be a six-month contract, his big break and a lot of money. He was going to come home afterwards and buy a place in the UK. Or, if things were going exceptionally well, establish himself out there and Morven was going to join him.'

Intrigued, Lily carried on drizzling balsamic vinegar on the salad.

'And I'm guessing that hasn't happened?' she said casually, scattering chopped walnuts on top.

'That was eighteen months ago. Nate finished the contract then was offered another six months. He also moved in with a woman he met at work.'

Lily picked up the plates. 'And there isn't room for Morven?'

With a pained expression, Sam opened the door to the dining room to let her through. 'Apparently not.'

They sat at the table. 'That's rough on Morven,' she replied, understanding now why the teenager might be feeling pretty pissed off.

'It is. She's confused, upset . . . rejected.'

'I bet.'

'She also loathed my brother's new girlfriend, Grady, on sight.'

'They've met?' Lily said in surprise.

'Only over FaceTime. That was enough.'

'So, Morven's with you for the time being?'

'Yes. She doesn't want to live with me and she doesn't want to live with Grady. I'm afraid Morven's mum, Holly,

114

didn't feel able to care for her. She and Nate had a fling when she was over here for a holiday. She married young and then fell pregnant with Morven. Her husband refused to bring up another man's child and issued her an ultimatum so Holly decided Morven was best off staying with Nate.'

Unlike Sam himself, Lily thought, who *was* bringing up another man's child, even though the circumstances were very different. 'That must have been incredibly hard for her,' Lily said, trying to imagine having to give up your baby. 'And no wonder Morven feels confused and rejected . . .' Lily found her heart thawing towards the girl. 'What does she want?'

'If I knew that, I'd be able to predict the Lottery numbers.' He shrugged. 'I don't know because Morven doesn't know.'

They continued the meal for a while, talking about the food, where the cheese and leaves had come from.

'It's Morven who created the artwork in your cottage, you know,' Sam said.

Lily thought back to the evocative collages of Scilly that hung in her room. They were original and haunting.

'They're all her work?' she asked, rethinking her initial assessment of the truculent teenager.

'All her own. She loves art. Mixed media is her big thing. She's just finished her A-level Art course and she's on track for a top grade.'

'She's a talented kid,' said Lily, thinking of the contrast between Morven and Tyrone, who'd virtually copied the style of a best-selling designer rather than trying to create something original.

'She is that.' Sam's eyes lit up with pride. Lily couldn't help thinking that Nate should be here to feel and show that pride. 'Unfortunately, that's another source of conflict. She can't decide what to do next. She'd have to go to the mainland to study Fine Art – at Falmouth University – but she hasn't applied for a course, so that's off for this year. Now she'll have to stay on the islands until she can reapply. It's why she's working for me here. Reluctantly.'

'She must be so hurt and confused. I felt the same way at that age, but for different reasons. I didn't fit in with the crowd at school, that's for sure. I loved making things but some people thought it was weird I had a market stall. Even then, I suppose I was focused on being an entrepreneur rather than on pop stars and boyfriends!'

And had never really given time to romantic relationships ever since, she thought.

Sam smiled and then said: 'So you've been running at a hundred miles an hour since your late teens?'

'In one way, probably, and lately, this big business opportunity has come up and it needs all my focus.' She didn't elaborate on the details of the supermarket offer, mindful she was supposed to be taking a break – and because she sensed an opportunity to find out more about Sam while she could. She only had tonight.

'Coming on top of your loss, it's no wonder you're shattered,' he said. 'A series of blows saps your resilience until one day, all the stress catches up with you and floors you.'

'Literally, in my case,' Lily said, gently shaking her head. 'You sound as if you understand?'

He answered quickly, as if keen to skate over his comment. 'I spent every hour renovating this place and had to hand over the reins of my building business to a friend. Then Nate decided to leave Morven at my door as if she was an item of left luggage – with no indication of when he'd collect her again. I feel I'm failing at all of it: the business, the retreat, being a surrogate parent.'

'I don't think I could have juggled all of that stuff at once, especially the parent bit.'

'I had no choice,' he said bluntly. 'I love Morven and want the best for her, but she's not my daughter and I'm too old to be her friend. To be honest, I feel as if I'm failing her on all counts.'

Lily hesitated before replying. 'I love my nieces too, and I understand the feeling of not being able to replace their mum, but I've no experience of teenagers. Does Elspeth help you much?'

He gave a wry smile. 'My aunt is a wonderful woman. I couldn't have managed without her, but she has the café to manage. She's even further removed from Morven's generation than I am, though sometimes they seem closer together than I am with either of them.'

Lily thought back to the conversation on the quay. 'Does Morven believe in all the myths and legends about Stark? It sounded as if they have something in common there.'

'When it suits her and when she wants to gang up on me

with Elspeth. They are alike in many ways. Independent, artistic, they say what they feel without a filter.'

'I've experienced that. I know I'm the last person to give advice but you shouldn't be so hard on yourself. You've so much on your plate and Nate's left you in the lurch. Maybe you need a retreat too? From Stark, I mean.'

'Like you, I don't have the time. I'm here to stay,' he said, gathering up their plates. 'I'll go and work my magic on the tortilla.'

Lily was back at her cottage by ten. Sam had said she should be up and packed by seven a.m., so he could catch the tide to take her straight by boat and buggy to Tresco heliport where she could be on standby for the first possible flight.

She knew she should get some rest after what had been an emotionally and physically exhausting day, yet it was impossible. The endorphins still pulsed through her despite two large glasses of wine.

She threw open the doors of the cottage and stood on the terrace. Overhead the stars were just coming out. They twinkled in a vast sky, casting a silvery light over the sand flats that separated her from Bryher and the other islands. In the distance, the lighthouse on Round Island winked with soothing regularity.

This was the last daylight in the whole of Britain, the far western edge of her homeland, and she and Sam were the only two people on the planet to enjoy it.

An electric thrill shot through her, the kind that she used to experience when she'd painted or sewn something as a child. Knowing she couldn't sleep, she went back into the cottage, made hot chocolate and brought it outside, along with pencils, watercolours and paper.

She had to capture the scene and started to sketch a faint outline of beach, sand flats and the low hills of Bryher surrounded by islets floating in a silvery sea.

Working quickly, she fought against the urge to criticise her work, or rip it up, knowing that she would never be able to do the scene justice, but the vital thing was to carry on. As her eyes adjusted, little details came into focus: white-walled cottages gleaming in the twilight; the jetty where she'd arrived and been so sharp with Sam.

Dipping her brush in a deep ultramarine, she cringed. Now she knew him better, she regretted her impatience and rudeness.

So much of what he'd shared with her had struck a chord. He'd had to step into his brother's shoes to care for Morven. He'd said he had no choice, but Lily didn't buy that. He'd taken her into his home and life because he cared and was now doing his best to juggle starting his business with looking after a troubled teenage girl.

Whereas Lily had been so busy working that she'd literally forgotten her two nieces existed.

She laid down the watery painting as lightly as she could. She was as rusty as the old mooring post on the Stark quay: it was an age since she'd used her creative skills for pleasure. She felt envious of the makers whose work she marketed ... it was a feeling she'd suppressed while running the business, yet now it surfaced. The wild seascape of

Stark had certainly rekindled that creative flame, even if it had almost finished her off too.

How could she make more time for her own creative passions again? Even if her drawings and paintings weren't good enough to sell, they were still valid. How could she make more time for the stuff that mattered the most – her nieces and her family – as Sam had done?

How could she make enough money to do all the things she wanted and carve some space in her life for *her*? Slowly but surely, she'd allowed work to hem her into a corner until she was left with only the tiniest patch of dry land to stand on and no room to move.

The dilemma, like the sky and ocean in front of her, was too big to capture or resolve.

With no phone beside her to remind her of the time, only the fact it was too dark to work stopped her. The stars were fully out now, a milky network twinkling from a vast sky of deepest blue. Such darkness was alien.

Lily went inside, stunned to find it was after midnight.

She held her painting out in front of her. The colours, she admitted, were beautiful: ultramarine, silver, teal, even a tiny hint of pink had crept in. It must have been the reflection of the sun over the horizon at the last moment of light – she couldn't remember adding it.

It was then she noticed through the window a figure lit up by moonlight: a figure who wasn't in her painting as he'd only just appeared, standing on the edge of the cliff, with his back to her.

It was Sam, shoulders hunched and hands in pockets,

staring out to sea, as if he was looking for something – or someone – in the vast night sky, with the weight of the world on him.

Her heart ached, recognising a lonely, lost soul.

Before he could turn around and spot her watching him, Lily put the painting down on the coffee table and stepped away, suddenly feeling as weighed down as Sam. Was it due to exhaustion or a delayed reaction to today's trauma? Was it from a sense of loss – of Cara and, ludicrous thought, having to leave Stark . . . and Sam?

Damn it. This was the second time she'd cried in two days! She'd been beginning to think that the break had done her good, despite the fact she'd almost died. But this solitude and introspection wasn't good for her.

It was making her emotional, and weak – neither of which would be any help in securing the future of her business and protecting the livelihoods of her team and makers. No matter how seductive Stark might be, how compelling its owner, it was an escape from reality – and while Lily resolved to make more time for herself in future, right now it was more important than ever that she step up and take the helm again.

Chapter Thirteen

'You're up early.'

At six-thirty a.m. Lily was in reception with her bags, startling Sam who was emerging from the kitchen carrying a paper bag.

She was back in her travelling outfit of blazer and jeans.

'I'm always up at this time and I didn't want to delay you for a moment,' she said, firmly but politely.

'Thanks,' he said. 'And you'll be delighted to know that there's a place for you on the nine a.m. flight.'

'That's lucky,' Lily said, not feeling delighted but rather relieved that she was going back to normality. The emotions that had been stirred up by their near-drowning were still churning away, even though she was putting on a professional exterior.

'Not really. One of the islanders agreed to delay their trip until tomorrow.'

'Oh . . . are they OK with that?'

'It was one of the gardeners at the abbey. I guess she wouldn't have done it unless she was,' he said.

'But she won't miss anything important?' Lily said, feeling guilty for interrupting the gardener's plans.

He shrugged. 'All I know is that the helicopter booking

office asked around and someone volunteered when they heard you urgently needed to go home.'

'I suppose it's not strictly *urgent* but . . .' Lily hesitated, feeling guilty for inconveniencing anyone. 'Will you please thank her for me? I really do appreciate it.'

Sam nodded curtly. The bond between them seemed to have dissolved on his part too. He must be embarrassed about the emotional discussion they'd had the previous evening.

He held up the paper bag. 'Anyway, I made a packed breakfast for you to have en route,' he said gruffly. 'It's only pastries and juice, I'm afraid, but you'll soon be back to civilisation. Well, Penzance anyway.'

'You needn't have gone to the trouble,' Lily said politely, deflated by the re-emergence of the more reserved Sam Teague.

'You're my guest, the least I can do is provide breakfast. Now, as you're ready to go early, we'll get underway, shall we?'

'Yes. Of course.'

While Sam locked the door to reception, Lily waited outside, drinking in her final moments of the view from Stark. The sun was shining amid a few fluffy clouds. The sand flats she'd painted the night before were now covered by water, with only rocky outcrops visible above the surface. Several yachts were moored in the channel between Bryher and Tresco, where its twin castles stood sentinel on either side. It was like a scene from a fairy tale.

All of this natural beauty had been hidden under the fog

when she arrived, tantalising her – Lily was struck by another thought, even more outrageous than the one where she'd felt she might miss Stark and Sam. Was it possible that they hadn't survived the near-drowning and, instead, had woken up in heaven?

'Happy to be going home?' he said, obviously noting the smile on her face.

'Yes . . . I – I need to get back to work, but I was just thinking of something else. It doesn't matter.'

'Let's get you on your way then,' he said, setting off down the path to the quay.

The sun was warm and she didn't need the blazer but donning her city clothes had been meant to help her feel more like herself again.

Would she ever feel like herself though? She wasn't quite the same person who'd arrived, vowing to step off the treadmill – as soon as she'd finalised the deal.

But who am I really? Lily thought, alarmed again by the way in which the foundations of her life had been shaken in just a few days.

The *Hydra* bobbed in the harbour below, the turquoise sea separating her from Tresco and the heliport. It was so beautiful, day or night.

Lily came to a sudden halt.

'Wait!'

Sam turned, an anxious look on his handsome face. 'What's up?'

'I left something behind but – oh, it doesn't matter.'

He nodded. 'Your phone. I'm sorry, I should have remembered. It's still in my office.'

'My phone?' Lily blurted out. 'Oh, God yes. I'd forgotten about that too. No, I meant something else.'

'Something else?' Sam looked astonished. 'More important than your phone?'

'No. No, of course not,' Lily said, embarrassed and shaken that she'd forgotten her mobile completely. 'It's only a watercolour I did last night. It was rubbish anyway. Bin it, would you?'

He shook his head. 'No, I won't. You must take it home.'

'*Must?*'

'Yes,' he said firmly, showing the steely side she'd glimpsed from time to time. 'I'll retrieve your phone while you get the painting.' With that, he marched back into the hub and handed the cottage keys to her.

Lily went inside again and found the sketch pad abandoned on the coffee table, the painting now dry.

Funny, but the scene looked even better than she'd thought last night when she'd cast it aside. The colours were more vibrant than she'd remembered and although it was hardly accomplished, it had something: a soulfulness and yearning for something bigger than herself.

'Stop it, Lily!' She spoke the words out loud. Stark had forced emotions to the surface that she'd suppressed and she hated feeling out of control or doubting herself. She lived her life like she ran her business: there was no room for doubt or regret. Still, she couldn't bear to leave the memory of Stark behind so she took the sketch pad back to reception.

Outside, Sam was pacing up and down, talking on the radio.

Probably some detail about the flight, thought Lily, but as he turned to face her and lowered the radio, she saw that his face had turned pale.

'What's the matter?' she said.

'That was Morven. I'm afraid I have some bad news.'

'What? For me? Oh my God, is it my parents? The girls?'

'No, they're all fine as far as I know. It's not your family, it's you.'

For a split second, Lily's fears that she really had woken up 'on the other side' took hold of her again before she snapped back to reality. 'Me? How can it be me?'

'Morven's been online. Someone must have seen the kayak accident and jumped to the wrong conclusion. Your obituary is all over the web. According to the Internet, you're dead.'

Chapter Fourteen

Lily sat in the Quayside Café on Bryher hunched over Morven's laptop. Her hands were shaking and she felt sick.

What she'd managed to see on her phone, once she had a signal on Bryher, was even worse when she saw it on the site of a tabloid newspaper. Not on the front pages, but towards the back: in the space where they wrote about dead people.

Obituary
CONTROVERSIAL FOUNDER OF 'LILY LOVES' DIES IN BOATING ACCIDENT

The self-styled 'Crafty Queen', Lily Harper, died in a boating accident yesterday while staying at Stark Island, a luxury retreat in the Isles of Scilly.

Harper started her first business while at school, making jewellery and accessories she sold from a market stall in a Staffordshire town. After moving the Lily Loves business online, she built the high-end craft and gift business into one of the UK's up and coming brands. Her gift range, featuring products all hand-made by independent craftspeople, had legions of devoted fans.

However, behind the cosy image of her brand, Harper had a reputation as a workaholic with a ruthless streak. Her appearance as a guest judge on last year's *Great British Craft Show* gained her notoriety when her now-infamous remark that contestant, Tyrone Poundbury, was 'completely devoid of talent' led to him quitting the show in tears.

'But I never actually said that!' Lily protested. Her stomach was churning but she was unable to stop reading.

Tragedy stalked the Harper family after Lily's elder sister, Cara, died in a car accident almost two years ago, leaving a widower and two young children.

Lily Harper was single and is survived by her parents and her two nieces.

Lily Jane Harper, 23 August 1989 – 5 June 2024

Pushing the laptop away, she sat back in her seat, shaking like a leaf.

'Oh, God . . .' The headline leaped out at her again, her own death announced in large black font. 'Why has this happened? *How* has this happened? Haven't they checked their facts?'

'Have they just made it up?' Elspeth said. 'Surely you can't just say that someone has drowned? That's ridiculous!'

'Well,' Lily said, her stomach churning but knowing she had to come clean, 'Sam and I did have an incident in a kayak yesterday.'

'An incident?' Elspeth said, clutching the arm of a chair.

'I got cut off by the tide at Tean Porth, but luckily he was out fishing in his kayak and came to rescue me.'

''Kin hell,' Morven muttered.

Elspeth collapsed into a chair. 'So you *did* almost drown.'

'Not really,' Lily said, terrified that if Elspeth knew the full truth she might have a heart attack. 'But it was scary.'

Elspeth fanned herself with her hand. 'Well, someone must have seen you in the water and thought you were a goner! They might have started the rumours.'

'How could they? There was no one else there . . . unless . . . there *was* a yacht sailing near the cove. They were too far off to call to but maybe they saw us.'

'Why didn't they call for help if they thought you were drowning?' Elspeth cried. 'And why did they go on the Internet and tell people you were dead without making any attempt to find out for sure? What's the world coming to?'

Morven shrugged. 'People do that all the time, Auntie Elspeth. It's normal now. I'm surprised no one filmed it.'

'*Filmed* someone drowning?' Elspeth cried. 'That's never normal in my book. It's certifiable!'

'Morven's right,' Lily said. 'Believe me, some people would do anything for their five minutes of fame on social media. I'll get my team to try and find out how this happened, but the important thing is that Sam and I are *fine*.'

'Sam?' Elspeth threw up her hands in horror. 'Was he in danger too?'

'Well . . . yes, but we're *not* dead. Clearly. It sounds like this is a rumour that's been blown up out of all proportion and has gone viral.' Even as she comforted Elspeth, Lily's heart sank further – if that was possible.

Morven reached over and clicked on another tab. 'There's a longer article on here,' she said, opening the online site of a different newspaper. 'With a quote from your friend.'

'What friend?' Lily said, almost adding she had no close friends . . . and feeling sick that she even had to remind herself of how many mates she'd lost touch with lately.

Morven angled the laptop so Lily could read the article.

'Lily was the proverbial swan,' says Amelia Parker, long-time friend of Harper and former marketing director of Lily Loves. 'To the world, it looked as if she was gliding serenely through life yet she was always racing around in pursuit of the next big thing. Under her cut-throat and ruthless business image, she could sometimes be a loyal and generous person. It's a dreadful shame that the wider world never got to see the real Lily.'

Parker added: 'I urged her to slow down several times for the sake of her mental and physical health. Her family will be completely devastated.'

'Not very nice of your friend to say that about you,' said Morven helpfully.

'She's not my friend,' Lily murmured, recalling how Amelia had left Lily Loves. They'd been colleagues but not mates and Amelia had quit of her own accord for a promotion at a bigger company. Lily had found her rather aloof and had never quite trusted her, but they'd always got on well enough. *Under her cut-throat and ruthless business image* – that was a strange thing to say when someone had supposedly died. It hinted at a hidden agenda. Had Amelia secretly hated her? Did other people in her team feel that way – her friends and acquaintances?

Lily's stomach knotted at the thought.

'I doubt it'll be on there long once they realise you're not really dead,' Morven said. 'But I got a screen shot. In case you want to sue them.'

'Morven!' Elspeth said, handing a mug to Lily, her green eyes full of concern. 'You've had a terrible shock, Lily. Anyone would turn pale. I've put sugar in it,' she said before glaring at Morven, who was grinning at Lily from the opposite side of the table. 'Morven, make yourself useful and fetch some of my ginger fairings!'

'Thank you.' Lily sipped the sweet tea. Words and phrases from her obituary and some of the comments under the news stories kept flashing through her mind like a neon sign she couldn't turn off.

'Driven and ambitious' – she'd have used those to describe herself. Yet 'notorious', 'controversial' and 'heartless'? She'd never been heartless or sought notoriety. She cared about her staff and the makers – and her customers.

She didn't even dare look at social media. Those words would not be the kindest things she read about herself, judging by what had happened after the *Great British Craft Show*.

'You'll be wanting to speak to your family,' Elspeth said.

'I've already sent a message on my phone, saying I'm fine. It was the first thing I did the moment I got a signal.'

Luckily, her parents hadn't seen the reports, though Richie had sounded hysterical with relief when she'd called him. She'd managed to reach him and asked him to get hold of Étienne as soon as he could. He'd managed to message Étienne but Lily still wasn't sure her brother-in-law had seen any communication at all – in the media or from Richie.

What must he think if he'd only heard the worst?

Lily's stomach turned over but she could do nothing until she heard from him.

In the meantime, Richie was busy issuing a statement that she was alive while marshalling the PR team to contact editors and have the story removed. Now she'd have to get involved in a long exchange of messages with people who wanted to know the full details.

Lily heaved a deep sigh. 'This is a nightmare.'

Sam walked into the café and Elspeth flew to him, holding him tightly. 'Sam Teague, you never mentioned you'd been involved in this accident with Lily!'

'We're fine,' he said, avoiding Lily's eye. 'There was nothing much to tell and I didn't want to worry you, Auntie Elspeth.'

Morven clattered a biscuit tin onto the table. 'It's all over social media too. People are saying some horrible things.'

'Can't you find something useful to do?' Sam shot back.

'Useful? It was me who called you about Lily being dead,

loaned her my laptop and brought the biscuits. What else do you want?'

'And I'm very grateful you were on the alert,' Lily said, trying to stem the rising storm. Morven was a pain but the last thing Lily wanted was a full-scale row between her and Sam. She pushed the laptop aside. 'Thank you. I'll be out of your hair now. I'll use my phone to deal with things from here.'

'We should set off to the heliport if we're to catch your flight,' Sam said anxiously.

'Yes, of course,' Lily said, remembering that she had been on her way home when the news had broken. She'd almost forgotten in the chaos. 'The sooner I'm back in London to sort this out the better,' she declared.

Minutes later, Sam was motoring the few hundred metres over the channel from Bryher quay to Tresco, where a golf buggy was waiting. He accompanied Lily and her luggage on the five-minute ride to the heliport. Her phone was constantly ringing. She recognised some of the names as press contacts she'd given interviews to in the past. They must now want a scoop on what it was like to come back from the dead.

Ignoring them all, she managed to speak to Richie, who seemed almost excited by the whole drama.

'I've arranged a car to meet you at Penzance and bring you straight to London,' he said. 'It's all in hand.'

'Thank you,' Lily said.

'You'll be back by mid-afternoon. I'm sorry for booking that horrible place. I should never have done it!'

The moment the golf cart stopped, Lily jumped off, still talking frantically to him.

'Richie – it's OK. It's not your fault. You were doing your best and Stark isn't hellish,' she said, trying to lower her voice so Sam wouldn't hear. 'It was OK. More than OK until – well, until things went a bit wrong.'

'Hun – you almost drowned there!' Richie bellowed.

'I was *OK*,' Lily insisted, while feeling guilty for lying.

Rotors whirred, drowning out Richie's next words.

'Sorry, I can't hear you now. The helicopter's landed. It's my flight to Cornwall. Message me if you need to but I'll be off the helicopter very soon.'

Sam was by the helicopter hut talking to the gardener Lily had spoken with when she'd first arrived. Other holidaymakers wheeled cases, chattering excitedly. Tanned staff from the Tresco resort hurried to and fro with luggage and boxes.

One man hugged a woman and two kids; locals bidding farewell, Lily guessed. She wondered where the lady who'd given up her seat was and felt a fresh pang of guilt.

Being ambitious was nothing to be ashamed of, yet she *had* been prepared to do almost anything to get off the island.

The rotors died and Sam rejoined her. 'There's a short turnaround and then you'll be off,' he said. 'Which will doubtless come as a huge relief to you. I'm sure you can't wait to see the back of Stark and us.'

Lily wasn't quite sure if he was joking. She was never sure where Sam stood, but she had a suspicion that under the cynicism, the mood shifts, lay some past trauma he wasn't prepared to share with her. His gaze turned over the water to where Stark slept in the sun, light glinting on the cottages of the retreat. She felt a sharp tug at her heart and recognised it at once: loss.

Her phone rang again and, as she answered it, two voices rang out in unison.

'Auntie Lily!'

'Hold on, girls!' Étienne's voice, sounding uncharacteristically sharp. 'Lily! Thank God you're OK!'

'I am. You got my message, then?'

'Yes, but I was in theatre so didn't have my phone. Soon as I came out, one of my colleagues on the night shift was outside and told me she'd seen the obituary.'

'Oh, God, no.'

'It's OK. Fortunately, she's highly sceptical about the Internet at the best of times and tried to calm me down and then I got to my phone and saw your message about half a minute later.' He paused then said hoarsely, 'But for those thirty seconds, I was absolutely petrified we'd lost you.'

Not as petrified as I was, she thought, stung by the horrific memory of Sam being washed out of the kayak.

She shuddered.

'I'm OK. There was an incident but the owner of the retreat was out in a kayak and spotted me. The sea was rough and we got into some bother, but it was all fine,' she said briskly. 'I've spoken to Richie and the PR team are trying to find out the exact details but they think some idiot on a boat must have seen it happen.'

'And decided you were dead?' Étienne said in astonishment.

'I don't know what they thought. Maybe they only saw part of what happened, or exaggerated, or just decided to make up a story for the hell of it.'

'Words fail me.'

'I know,' Lily said. 'But whoever started the rumour, it was picked up by all and sundry, spread by that shitty gossip site before it went viral.'

'But how did an actual obituary end up online?'

'Some news outlets prepare them in advance, even for young people. Richie found out an over-keen intern released mine before double-checking I was actually dead.'

Étienne swore in French but Lily understood *exactly* what he meant.

'Apparently, it's happened loads of times before. I'm in the best company. There's Beyoncé, Miley Cyrus, the Pope . . .'

'I suppose you should be flattered, then,' he said sarcastically.

'I'm not. At least Richie's managed to have the obit removed from the newspaper but the press are still hounding me for quotes. And that business from the TV show has been dragged up again too,' she added, feeling despondent.

'You're in the best place you could possibly be right now. I should hunker down there until the heat dies down, if I were you. Don't rush back.'

'I have to. The helicopter's leaving soon . . .' Lily looked out over the channel to Stark, which did seem like a haven.

Over there she could escape from the Internet, the phone calls . . . but she still had to deal with the fallout from the press story. Running away and letting Richie face it alone wasn't fair.

She could go back to Stark, of course . . . she *should* allow herself a proper break here. Its beauty was breathtaking and, apart from fog and a near-death experience, she had found a peace there she hadn't experienced since Cara had died. Stark had reawakened her creativity and uncovered raw emotions she'd buried very deeply. Perhaps she'd needed that safety valve to let them out and still did . . .

A uniformed pilot was talking to some of the holiday-makers outside the hut. He seemed to be checking names. She spotted Sam glancing at his watch and trying to catch her eye.

'Lily, before you go, I must let the girls have a word or I'll never hear the last of it,' Étienne said.

'Put them on quick,' Lily replied, trudging over to join Sam. Her legs felt as if they were made of lead.

The questions flew at her like serves from a Wimbledon champion. Lily cowered on her side of the net, with the two girls firing aces so fast she couldn't even tell who was speaking.

'*Auntie Lily! Are you having a loverly holiday?*'

'*Have you been in the sea yet?*'

'Er . . .' she said.

'*Have you seen a sea monster?*'

'*Can we come and see you?*'

'*Daddy needs a holiday too.*'

137

'*Daddy says there's a story on the Internet about you that people have made up. Why have they done that?*'

'*Daddy said it's gone viola.*'

Lily was half-laughing, half-crying. 'It's a silly mistake. It's rubbish.'

One phrase from the obituary had hammered itself into her brain harder than any other.

A dreadful shame that the wider world never got to see the real Lily.

But who *was* the real Lily?

Was being a ruthless, driven businesswoman all she wanted to be known for? What about a beloved friend and auntie, a loving daughter, a good *partner*?

The roar from the helicopter throttle was almost deafening, but Lily couldn't move.

What if this – now – was her second chance? Not the kayak accident but *this* moment? What if this was *the* opportunity to take stock of her life?

To think and to breathe?

To *change*?

'I don't think I can come home . . .'

'What? What did you say, Lily?' Étienne's voice was faint against the sound of the propellers.

'I think I'll stay here for a couple of weeks. I – I do need a proper holiday.'

'Of course you do, my love. We've been trying to tell you that.'

'Yes . . . but will you bring the girls to see me?'

'I'll see what I can do.'

Sam was now at her side. 'Lily, we *have* to go.'

'I'll call you later. Love to the girls.' She shut off the call and stared at him.

'The helicopter's boarding,' he said. 'You must go *now*.'

'I don't want to go.' A new certainty pumped through her veins.

'What do you mean? The flight's about to take off.'

'I know, but I'm not ready to get on it. I said I'd take a proper break and I'm going to. I can sort things from here. Richie can be in charge at the office. The business won't implode in less than two weeks.' She was almost breathless in her haste to get the words out.

The roar from the helicopter grew louder.

Lily raised her voice and held Sam's arms, almost pleading with him. 'I'm sorry for all the trouble I've caused you but, please, I *need* to stay here.'

Chapter Fifteen

'You have *got* to be joking. She can't stay here!'

'Morven, for God's sake, keep your voice down. *She's* outside. And, by the way, if you can't be civil to her – to Lily – then you and I are going to fall out properly.'

'OK, but don't expect me to wait on her.'

Sam stiffened. Morven had gone too far. 'No one will be waiting on her,' he said sharply. 'Lily is more than capable of looking after herself, believe me.'

'Wow, Uncle Sam, steady on. You sound as if you actually like her.'

'She's very nice when you get to know her,' he said, wishing he hadn't defended Lily quite so robustly. 'You've no idea what she's been through.'

Morven burned him with a laser stare. 'So, basically, you fancy her?'

Thrown off kilter for a beat, he managed to recover. 'If you carry on like this, I'm going to call your dad and make him come back right now.'

Morven tossed her hair and laughed. 'He wouldn't come back if *I'd* almost drowned in a kayak accident. He couldn't give a toss about me, only himself and The Gorgon.'

'That's not true,' Sam said, gathering all his patience. 'He *does* care, and you can't blame Lily for what's happening in your life.' He decided not to refer to Grady at all.

Morven's eyes gleamed with unshed tears. He'd said the wrong thing again.

With a vicious rattle, Morven flounced through the bead curtain that led to the kitchens. He saw her disappear out of the café's rear entrance, headed who knew where. At least she couldn't go far, trapped as she was on the half a square mile of land.

Sam couldn't be irritated with her for too long. She was clearly hurt deeply by Nate's neglect. Sam also feared that Morven might be right: although he was sure Nate loved his daughter dearly, his brother's priorities had gone seriously off the rails.

He'd have to call Nate again, and find out when – oh, God, *if* – he was coming back for his daughter. If ever Nate decided to leave her for good – following on from her mother's vanishing act – Sam didn't know what he'd do.

What with Morven and the retreat to deal with, Sam would have liked to flounce off and hide away himself, but he was meant to be the grown-up here.

Lily was waiting outside on her mobile again, of course. He'd only just managed to persuade the ground crew to off-load her bags before they'd taken off without her.

'I'm so sorry for the about-turn,' she'd said with a desperation that had disarmed him. 'I really do feel bad about all the drama and inconvenience, but I've changed my mind. I need to stay here. Sorry, I have to take this call. We can talk later.'

There had been no time to hear the finer details of her sudden change of heart. Sam had been busy soothing the crew and grabbing back her bags.

Only when he'd retrieved them and ushered Lily into a golf buggy and over to his waiting boat, had he been able to talk to her properly.

'I'll tell you more when I've finished sorting this out, but I'll be staying for the full two weeks as originally booked. That's OK, isn't it?' she asked.

'Well, yes . . .' Cowrie Cottage was the only one he'd booked out so far, but when he'd thought Lily was leaving, he'd made plans to spend the next few weeks finishing another two. He wanted to throw himself into the work and be free from his hosting duties, cooking and cleaning.

He wasn't sure how he was going to cope. On a practical note, he hadn't slept in his own bed at Hell Bay House, his home on Bryher, for days. Morven had had the run of the place, and God knows what she'd been getting up to on her own. Elspeth had said she'd seen young people coming to and fro and heard music until the small hours. Sam would have to go back there and check the place hadn't been turned into a rave venue before he took Lily over to Stark.

And now it would just be the two of them, alone together. There was no doubt they'd forged a bond since the accident and she'd overturned many of his expectations, but spending so much time with her might mean growing even closer.

Look what had happened the last time. It had ended in tears, bitter tears . . .

Sam shook himself. None of this was going to help him behave as a professional host for the next two weeks. He had to get a grip.

Lily was sitting outside the Quayside Café, talking to Elspeth.

'Ah, Sam!' His aunt greeted him with a broad smile on her face.

To his relief, Lily looked happier too. 'Elspeth says I'm welcome at the café any time I want to be in touch with the outside world.'

He hid a smile. The outside world made Scilly sound like Mars.

'And I can try out her coffee while I'm here. And possibly the cakes. The brownies were delicious.'

'You haven't tried the lemon drizzle yet,' Elspeth said. 'Or the coconut and lime sandwich, or the cheese scones. I do brunch and lunch as well as cream teas.'

'Stop!' Lily cried. 'I'll go home the size of a house!'

'You need fattening up,' Elspeth said. 'Doesn't she, Sam?'

Lily stared at him expectantly.

'I – er—' he floundered, feeling that Lily needed a good dose of his aunt's cakes.

'It'll be OK for me to pop over to Bryher, won't it? When you come for supplies and stuff?'

'Yes, of course.' He bit back a lengthy response involving tides, rocks, running the retreat, cooking for Lily, working on the unfinished cottages . . . before realising he was meant to be a host. 'Do you mind,' he said as brightly as he could, 'if while we're here we pop in at my place, quickly? I need some clean clothes and to check on the house.'

'Not at all,' Lily said, equally as brightly. 'Be my guest.'

Hell Bay House had stood for over a hundred years on a low grassy field beside the shore. It was separated from the bay itself by a freshwater pool and low rocky outcrops. In the distance beyond was Stark. He could see the cottages from here and even the ladder propped against one of the four unfinished units. Hidden at the rear were a concrete mixer and building materials.

It struck him that he was very far from having the retreat ready for visitors. Neither the facilities nor the infrastructure were ready – and, most worryingly, neither was he. It seemed arrogant of him now to have rejected Lily's offer of advice, yet he stood by his principle: she was on Stark for a proper break, not to talk business.

He just hoped that there were no more dramas to come while she was his guest.

The press reports surrounding her accident hardly showed the retreat in a good light. One had called it 'half-built' and words like 'deserted', 'isolated' and 'abandoned' had been used along with a mention of 'the plague and leprosy' in reference to the pest house. None of it was an actual lie, but together it made Stark Retreat sound like a few shacks on a pestilent lump of rock where guests weren't safe.

'OK. I'm ready,' Lily said, switching off her phone. 'I've spoken to Richie and my head of PR. They're going to deal with the press now so I can fully relax.'

'Sounds like a plan,' Sam said, unsure if she really would stick to it.

'Shall we go to your house?' she said. 'I've put you to a lot of trouble already.'

'Not at all.' He showed her to a muddy old Defender parked near the slipway. Her eyes ranged around on the way, taking in the tiny settlement known grandly as High Town, with its flower-bedecked cottages, gallery and post office stores.

'I didn't know you kept a car here,' she said.

'Yeah, though it's ancient and it's never left Bryher since the day I bought it from one of the neighbours. I wasn't even born when it arrived here on the freight ship. Most people on the islands have some form of motorised transport, to shift stuff around. We give lifts to those who need them: the elderly, non-drivers and kids up from the boats.'

'Everyone looks out for each other, I can see that.'

'It's a small community – we wouldn't survive if we didn't. Of course, there's also a downside to living in each other's pockets.'

'No privacy,' she murmured. 'Ironic that I came here for that and the opposite has happened.'

'Yes, I'm afraid everyone probably knows who you are by now. You might have been better off in London where you could at least have been one among millions. You've clearly decided Stark was the lesser of two evils.' He added a smile as he said it.

'I didn't stay here because I had no choice. I felt it was what I needed to do.'

145

He nodded and stopped the Land Rover outside a white-painted place. 'Here we are. Hell Bay House.'

Lily slid down from the passenger seat and stared at the building. 'OK?' he said, seeing her eyes widen at the sight of his home.

'Yes. It's – well, Hell Bay. It doesn't live up to its name.'

Sam followed her gaze to his double-fronted house, the gardens thick with mauve agapanthus and towering echiums. Scallop shells adorned the low white garden wall. He'd helped implant them in the cement himself when he was younger and his parents and Nate lived here too.

'You should see it on a wild January night in the middle of a raging storm. Sand gets blown into the garden and you can feel the foundations shake.'

'The actual foundations shake?' Lily asked, eyeing the ocean with trepidation.

'It feels like it, but we're far enough back from the sea for safety.' He saw her eyes widen at the sight of the jagged rocks closed around the white sand bay like jaws. As the tide ebbed, Stark seemed to be almost within wading distance across the shining strand and shallow pools. So tranquil, so benevolent a scene . . . Nothing bad or tragic could ever happen here, surely?

'So far, anyway. Come on in. Make yourself comfortable while I sort out some stuff.'

Hell Bay House had once been the home of one of the better-off families on Bryher, amid a clutch of cottages owned by fishermen and modern bungalows built in the middle of the twentieth century.

The Teagues had made money on mainland Cornwall, initially from pilchard fishing, and had invested it cautiously, which had enabled them to buy the house at the turn of the twentieth century – and to purchase Stark from its previous owner, a bankrupt minor aristocrat who'd been given it by the Crown and had been desperate to be rid of it.

Although Stark had been left jointly to Nate and Sam by their grandparents, Nate had never shown an iota of interest in it and hadn't put in a penny of investment. He'd told Sam that he could have the place and keep any profit he made from 'the godforsaken rock'.

Lily lingered by the gate to look out over the sea.

'This view is . . . breathtaking.'

He glanced up, used to the panorama of navy sea, bone-white sand and a sky that could be anything from clear blue to leaden.

'I guess so. I suppose I take it for granted. Even so . . .' he said, allowing his gaze to rest on the clouds scudding across the sky and the terns landing on the pool '. . . I would find it hard to live anywhere else.'

'Hard or impossible?' she said.

'Very hard,' he said, reminded of a similar conversation he'd had on this very spot. He'd known she was leaving then, as he knew Lily would soon. Only this morning he'd convinced himself he'd be glad to see the back of her but now . . . he longed for her to stay so he could know her better yet that would be to risk liking her *too* much.

She shivered.

'Shall we go inside?' he asked.

She nodded.

'Lily, can I ask what really made you change your mind about staying here?' he said, back in the sitting room.

'I – I made a strategic business decision.'

'A strategic business decision?' He sat on the arm of the sofa, arms folded.

She turned away from the window. 'Yes.'

'I see.'

'I decided that now wasn't the time to go back. The press are hounding me, and yes, I do need more time to gather myself. My family want me to take a break too and, for all our sakes, I think I should do it. The past few days have been . . . challenging . . . and it's probably best if I allow myself time to fully process them.'

'That sounds very much like a corporate statement,' he said. 'If you don't mind me saying . . .'

'Does it?' She treated him to a self-deprecating smile. 'I guess it's hard to kick the habit. It *is* OK, isn't it?' she added.

'Of course. You're my guest,' he said, aware he also was putting on a front.

'And you won't mind me popping over to Bryher when I need to? I can get one of the scheduled boats to the other islands from there, so I won't be under your feet all the time.'

'It's your holiday. You can do what you like. Please, make yourself at home while I collect some things from upstairs.'

He needed clean clothes. Although there was a laundry room at the retreat, he wasn't sure he'd have time to do any washing. In search of clean underwear, he opened drawers, knowing he had an unopened pack of boxers somewhere . . .

Cursing under his breath, he opened the drawer at the bottom of the wardrobe. Inside was a tiny bunch of dried flowers tied with a blue ribbon.

His stomach clenched with sadness at the sight and the bittersweet memories they brought back – he still couldn't bear to part with them.

Sam covered them with clothes again and went downstairs, forcing himself to focus on practicalities and activity. He put his clean clothes in a dry bag by the front door and popped into the kitchen, taking fresh milk, juice and a few other items from his fridge. The boat was already loaded with cool boxes of fresh veg, meat for the freezer at Stark and enough fresh fish from Rory to last a couple of days. Lily would be pleased.

'The forecast's good. We shouldn't have a problem getting around,' he called as she re-entered the sitting room.

Lily was nowhere to be seen but the curtains were blowing in the breeze through the open French doors.

He moved quietly forward and saw her outside on his terrace, surrounded by agapanthus, hugging herself as if no one else ever would.

Sensing his presence, she swung round, panicked at being caught looking vulnerable. He was struck by how slight she seemed, how drawn and isolated. Was this the woman of steel, the 'evil bitch' described online? Because, while he was upstairs, he had glanced at the social media comments . . . and wished he hadn't. He'd wanted to confront every single one of the cowardly pondlife posting such vile comments.

Then he remembered she was the last person who needed a man protecting her like some misguided knight in tarnished armour. It was better to keep his distance: that way he couldn't be hurt.

'I hope you don't mind. I needed some fresh air after this morning. And the view was so incredible, I stepped outside.' She smiled. 'I can't see anyone but perhaps a long lens is trained on me.'

Sam was alarmed. 'You think reporters would follow you over here to Bryher?'

'I'm not that notorious,' she said, attempting a joke. 'No, they wouldn't bother and the fuss will die down quickly. There will be new people to hound and troll soon enough.'

'I don't know how you stand it.'

She shrugged. 'I have no choice. Or rather, I have to accept it if I want to be successful at what I do.'

'I suppose so.'

'You'll have to deal with reviews from guests and the press, you know? You can't run a place like Stark and not put yourself out there.'

'I realise that. But maybe I hadn't realised quite how much.'

'Look, I am supposed to be on retreat, but I can give you some tips . . . but only if you want me to. Not as a businessperson, but as a – friend?'

'A friend?' he echoed. 'I – I don't want to add to your stress.'

'It would be a pleasure.' Her eyes sparkled. 'If you think you can stand the heat?'

She'd disarmed him again, and he glimpsed the warmth under the exterior, a warmth he was seeing more of, more often. 'Will it be as scary as being a contestant on the *Great British Craft Show*?' he asked, deadpan. Lily playfully punched his arm.

'In all seriousness, I'd appreciate some advice. But first, shall we get you safely to Stark so you can settle back in? It's been a hell of a day and it's still only eleven a.m.'

'Let's hope it doesn't hold any more drama,' Lily said, with a smile that didn't quite reach her eyes.

She still looked pale and the image came into his mind of her staring out at Hell Bay, hugging herself tight.

There was so much more she wasn't telling him.

But then, there was so much more he wasn't telling her.

Chapter Sixteen

'Now, I don't want you to worry,' Lily said, taking her chance to call her parents again before she returned to the tech-free zone of Stark. 'But I thought I'd call to say that I've decided to have a proper break after all.'

While trying not to alarm her mother and father, Lily felt she owed it to them to explain more about the kayak incident but, even in her new spirit of honesty and openness, she couldn't bring herself to say just how close she and Sam had come to disaster.

She tried to focus on the fact that the accident had made her realise she needed more time to rest and relax while all the fuss died down.

'We're so glad you're taking a proper break,' her mum said. 'Keep in touch so we know you're OK.'

'Please be careful, love!' her dad added.

A lump formed in Lily's throat. 'I will do. Don't forget, I'll have no signal on Stark but I'm going to explore the other islands, so I'll call you then. Please try not to worry about me.'

With that, she'd switched off her phone and boarded the *Hydra* as Sam was waiting to take her back. She hoped that Richie and the team could deal with the press enquiries and she was going to check in with him by phone on a regular basis from Bryher.

Even so, the thought of letting go of the reins made her feel twitchy.

She rested her eyes on the twin hills of the island, trying to focus on the feeling of the sun on her face and the wind in her hair. Having made her decision to spend the rest of her two weeks on Stark, she now needed to be fully *present*, just as Sam had advised her to be when she first arrived.

Along with the nervousness about letting go, was there also a feeling of release? Of relief that, for a little while, she could let someone else shoulder the burden?

If only she didn't have to wrestle with the supermarket decision. While she'd been on Bryher, she'd found it impossible to resist opening an email from her contact at their head office, asking if she was OK. She'd put them off for now, saying she was fine, taking a holiday, and would set up a meeting for the moment she returned.

Lily sneaked a glance at Sam. Was his grim expression merely concentration as he piloted the *Hydra* towards the hidden jetty? Or was he less than thrilled that she was returning?

Admittedly, she'd changed her mind at the last minute and caused someone to miss their place on the helicopter. To mitigate this, she'd insisted on paying the fare of the islander who'd given up her place, apologising profusely for the trouble.

Yet under the veneer of politeness, Sam was definitely on edge. He certainly wasn't the relaxed man who'd shared a meal with her last night; the one who'd proudly shown her the island and later pulled her from the sea.

She flinched as the fender bumped against the wooden pilings of the tiny jetty.

Sam's mood might not be anything to do with Lily's behaviour at all.

'Here we are again,' he said and, without waiting for an answer, slung her bags onto the quayside.

She climbed off, carrying her blazer. As the sun had risen higher, she was far too hot in her jeans.

'You know, I think I'm going to have to get some new clothes now I'm staying. I didn't realise I'd be spending so much time outdoors and I haven't brought enough to last the whole stay.'

'There are some clothes shops in Hugh Town on St Mary's,' Sam said. 'Mostly T-shirts, sweatshirts and board shorts.'

'That sounds perfect. When you take the boat to Bryher tomorrow, would you mind dropping me off at the ferry for St Mary's? I don't expect a lift all the way,' she added hastily. 'I'm more than happy to find my own way round the island transport system.'

'If you're sure . . .'

'Sam, I use the Tube almost every day. I think I can negotiate a few boats.'

His eyes crinkled and he defrosted a few degrees. 'No problem. I'll take you to Bryher tomorrow.'

After changing into something more comfortable, Lily threw open the door of the cottage and went onto the terrace, breathing in the fresh air. Through binoculars she could clearly see the Quayside Café and the other buildings near the jetty: a boat shed, a yard full of masts, Rory's fish shack and a couple of holiday chalets. The pub garden was full of holidaymakers and Rory's red sail boat motored between the yachts in the Tresco channel.

She found the guidebook again, wanting to remind herself of the history of the island. She guessed it had been compiled by Elspeth with illustrations from Morven plus old photographs that showed a group of three Victorian ladies in extravagant hats and long dresses sitting next to the hearth in one of the cottages – could it be *her* cottage?

She shuddered, wondering how Mabel Teague would have felt to see her home turned into a tourist attraction, first for the visiting ladies and then for Lily herself.

She could see it wouldn't be popular with everyone. Should she feel guilty for being here? No, Sam was trying to make a go of it and she was supporting him.

She found Sam wheelbarrowing roofing tiles towards one of the unfinished cottage units, which had a mound of building materials at the rear. Transporting those across and up to the resort couldn't have been easy; no wonder he looked so fit.

With difficulty she dragged her eyes from Sam's own impressive structure to the guest cottages. The simple single-storey stone buildings each had a window either side of a door and were built of the granite boulders found all over Stark and its neighbouring islands.

Even though they were simply constructed, they looked

solid enough to withstand the worst the Atlantic could throw at them.

'How did they build their houses? Two hundred years ago, I mean.'

'Brute force. Those stones must have been shifted into place by hand, perhaps using ponies to help.'

'And how have *you* managed?' she asked.

'Same, only without the ponies.'

He smiled yet Lily wished she hadn't drawn her own attention to his muscular forearms and broad shoulders.

He wiped a hand over his forehead. 'I'll admit, it hasn't been a walk in the park. It's taken three years from the initial idea. My friend Aaron helped me at first and I can still call on mates to pitch in occasionally if need be. We brought equipment like the cement mixer and mini-digger over on the freight boat.'

'Freight boat? I'd no idea it was such a complex operation.' Clearly, Lily thought, she had a lot to learn about running a business in such a remote location.

'Each island has its own communal freight boat used to bring heavier supplies and equipment from the main port in St Mary's. As for the work here: Aaron helped with the roofing, and a local plumber and electrician fitted the bathrooms and restaurant kitchen. I paid them back by helping them with their own projects.'

'The fit is to such a high standard, it must have been quite an investment.' Lily was more impressed and amazed than ever that Sam had made the cottages so beautiful.

'It wasn't cheap. I used an inheritance from my maternal

grandparents to get started plus savings from the building business.' He cast a wistful eye over the unfinished cottage. 'We're nearly there. When I've finished the roof on this and made it watertight, I'll start painting the third and fourth ones. The second is drying out and only needs furnishings.'

'I could help you with that. Painting and furnishing.'

'No way. You didn't come here to work for me!'

'It wouldn't be work. I love getting hands on and I rarely have time now. I learned how to paint walls and sew from my mum and dad. You did say I could give you some tips, so here's one: if someone offers to work for you for free, then you should grab the help with both hands.'

'I'll think about it,' Sam said.

'Call it my therapy,' she said archly.

He hesitated and she could see he was very tempted. 'Like I said, I'll think about it. Now, I'll leave you to relax. And be careful while you're on the island.'

'I won't get cut off, if that's what you mean.'

A short time later, Lily gathered up her artist's materials and set off to explore the side of the island she hadn't seen the previous day. It was located below the South Hill at the opposite end from the pest house.

As she walked away from the retreat, the sounds of hammering and helicopters approaching Tresco were the only things to disturb the peace. Even they faded by the time she'd walked down the slope and was in the lee of the South Hill.

The zig-zag path turned and, suddenly, Tean Porth, with its handful of ruined cottages, came into view. They were a hundred metres or so back from a crescent of beach, its sand as pale as the moon, scattered with bleached driftwood.

Lily caught her breath at this thrilling glimpse into the past.

She walked down the path until she was on the flat grassy area the houses were built on. The single-storey cottages were very similar in layout to her own, but there the resemblance ended. These dwellings had no roofs or windows, and their interiors were almost overgrown with bracken, fern and foxgloves.

She stepped inside one, under the stone lintel. Sam had mentioned that the stones for some of the cottages might have been taken from even older structures: Iron Age homes and tombs. The sudden contrast between warm sun and deep shade made goosebumps stand out on her arms. The foliage and shadows created a dank chill that added to the gloomy atmosphere.

At one end of the cottage, the hearth still stood and was large enough to duck inside. There was a narrow walkway through the plant life, which must have been created by humans – though when, she'd no idea. Sam and his builder mates, probably, as he'd said they'd recently inspected the structures to see if it was feasible to convert them.

Lily stepped into the shadows of those Victorian ladies who had looked on Stark as a romantic tourist destination after its residents had been evacuated. She imagined them on their day trips, sitting by the ruined hearth with their picnics – quails' eggs, hams and fancy cakes, with servants in tow to wait on them.

'Oh!'

She let out a cry and flinched, before laughing at the sight of the crow she'd obviously scared from the hearth. It was only a bird . . . and even though this place was making her jittery, it was so atmospheric. She knew she had to paint it.

She found a large granite stone to sit on a little way above the cottages, which gave her a view of the tiny hamlet with the white beach of Tean Porth behind it and, in the distance, white breakers crashing against the rocks. She drew a rudimentary sketch then dipped her brush in the jar she'd half-filled from her water flask.

Soon, Lily was absorbed in her work, simply trying to enjoy the act of creating and not worry about the result. She'd have other days to draw and paint the scene, though it could never be quite the same as today or even this moment. With clouds, waves and light changing by the second, her painting would always be an amalgamation of multiple moments, never to be recaptured again.

A moment frozen in time, yet also lost.

Cara flew into her mind. Her sister would have been pleased to see her, sitting here, living for the day. Lily thought about Étienne, then . . . what must he have been through in that half a minute after his colleague had told him about the online reports?

He must have been devastated to hear of another loss in the family and by the thought of having to tell the girls that their auntie was gone.

To centre herself again, Lily heaved in a deep gulp of the air, scented with the tang of seaweed and flowers. The gulls' cries seemed shriller and when she sipped from her flask and savoured the cold water, filtered from the island well, it tasted pure and sweet.

Oh, yes, she was alive.

She laid down her sketch pad, the sheet pinned back, and delved into her backpack for the sandwich she'd insisted on making for herself in Sam's kitchen. Goat's cheese salad on a granary roll from the Bryher bakery.

It smelled so fresh and tasted divine. She was sure her senses had been sharpened by the island's brilliant light and pure air.

She smiled and reached for her flask. How fortunate she was to be living in such luxury, eating fresh food, never having to suffer hunger or thirst – unlike poor Mabel and her family. Her mouth was full when she saw it. She paused, and tried to swallow the food but it would hardly go down.

Goosebumps popped out on every inch of flesh.

Her hands shook as she abandoned her lunch on the stone. It couldn't have been . . . Her eyes had been deceiving her. A trick of the light, her imagination working overtime.

She'd been sure she'd glimpsed a strange shadowy figure at the far end of the ruined cottage, but now she looked again, it had vanished.

'Lily!' Sam called down to her from the roof of the top cottage when she hurried past, breathing as hard as if she'd won the Olympic hundred metres.

'What's up? Are you OK?'

Lily dropped her backpack on the terrace. Her latest painting hadn't been dry when she'd shoved it into her bag and dashed from the cottages. It would be ruined but she didn't care. Her only object had been to get away from the place as fast as possible.

Sam climbed down the ladder and was by her side in an instant. 'What's happened?'

'N–nothing. I was just a bit . . . s–spooked.'

'What do you mean, "spooked"?' He touched her arm, fleetingly, then added, 'Take your time.'

She had no choice but to take her time, needing to steady her breathing and process what she'd seen. Or *thought* she'd seen. Her blood had run cold when the shadowy figure had appeared: but it was probably her imagination working overtime. After all, she had been thinking about Mabel at the time and had had a stressful few days.

'I was painting the ruined cottages at Tean Porth,' she said, feeling rather foolish now. 'And it was probably a trick of the light, but I thought I saw someone inside one of them.'

Sam's eyes widened. 'Someone? Who?' he said, adding more softly, 'What did they look like?'

'I couldn't say. It was more of a shadow than a figure. Like I said, it could simply have been a trick of the light. It startled me, that's all.' Lily shrugged though she was still shaken. 'Maybe I've had too much sun today,' she joked.

Sam didn't laugh. 'Did you see any other signs of anyone hanging around? A boat on the beach maybe? Even a paddleboard?'

'No, and I also had a quick look inside the cottage before

I started painting. There was no one visible, though there was a trampled area up to the hearth.'

Sam nodded. 'I went in there a week ago with Aaron to see if we could salvage any of the stones for the refurbishments. We didn't see any signs of intruders.'

'Then I must have been mistaken,' Lily said breezily. 'I'd been concentrating hard on painting and thinking about the old islanders at the time so perhaps I'd imagined a ghost.' She rolled her eyes. 'Which it couldn't possibly have been because they don't exist.'

'No, they don't, and if there was someone there, it could only have been an intruder though I doubt anyone can be on the island now,' he said reassuringly. 'They can't land at the jetty as it's low tide. I suppose they *could* beach a boat at Tean Porth but you'd have to know the right spot, avoid the rocky reefs, watch the tides ... and I can see almost the whole island from the roof here.' He paused then said: 'Could it be the press or some deranged vlogger?'

'I doubt it. How would they get here?' she asked.

'Only with the help of an islander and I can't think of any local skippers who would agree to help them land on Stark.'

'And I'm already yesterday's news. I don't think a newspaper would spend that kind of cash to pursue me here. Honestly, I wish I hadn't let myself get spooked. I probably need a lie down!'

Sam smiled. 'Please don't worry. I'll take a good look round after dinner to check if I can spot anything amiss. Until then, lock your door if you don't feel safe.' He looked at her earnestly. 'You *are* safe. I'm only seconds away in the flat and I can lend you the spare radio if that would give you peace of mind.'

'You're trusting me with a *radio*?' She raised her eyebrows in mock surprise.

'Yeah. In fact, I think it's best if you keep hold of it so we can communicate wherever we are on the island. You can speak to base too.'

'Base? You mean Elspeth or Morven.' She rolled her eyes. 'I don't think I'll be bothering them.'

'It'll be fine. Look, I've finished what I was doing. I'll knock off for the day and start the prep for dinner.'

'Sam, I think we're going to have to share the cooking from now on. I don't need three-course meals every night.'

'You paid for decent food, not self-catering and waiting on the host!'

'Sure, but that's in an ideal world where you have a team of staff. Earlier, you agreed to take my advice. You need to recruit someone fast, but first, you need five functioning cottages. Let me help you achieve both those things. I can't spend all my time drawing and shopping. It's not me. After all, I am the Crafty Queen.' She said it jokingly but then added, 'Seriously, Sam, I did start my business because I like creating things. It would be great to spend some time cooking and getting my hands dirty so to speak.'

'Well . . .' She could see he was tempted. 'If you think it would help you relax.'

'Call it part of my therapy,' she joked. 'Or Project New Lily.'

He laughed out loud. 'If you put it like that, how can I refuse?'

'You can't,' she said firmly. 'Though while we're on the subject of fresh starts, can I make a suggestion?'

'Go on.' His eyes were wary.

'I won't be here to help forever and you need a business plan. Why don't you put the cottages on a booking site and set yourself a deadline?' she suggested. 'How long do you think you'll need to have the whole retreat ready for guests?'

'Six weeks would do it.'

'That means you'll be able to launch properly in August and have September and October to let them out. Will you stay open through the winter?'

'No. I'll close in December and reopen end of February when spring arrives. Transport becomes tricky in the winter months. There are no sailings from Penzance and the flights can be affected by bad weather. I'll also need to keep coming over here to make sure everything is maintained and safe. The winter storms can be fierce.'

Lily nodded in approval. 'That sounds like a good plan. Your staff will need a break, and so will you. How many are you planning on recruiting?'

'Initially, a chef and a housekeeper–manager.'

She considered for a moment. 'Good in principle, but I do worry that a housekeeper–manager post will be way too much for one person, bearing in mind your staff will need time off.'

'Hmm. You could be right. They'll have to live in, of course. I can spend my nights at Hell Bay House and they can each have their own studio flat. Let me get freshened up and we can talk some more about it over dinner,' he said.

'Good, and I'll cook tonight. I can do a mean mac 'n' cheese. How does that sound?'

'It sounds bloody amazing, frankly.'

His eyes lit up with a warmth and energy Lily hadn't seen before, and she had an inkling his buoyant mood wasn't entirely due to the mac 'n' cheese. Could it be because they were both finally feeling more comfortable in each other's presence?

Chapter Seventeen

Sam had already been up and breakfasted when Lily sauntered into the dining room, still groggy from a long night's sleep.

Last night he'd devoured two helpings of mac 'n' cheese, and they'd firmed up some plans for finishing the cottages and recruiting staff. He'd then gone straight back to work until dusk while Lily had retired to her room.

She had sat out on her terrace until sunset, then she'd gone to bed and didn't remember anything until she'd woken at eight. *Eight!* She'd almost fainted when she'd seen the time on her phone and then reminded herself that she was on holiday.

'Sleep well?' Sam asked, setting a cafetière on her table for one.

There was a twinkle in his eye that infuriated her – and that added to his charm. And how could she find cargo shorts, an ancient T-shirt and builder's boots so sexy? Her last boyfriend – she couldn't call him a 'partner' as neither of them had invested enough time in the relationship for that – had favoured designer jeans, loafers and a weekly trip to a Turkish barber.

In fact, she didn't have much experience of romantic

relationships at all. No amount of business acumen could help her navigate through the confusing feelings she'd been experiencing.

Once again, she thought of the obituary and the way the world had seen her. 'Lily Harper was single . . .' Those few words said so much. In her single-minded drive for success, she'd lost sight of the other things she wanted deep down: to find lasting love and, perhaps, have a family of her own one day.

'Lily?' Sam's voice, gentle and calming, brought her back to the present.

'I slept very well, thanks,' she replied, pulling a hand-thrown mug towards her.

'I'm sorry I shot off after dinner last night, but I needed to make the most of the daylight and thought you might like some time to yourself after the day you'd had.'

'It was fine.'

His intense gaze made her twitchy. 'You say "fine" a lot but yesterday must have been a hell of a shock, not to mention exhausting. The stuff that was being posted about you online was disgusting. What's wrong with some people? Why don't they focus on their own lives instead of dragging other people down?'

She gave a small smile. 'If I knew that I'd be a trillionaire. I'd like to say they can't have much in their own lives, but some of them seem to have it all: high-flying jobs, families. I'm sure they have mothers and partners and kids who'd be horrified to discover what their "amazing hubs" or "wonderful mum" was up to online.'

'I'd be ashamed if someone I loved was spreading that bile.'

Lily shrugged. 'I've had to stop trying to get inside their heads. I've had to let it go or it would have destroyed me. It nearly did . . .' She sipped her coffee. 'This is great. Where's it from?'

'A place near Land's End. The owner, Eden, roasts it herself.' He put a basket of croissants in front of her. 'We can talk about what happened if you like? I'm aware that playing the strong, silent type isn't the best way of approaching problems these days.'

Her heart did a flip. He sounded so earnest, so sincere, even though talking about her feelings must be the last thing he wanted to do.

'It's—' She bit back the word *fine*. 'What happened yesterday wasn't "fine" and what the online trolls had to say did bother me, but not as much as that obituary. Not as much as the comment from Amelia who isn't my friend, clearly. However, my team are dealing with the public stuff and I'll just have to suck up the rest. I can't let it derail me, otherwise the haters have won.'

She selected a pastry from the basket, feeling the need to curtail any deep conversation in case she let her emotions get the better of her yet again. 'Thanks for your concern. I'm looking forward to my break here and to starting again. And I think I'll begin with this delicious-looking croissant.' She smiled, making light of the situation, but it was just moments before she was deep in thought again.

Starting again . . . Starting what *again?* She'd said she didn't want the experience to derail her, and yet she couldn't get the comments out of her mind.

Driven, ruthless, cut-throat . . . the world doesn't see the real Lily.

It didn't really matter how other people saw her. It was how she saw *herself*.

The world had given its verdict on her and she hadn't liked it much, but did she want to change it? Wouldn't that be playing into the hands of the people who'd judged her?

Surely she *must* follow her own path – and hopefully, over the next couple of weeks, she could find out where that might lead her.

'So, what's it to be then?'

Resplendent in a lilac-and-orange kaftan, Elspeth opened her order pad at Lily's table at the Quayside Café. 'Coffee? Cake? A full Scilly breakfast?'

Lily laughed. 'I've already had a great breakfast on Stark. Sam seems determined to feed me up, but I could squeeze in one of your wonderful brownies. And a mocha if you do them?'

'Of course we do mochas,' Elspeth said with pride. 'And I baked a fresh batch of brownies this morning so you're in luck. All coming right up.'

'Thank you,' Lily said.

Elspeth bustled off as four young people arrived for breakfast. From the conversation, she gathered they were students staying at the campsite. Each island had its own passenger boat, and there were more that plied their way from St Mary's. However, it was too early for the tourist ferries so the quay was busy with islanders loading up their own vessels.

Lily felt privileged to be there with them. There could only be a few dozen people staying overnight at the single hotel, bed and breakfast and handful of holiday homes. A sprinkling of holidaymakers were out for early strolls or dog walks but apart from that, the shores were deserted. The sands sparkled in the morning sun and the rocks glistened with green weed.

The tide was still going out leaving the shore washed fresh – the slate wiped clean, just like her life after her near drowning.

She was finding it almost impossible not to peek at the messages on social media about her 'death' and had to keep reminding herself that her team were dealing with those. Part of Project New Lily involved not constantly trawling through social media and being kind to herself, as much as to the people around her.

Shortly afterwards, Elspeth returned with a steaming mug topped with cream and marshmallows and a large slice of brownie. Although the June sun was warm, the breeze was fresh and Lily was glad of the fleece Sam had loaned her because her blazer and thin cotton sweater weren't warm enough.

It swamped her but she was grateful for it until she could go over to St Mary's for some more suitable clothes to withstand the vagaries of the Atlantic weather.

'Here you go. I didn't know if you wanted the works on

the mocha so I added them anyway. You can scoop it all off if not,' Elspeth said.

'I haven't had the works for as long as I can remember. My nieces would love this,' she said, hoping Étienne would somehow be able to bring them over for a visit, if not during her stay then at a later date. She admired the low white-washed building with its blue-painted woodwork, perfectly at home in its island setting. 'Your café is so lovely.'

'Thank you. It used to be a boat house but was extended and converted into two cottages. Twenty years ago, a family turned part of it into a café.'

'How long have you had it?' Lily asked. 'I don't mean to keep you from your work,' she added hastily.

Elspeth sat down at the table. 'I can spare a couple of minutes before the first ferry arrives. My assistant Barney can hold the fort for now. I took over the café after I split from my husband five years ago,' she said. 'I was only sixty-two and I needed to make some money. I'd always wanted a café but Him Indoors was never keen on me having my own job – or life. I think he wanted to keep my nose to the grind-stone doing his accounts.' She rolled her eyes. 'Instead, I left him, took on this place, and we're doing well.'

Lily's admiration for Elspeth grew. She might believe in folklore but she was also a practical businesswoman in tune with her customers. 'I hope he's seen how successful you've been.'

'Oh, he has. He's even tried to inveigle his way into my life again but I'm having none of it. This is my place now and I love it!'

Lily breathed in the clear air. 'The view is incredible.'

From her elevated position, she could see right across the sparkling channel that separated Bryher from Tresco, with its neat holiday cottages and gallery. To her left was Bryher's only pub and – less encouragingly – a large rock with a gibbet-like structure on the top.

Elspeth must have seen her shudder. 'Is that a real – er – scaffold?' Lily said.

Elspeth laughed. 'No, it's only a replica. Someone's little joke, not that I find it so funny. Some say that there was a real gallows up there during the Civil War. That's Cromwell's Castle opposite,' Elspeth said, pointing out the round turret perched on a rocky outcrop on the Tresco side of the channel. 'Some people say it was built to imprison mutinous sailors. Others joke it's for tourists who outstay their welcome.'

Lily gave a mock gasp.

'Present company excepted, of course.' Elspeth's eyes gleamed with mischief.

'Oh, I don't know,' Lily said. 'From what I'm reading online, there are plenty of people calling for me to come to a sticky end. It feels like being put in the stocks while the angry populace throws rotten veg at me.'

'It must have been horrible but it will pass,' Elspeth said, patting her on the arm. 'And this is the best place for you to hide away.'

'Even Stark? I thought you were against Sam opening up the retreat?'

'I am. I asked him not to. I was worried no good would come of it.'

'And now you've been proved right?'

'Maybe. Maybe not. You and he survived, didn't you? No matter what I think about Stark being left undisturbed, I would never want my nephew's business to fail – or anything worse to happen. I'm relieved you both came out of the sea alive. Perhaps the experience will make him think twice.'

'You really believe the island is haunted?'

'I believe there's a dimension of our existence that defies physical proof – so far. In other words, I like to hedge my bets when it comes to the supernatural!' Elspeth's smile faded. 'The main reason I'm worried about Sam taking on the renovation is because he's had so much on his plate lately. He's still a partner in the building company, he has Morven to deal with and he's never been the same since Rhiannon left.'

Lily breathed in sharply. 'Rhiannon?'

'His fiancée. *Ex*-fiancée. She used to be a district nurse on the islands. The family used to live on Bryher and her cousin still does . . . Rhiannon and Sam were very close, but she's been gone eighteen months.'

'Oh . . .' Lily floundered. 'I – er – didn't know that,' she said, trying to sound casual while her mind raced. So, Sam was nursing a shattered heart from a broken engagement with a local woman. That explained a lot . . . the moodiness, the hint of sadness beneath the stoic exterior.

'He likes to keep his private life private,' Elspeth said.

No wonder he found it difficult to play the cheery host if he was still getting over a relationship – getting over the woman he was going to marry, Lily thought. That night when she'd seen him staring out to sea: was he hoping that Rhiannon would come back?

She was about to try and find out more when Elspeth rose from the table.

'I should stop gossiping. Things are going to get manic round here any time now.'

'Do they ever get manic on Bryher?' Lily joked, but then noticed the tables around her filling up rapidly. People were bagging seats, browsing menus and filing into the café.

'When the first tourist boat arrives, it's like a pack of seagulls fighting over a chip wrapper, but I like to be busy. My bank balance needs it!'

Elspeth moved to a nearby table, taking an order for breakfast from six people with walking poles and rucksacks.

Lily finished her mocha and wrapped half the brownie in a serviette to enjoy later.

It felt odd to see Elspeth and her team buzzing around her, serving customers, while she simply sat and enjoyed the view. She thought of her team working away in London . . . should she check in?

No. She had to resist the urge. Richie would call or message if there was anything urgent. Instead, she took a selfie on the quayside and sent it to her parents and Étienne, to show them she was fine and could now communicate with them when she wasn't on Stark.

A few hours later, Lily returned to the café, having explored the island of Bryher. She'd watched the waves crashing against the rugged northern cliffs and sat in the sun on the white sands of Rushy Bay. She'd also called in at the post office and gallery, buying several postcards and two cute ceramic baby seals for Amelie and Tania.

She wrote her cards while eating some of Elspeth's fresh fish tacos, which were worthy of a five-star review. A couple with two Labradors had chatted to her and Lily had managed to smile when one of the dogs licked her hand enthusiastically.

She'd always been a little afraid of dogs after an incident when a large and snarling one had trapped her inside some public toilets in the local park as a child. Her parents had had cats, all of whom she'd loved, and the twins were always trying to choose guinea pigs and kittens for her from rescue sites.

Lily was far too busy to keep a pet in her London flat, even if she'd been allowed.

When the Labradors left, she went inside for an espresso, admiring the artwork on the walls. Some of it, though unsigned, bore Morven's poignant stamp while other works had the artists' names on them.

Lily waited for her coffee at the counter and spoke to Barney, a pink-haired Kiwi on a gap year.

'Who made the cutlery holders?' she said, pointing to the ceramic pots full of serviette-wrapped cutlery. They'd been glazed in deep green and teal and bore an impression of seaweed fronds.

'Mate of Morven's, I think.' Barney handed over her drink, an expression like a gloomy bloodhound's on his face.

'Damien? No. Damon. I always get confused with that kid in *The Omen* – the one who's the son of Satan.'

Lily bit her lip to avoid spluttering with laughter. 'Thanks, Barney,' she said, leaving a tip before heading back out into the sun.

When she sat down, she saw Morven on the opposite side of the terrace, deep in conversation with a tall, slender, very beautiful young man of around her age. He had the brooding, angsty looks that were scouted by modelling agencies in London. That was unlikely to happen here on Bryher. But in any case, he and Morven looked thick as thieves, as her mum might say.

Lily wondered if the teenager was Morven's friend Damon who'd made the pots for the resort. If so, he was very talented. Should Lily tell him?

Before she could even think about getting up to do so, Morven spotted her and scowled before pulling her friend by the elbow and leading him away from the café, as if Lily had the plague and he might catch it.

She sighed behind her espresso cup. Part of Project New Lily included a vow to be kinder to her fellow men, but it was proving to be more difficult with some people than others. And after what she'd heard about Sam and the mysterious Rhiannon, perhaps she needed to be more understanding of *him*.

Rhiannon must be quite a woman to leave him broken after all this time.

Chapter Eighteen

The following day, while Sam had arranged to meet up with his business partner Aaron for lunch in the pub on Tresco, Lily had gone for a day out in 'the metropolis' as she called Hugh Town, the small capital of St Mary's.

To Sam's great relief there had been no further accidents or incidents on Stark and he was beginning to think that they would both get through the rest of her stay unscathed.

He and Aaron had just demolished two large ham sandwiches and his friend took an appreciative sip of his second pint.

Sam hid a smile at the sight of flecks of foam in his friend's beard. He didn't give a toss about appearances. His mate was a 'unit', with archetypal sea captain looks that he cultivated with relish. He and Sam had been to school together and rowed in the Bryher gig crew until Sam had embarked on the renovations.

After chatting about boats and work and rugby, Aaron asked if there was any sign of Nate coming back.

'Not at the moment,' Sam said, having wondered the same thing several times a day recently. Perhaps his friend had asked to meet him precisely to give him a chance to talk about this.

Aaron nodded thoughtfully. 'How's Morven coping?'

'She's not, if I'm honest. She feels abandoned and I don't blame her.'

'Nate needs to step up – if you don't mind me giving my opinion.'

'He does and I don't.'

'Know what you need, mate? You need a break. A bunch of us are meeting up at the Rock Inn after rowing practice tomorrow. You should come.'

'If only . . . I'm on host duties.'

'For this woman who was in the papers? The dead one,' Aaron chortled. 'She can manage alone on the island for one evening, can't she?'

'Hmm . . .'

'Or you could invite her along?'

Sam laughed out loud, drawing raised eyebrows from his friend who remarked: 'What's up? Not her scene?'

'I doubt it. I don't know . . . I really can't leave a guest on her own.' He thought of Lily's encounter with the 'shadow'. Though it was tempting to dismiss it – whatever it was – as her being understandably on edge, Sam wasn't going to fall into that trap. Lily didn't strike him as the sort of person to mistake the evidence of her own eyes, and it was – just about – possible that someone had landed on Stark without his knowledge.

'She's had a crap time lately and, between you and me, that kayaking incident was a far closer shave than is being made out.'

'Really?'

'Yep. Don't let on to anyone because there's been enough drama around it but I thought we were both goners.'

Sam relayed the details of the accident to Aaron, who blew out a long breath.

'Jesus, I'd no idea it was that close.'

'It was, and it was Lily's decision to play it down in public. She doesn't need any more press attention and, if I'm being honest, I don't need the retreat to acquire a bad reputation. Not now it's almost up and running.'

'That sounds positive. How's it going?'

'Cottage two is virtually ready, bar a bit of decorating.' Sam held back the fact that Lily had offered to help with that. 'Cottages three and four are watertight and need more work inside.'

'Hmm. Do you want me to come and lend a hand? Help you with the heavy work, do some painting?'

'You must be too busy.'

Aaron grinned. 'Always, but I can spare the time especially on these light nights. I haven't forgotten how you helped me out in that storm. Me and the kids would have been sleeping under the stars if you hadn't spent days rebuilding the place with me.'

'You don't owe me anything,' Sam insisted.

'I know that, but I want to help. I might round up a couple of the crew too. Danny the decorator owes me a big favour.'

He slapped Sam's back, causing his Coke to spill over the table and make it even stickier. 'Come to the Rock. Bring this Lily. I'm sure we can handle her. The question is, can she handle *us*?'

'Believe me, Lily could handle anyone,' Sam said, feeling a smile creeping onto his lips.

Aaron's eyes widened. 'Oh, really? Impressed you, has she? She sounds like quite a woman. I haven't seen you take an interest in the female species since Rhiannon.'

'Lily's a guest,' Sam countered, alarmed that he'd revealed too much. 'It's my job to take an interest.'

Too late. Aaron had scented blood. 'Whatever you say, mate,' he said, picking up his glass with a knowing smirk. 'Whatever you say.'

After lunch, Sam zoomed back to Bryher and drove to Hell Bay House where he'd arranged to FaceTime Nate.

Ten minutes into the conversation, he was ready to hurl the laptop across the room. It was early-morning in California, mid-afternoon at Hell Bay House. Nate was sitting by the pool in a pink shirt, his Aviators pushed back on his gelled hair, an espresso cup on the table. They'd waited until Morven was out visiting friends so they could have a frank conversation.

'Nate, if you are going to take this new contract, you need to decide ASAP. Morven needs you. You can't leave her in permanent limbo. It's bad for her self-esteem, and it's affecting her mental health.'

'Don't I bloody know that! She won't even talk to me,' his brother complained.

'Only because she feels that you won't listen to her and don't care!'

'That's out of order, Sam! Of course I care. I love her. She is *my* daughter after all.'

'Then start bloody acting like a father to her!'

Nate's eyes narrowed and his lip curled. Sam knew he'd hit the rawest of nerves.

'I'll let you – and my daughter – have my decision as soon as I possibly can, but it's not as simple as you might think, from your cosy little backwater. What I decide affects more than just my future. Be glad you've only yourself to think about.'

'Oh, yeah, I have no worries whatsoever!' Sam snapped.

'Maybe,' Nate said smoothly, 'it would be better if you had someone special in your own life so you understood the pressure I'm under. I have to think about Grady's needs too, you know, as well as Morven's.'

Sam exploded. 'How the hell would I be able to have "someone special" in my life, Nate, when I'm already juggling a business and your daughter?'

'Hey! Calm down! I didn't mean to touch a raw nerve. I know Rhiannon hurt you badly. But she's gone, Sam. Accept it. You need to move on and find someone new.'

With great difficulty, he reined in his temper. 'I've work to do. I can't waste time sitting in the sun drinking coffee. Just make your mind up about Morven before it's too late.'

He ended the call, sitting back in his office chair in frustration. Perhaps he'd gone too far in implying Nate didn't care about Morven, but drastic action was required. She needed her dad – and if Nate wasn't coming back, God forbid, she needed to know so she could try to come to terms with it.

Sam also needed to come to terms with stepping in as her parent, if that's what had to happen. He couldn't keep leaving her with Elspeth, or making sure she was staying with trusted friends, as he'd had to over the past few weeks while he was working on the retreat. He hadn't spent a night at home since Lily had arrived.

'Was that Dad?'

Morven stood in the open French doors, her arms folded. He hadn't seen her come in. That girl was like a ghost, and she had superhuman hearing. What had she heard?

'Yes, it was.'

'I don't suppose he's coming home?'

'He's making a decision very soon.'

She smirked. ''Course he is.'

'He knows how important it is for you to be together. How important *you* are.'

'Did he say that?'

Sam hesitated and decided to be honest. 'He reminded me that he's your father, not me.'

Perhaps thrown for a moment, Morven shook her head. 'He needs to remind himself.'

Sam almost didn't recognise Lily when he met her at the *Hydra* a little while later.

She was dressed in cargo pants and a hoodie, with a bucket hat on her head.

'Hello!' she said, lifting up two carrier bags. 'I've been shopping!'

'I can see that,' he said, amused to see her in casual mode.

Her eyes were bright with excitement and seeing her so bubbly gave Sam an equal buzz. Along with his pleasure at seeing her smile, he also realised that he cared about her welfare perhaps more than he ought to, considering she was a guest.

On the way to Stark, she filled him in on her trip to the Scilly capital.

'It was heaving. The boat over from Bryher was packed and that big boat was in port – the *Scillonian*. Half the passengers must have been milling around the streets.'

'Some of them come for the day or hang around in town until they can get into their accommodation,' he replied, amused to be seeing the little town through fresh eyes.

'I managed to get a table outside a café at the back of the beach. Their salted caramel brownies are almost as good as Elspeth's. *And* I found a place selling books.' She showed him a bag from the Bourdeaux gift shop. 'It's been so long since I made time to read a novel. Though maybe I shouldn't have chosen a crime thriller set on Scilly! Can you believe this one's called *Hell Bay*?'

Sam smiled. He'd read the Kate Rhodes book himself, amused to find his home turned into a setting for violent crime and psychopathic killers. 'It's very good,' he said. 'I just hope it doesn't make you want to board the first flight out . . .'

With a gleam in her eyes, Lily shot him a look that made him melt inside.

'Don't worry,' she said silkily. 'I can separate fact from fiction and I decided against heading for the airport!'

Just in time, Sam pulled back on the throttle and turned the boat away from a hidden reef he'd almost skimmed. Lily's cheeks were tinged a soft pink by the sun and he loved – but wouldn't dream of telling her – the freckles sprinkled across her nose. Elspeth would say his home cook-ing was doing his guest good too, but it was the easing of tension that made the most difference. Her body had relaxed, the dark smudges under her eyes had gone, along with the strained expression.

It was so tempting to try and get closer to her and find out about the real Lily.

Sam reminded himself that the first rule of hospitality should be: don't get emotionally involved with the guests. After having his heart broken by Rhiannon, his first rule ought to be not to get involved with *anyone*, especially not someone from a different world who could only ever be passing through his life.

Chapter Nineteen

'Um . . . I've been invited to the pub.'

Lily was halfway up a ladder and about to reload her roller with Misty Morn emulsion when Sam made this apparently significant announcement to her.

That evening, over dinner, they'd had a discussion and he'd finally agreed she could help him finish Cottage Two – now known as Samphire. Cottages Three and Four – Starfish and Scallop – were also well on their way apart from bathroom tiling and painting.

'Or should I say "we"?' he added, carefully brushing paint above the skirting board and still not looking at her. 'I met up with my mate Aaron earlier and he said the gig crew are at the Rock Inn tomorrow. He invited you to join us.'

'He invited *me*? Are you sure? He doesn't know me.'

She descended to floor level where Sam had risen from his knees.

'He's heard about you,' he said. 'I'm afraid everyone has but that's not why he asked. He knew you were staying on the island and thought you might like to come. I did say you were here for peace and quiet but that I'd pass on the invite.'

Lily resisted the urge to tell him he had paint on his nose, or worse, to wet her finger and wipe it off. How could he look so gorgeous in a ripped T-shirt and paint-splattered shorts? Even the fragrance of turps on his top was sexy.

'He probably thinks you wouldn't leave me here, if I refused?'

'No! Absolutely not. I mean . . . of course I wouldn't leave you alone even though I'm sure you'd be *fine*.' Sam was clearly tying himself in knots. 'He was only being friendly. They're like that, the rowing lot. I used to be in the crew until I got wrapped up in this place.'

'I know the feeling,' Lily said. 'I used to meet up for dinner with a group of women from my Pilates class. I enjoyed it but that was over a year ago. After I was too busy to go along five times in a row, I stopped getting invites. I think they started a new WhatsApp group without me and I can hardly blame them.' She sighed. 'I need to get in touch again, make a commitment. When I get home.'

'Why don't you do it now?' he said. 'In just over a week you'll be back in London.'

Why did he have to remind her of the precise timeframe? Lily was already thinking of how things would be when she went back, the hurtling around and lurching from one task to the next. For some reason, she felt jittery at the prospect.

'Are you counting the days?' she said lightly.

'No. No, of course not,' Sam said, then frowned. 'You OK?'

'Yes. Fine. Apart from the paint smell and all the crouching and climbing. It's been ages since I got hot and sweaty outside of a gym.'

'You look great to me,' he said. 'We've virtually finished the work,' he added gruffly. 'Come on, let's have a break and some air.'

Lily washed her hands, still glowing from his compliment and even more amazed he'd made it, considering what stared back at her from the en suite mirror. She was wearing an oversized pair of decorator's dungarees over a vest top, her hair tied up with a scrunchie. It was humid and she hadn't looked so dishevelled for months.

Back outside, Sam stood on the terrace with two chilled bottles from the cottage fridge. The sun shone down half-heartedly through the haze, and the isles and islets seemed to lie becalmed in the glassy sea.

A drink of chilled water helped to cool her down. Samphire really was almost ready, its furniture already in the centre of the room, wrapped in dust sheets and plastic.

'So, you'll definitely be coming to the pub?' Sam asked again, standing beside her.

'As long as you're sure your friends won't mind, then I'd love to.'

His face lit up briefly. 'Great. Of course they won't mind . . . as long as you're prepared for a bit of banter. I can't guarantee much tact and diplomacy – especially from Aaron.'

Lily smiled. 'Oh, I think I can deal with a bit of banter.'

Half an hour later, they'd finished the room. Sam left the doors and windows open and went to clean the trays and brushes while Lily had a quick shower. It was her turn to cook that evening and she was making *poisson cru* with salad and fries. The fish had been caught by Rory that morning and was already marinating in coconut milk. Cara and Étienne had taught her how to make the Polynesian speciality. It was almost the last recipe in Lily's dwindling repertoire.

Rubbing her hair with a towel, she opened the French doors of her cottage to dry off in the late-afternoon sun.

'Oh, God!'

Her heart thumped when she saw the message – sign – *warning* – that had been left on the bistro table.

Someone had carefully arranged beach pebbles into a word:

LEAVE

The hairs on her arms stood on end.

Unless there were some very clever seagulls around, those pebbles couldn't possibly have found their way there accidentally.

She was ready to run across to Sam's flat but stopped. He'd probably feel he should gallop to the rescue. He'd worry that Stark wasn't secure or safe for her and he didn't need that just when he was pushing on to finish the place.

She didn't need anyone, least of all him, to take care of her. She'd lived in London for over a decade; she could handle a prankster . . . even a rogue reporter trying to scare up a story.

If it was a prankster, the message was hardly funny. Someone didn't want her on the island or else wanted to create trouble.

Lily dismissed the notion and locked her door. Despite

her bravado, she was rather relieved that she had been included in the pub excursion. She certainly didn't fancy staying on Stark on her own.

Thursday's plan was to eat at the Rock, rather than going back to Stark. She'd thought about taking along her sketch pad, to capture the view of Cromwell's Castle over the channel between Bryher and Tresco. She decided she didn't have time and anyway, she didn't fancy focusing on the gibbet after yesterday's unpleasant message.

After taking a photo of the pebbles on her phone, she'd gathered them up and thrown them onto the grass outside her room.

During the day, she threw herself into getting hot and sweaty again as she and Sam unpacked and rearranged furniture in Samphire before adding the small stock of artwork, lamps and cushions.

'Morven's artwork looks great in here. The cottage needs to be easy to clean and uncluttered, but it is still rather bare. I saw some lovely pieces in the galleries on St Mary's and at Bryher post office. They'd be a good start. If you have the budget, of course.'

'I have a small budget, yes,' Sam said warily.

'Then would it be OK if I did some shopping for you? I could order some pieces from Lily Loves but we should use local suppliers for preference. I promise I won't go over budget.'

Finally, he smiled. 'Oh, I know you won't.'

Sam had a couple of errands at the dock so Lily found a

quiet table outside the Quayside Café and put in a call to Richie via FaceTime.

'Hello,' she said, amused to see him lounging with a mug of coffee and looking very comfortable. 'Is that my office chair?'

'Yes, I didn't think you'd mind me using your desktop.'

'I don't – have you adjusted my seat?'

'Of course. I'm a foot taller than you. I promise I'll set it up for you before you get back, hun.'

'Make sure you do,' Lily said then smiled. 'I'm joking. How's it going?'

'OK. Fine. I've set up a meeting with that indie gift shop chain. I know you weren't sure they were the right home for the brand but they seem so keen. And the owner is such a sweetheart. She's got a *gorgeous* cockapoo just like Jakob's. I've seen it on their Insta feed. That's why the business is called Cockahoop,' Richie explained.

Lily was about to comment that just because someone was a sweetheart and had a gorgeous dog, it didn't necessarily make them a good business partner, but stopped herself. Richie's eyes were lit by a zeal that was firing ideas in her brain.

She'd been wrestling with her misgivings about the supermarket deal all morning. Cockahoop was a fraction of the size but might – just might – be a much better fit with the cosiness of her brand. Perhaps Richie's instincts were more on the money than she'd thought.

'Are you cross that I said we'd meet them?' he said anxiously.

'No, I'm not,' Lily said, thinking that she could never be cross with a generous soul like him. 'It can't do any harm. I didn't know she'd named the business after her dog. I like it . . .'

'So, you want me to delay the Cockahoop meeting until you come back?' he asked.

'Why don't you take it? You can handle it, can't you?'

'Well, yes, but . . .'

'But what?'

'Nothing. Only normally you like to be on top of every detail.'

'Richie, I'm supposed to be on holiday – a holiday that you practically forced me to take.' She added with a smile, 'I'm joking again, though as we're discussing the issue, you've handled everything that's come your way perfectly well. As you seem to have a rapport with Cockahoop, I think you should call them and set up an initial meeting. Now, you go home to Jakob. I'm off to the pub.'

His jaw dropped before he said, 'Off to the pub? At five p.m.?'

'Yes. For fish and chips and a night out with a hunky rowing crew. You'd love it,' she added mischievously.

'Too right I would!' he exclaimed, then added, '*If* I wasn't in a very meaningful relationship already, of course.'

'Of course.'

'Try to send photos though . . .' Richie's voice had a hopeful lilt.

Lily cut the FaceTime, enjoying the open-mouthed amazement of her PA a little too much. Her stay had shown her that the world wouldn't end without her – that for a while, at least, her team could handle things better than she'd dared to hope.

While she was delighted and relieved to see how well they were doing, she couldn't help but wish she'd trusted them enough to delegate more in the past. She might not have missed quite so much of her own life if she had.

Chapter Twenty

The Rock had the best location of any pub anywhere on the entire planet, Lily decided as she approached it from the direction of the Quayside Café.

Situated on the channel that separated Bryher from Tresco, it stood on the edge of the white sand beach. On this balmy June evening, the granite inn was bustling with locals and holidaymakers. It was also fish and chip night and a 'supper boat' had arrived from Tresco especially for the occasion, making it even busier.

Sam waved at Lily from outside the pub where the crew had gathered around an outside table. Even from a way off, she could sense their closeness, laughter ringing out and people slapping each other on the back.

Her stomach knotted and her courage faltered. She was used to meeting strangers in her job but these were people who might only know her via her TV or online reputation. Those harsh comments online could have given them a pretty awful view of her, one that might be hard to overcome. What if they were expecting the ruthless witch some people had painted her as?

She stiffened her spine. There was nothing she could do

but be herself: her real self. Pasting on a smile, she walked on and met Sam a few yards from the table. Despite what she'd told Richie about them being hunky, the rowing crew comprised a mix of men and women, all tanned and strong of arm but of various shapes and sizes.

'This is Lily, guys,' Sam said chirpily. *Too* chirpily?

'Hi,' Lily said, grinning fit to burst while feeling like a specimen under the microscope.

Sam introduced the gang to her, accompanied by banter and laughter.

Even though she was used to remembering faces and names, Lily was so nervous the new information flashed by in a blur.

Fergal: Irish, ginger and drinking a lurid cocktail. Penny: smiley, blonde bob, sixty-plus? Suman: tiny – how did she row miles in Atlantic swells? A married couple called Ivanka and Mike who ran the post office stores and wore matching bandanas. Bruce – not his real name, according to Fergal – who knew? – but an Aussie so he was now stuck with it. Several others . . .

She'd smiled and laughed during the introductions, aware she must not try too hard to dispel any image they might have formed of her from the press.

'And this is Aaron,' Sam said finally with an eye roll.

Aaron was a man mountain with a bushy beard. He raised his pint glass to Lily and met her with a head-on gaze as if he was facing off to her in a scrum. He was smiling yet Lily was slightly shaken by his direct scrutiny.

'Great to meet you,' he said. 'I've heard a lot about you.'

'Everyone's heard far too much about me,' she quipped.

To her relief the crew were all polite enough to laugh.

'I meant from Sam,' Aaron said.

'Ignore him,' Sam said, squeezing into the space next to his friend so that Lily could have the end of the bench. 'Though that may be quite difficult.'

Aaron roared and didn't seem the least bit offended. 'It's good to meet you, Lily,' he said.

'Likewise,' she said lightly, while realising just how under the microscope she still was.

After the introductions, some of the others started discussing the next gig race, leaving Lily to talk to her nearest neighbours on the table, Aaron, Sam and Penny, who broke the ice by asking how her holiday was going.

'Are you finding enough to do on the islands?' Penny said.

'More than enough,' Lily said, glad of a more normal question yet still aware that Aaron and Sam were listening. 'I've been shopping on St Mary's and browsing the galleries. I've walked, sunbathed, done some sketching and painting.' She gave what she hoped was a winning smile. 'Pretty much the same things everyone else does on holiday.'

'Apart from almost drowning?' Aaron said, deadpan.

'That kayak thing was a gross exaggeration,' Sam muttered. 'The press are a bunch of arseholes.'

'OK, mate. It was a joke. I'm sorry for bringing it up,' Aaron said to Lily, sounding genuinely apologetic.

She looked him full in the eye. 'It's fine and Sam's right. The press often have a very loose relationship with the facts.

It's what sells papers and gets clicks. I know that better than anyone.'

Aaron nodded but Sam wasn't mollified. 'Isn't it your turn to get a round in?' he growled at his friend.

Before he could reply, Lily rose to her feet. 'I think I'd better do that. As I'm the newcomer.'

Penny also stood up. 'I'll give you a hand,' she said. 'It'll be a big tray.'

'Thanks.'

Lily headed inside the pub with Penny following. She didn't care how big the tray was. She'd take any excuse to get away from Aaron and Sam for a few minutes so she could gather herself. While grateful for Penny's offer, she'd rather have gone by herself.

'Aaron can be a bit full on,' Penny said, giving the other half of the order to the barman after Lily had managed to remember her half of the table. 'But he's got a heart of gold.'

'They're business partners, aren't they?' said Lily. 'I heard he's going to help finish the other cottages.'

'Yes, he's been a good friend to Sam when he's needed it most.'

'Oh?' Lily was torn between wanting to know what had happened and her desire not to appear too interested in her host's private life. Dare she ask more while she had Penny to herself and the bar staff were making up the mammoth order?

Frustratingly, Penny seemed more preoccupied with settling the bill. 'Are you sure you want to pay for this lot and not go halves?' she said when Lily took her debit card from her bag.

'I'm happy to get a round in. It's nice to have been invited along, if I'm honest.'

'If you insist then,' Penny said, then lowered her voice. 'As for being invited, it's the first time in ages that Sam's brought anyone – especially a woman – to rowing drinks.'

Lily laughed, yet this information gave her a thrill of pleasure. 'Only because I'd be trapped on the island otherwise. I'm sure he feels guilty. To be honest, I think Aaron pushed him into inviting me. Probably curious!'

'That sounds like Aaron, though Sam would never be pushed into doing something he didn't want to. He's a lovely man but he can be so stubborn.'

'Really? I'd never have guessed . . .'

Lily waited for Penny to elaborate further on Sam's character or to mention Rhiannon but she merely smiled, keeping any information she might have firmly to herself. 'Like I said, Sam is a lovely man.'

Lily gave up on gleaning any more information and moved on to the subject of the island instead: 'Between us, I jumped at the chance to come over to the pub because,' she whispered, lowering her voice, 'it would be a little bit spooky spending the evening on Stark on my own.'

Penny nodded in agreement. 'Hmm. I can well believe it. It's a gorgeous place but it does have an atmosphere, doubtless stoked up by generations of old wives' tales that have been as exaggerated as your alleged near-death experience.'

Lily gave a faint smile, feeling slightly guilty about concealing the truth.

'Ah, the drinks are here,' Penny said. 'And dinner will be ready soon, but before you leave tonight, I'd *love* to know more about your painting and crafts. I'm a ceramicist – no, don't worry, I'm not angling to have my pieces stocked on your site – but I *am* in charge of the summer craft fair here. I'd like to pick your brains about how we can make the most of it.'

'I'll do my best,' Lily said, following Penny back to the table with the trays of drinks. Fortunately, by the time they returned, the talk had moved on to rowing. They were all busy discussing their performance in practice and the upcoming gig race.

Lily sipped her half of cider, listening to the banter flashing to and fro and feeling as if she'd been let out of jail. The focus was off her. Phew.

Even so, when anyone spoke to her, she felt she was weighing her words before she said them and examining them after they'd escaped her mouth. She wanted Sam's mates to like her but, more than that, she wanted them to see the real Lily – not the one who was constantly trying to live up to being the head of a successful business or how she thought a CEO should act.

She didn't want to let Sam down and had to actively avoid watching him and thinking how attractive he was. His eyes lit up when he laughed; he was about as relaxed as she'd ever seen him.

He caught her eye and treated her to a hesitant smile that she returned with a broad one. He must be feeling relieved that the evening had turned out well, that she'd fitted into his world for a few hours at least.

Penny had said Sam had really needed Aaron's support. Was that to do with Rhiannon? Lily knew very little and had wondered about her so much that her name had assumed an almost mythic quality.

Had Sam forced his ex away? Lily herself had seen how he could be a little obsessive, deciding to renovate the retreat at any cost – even to the detriment of his own wellbeing. However, she could hardly judge him for being driven. He seemed to act from a strong sense of duty and had risked his own safety to haul her from the water. The memory made her shudder.

There were two sides to every story. Dare she ask Elspeth?

'About time!' Aaron declared. 'Did you have to go out and catch the fish after we ordered?'

'You cheeky sod!' Kirsten, the landlady, exclaimed. 'I can take it all away again, you know.'

'Only joking,' Aaron said.

'Aaron, I should shut up and eat before Kirsten chucks us all out,' said Sam.

Soon, they were all tucking into the best fish and chips Lily had ever eaten. It turned out the fish *had* been caught that morning and the potatoes dug up that day by Ivanka's brother-in-law on St Martin's. Lily washed the meal down with a large glass of wine from the same island. She was beginning to feel pleasantly relaxed, her guard slipping further.

Talk turned to the work on the retreat.

'Do you mind staying in a building site?' Ivanka piped up.

'Well, it's not a building site any longer. Samphire is almost ready to let and we only have the tiling to finish on Starfish.'

Several pairs of eyes turned to her.

'*We?*' Aaron said before giving Sam a hard look. 'Don't say he's been making his guests work on the cottages?'

Lily sensed Sam stiffen beside her, a heartbeat from jumping to her aid.

'Wasn't that the whole plan? For guests to work for their bed and board?' she said innocently. 'You do know I can't stay too late because I have a toilet to plumb in tonight, and tomorrow I'm learning how to work the cement mixer.'

The others around the table erupted into guffaws.

Aaron found himself wrong-footed then laughed. 'Nothing would surprise me.'

Lily treated him to a sweet smile. 'To be honest, I *have* been offering my unsolicited advice. I was really impressed with the beautiful artwork in the cottages so I've been suggesting some decorative ideas for the two Sam's renovating at the moment. There are some wonderful pieces in the galleries here on the islands that would be perfect. It's a very talented community.'

'Any advice on decorating the cottages is fine by me,' Sam said firmly.

Lily tried not to catch his eye and, as she'd hoped, Aaron's interest in her faded as she enthused over the local art scene.

The conversation moved on to whether anyone wanted a pudding.

Inside, Lily heaved a sigh of relief that she'd managed to deflect attention from her slip-up. Hopefully none of Sam's friends now thought she was actually helping him renovate the cottages. Even if it *were* true.

Declining a pud on the basis of being stuffed with fish and chips, Lily went to the Ladies. Penny was washing her hands. When Lily came out, the other woman had waited for her outside the bathroom.

After a couple of comments about the food, Penny changed tack. 'I hope you don't mind me saying this,' she said.

Lily's stomach tensed. When someone started a conversation with that phrase, it generally meant she was going to mind quite a bit.

'It depends,' she said lightly, with a smile on her face.

'Oh, don't worry, it's nothing bad! When Elspeth said you were much nicer in real life than on that TV show, I was sceptical.'

'Oh? They edited out all the supportive things I said. I was horrified when I saw the finished result.'

'Yes, I should have realised that. My partner did an interview for a news programme on fishing and they made her come across as a total whinger who wanted all of the perks of living in paradise and none of the downside.' Penny sighed. 'I can now see the same thing probably happened to you but on a much bigger scale.'

'You could say that,' Lily quipped, sensing Penny had

more to say but was chickening out. 'You were going to tell me about the craft fair?' she encouraged.

'Oh, yes.' Penny was growing redder. 'As I said earlier, I'm in charge of organising it. It's held in the community centre the Saturday after next. Most visitors to the island have to pass the hall and some will come over 'specially with the market as the main attraction.'

'It sounds great and I'd love to come . . .' Lily said, realising there was a major problem with the plan. Two in fact.

'Really? Oh, you'd love it. You're right, we *do* have some incredibly talented artists and craftspeople. The craft fair is one of their major opportunities to sell and showcase their work. *Everyone* looks forward to it. We have around thirty exhibitors and most of the island craftspeople try to come. There's jewellery, pottery, textiles, mixed media, woollen accessories, hand-poured candles. Only handmade items are allowed, created here on the islands – which I'm sure you'll approve of!'

Penny sounded so enthusiastic and her comment about handmade items chimed with Lily's current dilemma regarding the supermarket deal.

'It sounds wonderful,' she said, wondering how she was going to break the news that she would be back in London by the time of the event.

'I realise it's a big ask but – would you consider being the VIP guest? You could officially open the market and perhaps draw the raffle? Meet some of our makers and chat to the punters too? I'm sure they'd love it.'

'I'm probably the last person they'd want to meet! I'd

scare everyone off.' Even though Lily was joking, her laughter only masked her anxiety. The recent online trolling had triggered it, but she so didn't want to let Penny or the islanders down.

Penny squeaked in horror. 'Yes, but I know you aren't scary at all and so will everyone who meets you. If you did come, it would add a touch of . . .'

'I think notoriety is the word you're looking for,' Lily supplied.

'Exactly. It would be bound to boost attendance by a mile!' Penny trilled.

Lily was torn in two yet found it impossible to burst Penny's bubble. The craft fair was exactly the sort of event she'd have loved to be part of, and she guessed it was a major honour to be asked. Even so, the prospect of being the centre of attention at a public event was making her stomach churn.

What she should have said was: 'I'm sorry, but I won't be here then.'

Giving a perfectly reasonable excuse was the sensible answer. Changing her plans would be complicated and it would be stressful to face everyone so soon after the latest news stories. Yet by staying away, she would be denying herself the pleasure of doing something that lay at the heart of her business and her life: arts and crafts and supporting the people who made them.

Penny must have sensed her misgivings. 'Of course, please don't feel obliged at all,' she said. 'It is a huge cheek . . . and honestly, no one would ever know I'd asked you.'

'No, no,' Lily said hastily, keen to help this kind woman as much as she could. 'Um . . . I'm not quite sure what my plans are yet. I mean, I haven't firmed up exactly when I'm returning to London, but if I'm still here, yes, I'd like to.'

Penny exhaled in delight. 'That would be amazing. You see, the fair isn't only about sales on the day, but about raising the profile of craftspeople – it can lead to online orders and commissions or having their work in galleries.'

Lily fully understood. She'd started at craft fairs. She'd had a market stall. She knew how hard it was to find places to showcase and sell your work, how hard it was to get started and make a living. That's why she'd started Lily Loves, to support makers and give them a platform. It was about following her passion and the fact she was able to make a living out of it was the unexpected bonus, though she recognised some of that passion might have become lost along the way recently.

'Look, I'll be honest with you, I do have a flight booked the day before but this is important. For you and the makers – and me.'

Penny held up her hands in horror. 'Oh, I couldn't inconvenience you that much!'

'I wouldn't offer if I didn't want to,' Lily said firmly.

'I feel bad for asking but it would be *wonderful* if you could come!'

'Tell you what, I won't make any promises now. I need to talk to my team first, to make sure I won't miss anything vital at work and see how feasible it is to alter my travel arrangements. I will get back to you by tomorrow evening.'

Lily looked over to Sam whose laughter had attracted her attention. He looked so happy and gorgeous that her stomach did a flip. He caught her eye and tilted his head enquiringly, guessing he was being talked about.

A shiver ran through her. Penny had just handed Lily the perfect excuse to stay longer with him . . . it was both thrilling and scary to realise how much she wanted to stay.

'I also need to ask Sam if he can put up with me for an extra weekend.'

Penny slid a look towards him and smiled. 'Oh, I think he'll be more than willing to oblige.'

Chapter Twenty-One

The dull roar of the *Hydra*'s engine had a strangely comforting effect on Lily on the way back to Stark.

Sitting in the seat next to the helm, she had a fantastic view as they bounced over the waves, sending spray flying high into the air.

'How did you fare with that motley crew?' Sam asked once they were in the middle of the channel, as if it was now safe to speak without his friends overhearing. 'I hope it wasn't too much of an ordeal?'

'Did it look like one?' She was amused and quite touched by his concern.

'No, but together they can be a bit much. I was worried the rowing talk might send you off to sleep.'

'No, but the local wine and cider might. It was honestly fine – I just don't like being the centre of attention.'

'I was worried that it might be a baptism of fire,' he said.

'Sam, don't stress. It was a few drinks in a pub.' Anyway, she'd be gone soon. Even if she didn't make a good impression, she'd never have to see them again. Yet she did care what they thought of her, and that had never bothered her before. Why now?

'Anyway, it doesn't matter what they thought,' Sam continued. 'I don't want you to have to try too hard.'

'After the bad press I had, I always have to.'

'No, you don't,' he said, turning away from the sea to look straight into her eyes. 'Not with me.'

Lily's stomach did a double flip that had nothing to do with the waves. She knew he meant every word: that she could be completely herself with him. If Sam hadn't been carefully steering the boat between treacherous rocks in the twilight, she might have done something she regretted: like kiss him.

'I know,' she said, keeping her hands firmly on the seat. 'And that means a lot to me. I confess I wasn't in love with Stark when I first arrived.'

'You don't say?' he commented with a wry smile.

'But I am now. It's beautiful and I'll be sorry to have to leave.' She hesitated for a moment. 'In fact, I want to talk to you about that.'

'Oh?' He glanced her way, in between negotiating the safe channel between the rocks.

'How would you feel about me staying a little longer?'

'Longer?' The boat wobbled and he adjusted the wheel. 'How much longer?' he said once she was back on course.

'Only an extra few days. Don't worry, I'll be out of your hair after that. You see, Penny asked me if I'd stay and help her launch the craft fair and I said I'd have to ask you. It would mean delaying my flight yet again, and I absolutely do *not* want to disrupt anyone else's plans, but if it is possible and you can put up with me for another weekend, then I feel I ought to help. Actually, I *want* to help. I got my first start in business at craft fairs and I know how hard it is to build a profile and make a living from your own products.'

'That's very kind of you,' he said.

'Is it?'

'Yes, especially after the battering you've had at the hands of the press lately. I'm sure Penny and all the craftspeople will appreciate it.'

'I hope they don't see me as muscling in,' she said, experiencing a flutter of anxiety again.

'They won't. Not once they meet you.'

The flutter turned into something much more pleasant.

Hoping she wasn't doing anything as gauche as blushing, Lily went silent while Sam reined back the throttle on the approach to the jetty. He needed all his concentration to steer the *Hydra* through the narrow entrance. Perhaps she should have waited to ask him until they were safely on Stark.

With the boat alongside, he jumped off.

'I'll help tie up,' she said, as he secured the bow rope to an old iron post.

'OK.' He threw the rope to her and she looped it around the cleat on the stern, tying it off with two hitches.

'I've been practising,' she said. 'With the curtain cord in my cottage.'

He laughed. 'We'll make an islander of you yet.'

Finally, they were together on the quay, in the deep blue twilight of a June evening.

'I have no problem with you staying on,' he said.

'I also thought it would give me the chance to help you finish Samphire and Starfish.'

'It would, but you don't need to do that. What about your own business? Aren't you desperate to get back to it?'

'Not as desperate as I was,' she said, walking by his side up to the retreat, conscious of his quiet, solid presence beside her. It felt good, yet she was also conscious of the supermarket deal looming in the corner of her mind.

'Is that a good thing?' he asked.

'When I arrived, I didn't want to let go. Not even by a millimetre. I was clinging onto the business, my work – to all kinds of things – so hard, I was exhausted. I had to let go, let myself fall a little way, to realise that.'

They stood side by side, gazing out over the Atlantic where the horizon was still tinged with pink, a reminder of the day that had passed. Soon, the sky behind them would lighten again, hinting at a new day full of possibilities.

Lily had to seize them.

'You understand what I'm saying?' she said to Sam.

He let his eyes rest on the horizon. Lily waited, her pulse beating faster, hardly daring to imagine what might happen next.

'I'm pleased you're staying,' he said, with a brief smile, before stretching and yawning. 'Now, it's late and I'm knackered. I think I'll get an early night. I'll take you to Bryher first thing so you can try to rearrange your flight.'

To her relief, he didn't add 'again'.

The next morning, Lily lay awake for a good while, wondering whether she'd made the right decision to stay – and why Sam had blown hot and cold the evening before. Were his mood swings the result of his break-up with Rhiannon? Had one woman left such scars on him that he was too scared to open himself up to another?

Lily wouldn't know unless she asked him straight out and she wasn't going to do that and risk shattering the fragile connection they'd built – or that she thought they had. She wondered which Sam she would see today: wounded lover, tender man or reluctant host.

In the end, he was polite and pleasant over breakfast but seemed preoccupied. She'd heard him talking on the radio to Aaron about soil pipes so decided she was being over-sensitive and that Sam was too busy worrying about finishing the bathrooms to give much thought to anything else.

He dropped her at the Bryher quay and immediately headed over the channel to Tresco where he said he was meeting Aaron.

Lily had her own list of tasks and the first was to break it to Richie that she wanted to stay on for the craft fair. Boss she might be, but she had an inkling he wouldn't understand why she was staying away to open a few market stalls. She kept privately questioning the wisdom of her decision and was steeling herself before the call with a slice of carrot cake on the café's terrace.

In the event, the surprise WhatsApp video call she received from Étienne felt like fate.

'Hello, Lily! Thank goodness I got you,' he said, sounding almost out of breath. 'My God, that sky looks blue. It's pissing down here, which is why I'm standing under the car-park machine shelter outside the hospital. Now, listen up,' he said, holding up a Greggs paper bag. 'I've got exactly ten minutes to down a cappuccino, eat a cardiac-inducing doughnut and ask you a bloody enormous favour.'

Did he need her to dash home for some emergency? He sounded agitated – or perhaps he was simply buzzing from adrenaline, sugar and caffeine.

Lily's stomach clenched. 'Are the girls alright?' she said with sudden alarm, knocking her cake fork onto the terrace.

'Oh, they're fine. They're more than fine. They're bouncing off the bloody ceiling and that's why I'm asking you a favour. Look, a miracle has happened: the teachers are on strike the Friday after next.'

'And that's a good thing?'

'Yes, because I also have the weekend off duty and a day owing . . . so basically, we could come and see you. We'll need a place to stay, though, and I haven't even checked if there's any way of getting to you, but the girls have already worked it out and seem to think they can click their heels three times and be beamed up to you. Now I've said all that, it's probably a ludicrous idea . . .'

'Not ludicrous. It sounds absolutely amazing. I'd love to show you Stark but I was supposed to leave the island that day.'

'What? Oh, shit.' He pulled a face. 'I'd lost track of time. Sorry. Forget it.'

'No, Étienne! I can alter my flight home. If you can get here, you and the girls could have Samphire Cottage because we've almost finished renovating it.'

'*You've* been renovating a cottage?'

'Only the odd lick of paint and some styling. And don't worry about flights – I'll talk to Sam and Richie. Between us all we'll get you here. I want you to come *so* much and actually it would fit in with some new plans. I've been invited to open . . . to help with a craft fair next Saturday so I was planning to stay on a few more days.'

'You're opening a craft fair?' Étienne echoed, his brow creasing in concern. 'This all sounds like serendipity, but Lily, are you absolutely *sure* we're not causing you trouble by disrupting your plans? What about work? The business?'

'The business? Oh, that can wait for a couple of days. I'll phone Richie and sort it.'

He peered at her. 'Lily, are you *sure* you're OK?'

'Why?'

'Because . . .' he began, before murmuring, 'Nothing. Don't worry. If you're certain we won't add to your stress, we'd love to come. Now, I need to eat this doughnut and get back to the blood and guts in A&E.' He held up the doughnut, squeezing it so the jam oozed out.

'Do you mind not doing that, please?' Lily muttered.

He gave a wicked grin. 'Send me the details when you can, but please don't pile pressure on yourself over this visit – you sound as if you've enough on your plate already. I won't tell the girls until it's all arranged. They'd be totally wild with excitement and refuse to sleep at all.'

Lily ended the call and heaved a sigh. She was ecstatic at the prospect of seeing the twins, yet her elation was tinged with dismay. Étienne was astonished she was putting anything other than the business first. Perhaps, she thought with sadness, he didn't trust her to keep her word.

Well, this time, she would. She'd move heaven and earth to make sure Étienne and her nieces found some way of reaching Stark – and she would also show the islanders that she was far from the person portrayed on TV.

Nothing would stand in her way.

There was more serendipitous news later that afternoon that made Lily feel she was obviously *meant* to stay. One of the islanders had been offered a last-minute medical appointment on the mainland and was only too keen to take her place on the Friday flight.

Sam had put the word out to Elspeth via the radio the previous evening. By now, everyone on Bryher – and probably beyond – would know she was staying longer. Any illusion of privacy was blown out of the water, but that couldn't be helped. She was, after all, going to be the star guest at the craft fair.

Étienne had managed to get spaces for him and the girls on a late afternoon plane from Exeter for the following Friday, so they were sorted. She only needed to ask Sam if they could stay at the retreat, but first she needed to text Penny to confirm she'd be able to attend the craft fair, and then call Richie.

He was lounging in her office chair, his West Bromwich Albion mug on her desk. Lily decided not to say anything about him having commandeered her office temporarily.

'Hello, you look very well,' he said cheerfully. 'The seaside is doing you good. Sea air is a tonic for all ills, my nanna says.'

'Your nanna is a wise woman,' Lily replied. 'Actually, I've been busy painting.'

Richie beamed. 'Oh, how lovely. Watercolours?'

Lily laughed. 'Um, a bit – though yesterday it was emulsion.'

Richie pouted. 'Emulsion . . . okayyy. Was it some kind of experimental art class?'

'In a way,' Lily said, feeling rather guilty for teasing him. She didn't think he'd understand if she admitted to helping paint the cottages. 'I didn't call you to tell you about my artistic efforts. There's been a slight change of plan.'

'*Slight*?' His expression turned wary. Lily knew she was throwing him a succession of curve balls. Well, it would do him good. She'd been too predictable over the past few months.

'Yes, Étienne wants to bring the twins over for a long weekend, but it means I need to stay on until next Monday. I've already amended my flight home. Another islander wanted to swap as it suited them better so that's fine. I don't think there's anything you can't handle, is there? I can do all my scheduled meetings over FaceTime.'

'Oh . . .' He was clicking the top of his lilac biro anxiously. She knew that look. 'I'll double-check. The director of our ad agency is coming in to present the Christmas campaign but we can take the meeting if you like.'

'Are you sure?' she asked.

'We can handle it and brief you later . . . only I thought you'd like to know as you usually want to be in the thick of those meetings.'

Lily loved meeting – and grilling – the ad agency creatives but she couldn't be in two places at once, and while the prospect of missing the next one gave her a flutter of anxiety, she squashed it down. 'I'm sure you and the team can deal with it very well. I have total confidence in you.'

Richie's lips parted in amazement. 'You *do*?'

'Of course. Now, if anything genuinely *urgent* crops up while I'm on Stark, there's always the radio. You have Elspeth's number, and she'll contact Sam and me if necessary. So, we're good?' she added firmly.

'Yes, I think so . . .' Richie's pen-clicking increased in tempo. 'You'll be back in the office a week on Tuesday, then?'

'Of course.'

'OK, then. See you soon.'

She knew Richie too well. The hesitation in his voice, the frantic clicking – he was wondering if she would be going back at all.

Judging by the butterflies in her stomach, Lily was wondering the same.

Immediately, she dismissed the very notion. Giving up her business wasn't an option. Too many people depended on her. She loved being her own boss and she'd worked far too hard to reach this point, to pack it in.

Yet she was also determined that her real obituary – no matter how far off it might be – would not read like the one that had been prematurely released.

Richie cut into her thoughts. 'Is there anything else, hun?'

'No, I don't think so. I'm happy to leave everything in your capable hands. Byee!'

She ended the call, grinning like a Cheshire Cat at the look of amazement on his face.

Now, all she had to do was ask Sam if Étienne and the girls could stay at the retreat. To think, only days ago she'd have moved heaven and earth to leave this place. Now, she was rearranging her life so she could stay.

Chapter Twenty-Two

On Saturday morning, Sam was up at five-thirty, taking advantage of the fine dry morning to put some final touches to Samphire. All it needed was some bathroom fixtures and fittings, which he could complete before making breakfast for Lily.

In the end, she had beaten him to it, turning up with a flask of coffee and a bag of pastries that made his mouth water. Lily herself looked edible to Sam in her denim cut-offs and an oversized T-shirt he'd loaned her.

She rattled the paper bag. 'Found these in the freezer and bunged them in the oven,' she said. 'I baked three for you, thought you'd be hungry.'

'You thought right,' he said. 'Thank you. I was ready for this.'

They ate on the terrace, watching the sun climb higher and the glittering sand flats appear as the tide retreated.

'Thank you for letting Étienne and the girls be your first guests in Samphire,' she said. He had agreed to let them stay in the cottage and had let her use the radio to get a message to Étienne.

'It's not a problem. They can be my next guinea pigs.'

'They'll be so excited! I can't wait to talk to them later

when they're back home from school. Their nanny is going to set up a FaceTime. Étienne works such erratic hours as a doctor, and my parents live too far away to be more than occasional babysitters, so he has to have a live-in nanny.'

'It must have been tough for him, suddenly being a lone parent.'

'I don't know how he's coped. He's wrestling with his own grief yet having to put on a brave face for the girls and hold down a tough job.' She smiled at Sam. 'You'll like him,' she said, with steel in her voice. 'Everyone does.'

Sam got the message that liking Étienne was non-negotiable. Briefly, he experienced a pang of jealousy and wondered if Lily felt something more than brotherly love for the man. Then he dismissed it: even if she *did* have feelings for her brother-in-law, it was none of Sam's concern. He wanted her to be happy – and she could never be happy with him.

There had been moments when he'd sensed a spark between them – moments when they'd been working together, eating together, laughing together and putting the world to rights. She was devoted to her family, cared about her employees and was deeply loyal. All of those things he valued and shared – yet he was acutely aware she was only in his world for a fleeting time, living a fantasy that he dared not allow himself to share.

He was providing that escape: he should be thrilled it was working and forget the cost to himself.

'Sam?'

Lily was on her feet, flask and mugs in her hands and a serious frown on her pretty face.

'Far be it from me to crack the whip but shouldn't we get back to work?'

He laughed out loud at the ridiculousness of her statement. 'I am dreading the reviews you're going to post: I almost drowned, had to cook for the hotel boss and build my own room!'

'I haven't had to build my own room,' she said with a cheeky smirk that sent the temperature soaring. 'But I am having to build one for Étienne and the girls.'

Sam couldn't deny this and he was extremely glad of the help. Samphire was a suite, like her own cottage, with a bedroom and separate lounge area. Lily insisted on making up the bed and left a spare duvet and pillows in the sitting room for the twins.

'Amelie and Tania are going to love sleeping on this sofa bed. I doubt Étienne will get much sleep though. They'll be hyper with excitement.'

'You'll have to take them for a very long walk.'

'I'd like to take them rock pooling,' she said.

'I thought we could have a fire on the beach after dinner, toast some marshmallows, hot chocolate . . .' Sam said. 'Maybe something a bit more exciting for the grown-ups.'

'That would be fantastic.' She held up crossed fingers. 'I just hope the weather stays fine so their flights take off and they can see how lush the islands are.'

On Sunday they worked until lunchtime before Sam insisted that Lily take a break. Already he felt a huge weight had lifted from his shoulders with two cottages complete and the cavalry arriving to finish the third and fourth. Aaron was coming over the following day, along with an electrician and plumber.

Lily had urged him to start advertising all the units on the hotel booking sites. At her instigation, he'd also advertised for a seasonal chef and housekeeper, both locally and more widely on hospitality recruitment sites.

Lily made herself a sandwich for lunch and, at Sam's insistence, took herself off for a break. He shifted some boxes of slate tiles to Starfish, meaning to finish the stone planter he'd built on the terrace.

He saw her strolling down the slope from the South Hill, wearing her bucket hat, carrying a bag with her sketch pad and paints. She looked relaxed – jaunty almost – and he was glad to see it. A moment later, she vanished amid the foxgloves and bracken.

The temperature rose but he had to push on, so he slathered on more suncream and fetched an old cricket hat of Nate's. His brother had played for the island team for all of two games before he'd grown bored of 'having a rock chucked at me'. He'd been a decent batter too, but couldn't be bothered to stick at it. Only computer games had ever held his interest.

Time ticked by and the sun felt even hotter. Sweat trickled down Sam's neck and his arms ached but the planter was finished. He swept up debris from the terrace. Once Aaron and his mates had spent a week at the retreat, Starfish would be ready for letting and Sea Holly and Scallop on their way, making a quintet of cottages in all. Maybe he could even invest the revenue into developing the ruined ones by the bay.

He checked his watch. Wow, it was past four! He picked up his flask for a drink of cool water.

'Sam!'

Lily's shout reached him on the terrace. Sam dropped a slate on the ground and took off around the side of the cottage.

There she was: scrambling up the slope from the middle of the island, gasping for breath. He hurtled down to meet her and she flung herself into his arms.

'What's happened?' he said, holding her tightly.

'I saw it again! In one of the old cottages. This time, it wasn't just a shadow, I'm *sure* it was a person.'

'Jesus. A person? It – they didn't hurt you?'

'No.'

'Was it a man or a woman?' he asked, still holding her, but gently. Her breathing gradually steadied.

'I'm not sure. I know that sounds silly, but it was just a fleeting glimpse in deep shade. I went inside there to sketch the foxgloves around the hearth and the figure dashed across the open doorway. It *was* a real person, Sam. I shouted after them. Asked who they were. I wanted to go after them but I – I didn't think it was a good idea, so I just left everything in the cottage and ran up here.'

'You must have been petrified.' He swore. 'I'm going down there to find them right now!'

'No, please.'

'Why not?' he said, his blood boiling at the thought of someone upsetting or even threatening Lily. 'I'll have to tell the police. The chief inspector, Ben, is a friend of mine. He'll take it seriously.'

'No – don't! I don't think they mean any harm. They probably only want to prank me.'

'Scaring you isn't funny!'

Sam folded her to him until her breathing steadied. It felt so good to hold her, to comfort her. She lifted her face away from his shoulder and looked up at him. Too soon, she would pull away from him and this moment would be over, this moment that he wanted to stretch out forever.

She tilted up her head and he lowered his face to hers for the kiss that he hadn't realised he'd been craving. He wanted to kiss her, even though it might lead to more and make things harder when she left.

Her lips brushed his and then she was out of his arms, leaving him feeling empty.

'God, talk about being spooked . . .' Her cheeks had turned pink. 'I'm sorry.'

'Don't apologise,' he said gruffly, torn between disappointment and relief that the kiss had ended so quickly. 'It must have been a horrible shock. And look, you've fallen into the brambles.'

Moving even further out of his reach, she glanced down at her scratched legs. 'I was in a hurry to get away but I'm fine, honestly. It's my sketch pad and paints I'm worried about. I left them in the old cottage.'

'I'll get them.' Anger welled up inside him. 'And I *am* going to find out who's behind this! Prankster, my arse!'

Lily's laughter was edged with embarrassment. Had her

scary encounter made her nervy or was it her reaction – their joint reaction – afterwards? 'Are you still sure no one could reach the island?' she asked. 'I've seen an old photo with a rowing boat drawn up on the beach, in one of the books in the cottage.'

'Like I said, it's possible by kayak or rowing boat in the right conditions and I agree it's someone real,' he said briskly. 'Do you have any idea at all of what they looked like?'

'Not really. I am sorry. I heard the bracken rustle and I heard them breathing, then saw them dash across the open doorway. They were wearing dark clothing and it was difficult to see detail in the shadows. I guess they could have had a hoodie on, or a coat.' She hesitated. 'I'm really not sure.'

'The only idea I can come up with is it's someone who wants to cause trouble. Whether it's a journalist or locals who don't like the idea of the development here, I have no idea. I'm going to have a bloody good look round right now. You stay here. Lock the door if you want.'

'I'd rather come with you.'

'Fine. Let's go together, but we'll get you cleaned up first and I'll make you a cup of tea.'

'I'd rather have a coffee with some of that island rum from the cottage.'

'I'll come over and make you one now. No arguments.'

Sam made the drinks while Lily washed herself in the bathroom and daubed some antiseptic cream on her legs. Sam was seething with whichever idiot – or idiots – had decided to frighten his guest. How could he open the retreat while this was going on? How could he guarantee that Lily's family would be safe?

Plus, there was now the added complication of that kiss – if it was a kiss? He'd felt her lips brush his, tasted lip gloss.

He remembered his decision not to get emotionally involved with the guests. It followed he shouldn't kiss them either. He was teetering perilously close to throwing the whole rulebook out the window . . .

When Lily emerged from the bathroom, she looked calmer.

Sam reverted to brisk practicality and handed over the coffee. 'I made one for me without the rum.'

'Thanks. Look, I really don't want to be any more trouble,' she said. 'It's funny that it's only me who sees them.'

'They're probably worried I'd recognise them if they're from round here.'

'Maybe . . . but there's something else I haven't told you. Somebody left me a sign on the terrace table a few days ago. A message spelled out in pebbles.'

'What?' His stomach clenched. 'Why didn't you say anything?'

'You were busy with the cottage. It didn't seem that bad at the time but now, having almost come face to face with an intruder, it does feel like I'm being singled out.'

He wanted to hug her again but didn't dare. He was, however, determined to keep her safe.

'What kind of message was it?' he said, a chill seizing him.

'Well, the pebbles spelled out LEAVE.'

'Right. That's it,' Sam declared, firing up with anger and protective instinct. 'We're getting off the island. I'm going to take you over to Bryher before dinner. We can stay at Hell Bay House for the night.'

'Oh, that's not necessary.'

'It is until I get to the bottom of this,' he said firmly. 'I want to make sure that there won't be any disturbance when your family arrives.'

'But I can't stay in your home!'

'Yes, you can,' he said, determined that nothing else would go wrong. 'Pack your bag now. We're leaving.'

Chapter Twenty-Three

Lily felt it was strange to be spending the night at Sam's home, though she wasn't going to object again because the appearance of the intruder had genuinely spooked her. Someone had it in for her, enough to make a difficult landing on the island and risk being seen.

Elspeth was waiting on the quayside when they arrived, and hugged Lily tightly.

'Oh, you poor thing!' she said, while Sam tied up. 'Sam says you've had a terrible fright.'

'It was just a scare. I'm OK.' Still cringing with embarrassment, Lily was determined to downplay her encounter, especially with islanders hanging around the quayside, their interest piqued by Elspeth's display of concern.

'I can't think who would be stupid enough to try such a thing. It's sick!'

'They probably think it's funny.'

'Well, I don't. Come on, I brought Sam's car down for you so you don't have to walk.'

Lily was mortified. She could manage the fifteen-minute walk to Hell Bay House. People would think she was a real diva, expecting to be chauffeur-driven such a short distance.

'That's very kind but, honestly, I wasn't hurt. Whoever it was rushed away pretty fast when they saw me.'

'Well, you jump in the car anyway,' Elspeth said, walking with her to the Land Rover. 'We'll drive down there together.'

Sam joined them. 'I'll be along in a bit. I need to have a word with Aaron about the electrician,' he said.

Elspeth drove, insisting Lily sit in the back, like royalty. Minutes later, she was walking into Hell Bay House. She couldn't help but wonder if Rhiannon had stayed or even lived here with Sam before she'd left. Lily still only knew the barest details: that Rhiannon had departed suddenly, with no explanation that Lily could fathom.

Elspeth walked into the house, calling, 'Morven! Are you here?'

Oh, God, Morven. Lily had forgotten she'd be invading the girl's home as well as Sam's.

'I'm in here,' Morven called. 'Working.'

Elspeth marched into the lounge, with Lily dragging her feet behind. 'We have a guest tonight. Lily's staying over . . .'

Morven sprang up from the sofa, her iPad slipping onto the rug.

'Why's she staying here?' The girl stared at Lily as if she'd landed from Mars.

'Sam invited Lily,' Elspeth said angrily. 'She's had a bad experience on Stark.'

Morven retrieved her iPad and wrinkled her nose as if she'd found a large spider on the carpet. 'What kind of bad experience?'

'Someone's been leaving messages and hanging around Tean Porth,' Lily said.

Elspeth faced up to her great-niece. 'You wouldn't know anything about it, would you?'

Morven scoffed, 'Why would I know anything about it? Why does everyone think I'm involved whenever shitty stuff happens?'

Grabbing her tablet, she dodged past Elspeth and skulked out of the French doors.

Elspeth closed her eyes in despair. 'I am so sorry about that. She's so awkward these days, neither of us know what to do with her.'

'It must be tough with her dad away,' Lily said, trying to summon up some empathy.

Elspeth sighed. 'It's awful for her. I wish I could get my hands on Nathan and show him the damage he's doing to his daughter by keeping her in suspense all this time. Poor Sam is having to bear the brunt of it . . . Still, at least she's said she doesn't know anything about the mystery intruder, that's something.'

Actually, thought Lily, Morven hadn't answered the question at all.

Elspeth scraped up a smile. 'Anyway, would you like to come upstairs and I'll show you to your room? I'm sure Sam won't be too long.'

Lily went up the stairs, feeling the polished oak banister under her palm. The house had triple windows on both elevations, letting in loads of light. Everywhere there were comfy sofas and cosy nooks, bookcases and prints.

'It's good of you to have me.'

'Sam wouldn't want you to feel uncomfortable. I wish I'd never mentioned disturbing the spirits. Although I'm certain the island holds echoes of its past residents, I don't think they'd come back 'specially to stalk guests. I'm sure the figure you saw is just some prankster.'

Lily had to smile. 'I don't think it was a ghost and I'm not sure Mabel Teague would decide to leave a message in pebbles for me.'

'I doubt poor Mabel could even read and write,' Elspeth said as she opened the door of a room at the front of the house, above the lounge. 'Here you go. It's only a single, but it's always ready for guests and the bathroom is right next door. Nate stayed here the last time he came back to see Morven.'

'It's lovely. Very welcoming,' Lily said, feeling comforted by the sight of the white duvet, Lloyd Loom chair and pastel colour scheme. It was fresh but soothing. 'What a pretty chair.'

'I'm glad you like it. The chair was Sam's grandmother's. His parents left it here when they moved to the mainland. Morven painted it green – pistachio she calls it – and made the cushion.'

'It's beautiful,' Lily said, admiring the tapestry cushion, though wondering if it might explode when she sat on it.

She put her bag on the rug beside the bed and crossed to the window. Her room must be right over the porch, giving a view of all the comings and goings – and Hell Bay itself, with Stark looming mysteriously over the channel. Was anyone on the island right now, flitting about the hearths and leaving messages on her terrace?

She almost shivered but instead said enthusiastically, 'What a view. It makes a change to be looking over at Stark.'

Elspeth had joined her at the window. 'Yes, it must.'

Evening sunlight glinted off the windows of the cottages and reception hub. 'I can see all the cottages from here.'

'You can. Sam says you've been helping to renovate them.'

Lily laughed. 'Renovate makes it sound as if I'm brick-laying and roofing. Sam's done ninety-nine percent of the work already. I'm just lending a hand with the finishing touches to Samphire and Starfish so he can open them to visitors.'

Elspeth sighed. 'I'm glad he's agreed to accept some help. I didn't want him to re-open the island mainly because I've been worried he's heading for a nervous breakdown. It's such a lot of work and responsibility. I think he under-estimated how much. And he puts so much pressure on himself.'

'Perhaps that's true, but he's now fully aware of what's involved, which is why he's going to recruit some experi-enced staff,' Lily said soothingly. 'The chef from the St Agnes Bistro is interested since the owner retired. Sam's already placed ads with the recruitment agencies for a housekeeper too.'

Elspeth patted Lily's arm. 'Thanks for helping him. He finds it hard to admit he needs it.'

'I'm no expert at hospitality, and he was dead against me getting involved initially. I just can't stop myself.'

'You're both as bad as each other, but he needed the

support. I'd do more if I didn't have the café.' Elspeth's green eyes searched Lily's face. 'He'll miss you when you're gone.'

Lily laughed. 'I've only been here ten days.'

'That's long enough to miss someone. In more than one way.'

Feeling her cheeks glowing, Lily glanced away and fixed her eyes on her overnight bag. 'Should I unpack then come down and help you start dinner?'

'Oh, there's no need for that. I can manage.'

'It would be no trouble,' Lily said firmly, determined that Elspeth wouldn't have extra work to do on her account. 'I've enjoyed cooking while I've been here. I don't have time at home and, believe me, I need the practice. I've run right out of my go-to recipes and I could count them on one hand.'

Elspeth relented. 'Well, if you'd really like to. I was going to make a one-pot chicken and asparagus thing. It's my mother's recipe but I make it as a traybake 'cos it sounds trendier. We serve it at the café on Sundays sometimes. You could add that to your list.'

'Sounds great. I'll go home and make it for my mum and dad. Amaze the lot of them . . . I don't get home enough but I *will* make time from now on. That's one of my post-retreat resolutions.'

Elspeth looked amused. 'Well done, but don't make *too* many, will you? Stick to a couple that really matter and just try your best. You don't want to add not being the perfect chef or the perfect daughter to the list of things you can beat yourself up about, now do you?'

Lily felt a lump forming in her throat. Cara had always found time to visit their parents. Cara also found time to be a mum and to save the lives of other people's children. Lily, however, was hellbent on sourcing the perfect bud vase for your hall or those handmade gin tumblers you'd been seeking forever . . .

'No,' she said, stricken with the guilt Elspeth was trying to assuage. 'You're right.'

Elspeth patted her arm. 'Come on, let's cobble together a not-perfect dinner and enjoy not being invited on *Masterchef.*'

Lily shook herself out of her mood. If she really wanted to change her life and honour Cara's memory, wallowing in self-pity was not the way. Change should start now. She forced herself to enjoy the process even if she kept thinking that she should be cooking with her own mum – though her mother, Ailsa, was as big a fan of the ready-meal aisle as Lily herself.

Her parents led busy and fulfilling, yet fairly ordinary, lives. They'd always seemed very happy together, providing a loving home for Lily and Cara. There had been plenty of joy and happy times in the small Staffordshire market town they'd grown up in. It was a quiet place where nothing very exciting happened, but their modest home had always been full of laughter. Her parents had given Lily and Cara a stable upbringing and encouraged both their daughters to pursue their dreams, finding time to take them to their clubs, play games, console and celebrate with them.

Along the way, Lily had somehow lost sight of how precious time was – how precious *they* were.

That would all change, she decided, and was already looking forward to impressing her parents with her new-found culinary enthusiasm.

For now, while she chopped and fried, diced and measured, she shared Elspeth's reminiscences of her younger days. It turned out that Sam had known her mother briefly – his great-aunt – when he was a young boy. Nate had too, and remembered her far better, being five years older.

Delicious aromas of onions and chicken filled the house by the time Sam returned.

'Smells great,' he said with a surprised look at Lily. 'Can I help?'

'We've done most of it now,' Elspeth insisted. 'Too many cooks and all that.'

'I'll lay the table, then. Where's Morven?'

'In her room, talking to her friends,' Elspeth said. 'Can you go up and tell her dinner will be ready in ten minutes?'

'Yep. I'll have a shower while I'm up there, so I'm fit for company after working on the cottages all day.'

Lily was dying to say 'You look more than fit to me', but kept her mouth firmly shut, and contented herself with innocently rinsing purple sprouting broccoli in the Belfast sink. The thought of him stripping off his shorts and T-shirt and stepping into a steamy shower was enough to send her temperature soaring.

'I'll give Morven notice now and check on her again after my shower,' he said. 'See you in ten.'

Lily had forgotten what hard work it was making sure all the elements of a meal for four were ready at the right time and served up hot. She'd also whipped up a hasty Eton Mess made with strawberries from Elspeth's garden and some meringues left over from the café service.

'The bakery makes them 'specially for us,' Elspeth had said, handing over a paper bag. 'There's some cream in the fridge. Give it a quick whip and squish it all together. You can add a drop of the blackberry cordial on that shelf if you like. I made it last summer.'

With the Mess suitably squished and chilling in the fridge, Sam came downstairs with wet hair and his clean T-shirt sticking to his still-damp chest.

'Morven *will* be on her way any minute,' he muttered, giving the impression that she'd been as difficult to shift as chewing gum from a pavement.

Although she wanted the family to be together, Lily was also nervous of Morven's reaction to her over dinner. The girl was probably dreading their evening together even more than Lily was.

For the time being, she focused on carrying out the tray-bake to the table. The chicken was cooked beautifully, falling apart, dotted with melting mozzarella and asparagus that had turned crisp at the tips. It smelled divine.

'Spuds!' Elspeth barked, blowing a strand of hair out of her eyes.

'Yes, chef!' Sam carried the tureen of new potatoes, scattered with mint, into the dining room.

Lily followed with a dish of broccoli and they were ready.

Elspeth brought out a large jug of elderflower cordial filled with ice and heaved a huge sigh.

'Righty-oh. Let's dig in . . . where is that girl?'

'*She's* here.' Morven slouched in through the door, a pair of headphones round her neck. She sniffed. 'What is it?'

'Thought you weren't coming,' Elspeth replied.

'I'm not hungry,' she said, sliding onto a chair.

'Then you can sit and watch us tuck in,' Elspeth said. 'Pass those spuds, please.'

Sam exchanged a pained glance with Lily, who felt rather sorry for Morven, being summoned like a kitchen maid, even if Elspeth meant well.

In the end, Morven relented enough to try a portion of chicken with two helpings of potatoes and then push a spear of tenderstem broccoli round her plate.

Sam was on his second portion of everything. 'This is delicious, Auntie Elspeth.'

'Lily did a lot of it – and can you please stop calling me Auntie? It makes me feel old.'

'You *are* old, though, Auntie Elspeth.'

Lily stifled a gasp.

'No need for that, Morven!' Sam said.

'Well, actually, she's right. Sixty-seven must seem old to a seventeen year old.'

'I didn't mean to be rude,' Morven protested and, for once, Lily believed her.

She gave her a sympathetic look but Morven ignored it.

'Is there any pudding?' she muttered.

'Yes, Lily's made an Eton Mess.'

'Hmmph . . . Can I take mine upstairs?'

'Not yet, if you don't mind. Let's wait until everyone's finished.'

Morven stabbed at her broccoli. 'I wonder what the ghosts on Stark are having,' she murmured with a sly grin.

'Morven . . .' Sam warned.

'Spook-hetti, I should think,' Lily said, cutting up a potato. 'Followed by I Scream.'

Elspeth giggled and Sam grinned.

Morven stared at her. 'That's so lame.'

'My nieces told me the jokes. They love ghosts. Maybe they'll see one when they visit next weekend.'

Morven's jaw dropped. 'Your nieces? They're coming here too?'

'Lily's family are coming to stay,' Sam said, a core of steel in his voice. 'Her brother-in-law and his little girls.'

'B–but where are they going to sleep?' Morven stammered. 'Not here! There's not room.'

'On Stark. Samphire is ready now, thanks to Lily's help, and Aaron and the gang are coming over to help me finish Starfish.'

'*You've* been building?' Morven made no attempt to hide her incredulity as she stared at Lily.

Out of the corner of her eye, she saw Elspeth, knife and fork poised, ready to jump in and tell off Morven for her rudeness. But Lily could fight her own battles.

'I wouldn't say building, but I have been doing some painting and styling. I enjoy turning my hand to all kinds of creative stuff, much like you do.'

Morven opened her mouth and shut it before attacking her broccoli spear as if it might leap up and stab her.

After the main course, she scuttled upstairs with her Eton Mess. Clearly her dislike of Lily was trumped by her love of desserts.

Lily was too full to eat any pudding. Sam, however, demolished a large bowlful and Elspeth declared it 'smashing'.

The three grown-ups retired to the terrace overlooking the bay, where clouds were gathering over Stark.

'There's a storm forecast,' Sam said, shading his eyes as he stood on the paving stones. More dark clouds had marshalled on the horizon behind the island, making Lily doubly glad to be at Hell Bay House.

Elspeth rested her feet on a padded recliner. 'If anyone is over there, I hope they get soaked to the skin!'

'Do you think there will be?' Lily said, getting up and standing by Sam.

'Feck knows.'

'Sam!' Elspeth cried out in horror at his language.

Lily was amused that he'd let down his guard enough to swear in front of her. She was clearly no longer seen as just a guest. That sent a frisson of excitement and satisfaction through her. She might not be part of the family, but she was on the verge of becoming a friend.

Chapter Twenty-Four

Sam made coffee and they drank it on the terrace while talking about the craft fair. Elspeth said that it was the highlight of the year for a lot of the artists and craftspeople and that Morven had planned to share a stall with Damon.

'Penny Bannister was a bit cheeky asking you to help,' she observed.

'I didn't mind,' Lily replied. 'I love being able to support local makers,' she said, hiding the fact she was still apprehensive about the public speaking aspect of the event.

'Yet you had to change your plans?' Elspeth said, with a shrewd sideways look at her.

'Yes, that was a logistical challenge,' Lily said, and added, 'though I was highly motivated once I heard Étienne and the girls were coming.'

While they'd been cooking, Lily had told Elspeth what had happened to Cara.

'I bet. You must be very close, especially after losing your sister,' Elspeth said gently.

Out of the corner of her eye, Lily spotted Sam taking an interest.

'I feel I've had to step into her shoes in some ways.' She

stopped, emotion welling up again. 'Not that I've done a very good job of it. Or any kind of job.'

'I'm sure that's not true.'

'It is. And that's one of the things I'm going to change when I get home. I *will* make more time for them, no matter what. I'm going to promote my PA – not that he knows it yet – and give him and the team more responsibility. I'm going to spend more time with my family and – um – perhaps try a bit of self-care.'

Unexpectedly, Sam didn't smile at the phrase.

'Fasten your own oxygen mask first, eh? Without doing that, you've no hope of helping those around you.' Elspeth nodded in approval. 'I learned that along the way.'

'It's something I've realised since I've been here. I needed to take a step away from the everyday and draw in a deep breath to give myself some perspective,' Lily said, looking at Sam as she spoke. 'And Stark's given me an opportunity to do that.'

'Good.' Elspeth eased herself out of the lounger. 'I think I'll go home. It's been a long day. What's your plan for tomorrow?' she asked Sam.

'I'm going back to Stark with Aaron. We're going to scour the island and see if we can find any trace of this uninvited visitor. Lily, would you mind staying here until I have news?'

'Not at all . . . I can go straight to the café. In fact, I'd tentatively arranged to meet up with Penny to find out more about the craft fair, so it suits me.'

'Great,' said Sam, sounding relieved that Lily wasn't

going to put up a fight to join him ghost hunting. 'I'll walk you home, Auntie Elspeth.'

Elspeth rolled her eyes good-naturedly. 'I think I can safely make my way two hundred yards down the path. You stay here with Morven and Lily. I'll see you at the café in the morning,' she added to Lily. 'Now, goodnight and sweet dreams.'

Lily thanked her for dinner with a hug and watched her walk out of the garden and towards her cottage.

'I'll message her as soon as I think she should be home,' Sam said. 'She'll go mad if I follow her.'

'Have you been worried about her before?' Lily asked.

'No . . . and I'm being paranoid, I suppose. Contrary to the crime novels, serious trouble is incredibly rare here.'

'Let's stay out here until you know she's safely home,' Lily suggested.

Two minutes later, Elspeth herself sent a message saying she was back in her cottage and that Sam should stop worrying.

'That's easier said than done,' he murmured.

'Tell me about it,' Lily answered. 'Shall we go inside?'

The sky was still light at ten o' clock and Sam had left the French doors open to make the most of the long day. The scent of the sea blew in and gradually the birds settled in their roosts, leaving only the rustle of leaves and low rumble of the sea to be heard. Occasionally, music drifted down from Morven's room.

He turned on the lamps and they sat talking about the

cottages and his plans. He also apologised for Morven's behaviour when he was sure she was out of earshot, but Lily told him not to worry.

'I've invaded her space,' she said. 'It's hardly surprising she feels painted into a corner. Have you heard any news from your brother about coming home?'

'Not since our last chat. He knows he can't keep Morven dangling any longer. She's got to decide what to do about her further education once she has her A-level results and needs to focus on that if she's staying on Bryher. It's been disruptive enough to have to board on St Mary's in the week, without her father staying away for so long.'

'Where did they live before he went to the States?'

'In a bungalow near the community centre. It's rented out as a holiday let at the moment. He was able to work remotely from Bryher as a freelance games designer. His main client was based in Exeter and Nate managed by making monthly business trips to their office. It worked well.'

'Until he went to LA?' Lily said. 'Are you worried he might not come back for Morven at all?'

'Sometimes, yes.'

'Poor Morven,' Lily murmured, putting herself in the teenager's place. 'No wonder she feels all at sea. And even her home has been taken over by strangers.'

'You don't mean you coming here?' Sam said.

'No, I actually meant that her real home – the bungalow – is rented out.'

Sam looked relieved. 'Good, because you're not a stranger. I invited you here as my guest – as more than a guest, as a ... friend. This is my home, and Morven will have to put up with it.' With that he got up, gathering empty mugs. 'I'm going to put these in the dishwasher and then I think we should both get an early night.'

As Lily got ready for bed, a tingle ran through her. Sam had been adamant she was more than a guest, although she wasn't sure that 'friends' covered the relationship between them. She'd replayed the kiss often and couldn't help thinking he was ready to reciprocate.

Even now, she found it impossible not to picture him lying in bed a few feet down the hall – even closer than when they were together on Stark. Did he wear pyjamas? Somehow, she couldn't imagine it ... she hoped he wouldn't forget that she was in the house and go wandering to the bathroom, with nothing on ...

The touch of his lips ...

Needing a distraction from such thoughts, Lily decided to go outside to message her parents but the lure of the screen was no match for the scene in front of her. The scent of wild honeysuckle reached her and the moon shone down, creating a shimmering path across the channel, painting Cromwell's Castle in a mysterious silvery hue. She smiled to herself: everything surrounding Stark was mysterious.

The wind whispered against her cheek, like the brush of Sam's lips on hers, the touch of his hand. Perhaps the moon wasn't as beautiful as she thought, nor the honeysuckle as delicious. Perhaps she was experiencing everything with such intensity because she'd almost died or because ...

'Hey! You!'

Lily jumped.

Morven stepped out of the French doors and glared at her.

'I presume you mean me,' Lily said evenly, not needing her business skills to recognise a cobra about to strike.

'We can manage without you. We did before,' Morven said, coming closer. 'You take over Sam's project, you want to interfere with the craft fair, move into our house . . . You just *have* to be the boss of everything, don't you? Well, the island doesn't need you! None of us do.'

For a nanosecond, Lily thought about explaining that she'd had her arm twisted to help at the craft fair, and that Morven was being ludicrously unfair – not to mention incredibly rude.

Instead, she threw her teenage nemesis a winning smile. 'Well, perhaps *I* need *it*.'

Morven marched back inside and headed upstairs, turning up her music so loud that the floors were practically vibrating. Lily knew there was no point going to bed with that row going on.

After closing the doors behind her, Lily went back into the sitting room.

Sam walked in from the kitchen and winced. 'I'm sorry,' he said. 'I'll go up and have a word.'

Not long after, the music stopped. As a teenager, Lily had done the same herself a few times and, despite Morven's rudeness, she could understand the girl's frustration. She must feel that the only control she had over her life was through the volume of her sound system.

'It's safe to go up now,' Sam said on his return. 'I'll lock up.'

Wondering if he usually locked the doors, Lily went up to her room and was soon lulled to sleep by the sound of the waves breaking on Hell Bay.

When she woke, it was to sounds that were anything but soothing.

Shouts reverberated through the house, along with heavy footsteps on the stairs. Morven must be thumping around, possibly spoiling for a fight over breakfast.

Lily got up and pulled on a hoodie over her pyjamas. She opened the door a crack to find Sam just emerging from Morven's room, raking a hand through untamed hair.

'Is she up there?' Unexpectedly, Elspeth's plaintive cry came from the hall below.

'What's the matter?' Lily said.

Sam's face was grey with anguish. 'It's Morven,' he said. 'Her bed's definitely not been slept in and she's nowhere to be found.'

Chapter Twenty-Five

Lily got dressed as fast as Superman and ran downstairs to where Sam was pacing up and down the hallway.

Elspeth was also there and Lily discovered that Sam had called her after finding Morven's room empty and no sign of her in the house. He'd gone back to double check her bedroom when Lily woke up.

His aunt was now on the landline, sounding panicked. 'No sign of them at all? . . . OK. Thanks . . . Yes, she probably has . . . Yes, I'll call back if I hear anything.'

Sam looked disappointed. 'Not at Rowena's, then?'

'No. Her mum says Row spoke to her on FaceTime but that was much earlier, probably when Morven took the pudding up to her room.'

Sam burst out: 'Where the hell is she in this weather?'

For the first time, Lily registered the rain blowing against the windows. The mayhem inside the house had blotted it out.

'What about her friend Damon – might she have gone to his?' Lily suggested.

Elspeth shook her head. 'Already tried his house. He's out fishing with his brother now, though his mother reckons he was in all night before that, "for a change". She thinks he's got a secret girlfriend.'

'And that could be Morven?' Lily said.

'I don't know about that,' Elspeth said. 'They're thick as thieves but I've never seen them canoodling. They seem more like brother and sister – or a gangster and his moll, always plotting something.'

Lily's cogs whirred. 'So, Damon's been out a lot at night . . . I could be way off here, and please don't be offended, but have you thought that he – or Morven – could have had something to do with the intruders on Stark?'

'Yes, and I dismissed the idea,' Sam said, then grimaced. 'I'd assumed she couldn't get across there on her own but . . .'

'She wouldn't dare go that far!' Elspeth cut in, sounding horrified. 'Sailing over to Stark and trying to scare you? I can't imagine why.'

'I can,' Lily said. 'In fact, someone left a very specific message on my terrace.'

'What?' said Elspeth. 'You never mentioned that.'

'It said LEAVE – very neatly spelled out in pebbles. It could have been framed as a collage to be honest.'

Elspeth clapped her hands to her face. 'Oh, I hope it wasn't Morven! It's so dangerous crossing to Stark.'

'Yet Damon was brought up on the islands,' Sam murmured. 'He has access to a boat and he's been out a lot with his brother so he knows the coastline well. Maybe they're both on Stark now.'

'Unless they've run away together and I've been

completely wrong,' Elspeth said. 'Should we check the flights and ferries?'

'They don't have the money to book flights and go off together,' Sam said. 'As far as I know.'

'And if he's been in all night, he can't have run off with Morven,' Elspeth said. 'Listen to that rain. Oh, God, what if she's come to harm?'

The colour drained out of Sam's face. 'Nate . . . I have to let him know she's missing.'

Elspeth squealed, 'Oh, no. Don't. Can't we hang on a bit?'

'She's his daughter. I can't keep a thing like this from him.'

Lily stood by feeling helpless and unwilling to voice something that had been niggling her . . . yet she had to get it off her chest.

'Look, I apologise in advance if this is unhelpful, but if she *is* the culprit then maybe she's gone to Stark again. She was pretty upset last night. I wasn't going to tell you, but she – um – had a go at me.'

Sam pressed his lips tightly together before murmuring, 'What did she say?'

'She was annoyed because she thought I was taking over, at the retreat and the craft fair . . . I think it was the last straw when she saw me in her own home too.'

He closed his eyes briefly. 'I didn't realise she was that upset. I *should* have realised.'

'I think she may not even recognise how upset she is herself,' Lily said gently.

Elspeth sat down heavily on the oak bench in the hall. 'This is Nate's fault.'

'No, it's mine, for not listening or seeing the signs. If anything has happened to her or she's done anything . . .' Sam said '. . . I'll never forgive myself as long as I live. I have to tell Nate and now.'

He marched off to the study.

Elspeth leaned back against the wall. 'I won't forgive myself either. I should have realised the state she was in. I know she can be awkward but it's out of character for her to do something so daft as trying to scare you off Stark – or take the risk of going over there without Sam.'

Lily heard him speaking from the study. She could hear another male voice, taut with anguish, and an American woman shouting, 'Nate? What the actual fuck has she done now?'

'We don't know she has yet,' Lily said, 'I just have a hunch. If she wanted to hide away from us, for whatever reason, there aren't many places she could go without money.'

The door to the study slammed shut, but they could still hear raised voices.

Elspeth sighed. 'And now Sam and Nate are at each other's throats. This is a disaster.'

Lily sat down next to her and patted her hand. 'While we're waiting for Sam, why don't we have a think about other places Morven might have gone to – we can make a list and check those as well as Stark?' She hoped to distract Elspeth by focusing on practical things they could do.

'She could have got to one of the other islands . . .

Although the passenger boats were finished by dinnertime and she must have left long after that.'

'She'd have had to have help, then?' Lily offered.

'That's what bothers me! If she isn't around Hell Bay or on Bryher, how did she get across the water? If she even made it . . .' Elspeth was now in tears.

Lily pulled a tissue from a box by the phone and offered it to her. 'I'm sure she'll be alright,' she said, comforting Elspeth. 'She seems very resourceful and smart to me.'

A couple of minutes later, Sam marched out of the study.

Elspeth pushed herself to her feet. 'Oh, Lord, what did Nate say?'

'He'd almost gone to bed and was in pieces when he heard. I almost wish I hadn't FaceTimed him and seen the look on his face. I've never seen him so scared, but what could I do? Not tell him for hours until we find her – if we find her?' Sam stopped speaking, frozen with anguish.

'We *will* find her. And you had to tell him,' Lily said firmly. 'And we – I – had a thought. Do you think Morven could be on Stark right now? Even if she hasn't been messing around on there, she might have gone now as she knows it so well. Maybe she thought she might stay in one of the cottages.'

Sam looked thoughtful. 'That's possible. She does have a key . . . I had one cut when she was going to help me with the changeovers. I don't think I ever had it back.'

'That's where she'll be then!' Elspeth said. 'Hiding in one of the cottages!' She seemed so relieved, Lily hoped this was right.

'We don't know that for sure, Auntie Elspeth,' Sam said gently. 'But it's worth a look. While we drive to the quay, can you call around a few mates?' he said to Lily and his aunt. 'The rowing crew will help. I'll give you the numbers from my phone. Ask them to help in the search.'

'Shall we ask one of them to stay on Bryher and phone the heliport and ferry terminal?' Lily suggested. 'And send a few more to hunt around Bryher itself and spread the word among the islanders?'

'Yes. Good idea.' He flared into action again. 'Meanwhile we'll go over to Stark. Elspeth, what do you want to do? Come with us or stay?'

'Come with you,' she declared. 'I'm with Lily, I think Morven's on Stark.'

'I agree with you both . . .' Sam said, adding with renewed energy, 'and if she is still on the islands, and I think she has to be, we'll find her.'

Half an hour later, most of the rowing crew and a dozen other islanders had gathered at the quayside with Sam, Lily and Elspeth. Word had spread like wildfire. Bruce was coordinating the wider search effort on Bryher. Rory took the gig crew in his boat while Sam motored off in the *Hydra* with Elspeth and Lily.

The boat thumped over the waves, water flying up, wipers swishing wildly. The rain was horizontal and the wind whipped up whitecaps. It was a horrible day to be outdoors.

Elspeth huddled in a corner of the cabin, holding on tight to the seat. Lily sat next to Sam, trying to ignore the jagged rocks lurking on every side.

Sam slotted the boat into the little harbour at Stark, cut the engine and leaped ashore. Ignoring the driving rain, Lily hitched the rope around the bow cleat. 'What about the others?'

'Rory's moored offshore and launched his RIB. He's brought his own radio and a spare for the search party.'

'She could be in reception or your flat,' Elspeth said, rushing up the path from the jetty like a woman half her age.

Penny arrived not long after, rain dripping off her yellow waterproof.

'The others are on the quay but I thought I might be able to help up here. Make tea, run errands . . .' she said.

'Thanks, Penny.'

The moment Sam tried the door of the reception hub, it was clear Morven wasn't there.

'It was still locked,' he said, walking inside. 'Come on, let's check the cottages. Elspeth, would you and Penny mind staying here on the radio, please, in case she turns up on another island? We'll only be a minute.'

'I don't want my aunt out in this weather,' he said to Lily, who wondered if Sam was also worried in case they did find Morven – and not safe and well.

She shuddered at the prospect and crossed everything that nothing like that would happen. She dreaded him having to go through what she had when they'd lost Cara. However, thinking the worst would help no one, so Lily focused on the search.

Even as they approached Cowrie, her hopes faded. It looked as shut up and unoccupied as when she'd left it. The moment she tried the door, her fear was confirmed.

'I suppose she might have been inside and left,' Sam said while Lily unlocked it.

'Morven!' she called, inching open the door, longing to find the girl asleep on the bed, hair spread over the pillow, like Sleeping Beauty. 'Are you here? It's OK . . . you're not in trouble.'

There was only silence and the stuffiness of a room that had been shut up for a day.

'Is she here?' Sam marched in behind her.

'No one's been in since we left.'

'Nor the other cottages. As far as I can tell, everything looks the same.'

It was clear that no one had been inside the unfinished cottages and Aaron reported no sign of Morven or anyone else around the retreat area in general.

Sam despatched Fergal, Aaron and Ivanka to search the island's coastline. Lily grew cold when he mentioned the numerous indentations, sea caves and cliffs.

'I didn't want my aunt to hear that,' he said just before they went back into reception.

Elspeth was sitting on a sofa, looking exhausted and grey-faced.

At Sam's appearance, she burst out: 'Is she here?'

'I'm afraid there's no sign of her in any of the cottages.'

Elspeth let out a sob.

Penny was next to her, patting her arm. 'It'll be OK, Elspeth. We'll find her.'

'We will, I promise,' Lily said, before she left, armed with one of Sam's spare handsets.

'I'm going to check the ruined cottages by the bay. There are a couple of Neolithic chambers hidden in the bracken. She could be hiding in there,' said Sam.

'Chambers?' Lily shuddered, hoping he didn't mean tombs.

'Elspeth mentioned them. Morven takes an interest in the ancient history of the islands so I'd better check just in case.'

'I'll do the pest house then,' Lily said, suppressing a shiver as the rain hammered down like stair rods.

'OK. Lily . . .' he said, touching her arm gently '. . . thank you. You didn't ask for all this grief when you decided to come here.'

'Thank me when I find her,' she said, with more conviction than she felt inside.

Lily pushed the radio deep into the pocket of her waterproof and scrambled down the hill as fast as she could without tripping over hummocks and brambles. The pest house was a grey blur through the rain. Part of her couldn't imagine anything awful happening in such a peaceful spot as Stark, yet this place had been built for death . . . how horrible!

She moved carefully as the paths were muddy. Occasionally, the shouts of the others drifted to her on the wind. If Morven was hiding out, she must be petrified, being hunted like prey. Unless she was enjoying all the drama. Lily fervently hoped it was the latter.

She stopped a few metres away from the pest house, listening for any sound. A shiver ran through her at the prospect of what she might find. If Morven had been here all

night, even though it was mild, it was slippery and wet . . .
what if she'd tripped and hurt herself?

Or what if she *wasn't* here – or hadn't even made it, trying
to pilot a boat alone? What if she was under the cold sea, like
Lily had been?

'Morven!'

Her desperate shout echoed off the walls but was met
with silence.

'Morven! It's Lily. I know you don't want to be found but
people are worried.'

She lingered outside the pest house, listening for any
hint of another human presence: the rain was almost horizontal, soaking her face. Her legs were red and cold.

Lily shouted again in frustration: 'Morven, for God's
sake, if you can hear me, will you come out before I die of
hypothermia?'

A snort came from the interior of the house.

'It's always about you, isn't it?'

Chapter Twenty-Six

A bedraggled figure appeared in the open doorway. 'You'd better come in.'

Resisting the urge to shout in relief, Lily stepped over the broken stone in the threshold of the building. Morven retreated to the shelter of the stone hearth where there was also a camping stove, a sleeping bag, a metal mug and an empty Pot Noodle tub.

'Don't say you slept here last night?' Lily said.

''Course I did! I've stayed on Stark before.'

'On your own?'

'With Damon. And *no*, there's nothing going on between us. Not like that. We're both seventeen so we could do whatever we wanted to, *if* we wanted to, but – and not that it's any of your business – Damon is gay.' Morven rolled her eyes. 'He's in the closet at home so don't tell anyone, but all his friends know. He can't wait to get to college.'

Lily let this outpouring settle. 'It's none of my business.'

Morven scoffed, 'You could have fooled me. You're out here hounding me.'

'I'm not hounding you. I'm here because I care what happens to you.'

Morven laughed and Lily braced herself for another

tirade but instead the girl said: 'You'd better come under here before you get too wet. The roof's barely there.'

'I don't think I could possibly get any wetter, but thank you.'

Morven sat down, knees tucked to her chest, under the hearth. With some difficulty, Lily squeezed in at the opposite side, relieved to be out of the rain – and ecstatic to have found Morven safe and well.

'You're going to tell Sam and Auntie Elspeth where I am, aren't you?'

'I don't have a choice. They're going out of their minds with worry.'

'Yeah . . .'

Lily thought of the radio in her pocket and went to pull it out.

Morven shrieked, 'Don't call them or I'll run away!'

Yet she couldn't go anywhere, Lily thought, but saw the panicked terror in Morven's face and kept her hands in view.

'OK, I'll hold off calling for a minute, but I *have* to let them know you're safe. They're so worried.'

'Just a minute more,' Morven said, her voice pleading.

'How did you get over here?' Lily asked.

'Damon brought me in his brother's boat before dawn. I met him at the quayside. His brother didn't realise I hadn't told anyone I was coming.'

Lily resisted the urge to scream. 'That sounds dangerous.'

'Not for us! Damon was practically born in a boat. I could pilot an RIB over here if I had my own. Sam won't let me use the *Hydra* or even practise. He says he's afraid something will happen to me. It won't. This proves it.'

'Yeah. I can see that. But why didn't you stay in one of the cottages? Sam said you had a key.'

'Because I was *hiding*,' she said as if Lily was stupid. 'And it wasn't raining when I first got here. And anyway, I forgot the key, didn't I?'

Lily saw the rucksack and camping lantern tucked in a niche under the hearth.

'Looks like you thought of everything else,' she said.

'I did. I can survive without anyone's help. I might just take off and leave. I'll hitch, find a job on the mainland or in London. You started without going to uni.'

'Yes, *but*,' Lily said carefully, 'I had a lot of help and support.'

'Your parents, you mean?' Morven said contemptuously, picking up a pebble.

'Yes, and I'm sure you would too. You must tell Sam – without blaming him – how you feel and what you want to do.'

'He's too busy . . . and that's the thing!' She tossed the pebble across the empty room, hitting the far wall. 'I don't know what I want to do.'

'Don't know, or are worried it'll all go wrong if you try?'

'It would.'

'Why?' Lily asked. 'Tell me what the "it" is that would all go wrong?'

Morven shook her head. 'You'll laugh.'

'Morven,' Lily said patiently, 'I'm the girl who told her

parents I didn't want to apply for uni. I wanted to run a market stall instead. No one had any idea that it would eventually lead to a successful business.'

'I *do* want to go to uni . . . to Falmouth, to study Fine Art.'

'Sounds like a great plan. Why can't you?'

'Because Dad's in the States and might drag me back at any moment, if he cares enough. Because someone's got to pay for it – and I can't ask Sam or Auntie Elspeth to help . . . they don't have the money and I wouldn't take it from them anyway,' she said fiercely.

'OK,' Lily said, aware that everyone else was getting drenched, frantically searching for Morven – yet also aware that this might be her only chance to find out how the girl really felt. 'Let's imagine, let's say in your wildest dreams, that you could afford it. That it wasn't a problem.'

Morven hugged her knees, avoiding Lily's eyes. 'I – I still couldn't.'

'Why not?'

'Because – I – because—' She kicked at an empty Red Bull can. 'I'm not good enough! That's why.'

'OK. You probably won't believe any of what I'm going to say but I'm not here to blow smoke up your arse.'

Morven laughed.

'You know I speak plainly. Too plainly sometimes.'

'Like, yeah!'

'So, I'll be honest. I've seen your work. Before I even knew who'd created the artwork on the walls of my cottage, I was impressed. Very impressed. You have heaps of talent;

your work is original and – affecting. It made me *feel* something. It has a power born of this landscape.'

Morven still wasn't looking at her, but she was listening. Listening hard.

'I would probably stock it at Lily Loves, even now.'

The girl's head snapped up. 'Probably?' she said indignantly.

Lily smiled. 'Ah, some artistic pride. I like it.'

'I don't care if you'd stock it.'

'That's fine, but you do care about going to uni. So, you are good enough, more than good enough, and you must follow your dream. There will be a way,' Lily said, hoping that Sam and Nate would agree. If not, she'd have to intervene. 'You need to have self-belief and to fight for what you want.'

Morven was silent, drawing in the ashes with one finger.

'I could try, I guess.'

'Could?'

'I *will* try. Look, I need to tell you something. It was me who was spooking you.'

Lily let out a mock gasp. 'Really? Who knew?'

'You might have guessed.'

'I didn't. Not until I saw the pebbles. You do have a distinctive style, Morven.'

'Shit.' She heaved a dramatic sigh. 'I'm sorry for scaring you.'

Wow! thought Lily. 'Can I ask why you did it?'

Morven couldn't meet her eyes, then muttered, 'I guess I thought you might be a stuck-up cow, from what I'd read

259

online. And you weren't very friendly when you first arrived at the quay.'

Ouch, thought Lily, remembering her obsession with the phone and rudeness to Sam afterwards.

'So, you disliked me and thought you'd spook me?'

'It wasn't just that!' Morven said then swallowed. 'I suppose I was jealous.'

'Jealous?' Lily exclaimed. 'Why?'

'Because Sam never has time for me. He never has time for anyone, but all of a sudden, he's all over you and everything is about you . . .'

'I'm his guest,' Lily said gently. 'It's his job to look after his guests.'

'Sure it is,' Morven said. 'And I feel stupid now, but I was worried that you and he were getting too close and you'd take him away and I'd be kicked out and have nowhere to go.'

Morven hugged her knees again and cast her gaze downwards. When she looked up, her eyes were shining with unshed tears.

Lily couldn't reply for a moment as a lump formed in her throat. Morven was exposed as a scared, lonely, abandoned child. Lily had experienced similar feelings after the business on the web, and again when it had resurfaced. She had a loving family and friends and colleagues who cared, yet she had felt that no one could understand her situation or what she was going through.

'That would never happen,' she said firmly. 'Never. He's a good guy, your uncle,' she continued, reminding Morven of their relationship. 'He'd move heaven and earth to help you. He's got so many people out looking for you now.'

After a dramatic sigh, clearly calculated to keep Lily in suspense, Morven nodded. 'OK. I suppose he must have been a bit worried.'

'A *bit* worried . . .' Lily restrained herself from swearing and blowing up the fragile bridge she'd built with the girl. Besides, Sam and Elspeth would make her fully aware of the anguish she'd caused, without Lily adding her thoughts. 'The most important thing now is letting Sam and Elspeth and your friends know you're safe. Believe me, they care about you more than you could ever imagine.'

Morven started stuffing rubbish into a bag and Lily joined in, aware of Sam and Elspeth waiting nearby, sick with anxiety. At any moment they might call the police.

'I'm going to call Sam on my radio to say we're heading to the retreat, OK?' she said finally.

'Yes.' Morven nodded, still looking apprehensive.

'Good.' Lily exhaled in relief and pushed herself up to her feet.

'On one condition,' added Morven.

'What's that?'

'You like Sam, don't you?' the girl said, her eyes gleaming with triumph. 'Admit it. You fancy him.'

'Morven!'

'True, though?'

Lily was in turmoil. There was no way she was admitting a personal detail like that to anyone. *Or to herself.*

'Yes, I like him, but today,' she said, deploying a

politician's tactic, 'is about you. Your welfare and your future. So, come on,' she added, 'before your auntie has a heart attack and your uncle goes out of his mind.'

Clutching her rucksack to her chest, Morven started to move towards the door, then said, 'Wait!'

Lily's heart sank. She gripped the radio, about to push send. What now?

'For what it's worth, that Tyrone deserved what you said. He is totally devoid of talent.'

Chapter Twenty-Seven

Lily set off for the retreat with Morven, making her radio call on the way.

'I knew they'd be like this!' the girl cried, seeing her aunt and uncle come hurrying towards her.

'It's because they love you,' Lily said, hoping Morven wouldn't run away again.

Sam grabbed his aunt's arm to steady her when she stumbled on the steep path. Behind them, Lily could see the search party from the gig crew in matching hi-vis vests.

'Oh, shit,' Morven muttered. 'I didn't think it would cause this much trouble.'

'People do care,' Lily said, wanting to point out that 'it' involved a young girl vanishing on a deserted island in the middle of the night.

'Morven! Oh, you silly, *silly* girl! I can't tell you what I've been imagining!'

Elspeth flung herself on Morven, hugging her niece so hard that she had to beg to be released so she could breathe. Sam stood by, stony-faced, though Lily had a strong feeling he was holding back tears.

'Where have you been?' Elspeth cried, still holding the girl. 'Don't tell me you rowed over here on your own in the dark? Oh, I'm so glad you're safe but why did you do such a stupid thing? Didn't you know we'd be out of our minds with worry? Sam's been beside himself.'

The flow of words left little chance for Morven to respond other than in grunts.

Finally, Elspeth released her.

Morven looked at Sam and said: 'I'm sorry. I shouldn't have done it.'

'Then why did you?' he said, before slipping his arm around her shoulders. 'Come on. Let's go to the flat and you can get warm and have something to eat. We can talk about this later.'

'Have you called Dad?' she asked.

'I had to,' Sam said.

She groaned. 'Oh, God. What did he say? Was he worried?'

'He was terrified,' Sam said. 'I haven't seen him cry since Grandpa died.'

Morven burst into tears herself and hugged Sam. 'Please don't say he's coming home?' she cried. 'I don't w–want him to come home because of this. That's not why I did it. I don't want to force him. I want him to come back because he chooses to.'

Sam patted her back. 'I know, sweetheart. Look, I need to get a message to him to say you're safe. You dry off and have a drink while I do that, then we'll go home and you can speak to him yourself.'

He caught Lily's eye over Morven's shoulder and mouthed, 'Thank you.'

Fighting back her own tears of relief, Lily said, 'I'll look after the search party. I bet everyone would love to be out of this rain.'

'Good idea,' Sam said.

Lily could see his shoulders relaxing and the tension ebbing from his taut features.

Elspeth took Morven's hand. 'Come on, trouble. I'll make you hot chocolate.'

A couple of hours later, the four of them were back at Hell Bay. The search team had dispersed to their day jobs, while Sam and Morven were on FaceTime to Nate. Lily had managed to have a very brief word with Sam and had passed on what Morven had told her about wanting to do Fine Art at university.

'It's really none of my business but I thought you ought to know.'

'Thank you for finding her and for persuading her to talk.'

'It was hardly a heart-to-heart but at least she's ready to say what she wants.'

Lily decided to give the family space, heading off to a belated meet-up with Penny to discuss the arrangements for the craft fair. Along the way, she battled pangs of guilt that she'd become so invested in someone else's family yet had drifted so far from her own.

Her journey stirred up other troubling thoughts too: she saw posters on walls and outside the post office, declaring that she was the 'VIP Guest' at the Scilly Summer Craft Fair.

Morven's words came back to her, even though they'd been retracted: *It's all about you.*

Lily didn't want the event to be all about her; far from it. She'd only agreed because Penny had said it would help get people through the door. However, it had also meant she had the perfect excuse to stay a little longer, to see her family – and have a few more days in Sam's company.

'Hello! Over here!'

Penny was waiting outside the community centre.

After asking for an update on Morven and the Teagues, she showed Lily inside. The first surprise was how new and spacious the building it was. The second was finding Damon and a couple of other teens playing pool.

He glanced up and away again quickly. By now, he'd have realised that everyone knew his part in helping Morven spook Lily.

She focused on the task at hand. 'The hall's much larger than I expected,' she said. As well as the pool table, a young family were hitting balls on a table tennis table and there was still room for chill-out spaces around the sides and ends.

'We managed to nab a small Lottery grant,' Penny explained, 'though we raised most of the funds to build it ourselves. Prince William opened it,' she added proudly, showing Lily an area at the rear with bookshelves and bean bags. 'Everyone can use it, holidaymakers as well as islanders. There are books, DVDs and toys to borrow – and loos, of course. We just suggest a small donation in return. It's used for weddings and parties, and we hold a doctor's surgery here once a week,' she went on. 'Rhiannon used to do a weekly clinic too . . . before she left,' Penny added.

'Oh?' Lily hoped to nudge her into further comment but she either didn't take the hint or decided to move the conversation on. 'In a place this isolated, we have to be as self-sufficient as possible.'

'I can see that,' Lily said, not daring to push the topic further.

'There's a kitchen too. If it's fine, we can move some of the stalls outside. There's a man who grows exotic plants for sale.'

'How many stalls have you got?'

'Thirty-four at the last count.'

'Thirty-four! I'd no idea there were that many crafts-people on Scilly.'

Penny beamed. 'We're a very talented bunch and since word got round that you were coming, every maker across the islands wants to be here. With such a big turnout, we're going to charge a two quid entrance fee.' Penny gave a wry smile. 'You were right that notoriety sells.'

'Unfortunately. Let's just hope everyone is disappointed that I'm not the ogre they're expecting.' Lily covered her nerves with a smile though her stomach was churning. 'At least I'll have my brother-in-law and nieces for protection. They're coming over to Stark for the weekend.'

'How lovely,' Penny said. 'Let me show you the play-ground. If your nieces are little, they'll love it.'

After finishing her mini-tour with Penny, Lily took the shortcut behind the post office store on her way back to Hell

Bay House. The view from there over most of the Isles of Scilly was panoramic. She had a reasonable idea of all their names now: St Mary's, Tresco, St Martin's, and even St Agnes to the west, with the Bishop Rock lighthouse marking the far western edge of Britain.

Her stomach tightened as she thought of leaving these huge skies and shimmering seas for the claustrophobic London streets. Or perhaps the decision she had to make about the supermarket deal was making it seem more claustrophobic. She'd had another email from the company that morning, asking her to set up a meeting where they'd discuss it with her team. She hadn't even told her team a deal was on the horizon.

Parking the dilemma for the time being, she walked straight off the path into the rear garden of Hell Bay House. Morven was in the kitchen window, chopping an onion – apparently preparing a recipe from TikTok, judging by the sounds coming from her phone. She didn't notice Lily who went round to the front of the house where a loud buzzing sound led her to Sam.

He had his back turned, giving Lily ten seconds to admire his tanned thighs and the way his biceps flexed as he skimmed a powered cutter along the hedge. His T-shirt was sticking to his back and perspiration glistened on his neck.

Already warm from her walk, her body went into meltdown.

He cut the power and lowered the hedge cutter.

'Hey there,' Lily said, her voice seeming loud in the sudden silence.

He turned, lips parting in surprise, eyes hidden behind Ray-bans. 'Oh . . . hello. I didn't know you were there.'

'I only just got here. Didn't want to scare you in case I caused an accident.'

With a smile, he laid the tool on the grass. 'I should keep your distance, I'm very hot and sweaty.'

I can see that . . . 'Same,' she said. 'I've just walked over the hill from the café.'

His gaze, even through the shades, seemed to burn into her. 'Hot and sweaty suits you.'

A tingle of desire shot through her. 'You too,' she murmured, fighting an urge to leap on him. 'Um . . . I saw Morven cooking in the kitchen.'

Sam rubbed his forehead and seemed thrown off kilter. Had he been fighting the same urge?

'Yeah. She's, er, making dinner for us. Do you mind staying another night here? I don't want to leave her on her own.'

'No, of course not,' Lily said, filled with relief that she wouldn't be alone with him on Stark. With the raging hormones he was stoking in her, she wasn't sure she could contain herself.

'Actually, I'm making dinner for me and my mates.' Morven appeared behind them, her T-shirt spattered with bright green pesto. 'Sorry to disappoint you but Auntie Elspeth said I could have them over for dinner. She's going to her Zumba class and then coming over to stay with me afterwards.'

'I didn't know about this,' Sam said sharply.

'It was Elspeth's idea. She said you'd be keen to get back to Stark and have a rest after all the drama.'

Sam exchanged a glance with Lily, as if to ask how much Morven had heard of their previous flirtatious banter.

'Don't stay here on my account. You need to carry on working. And before you ask, I won't run off again.'

'I'm not sure.'

'Not sure about me running away or about trusting me?'

Lily caught her breath. What a test from Morven: Sam's first, possibly only, chance to show he meant what he said. Lily guessed there was only one answer – but would Sam pass the test?

He smiled. 'If you're sure you don't want us to stay, and Elspeth is going to keep an eye on you, then why not?'

Morven snorted. 'I'll be keeping an eye on *her*. As she keeps telling me, she's not as young as she was,' she added cheekily. 'And I bet you're both dying to get back to Stark. You won't have to worry about the ghost tonight, will you?'

'Don't push it,' Sam said lightly but with a warning edge.

'Yeah, I know. I was a cow. It was shitty of me. I've said sorry to Lily and I'm glad we spoke to Dad. I didn't do it to make him come home but now that he is . . .' She swallowed. 'We can talk prop—'

A loud beeping from the house cut her off. 'Oh my God! That's the smoke alarm,' she shouted, streaking off towards the kitchen.

Sam heaved a sigh. 'I'd better go and see if she's burned the house down.'

'I'll come in, shower and pack my stuff,' Lily said, but

Sam was already jogging through the door, unable to hear her above the screech of the alarm.

With the house safe, and Morven preparing a fresh batch of bruschetta, peace was restored.

Lily had her bag packed again and hopped in the Land Rover to drive to the quay with Sam. On the boat over, he was even quieter than usual. He still looked gorgeous, but exhausted.

'Far be it from me to suggest this to the owner of a wellness retreat, but have you ever thought of indulging in a little self-care yourself?' Lily said, when they docked at Stark. 'You've been working on the cottages for months and worrying about Morven. Why don't you allow yourself some time to relax? I got pasties from the bakery. I thought we'd have those tonight.'

'Pasties sound great.'

After Lily had put them in the fridge, she found Sam outside the reception hub staring out to sea as if looking for the lost land of Lyonesse. He was so deep in thought that he didn't hear her approach.

'OK?' she said, joining him.

He turned quickly, as if startled by her presence. 'Yes. I think so. It's been a hell of a day.'

'It has. You can tell me to mind my own business if you like but can I ask how it went with Nate? Morven seemed more at ease.'

'He's coming back at the end of the month. He's taking unpaid leave from work to spend some time with Morven so they can talk face to face.'

'And Grady?'

'She's staying in LA.'

Wise choice, thought Lily, keeping her opinion to herself. 'It can't be easy for any of you.'

'No. I – when I had to tell Nate that Morven had gone missing, it was one of the hardest things I've ever had to do. I felt I'd failed in the most important job there is, keeping her safe.'

'You didn't fail.'

'No, but if anything *had* gone catastrophically wrong, I don't know what I'd have done.' He laughed bitterly. 'The irony is, Nate said he didn't blame me. He blamed himself for going to LA and then not making a decision about her sooner.'

Privately, Lily agreed with Nate's assessment, yet only replied: 'Morven wants to go to Falmouth but she's too afraid of failing. Did she tell you?'

'Yes, kind of. It's hard to get across that she'll probably be afraid of failing at something her whole life. That you have to feel the fear.'

'And do it anyway?' Lily offered.

'Yeah. Though that's easier said than done.'

'You've renovated the retreat. It's almost ready to open – properly. You've survived your first guest.'

'Yes, but you almost didn't survive us.'

'Yet I'm still here and I know how hard it can be to decide on the right path to take, in business and in life. I've got it wrong before, and I probably will again.'

And now, there was an added load on her mind: Sam and her growing feelings for him.

Tonight, however, her main task was to be present. With him . . . and at the weekend, with her family and at the craft fair.

Reality would come around soon enough.

'Are *you* OK?'

His fingers brushed her forearm, making her skin tingle. He'd been watching her, watching over her . . . tender and strong. He was exactly what she needed right now and that scared her because she'd have to do without his support in a few days' time. She'd be on her own as she had been before: an inaccessible island, lost in a stormy sea.

'Yes, fine,' she said, a heartbeat away from kissing him again. 'It's been a long day but I'm glad Morven is safe.'

'Me too.' Without warning, he dropped his hand and picked up their empty bottles.

'We both deserve a night off from worrying. Let's heat up these pasties and see what I can find to go with them.'

'Sounds like a plan,' Lily murmured, feeling bereft. Once again, he'd been about to get close to her yet had pulled back.

Lily might be opening up but as for her host . . . with only a few days left on the island, she'd started to question if she could ever break through the rock-hard shell he'd built around him. If she would ever know the real Sam.

Chapter Twenty-Eight

Bryher Quay was bustling when Sam loaded up the *Hydra* on Thursday morning with supplies for his weekend visitors. Over the past couple of days, he and Lily had worked super hard to finish the decorating and fittings.

He was quietly proud when she'd declared it looked 'sparkling and gorgeous' for their special guests.

It seemed strange to see Lily's face on posters all over Bryher, advertising the craft fair. It reinforced the fact that she was a minor celebrity and brought home to him how impossible it would be that a mere mortal like himself could ever make her happy.

Every time he was tempted to open up, to tell her he'd started to have feelings for her that went way beyond host for guest, the scars of the past yanked him back to reality: a woman from such a different world, only here for a matter of days . . . He cared too much for her to start a passing fling. It was for the best that he keep his distance entirely.

'Wait. I'm coming back to Stark with you.'

He'd been so lost in thought, he hadn't noticed Morven arrive.

'You want to come over?' he said, setting down a crate of

beer and wine on the stones of the quay. 'Haven't you spent enough time on Stark recently?' He couldn't resist it.

'Ha ha! Soo funny, Uncle Sam.' Morven curled her lip. 'I said I'd help with the cleaning and changeovers, which is why I'm here.'

'I thought you went off the idea when Lily turned up?'

'Yeah. But her family are coming so you'll need the extra help. Besides . . .' Morven looked sheepish. 'I thought she'd be a pain but she's not as horrible as she first seemed.'

'Thanks. I'll pass on your compliment to our guest.'

'She's not a guest though, is she?' Morven said. 'She's kind of . . .'

'A friend,' Sam supplied.

Morven snorted. 'Yeah. *Sure* she's your friend.'

'I meant *your* friend.'

'Stop winding me up!' Morven cried in frustration. 'Now the cottages are ready, we'll have real guests soon plus her family. You'll need help with the cleaning and making the beds so I'm offering again.'

Sam relented. Morven had stood enough teasing. 'That would be great but are you absolutely sure? I have advertised for a housekeeper but they'll need an extra pair of hands too. They can't be expected to deal with everything.'

'Yeah. I'll do it because as a cleaner I won't have to see the guests and I need to save up some money. And you need the help while I'm here on the islands for the summer . . . and maybe next year until I start university next September. *If* I do go,' she said, deflating suddenly. 'Because I might be somewhere else.'

Sam folded his arms. 'Wow. That's the best job application I've ever heard.'

Morven pointed her finger at him. 'Don't push it, Uncle Sam.'

'OK. Yes, please, I'd appreciate your help,' he said, touched by her plan to save up for uni. Nate *had* to realise how badly his daughter wanted to study Fine Art but the decision was out of Sam's hands. 'But please try not to call me uncle. It makes me feel old.'

Morven smirked. 'You're old enough.'

Sam rolled his eyes, quietly glad she was her cheeky self again.

'Oh, look, here she is.' Morven flipped a thumb in the direction of the café where Lily was walking through the tea garden, laptop bag over her shoulder and a box in her arms. On this fine midsummer day, the sun was hot on any bare skin and Lily's cheeks had turned a nice shade of pink, not that he'd tell her. In a white vest top and her denim shorts, she looked as if she belonged on Bryher.

'Hello!' she said, breathing hard. 'Elspeth insisted on us having these sandwiches for lunch. Bruce made me have this cauliflower – don't ask me why – and Ivanka kind of strong-armed me into buying a jar of greengage jam from the shop. I don't even like jam . . .'

'I do,' Morven said, swiping the jar from Lily's box.

'That's lucky,' she said.

'Thanks,' Sam said, taking the box from Lily, thinking that she'd become part of island life faster than he would if he'd been a stranger. From initially loathing the place, she was now living the dream ... the fantasy. It was hard to believe he only had a few more days left with her. How long would it take for this escape from reality – this retreat from her real life – to wear off?

Morven climbed aboard after them.

Sam reversed away from the jetty. 'Will you want a lift home after you've helped or are you staying on Stark in Samphire?' he asked his niece, who was lounging on the rear seat.

'God, I'm not staying with you two. It's Nazim's birthday and I'm going to her party at the Tresco Inn. And before you ask, her mum has booked a jet boat to take everyone from Bryher there and back and she's going to drive me home to Hell Bay House after. Auntie Elspeth knows all about it in case you want to double-check my alibi.'

Lily hid a giggle. Sam rolled his eyes. 'OK. I'll bring you home for five, if that suits you?'

'I suppose that'll be OK. I'll need to get changed after helping with the cottages.'

On the way to Stark, above the engine noise, he caught snatches of conversation between Morven and Lily. They were talking about collaging, though much of it was lost on him.

He didn't see himself as creative unless you counted building walls and installing roofs. The construction part of his job was a means to an end, until he could reach the wood-work part of the project. It gave him deep satisfaction to design the built-in window seats and find the perfect pieces of timber for the shelves. He could lose himself while he carved and planed and fitted.

He wasn't about to have a stall at the craft fair, however.

His main pleasure on this trip was to see Morven engaging with him and Lily. He just hoped Nate didn't let her down. He wasn't sure how she'd react if his brother announced he was taking her off to LA to live with him and Grady. Sam couldn't get that video call out of his mind: Nate's shock, his tears and Grady's reaction: 'What the actual fuck has she done now?' As if Morven was only an irritation to be borne, not a potential step-daughter.

When they reached Stark, she was still talking happily to Lily.

'I could show you where I find the pebbles and shells. I know all the best beachcombing spots on Bryher and Stark.'

He winced. No wonder Morven knew Stark intimately after her antics . . . yet Lily answered her without apparent irony.

'OK. I'd like that.'

Sam sighed. He wasn't sure how much cleaning and bed changing would be done, though he supposed he should be grateful that the two of them were bonding over something rather than sparring with each other.

Sam spent the afternoon varnishing the woodwork in Starfish. Contrary to his expectations, Morven had helped clean the cottage, then she and Lily styled the bed with cushions and added a vase of fresh flowers grown in the garden at Hell Bay House.

'Is cauliflower cheese OK for dinner?' Lily asked when

Sam walked into reception after dropping Morven back home. 'Hope so, 'cos I've already made it.'

She showed him a dish with the veg smothered in a cheese sauce.

'Er . . . yes,' Sam said, hoping his stomach wouldn't rumble too loudly. 'I could do some steak to go with it. There are some in the fridge.'

'I spotted them.' She chuckled. 'Don't worry, I need more than cauliflower cheese too.'

He exhaled. 'I'm very glad you said that. You don't have to cook everything though.'

'I know I don't have to, but I want to. My recipe portfolio is expanding. I might book myself on a cookery course when I get home. You could offer courses here too. I've been thinking about it. Cookery, foraging, yoga, creative writing. There are so many talented people on the islands who could be tutors and you could charge a premium to the guests who attend.'

'That is a very good idea,' Sam said, feeling so comfortable in her presence that she could be his business partner – more even? What was happening here? Lily cooking for him and him cooking for her . . . her waiting at home for him as if they were living together.

He was thinking back to Aaron's comments and a veiled remark from the pub landlady, and to a conversation he'd had with Elspeth that morning.

'People are bound to gossip. You're alone on that island with her every night. Be careful, love. I like Lily a lot but don't get your heart broken again.'

'There's zero danger of that.'

Sam snapped back to the present. 'Let's get these steaks going,' he said more gruffly than he'd intended.

By dinnertime, a mizzle had blown in so they ate inside.

'I hope it clears up for Saturday. I checked the forecast and it's looking dry.'

He smiled. 'The forecasts don't mean much here. It was supposed to be sunny today but Elspeth's seaweed was damp this morning and she reckons she knew the rain was coming.'

'That doesn't give me a great deal of faith to be honest.'

He laid his knife and fork down. 'Rory said the Met Office long-range predicted a dry weekend.'

'Now *that* I can buy into. Penny has every eventuality covered but I so want the girls to see Stark at its best.'

'As opposed to not being able to see it at all?' he said. 'I'm sorry it was crap when you arrived. No wonder you were pissed off.'

'You couldn't help the weather.' Her eyes gleamed with mischief. 'Though you weren't exactly a ray of sunshine yourself.'

Sam remembered how tense and nervous he'd felt at taking in a guest when the retreat wasn't ready.

'I suppose I know you well enough now to admit I regretted accepting the booking pretty much from the moment I put the phone down.'

She rested her hand on her chin. 'Why did you, then?'

'Richie said you'd had a horrible time and were desperate for a break and I was gung-ho enough to think I could pull it off. I always think I can get more done than I have time for.'

'You're as bad as me, trying to do everything yourself. No man is an island . . .'

He'd cut himself off since Rhiannon had left. 'No, and I think I've realised that lately.'

He hovered on the verge of telling Lily that she was the reason he'd looked up at the sky again, instead of living inside the walls of his darkest thoughts. He'd realised that he'd been through a bereavement – a double one.

'After the kayak thing, you talked about loss.'

Lily's lips parted in surprise.

'I said I hadn't lost anyone, not in the same way as you, but perhaps that's not quite true.' The words froze in his throat, words he'd never said to anyone.

'Rhiannon was pregnant, but she had a miscarriage. The baby – our baby – died.'

'Oh, Sam.' Lily spoke softly. 'I am so very sorry. Truly.'

Her sympathy brought a lump to his throat. 'No one else knows she was ever pregnant.' Even as he spoke, he felt astonished that he was pouring out the most painful details of his life to someone he'd known for mere weeks, when he couldn't tell the loved ones he'd known for years.

'I'm here to listen,' she said. 'If you want to talk.'

His stomach flipped. In Lily's eyes, he glimpsed the good, kind person beneath the hard exterior shining through. She'd already shown him so much of her true self, she deserved some honesty from him.

'Rhiannon was about eight weeks gone and on a training

course in Truro so I wasn't even with her when she lost the baby,' he said, remembering the sense of helplessness that had added to his agony. 'The weather was bad – thick fog for days – so it was a while before she could fly home. She went through that on her own, apart from her colleagues being with her.'

'When was this?'

'First week of January last year. Not being able to get to her, to comfort her, was . . . awful.'

Sam looked down. He hadn't realised that Lily was holding his hand. He didn't let hers go.

'It must have been absolutely terrible for you,' she said.

'It was bad.' Torture, he remembered, to be trapped and unable to reach her. 'To be honest, I'd never felt more like leaving the islands forever.' He'd met her afterwards at St Mary's airport on a raw grey day when you could barely tell where the sea and sky met.

'She wanted a child so much. I did too, but it had taken longer than either of us had expected and Rhiannon blamed herself. When she finally conceived and then we lost the baby, it felt doubly cruel.'

'Life can be *so* cruel, without reason . . .'

Lily understood, Sam knew it. 'When we got home to Hell Bay, I told Rhiannon that we still had each other. I reassured her that the two of us would always be enough if we weren't able to have kids in the future. We were enough . . . enough for *me*.'

The pain of what happened next returned, almost as

sharp as when Rhiannon had first delivered the news that had landed like a bomb in his life.

'A few days later, she told me that just us wasn't enough for *her*. She said that she'd been having second thoughts about our relationship for a while and the baby had masked her doubts. She'd swept them aside when she thought we'd be a family, hoping that they'd go away once the child was born, but with only the two of us to focus on again . . .'

Sam broke off, to compose himself for a moment. 'So,' he managed, 'we split up.'

'Oh, Sam, that must have been so tough while you were still coming to terms with losing the baby.'

'It was very hard, I'll admit. I wasn't enough for her on my own and to realise she'd been having doubts for a while . . . I didn't know what to say or do. I felt like I was drowning, not knowing which way up I was, how to get through each day.'

'All of those feelings are completely understandable.'

Comforted by Lily's empathy, he took a breath and then went on. 'So she left. While she'd been away on the course, a friend of hers had taken a job in Adelaide and mentioned how badly they needed more nurses. Rhiannon decided to leave too. Nothing I could do would change her mind and she asked me to respect her decision so I stopped trying. Three weeks later she was on her way to Australia.'

'That's a huge change to deal with. So sudden, two losses on top of each other,' Lily said. 'You must have felt helpless and abandoned.'

'Both. I offered to go to Australia with her so we could give things another shot but she insisted I mustn't try to go after her.' Rhiannon's words came back to him again – he saw her face, tender and sad but resolute.

'Please don't. I need to make a fresh start on my own, far away from here. I could never rip you out of the place you belong to. You're as much a part of the landscape as the granite or the sand on the beach, Sam.'

'I am so sorry.' Lily squeezed his hand.

'I've been grieving, I suppose,' he said, still amazed he'd told her so much. 'And I let it go on too long.' He thought again of the flowers he kept in his room, ones he'd picked from a small meadow on Bryher to honour the loss of his child. A lump formed in his throat.

'Sam, if I can tell you one thing, it's that there's no time limit on grief. Be kinder to yourself.' She smiled briefly. 'Oh, no, listen to me acting like a self-help guru. Next thing you know, I'll be writing a book about how a near-death experience helped me to live again. *Actually*,' she said, tapping her finger against her lips and musing, 'that's not the *worst* idea I've ever had.'

Lily drew a smile from him, like water from a dry well. In the midst of wallowing in his misery, she'd turned on the sunshine.

'I'm joking,' she said, suddenly serious again and no longer holding his hand. 'You did all you could. You said you'd have been ready to leave Scilly if Rhiannon had asked you to.'

'I was desperate. I have travelled and worked abroad. It

was a fantastic experience but I love it here. Rhiannon was right, she was the wise one. I *am* part of the landscape. I would never have been happy to live away from here.' Even as he said it, he realised he was sabotaging any possibility of a relationship with Lily, however remote that had been before he'd told her about the baby.

'I now understand why,' she said. 'It's very beautiful. More than that, it's extraordinary. Unlike any place I've ever seen – not that I've seen that much of the world outside airports or hotel rooms.'

'Is that one more thing on the agenda for Project New Lily?' he asked, glad to shift the focus to her again. He felt wrung out.

Her eyes lit up. 'Yes, it is and the list is growing longer every day. Learning to cook, spending more time with the family, going to the gym, travelling the world, running the business. I can't do it all . . .'

'I think you could do anything you wanted.' He squeezed her hand. 'You're an extraordinary person, Lily. Unlike anyone I've ever met.'

He was no longer holding her hand. He was holding her in his arms and kissing her. Not a brush of the lips, a 'did-that-really-happen' moment – a deep kiss that made his spine tingle and wiped away every resolution he'd made not to reveal his feelings for her.

He took her hand and she seemed to know exactly what he wanted without him speaking. As the soft rain fell, he led her out of the door and to her cottage.

She stopped at the door.

PHILLIPA ASHLEY

'Wow.'

'Yeah.'

'What is this, Sam?'

'I don't know,' he said. 'You tell me?'

'It's . . . risky. Believe me, I *want* to walk through that door with you and stay in your bed all night. I *want* to wake up with you.'

His heart sank. 'But . . . there's a "but" waiting, isn't there?'

'I don't want to hurt you. I don't want to hurt either of us.'

His stomach knotted with dread. It was a little too late for this. He didn't want her to be kind to him. He'd already decided that he would take the consequences of stepping closer, of putting his hand near the fire again.

'You had your heart broken when Rhiannon left the islands,' Lily said. 'I'll be doing the same thing come Monday. I care too much for you to let this become something that would hurt you all over again. It's better if we leave it like this before the same thing happens again.'

'So, it's me you're thinking of?' he said, feeling numb with shock. 'Just *my* heart?'

'I don't want either of us to end up with a broken heart. We've both been through so much, I don't think I could take any more pain. You're not going to leave the retreat you've put so much into building. I'm not going to leave the business I've put so much into building.' She stopped to draw breath then went on, 'Please understand that doesn't mean

286

we don't care for each other, but we also don't want to give up on our personal passions – and neither of us should. That's not a good basis for any relationship.'

With that, she broke away, hurrying into her cottage before he could even reply.

Chapter Twenty-Nine

With enormous relief, Lily spotted the plane heading out of clouds towards the sunshine at St Mary's Airport.

Boy, she needed some light to focus on after the gloom of the previous evening. Had she been right to end the relationship with Sam before it had even begun? Or should they just have slept together and been satisfied with that?

She'd had little rest, turning the words she'd said to him over and over, wondering endlessly if she'd made the right decision to push him away. Surely it would have been worse for both of them to have started a relationship that might end in failure?

Even if they could overcome the physical distance between them – and solve all the practicalities – Sam sounded as if he was still grieving for Rhiannon and clinging on to the past. Lily might simply be a distraction for him – a brief moment of solace.

After finally finding someone she felt a deep connection with, why did it have to be a man who lived in another world and whose heart was still in the possession of another woman? It had felt kinder to use their differences in lifestyle and commitments as an excuse for a clean break.

The plane came into view, seemingly metres above the

cliff at the end of the runway, wings wobbling. Before she had time to think nervously about its precious cargo, it had dropped onto the tarmac and braked hard.

A minute later, the steps unfolded and Étienne and the girls were climbing down them. They spotted Lily immediately. Once they were off the runway, the twins broke away, pigtails flying in the breeze.

'Auntieeee Lileeeeeee!'

They ran into the terminal and launched themselves on her.

'Hello, you two! It's so wonderful to see you.' Lily felt emotion clog her throat. Her spirits soared. She'd always have Tania and Amelie, her beloved nieces. Nothing could ever change that.

Amelie, keen to be on the move as usual, danced around her while Tania gripped her hand like a vice.

Étienne arrived, face wreathed in smiles. 'I think it's safe to say they're pleased to see you. Thank God we're here. I don't think any of us has had much sleep since I told them we were coming for a visit.'

'Is this Stark?' Amelie said. 'Where's your cottage? Where's the café?'

A small voice beside her murmured, 'And the playground?'

'They've been on Google Earth,' Étienne said with a grimace. 'A lot.'

'Clever girls. The playground's on Bryher, darling.' Lily squeezed Tania's hand and addressed them both: 'I promise we'll visit it tomorrow.'

She was rewarded with little skips from the pair of them.

Finally, Étienne got a look in, kissing Lily's cheek. 'I hardly recognised you.'

'Oh, you're just saying that.'

'No, it's true. You've stepped out into the sun. What magic has this place worked on you in two weeks?'

'It's not magic. Only the sunshine, some fresh air and – er – exercise. You're a doctor, you know how it works.'

'It's more than that. Girls, there are our cases. Shall we collect them?'

While the girls retrieved purple and yellow wheelies from the shortest conveyor belt in the history of the world, Étienne smiled. 'This airport is like the little ones in French Polynesia. Look, there are even agapanthus and proteas.'

'It is beautiful and everything is bijou,' Lily said, when he'd picked his case from the belt. The girls skipped out of the terminal to a pick-up area where passengers were being shepherded onto waiting minibuses.

'Do we get to go in a bus?' Amelie asked, hyper enough to jump on the first vehicle wherever it might end up.

'No,' Lily said. 'We're waiting for Rory. He keeps a Land Rover on St Mary's and he'll take us to the quay where Sam's boat is waiting to take us to Stark.'

'Land Rovers? Boats to Stark?' Étienne looked delighted. 'I can barely believe it. You know, flying over the islands, I really thought I might be back in Mo'orea . . . the turquoise sea, the white beaches, and now the flowers and the boats ferrying us to tiny paradises.'

Lily patted his back. 'You wait until you feel the

temperature of the water, then you'll know you're not in the South Pacific. Let's go. Rory's just arrived.'

The journey to Stark was suitably exciting. The Land Rover trundled around country lanes into Hugh Town with its shops and galleries, and finally onto the cobbled quay.

Everyone thanked Rory and he let them out.

'That car smells funny,' Tania whispered to Lily while Étienne was unloading their bags, with Amelie helping.

'It's fish, sweetheart. Rory is a fisherman.'

'I don't like fish. Daddy says it's very good for us but I only like fish fingers and he says they're not proper fish.' Tania slipped her hand into Lily's again. 'Will we have to eat fish on the island?'

'Not if you don't want to,' said Lily. 'I promise.'

'Hi there!' Sam called from below. While they were unloading, the *Hydra* had come alongside the quay.

'That's our boat? Nice,' said Étienne.

'I'll give him a hand,' Lily said.

Leaving the twins with their father, she skipped down the steps onto the pontoon and helped Sam tie up.

Seeing him amidst her family was a shock. Normally she had no problem introducing people to each other. She'd done it at scores of meetings and conferences but this was different. Once again, she had the sense of her life not being quite real.

Étienne was a strikingly handsome man, yet she had only ever had brotherly feelings towards him.

Whereas Sam, tall, rugged and impossibly gorgeous, sent her stomach into a full gymnastics routine. That could be down to nervousness, of course. Would they get on? Would bringing her family here reinforce the fact that she didn't belong? Would Étienne realise how she felt about Sam?

Suddenly, Étienne and he were talking about boats and she hadn't even introduced them properly.

'Great boat. Looks like it has some oomph?'

'Yeah, I need it round here.' Sam's reply held more than a touch of pride.

'I had a fast RIB on Mo'orea. Ashore, a wrecked old Deux Chevaux van. No one cares about the car. It's your boat that counts there.' Étienne sighed. 'I miss that in London.'

Sam laughed. 'Wait until you see the wreck I keep for chugging around Bryher.'

Lily was momentarily superfluous to requirements and loved it. If she'd been worried that Sam might retreat into his shell because of their discussion the previous evening, there'd been no need. *Of course* she'd been wrong, she thought with a jolt. Sam would never let his personal feelings stop him from welcoming her family. Problem was, she liked him all the more for that.

'Come on, let's get on board,' she said, gathering the twins to her. 'Be really careful climbing on. I'll help you.'

Twenty bone-shaking, ear-shattering minutes later, during which time Sam had allowed Étienne to briefly take the wheel while the girls had screeched in excitement and terror, they were slipping through the rocks towards Stark jetty.

'You never let me do that,' Lily accused Sam while they were tying up.

'You never asked. You can once we're in the open water. I was keeping a close eye on Étienne.'

'I'll hold you to that,' she said, before realising she might not have the chance.

Étienne had helped the girls off the boat and they skipped ahead up the path.

He hung back. 'So, this is the magical island,' he said. 'Where the ancient ghosts still wander.'

'Where have you read that?'

'I can Google too, in my occasional coffee breaks,' he said. 'It does have an atmosphere . . . like Raiatea.'

'It's not the centre of civilisation and culture,' Lily said, referencing the island where Étienne had been born. 'Don't get too excited.'

'That's okay. I'm mainly hoping to get some sleep,' he said, nodding at the girls who were bouncing around outside the reception hub. 'Though I don't think I've got a cat in hell's chance.'

As it turned out, Étienne was wrong. After dinner, Sam and Lily took him and the girls for a little wander towards the highest point of the island. It was a warm evening, although the horizon was flecked with hundreds of clouds that looked like a sea monster's scales, according to Tania.

'They're cirrocumulus clouds,' Sam explained.

The girls tried to get their tongues around the word for half a minute then dissolved into giggles.

'Will they rain on us?' Amelie asked.

'No. They're not heading in our direction – and anyway, they usually don't mean rain.'

'Good. I don't want rain for the craft fair,' Lily said.

'I think it will stay fine,' Sam said.

Amelie yawned. 'I'm tired, Daddy. Can I go to bed early?'

Étienne let out a gasp.

'I'm not tired *at all*,' Tania declared but tugged at Lily's hand. 'Will you read us a story, Auntie Lily?'

'About the *ghosts*,' Étienne mouthed to Lily, causing Sam to suppress laughter.

Lily shot Étienne a glare. 'Come on, let's go back to your cottage and get ready for bed. Then I'll read to you.'

'I'll join you in a moment. Sam said he'd show me the pest house.'

'What's the pest house?' Tania chimed in.

'It's where he keeps his concrete mixer,' Étienne said while Sam smiled wryly.

Lily shook her head at the fib but was relieved. None of them wanted to be embroiled in tales of death and disease right before bedtime.

'Come on, then. Let's go home.'

It was funny, she thought, how 'home' became a movable feast when you were on holiday. A tent, a caravan, a cottage on a remote islet. Did Sam think of the flat on Stark as his home – or Hell Bay House? She immediately answered her own question. Almost certainly Hell Bay House.

Her thoughts drifted back to the previous evening: Rhiannon had decided Sam would never be happy anywhere else, that he could never change.

Yet Lily herself had changed . . .

The twins soon claimed her full attention. Herding them into pyjamas, persuading them not to eat all the chocolates in the hamper at once or trampoline on the bed, was a major feat.

'Can we have *Rainbow Fairies*, please?' Tania asked when they'd finally brushed their teeth.

Amelie produced her own book. 'I want *Unicorn Academy*.'

'Tell you what. Why don't we have a bit of each?'

Lily was reading from the unicorn book when Étienne joined them and by then the twins were half-asleep. She wondered what he and Sam had talked about: boats, probably, or power tools . . . or plague and leprosy.

He took the book. 'I can take over now.'

'We want Auntie Lily . . .' Amelie said sleepily.

Tania emitted a little snore.

'I think it's time to sleep,' he said softly. 'I'll finish this story and let Auntie Lily get her beauty sleep.'

'Why does she need a beauty sleep?' Amelie said.

'It's just a saying. An English saying. *Elle est parfaite*.'

'I'm very far from *parfaite*, as you well know. That was Cara.'

'No one is perfect, not even your sister,' Étienne said, with a bitterness that took Lily by surprise. He must be missing Cara very badly tonight. He took the book from her. 'Now, Sam could do with some help clearing up after us.'

Lily scoffed. 'I can't believe he would have said anything like that.'

'I deduced it. Like Sherlock Holmes.'

'Sure you did. I will go and offer, though.'

'I may just turn in early. Read a book myself. I'm knackered.'

'OK. See you tomorrow.'

'It will come round soon enough with these two in charge.'

When Lily returned to the hub, Sam had already cleared away and loaded the dishwasher. Alone with him again, she wasn't sure how to approach him. Last night had changed everything.

'Coffee?' he said. 'I can make one for Étienne as long as he doesn't complain that it's not like the good French stuff.'

'I think he might have fallen asleep already. I think he's shattered.'

'Holding down a job as an A&E consultant and a single parent? No wonder.'

'They have the nanny to help,' Lily said, sitting down opposite Sam. 'But you're right. It's tough parenting and having a full-time job. However old the kids are,' she added. 'I suspect Morven causes twice the angst the girls do.'

'Yeah. She does. Did. Hopefully . . . and I mean this in the best way because I do love her . . . she will soon be causing Nate the angst, though less of it since she decided to admit she wants to go to Falmouth next year. Thanks for helping her be able to tell us.'

'I didn't do anything.'

'You did. You managed to break down the wall somehow.'

'I didn't break anything down. Morven was tired, cold and desperate. I only happened to find her first and be someone outside of the family. To be honest, I'm amazed she didn't chuck her camping stove at me.'

'No, you're wrong. You're good with people.'

Lily laughed. 'Tell that to my army of Internet trolls.'

'You're doing it again. Deflecting a compliment.'

'Am I?' Lily said.

'And you shouldn't.'

'No, I shouldn't,' she said. 'OK. I'm good with some people, most of the time.' She remembered what Étienne had said: *No one is perfect, not even your sister*, and felt a ripple of unease. It had been an emotional time for her, for Sam, for the family. No wonder everyone was on edge.

'I think I'll have an early night. Very early,' she qualified. 'I've got a big day tomorrow.'

'You'll be fine,' he said firmly, with the confidence of someone who cares about you and can't imagine why others wouldn't feel the same. 'In fact, you'll be brilliant.'

Lily felt her cheeks glow.

'Thank you. I must admit, I feel a bit nervous at being on show after all the furore with the TV show and the press coverage of the accident. I wouldn't admit this to anyone else, but I've no idea what the reaction will be. I'm sure some people will think I'm taking over, like Morven did.'

'We'll be there, cheering you on. If you can win over Morven, you can work your magic on anyone.'

Even you? she thought, half regretting she hadn't taken things further after all.

297

'What time do you need to be at the community centre?' he asked, switching to practical matters – fortuitously, Lily decided, as her resolve was in danger of wobbling.

'It opens at ten but I said I'd arrive at nine-thirty.'

'We should leave here at nine, then. Is that too early for the twins?'

'Considering how hyper they are, I doubt it.'

'Early breakfast and we'll set off.'

Lily felt a rush of affection for him and was touched at the way he was tying himself in knots to boost her confidence.

'Sounds good. See you in the morning.'

She walked back to the cottage, with the sun in the background slipping towards a sea of liquid gold. It was an impossibly romantic evening. However, at least tonight she'd had the girls and Étienne as the best possible chaperones. Soon, she and Sam would be out of temptation's way.

Chapter Thirty

There was no sign of Penny when Lily walked into the community hall the next morning, although it felt as if practically every other islander was there.

The hall was packed with stalls and, as the weather was fine, several more had been set up on the sports field, including a garden ornament-maker, a plant stall and a coffee van housed in a converted horsebox.

Disarming smile pinned in place, Lily strode in, hoping Penny would appear from one of the many doors leading off the room.

'Can I help you?'

Instead of Penny, a formidable-looking woman in beige hiking shorts and a rugby shirt bore down on Lily and barred her way. 'We're not open yet. The fair doesn't start until ten. You'll have to wait your turn.'

The way the woman's voice carried, Lily was reminded of a fog horn.

'I'm not a visitor, I'm Penny's guest,' she said, holding out her hand. 'I'm Lily.'

Ignoring her polite gesture, the woman knitted her bushy eyebrows. 'Lily? Lily who? Penny never mentioned you.'

'Lily Harper. My name is on the posters.'

'Oh. Ah. I see.' The woman looked her up and down as if appraising a horse. 'My mistake. You're not as glamorous as I expected.'

'Why did you expect me to be glamorous?' Lily asked, amused and annoyed in equal measure. She'd agonised over what to wear from her small holiday wardrobe. In the end, she'd opted for a summer dress that Cara had once said she looked nice in, and a new pair of canvas sneakers.

'Oh, I don't know,' the woman boomed. 'I suppose I had an image ingrained in my mind. Penny said you'd been a celebrity judge on that craft show. I expected lots of eye-lashes, fake tan – that sort of thing.'

'Did you actually *see* the show?' Lily asked politely.

The woman snorted like a stallion. 'My God, no. I never watch that sort of thing. Don't watch much TV. Too busy unless it's *Countryfile*. Even that's gone downhill now. I'm Muriel, by the way. Muriel Cadogan, i/c visitor relations. It's my job to make everyone feel welcome.'

Lily almost snorted herself. 'Important job. Have you seen Penny?' She tried to look past Muriel's imposing person. 'I'm meant to be meeting her.'

'Muriel!'

Before she could reply, Penny jogged up, a little pink in the face. 'I see you've met Lily! Isn't it wonderful to see her?'

Muriel curled her lip dismissively. 'I'll leave you to it, then. I've got to read the riot act to the stewards. Stop them from letting any strays in before we open.' She checked her watch. 'In twenty-three minutes.'

Muriel sallied off, chest puffed out like a galleon with all its sails billowing.

Penny gave a little sigh. 'Oh, dear. I am *so* sorry I wasn't here. There was a problem with the PA system but it's sorted now. Was Muriel very terrifying? She can be rather intimidating.'

'She was a bit . . . forceful,' Lily said, laughing. 'But I can cope.'

'Phew. Good for you. Muriel always takes charge of logistics. She's really not the best candidate for customer relations so I try to encourage her to stick to putting up ropes and organising queues. Hopefully, you'll feel more welcome from now on. And if you've survived Muriel, the rest should be easy!' Penny beamed encouragingly. 'Come on. The other organisers are dying to meet you.'

Lily wouldn't have said 'dying' exactly, but there was a definite curiosity among the half-dozen or so volunteers who were helping at the fair. Unlike Muriel, they'd all seen the *Great British Craft Show* and a few looked wide-eyed with terror that Lily might suddenly pass a verdict on their hair or shoes. Evidently, she still had a *lot* of work to do before she convinced some people that she wasn't the ogre who had been portrayed in the TV programme.

On the other hand, she could only be herself.

By the time she'd met everyone and run through her duties – a very few words to launch the show, generally staying around to chat to people and then shaking hands at the prize-giving – the fair was almost ready to open and a queue of punters snaked down the side of the building.

Muriel's voice boomed out from the entrance doors.

'By my watch, it's time to open. Manpreet, you can unbar the doors and let in the hordes!'

Lily didn't see Manpreet but imagined her being trampled by hundreds of visitors eager to get first dibs on the ceramic dolphins, paintings and coasters adorning the stalls.

Moments later, people swarmed in, buzzing around like excited bees, and the noise swelled to deafening proportions.

Penny ushered Lily into the kitchen where several volunteers were already filling cups of instant coffee with hot water from an urn. There were hundreds of cakes and biscuits on trays.

'We ought to do the official bit quite soon, if you don't mind?' Penny said. 'Get it over with now we've got the punters inside.'

Lily's stomach did a somersault. It seemed so long since she'd addressed an audience outside of a small business meeting. She'd avoided all requests for TV and radio interviews since the show. She felt very warm and sweat broke out on the small of her back.

'Lily? Is that OK with you?' Penny asked, a panicked look in her eyes.

'Oh. Yes. Yes, good idea,' Lily said, feigning enthusiasm. 'Get it done now.'

'Great, we'll do it from the dais,' she said, leading Lily out of the kitchen towards a raised stage area constructed from the kind of wooden boxes you'd find in a school gym.

Lily followed Penny onto the stage. Some people turned their heads, but most were busy browsing the stalls.

'There's a microphone,' Penny said, picking up a lead and mic from its stand. 'I'll introduce you and then you speak.'

Lily's skin crawled. A *microphone*. 'It's not on yet, is it?' she whispered, feeling clammy and a little light-headed.

'Not yet. I promise I'll let you know. I'll say: "Please give a warm welcome to our very special guest, Lily Harper, founder of the fantastic online craft and gift brand, Lily Loves." And then you'll be live. Is that OK?'

'Oh.' Lily nodded, fighting to regain her composure. 'That's fine. Thank you. I just didn't want to . . . make a faux pas.'

'I quite understand,' Penny said gently, although Lily wasn't sure anyone could understand the humiliation and horror of being caught saying something she shouldn't in front of millions of people.

'You will be wonderful, you know. Look how many people have come to see you. There's no way we'd have had such a turnout without you.'

Lily did look. There must now be well over a hundred people in the room, probably more. Her heart was still beating far too fast and sweat trickled down her back. Why had she agreed to this?

At the rear, a small group caught her eye.

It was Sam and Étienne, with Amelie and Tania on their shoulders.

The two girls waved frantically and Étienne and Sam smiled broadly.

Lily almost burst into tears of relief. She had people she loved and cared for here and they were willing her on. They were what mattered, not what random strangers thought or said.

Penny's hand was on her shoulder. 'Shall we go for it?' she murmured.

Lily took another breath and let it out with a smile of relief. 'Yes. Let's.'

'Good morning, everyone, and welcome to the annual Bryher Craft Fair!' Penny said. 'This year is very special for two reasons. Firstly, we have a record number of makers attending. An amazing total of thirty-four!'

Woo-hoos went up.

'And secondly, we have a VIP guest to open the show and hand out the raffle prizes – several of which she has donated – later. Please give a very warm welcome to our very special guest, Lily Harper, founder of the fantastic online craft and gift brand, Lily Loves.'

There was applause and a few whoops and cheers which Lily guessed were from her fan club at the back of the room.

She stepped forward. 'Thank you, everyone, for that warm welcome. When Penny asked me if I'd open the fair, I'll confess I was a little reluctant.' Lily paused, scanning the room for a reaction. 'You see, I've been thinking a lot about talent lately . . .' she went on.

Someone sniggered and a few people gasped.

'And what it really means. I've concluded it's about

being truly yourself. About having the courage to be original and authentic, even though that might be challenging at times.' Lily paused, having spotted Morven watching her intently.

'I've been visiting the craft shops and galleries of the islands and enjoying the beautiful homeware and artworks in my accommodation. Now, I can see even more of them at this show. Frankly, I've been amazed. I've seen so much originality and skill here on these tiny islands that I asked myself: what can I possibly add to a fair that already showcases so many incredible artists and makers?'

There was applause and a low buzz of agreement. Someone said: 'Hear, hear.'

Lily carried on.

'I know you are going to love visiting all these stalls, meeting the makers and, hopefully, heading home with bulging bags full of beautiful gifts and artwork. So, without further delay, please get buying!'

A very warm round of applause rang out, accompanied by a few more whoops.

Lily handed the mic back to Penny like it was a hot potato.

'It's off,' she said.

Lily experienced a huge whoosh of relief. It was over and it hadn't ended in disaster.

'Good speech. I can see you've done this before,' Penny said.

'Not to an audience like this.' She felt like she'd just been let out of school for the big holidays.

'Good for you for doing it! It was a big ask after what you went through.'

'No problem. You're welcome,' Lily said. 'I'd love to go and look at the stalls properly now and mingle with the makers.'

'Off you go then,' Penny said. 'If you can fight your way through the hordes, as Muriel calls our customers!'

Lily thought that fighting her way through hordes would be a breeze after making her speech. She dived into the crowds, hoping to meet up with Sam and the family, but the place was so packed, it was like trying to find a mate at a music festival. Occasionally she caught a glimpse of Étienne or Sam but then, tantalisingly, lost them again.

People kept stopping her to chat to or pose for selfies, and she was fully aware that her main role was to speak to the makers and punters.

Delicious scents wafted from a stall selling candles, melts and diffusers concocted from flowers grown on the islands. There were pouches and cosmetic bags in sustainable fabric and lots of original artwork. She was particularly taken by a range of notebooks and stationery with gorgeous paintings of the sun rising over Stark. There were coasters adorned with puffins, scallop trinket dishes and baskets made from old fishing rope.

She could have bought so many things for gifts and resolved to order her birthday and Christmas presents from the makers when she returned.

She spoke to as many of the stallholders as she could, asking about their processes, their inspiration.

Each one was passionate about their work and the place where they lived. Some were well-established while others were still trying to carve their niche and make a living.

Her mind whirled with ideas. Of course, Lily also wanted to sign up some of them to the Lily Loves label, to see if they could sell their work through the website. She could envisage a new and unique range: Lily Loves Scilly.

Today wasn't the day.

She halted near a stall next to the canteen. Good spot, she thought, watching Morven and Damon. Their time stalking her on Stark clearly hadn't been wasted, judging by the collages and flat lays created from shells and pebbles and other materials.

One end of the stall was taken up by moody black-and-white photographs of local scenes that could have graced the cover of a grisly thriller. It was certainly an original take on Scilly.

She approached the stall and pointed to a flat lay of a fish made from colourful shards of plastic. Damon scurried to the far end of the stall, intent on 'tidying' a display of prints.

Morven wasn't so shy. 'He's too scared to speak to you but he is sorry,' she said, well within the hearing of her partner-in-crime.

'Apology accepted,' Lily said, quite pleased that Damon was scared of her. Served him right.

She picked up a fish artwork created in vivid shades of teal, blue and turquoise. It was both cute and original. 'I haven't seen these before.'

'I've just started working on them.' Morven curled her

lip in disgust. 'Plastic rubbish washes up everywhere but at least I can clear some of it up while I'm beachcombing and repurpose it. I found some of the plastic for this one in the bay by the ruined cottages on Stark,' she added, leaving Lily unsure if she was being provocative or not.

'Well, I really love it and I think I'll take it.'

Morven's lips parted in surprise. 'You're just saying that to make me feel good.'

Lily went to replace the flat lay on the stall. 'If it bothers you, I can leave it?'

'No!' Morven rolled her eyes. 'Do you *really* like it? It's one of my favourites.'

'I wouldn't have said so if I didn't. The colours are gorgeous and it will brighten up my office.'

'Your office. You're going back then?' Morven sounded genuinely amazed.

'Well, yes ... I have to. I'm leaving on Monday morning.'

'Oh.' Was that a hint of disappointment in her voice? Then she said, 'The fish is twenty-five quid, you know.'

'OK.' Lily mused. 'For a piece of original art made from found items, by a new artist, I'd say that was a fair price.'

'I should have charged more then!' Morven declared, putting the fish in a paper bag stamped *Morven's Creations*.

Lily swiped her card over the portable reader. 'You should ask Sam to hang some in the cottages. You could make them to complement the colour schemes in the bathrooms.'

'Yeah. Maybe I will.' Morven's eyes lit up. 'I can charge him a bit more for a special commission. I'll tell him.'

'I'm sure he'll be delighted.' Lily thought gleefully of Sam's expression when he heard that. 'I like Damon's photograph of the pest house by the way. I think I'll buy that too as a memento,' she said. 'You can pass that on to him as he's too scared to speak to me. I'll pick it up later.'

Clutching her purchase, Lily moved on, admiring silver jewellery, ceramics, textiles decorated with agapanthus prints, turned wood items, paintings, glass decorations and more. She bought a shopping tote made of recycled fabric to put her fish in and collected the print of the pest house from a sheepish Damon, who muttered something that sounded like a mash-up of 'thanksozthanksyeah' as he swiped her card.

Most of the makers had the open minds of artists and creative people. They seemed willing to give her the benefit of the doubt. Two told her that Tyrone from the craft show needed to hear the truth, and several posed for selfies. Occasionally she overheard phrases she wasn't supposed to.

'Oh, is that her?'

'She doesn't have much make-up on, does she?'

'I'm sorry but I don't think she was the right person to launch the fair.'

'Actually, she seems really nice and normal.'

'She seems lovely to me. She posed for a selfie and I like her dress.'

'She bought one of my bags!'

'Bet she rips off the makers.'

'I bet she's loaded. She could probably buy everything here – including the community centre and the islands.'

Er, no, not quite, thought Lily, but said nothing. She was fully aware how fortunate she was, and that she was privileged and wielded a degree of power, but she *had* started very modestly in life and cared deeply about the makers. She operated on what she thought was a very fair basis and was always open to discussion, bearing in mind she did have to make a profit to keep the business running. She could make a lot more – especially if she took the supermarket deal.

Yet wouldn't that go against the very values she'd championed here at the show: originality and individual creativity?

If she'd been reminded of one thing by the fair, it was how important individual creativity was. It was the passion of the artists and makers that reminded her of how she'd felt when she'd had her own little stall – and how satisfying it had been to support other artists' work.

'I get up early to catch the best light when it's still and I'm all alone. There's no point rushing though I've been up all night before a fair to create new stock to sell. I must be mad . . .'

'I source everything either on the islands or as close to home as possible. It matters.'

'I can't imagine doing anything else. Even if I made no money at all, I'd still paint or sew – but I have to eat and pay my bills . . .'

Their comments made her tingle with recognition because she herself had felt the same highs and lows, the joy and angst. She knew their problems and it was why she'd set up Lily Loves in the first place. It still was.

Running her business wasn't about making loads of money; it was about passion and integrity – words that meant nothing in themselves but everything if you backed them up with actions.

'Auntie Lilleeee!'

The girls had finally found her. Gathering them to her, she heaved an inner sigh of relief. Sam and Étienne arrived too, and their little group attracted attention. Lily didn't care, it was so lovely to be reunited with them again.

'Can we have lunch? I'm starving.' Tania patted her tummy with a dramatic sigh.

'Me too,' said Lily.

Amelie tugged at Lily's hand. 'Sam let me drive the boat!'

'Did he? He doesn't let me.'

'You sat on Daddy's lap and he drove the boat,' Tania said. 'He let *me* tie the knot.'

'Everyone helped,' Sam said firmly.

'Except me,' Étienne declared. 'But I am hungry so shall we find some food? What shall we have?'

'Cake.'

'Beans on toast.'

'No, I want cake.'

'*Poisson cru?*' Étienne offered hopefully.

'I can make that,' Lily said, sliding a look at Sam.

Étienne raised his eyebrows. 'Maybe we should have it for dinner then.'

'Let's have burgers,' Sam cut in to avoid a diplomatic incident.

'Yes, burgers! Burgers!'

The twins took hold of Sam's hands and forged ahead to join the queue at the barbecue.

'I see you acquired a new skill while you've been here,' Étienne said to Lily.

'I can make about six things. That's it. I couldn't let Sam do all the cooking and sit eating alone while he lurked in the kitchen – it was just weird.'

'If you say so.'

'Étienne, don't make more of this than it is.'

'I didn't even know there was a "this" to make more of.' He slipped his arm around her shoulders. 'It's wonderful to see you happy. I'm so glad you didn't rush home that first weekend. It would have been a tragedy.'

'Tragedy? That's a strong word.'

'Rejecting something precious when it might be your only chance in life to grasp it, is a kind of tragedy. Believe me,' he said wistfully.

Lily couldn't argue so she nodded and joined the girls in the queue for food. Deciding between hot dogs and cheese-burgers was so much simpler than deciding who was doing the rejecting: Sam or her.

Chapter Thirty-One

After the craft fair, Sam took them back to Stark for a camp-fire supper on the tiny beach below the main cottages. They all gathered driftwood for the fire and cooked fish tacos that even Tania ate.

Lily and Étienne lounged on rugs, beer bottles cooling in the sand beside them.

Sam had taken the twins beachcombing, giving Étienne and Lily a chance to talk. She had a feeling that Étienne might have asked him if they could have some time alone.

'The girls love it here,' she said.

'Who wouldn't?' Étienne replied, looking at the flames. Their light and that of the sinking sun lit up his face, and Lily glimpsed the melancholy behind the smile.

She wondered if he was thinking of her sister, and the bittersweet memories that came along with that remembrance. When he and Cara met, she had been working as a nurse at a clinic on one of the more remote islands where Étienne was running a small hospital. She'd said she wanted to experience life outside the bubble of her own little world.

She wanted to see other perspectives, experience other cultures, but after a few years, she'd returned to England with Étienne and they'd both worked at the same London hospital before she'd had the twins.

How cruelly her life was cut short, but at least she'd lived it. Done what she'd set out to do, found love, had a family.

'I hated it here at first. It was smothered in fog, chucking it down, and it felt like I'd been banished to Stark like one of the pestilent sailors,' Lily said.

He laughed. 'And now?'

'I love it, even when it rains. It isn't only the gorgeous beaches and the sea. There's something unique about the landscape, the peace. The people.'

Étienne threw another stick on the fire. 'People or person?'

Wrong-footed, Lily decided to pretend she hadn't heard. 'There's an honesty about them. All of them, even Morven. They are their own authentic selves.'

'I'm pleased you think that, but they probably have their secrets. Everyone has secrets, a part of them they want to keep hidden . . .' He broke off, a melancholy expression on his face that sent a chill up Lily's spine.

'Cara was perfect. Someone to live up to – not that I ever could,' Lily said, disturbed by Étienne's cryptic statement. 'And I can't imagine what she'd have to hide . . .'

That sad, wistful smile crept onto his lips again. 'If you're living your life by the standards of someone you think was perfect then please, dear Lily, don't. I worshipped your sister, but she wasn't a paragon.'

Lily grew cold at the expression in his eyes. It was so full of regret. 'What do you mean?' she said, though part of her didn't want to know.

'Before the car crash, Cara and I had been going through a difficult time. Our jobs – my job especially – consumed us. Being parents to twins, I suppose we both felt under a lot of pressure and Cara . . . well, she looked elsewhere.'

'*Elsewhere?*' Lily felt sick.

Étienne patted her hand. 'I am sorry to tell you this, but I think you should know. Now that you've made space in your life for something other than work, now you're stronger. Cara had a brief fling with a man from work. Another consultant. In fact, I knew him slightly.'

'No,' Lily burst out. 'I don't believe it.'

'I'm afraid it's true,' he said, gently but with deep sadness that brought a chill to Lily.

Tears stung her eyes. It was impossible to take in.

'And I have fully forgiven her. But at the time, we were considering a trial separation . . .' He sighed. 'Then before we could, we were separated forever and my heart was ripped to pieces.'

'Oh, Étienne! You never said anything about this.'

'Why would I? What would it do other than hurt your parents, the girls, everyone who loved her? But with you, right now, I think that it's more important to be honest. You must realise that no one is without flaw. Not Cara and not me either, because I didn't give her the time and attention she clearly craved. I know it must come as a shock but if your sister were still here, you would have found out.'

Lily hugged her knees, still numb with shock.

Étienne rested his hand on her back briefly.

'I had no idea,' she said, choked with emotion.

'No, and maybe we would have got back together. It might have been the wake-up call I needed – and she might have found that we were worth saving after all. I just don't know and now I never will.'

Lily's tears were hot on her cheeks. 'I'm sorry. For you and for Cara.'

He held her hand. 'You're not angry with me for telling you?'

'How could I be? I'm shocked because I'd no idea. I'd built up her memory into something so flawless. I didn't know . . .'

'She will always be my dear Cara to me. I still love her as much as ever, but you mustn't kill yourself trying to live up to her. I have deliberated about telling you this but I know she would've wanted me to, so that you can look at your life through a new lens and treasure the things that really matter. Treasure them right now. Promise me that?'

She nodded, dabbing at her eyes with one of the starfish serviettes left on the picnic blanket.

'At least you're missing what you had, even if it wasn't faultless,' she said. 'I miss what I've never had.'

It was the first admission she'd ever made to him – to anyone – that she might need a partner in life, someone to love and love her back.

'Lily, you must let someone in. I – you have no idea . . . Just don't ignore the gift in front of you. You mustn't let it – *him* – go.'

'Sam again,' she said, with a dismissive laugh. 'That can't come to anything.'

'It can if you let it. If you have the will. You *must* make it happen.'

'What if he doesn't want it? He's made that clear enough. How could our two worlds ever meet?'

'Cara and I made it happen and we lived on opposite sides of the world. You two live in the same country!'

Lily found that almost impossible to answer but eventually did. 'It isn't only geography.'

'Bullsheet,' he said, his French accent surfacing in the heat of the moment and making Lily giggle.

'What's so funny?'

'Nothing. Now, shhh. Sam's coming back with the twins.'

Down the hill they came, Sam with a broad grin on his face. He was flanked by Amelie and Tania who were swinging baskets, presumably full of precious things.

Étienne rose to his feet, hissing under his breath, 'I *will* be very cross with you if you do not take this chance.'

'Lily! We got beach treasure. Shells and a mermaid's purse,' Amelie shrieked.

'A dogfish egg case,' Sam said. 'From Tean Porth.'

'I found a cowrie.' Tania presented the tiny shell for inspection.

Lily picked it from her palm. 'It's beautiful,' she said, holding it like a diamond. It should be Cara sharing this moment, Cara looking at beach treasure, and yet it was Lily. She had been given a very precious treasure: the love and care of her nieces.

They held out the baskets with their shells and pebbles. 'Oh, let me see,' Lily said, smothering the emotion.

'Can we make pictures with it, like at the fair? Morven said we could do it.'

'We'll do that tomorrow,' Lily said. 'But now it's time for bed. Shall I read you a story?'

'Yes!' said Tania.

'Please,' Amelie added shyly.

'I'll take them,' Étienne said firmly but Lily was already on her feet.

'I'll sit with the girls. It's my last chance for some quality time. My last chance for a little while,' she qualified. 'Because from now on, things are going to be different.'

She didn't look at Étienne or Sam, not wanting to see a trace of doubt in their eyes. Because, she was pretty sure, neither of them believed her.

The girls were tired after the long day and fell asleep before she'd even read a chapter of their book. Lily went onto the terrace of their cottage, made a hot chocolate and wrapped a blanket around herself.

Below her, she could see the glow of the fire and two figures sitting side by side: Sam and Étienne. Two beautiful, strong men. One, a dearly loved brother; the other – the only man she'd ever wanted to matter to.

She'd already vowed to let go of so much in her life. How could it ever happen unless she handed over her heart too?

Chapter Thirty-Two

Everyone – apart from Sam – had a lie-in on Sunday.

Étienne and the twins arrived in reception moments after Lily herself to find two tables had been pushed together and laden with jugs of juice and baskets of pastries and cereals.

The scent of coffee came from the kitchen and Sam emerged, smiling.

'What would you like to do today?' he asked. 'I can take you anywhere you want in the boat.'

Tania was straight in. 'Can we go and see the castle?'

'Cromwell's Castle,' Lily clarified for Étienne's benefit. 'The one you can see from the café and Rock Inn.'

'I'd like an ice cream at the café,' Amelie said, adding significantly, '*please*.'

'We could do both,' Sam offered. 'I need to pick up some supplies from St Mary's and I want to swing by Aaron's yard on Tresco. So I could drop you off on the island and pick you up after lunch?'

The plan was set and mid-morning they were on their way along the coastal path from Tresco Harbour towards the castle, swishing at the foxgloves with grass stems. Being out with the girls was a breath of fresh air: leaving Lily a little space to focus on Étienne's revelation the night before.

A plaque explained how the sturdy round turret had been built on the orders of Oliver Cromwell to protect the channel between Tresco and Bryher from invaders.

On the water, yachts lay at anchor alongside Rory's fishing boat. A couple of paddleboarders sculled their way between the craft and tourists sunbathed on the beach opposite the Rock Inn.

Tania and Amelie climbed the steps onto the castle roof ahead of Étienne and Lily. They kept a close eye on them although the girls could only peer through the crenellations.

Tania wandered back to them. 'Can we live here?' she asked.

'What? Inside the castle?' Lily said with a smile.

Tania's eyes lit with excitement. '*Can we?*'

'Unfortunately not.'

'*Fortunately* not,' Étienne said. 'It would be very draughty in the winter without windows or carpets and there's no WiFi. Besides, how would I work in London at the hospital?'

Tania had the solution. 'Auntie Lily could live here and we could visit her. So, we can see our friends and go to *The Lion King*. Then we can come to the castle and Stark at the weekends.'

There you go. Simple. They've got it all worked out, Lily thought, hoping their lives would stay as uncomplicated for as long as possible.

Tania scooted off to join Amelie, who had found two substantial wooden sticks someone had left in the castle hearths.

Lily watched them start a sword fight, shrieking with

delight. 'It must be wonderful to be at the age where anything and everything is possible.'

'It still is,' Étienne said. 'If you let it be.'

'Maybe you're right. You know, Elspeth told me something the other day. As your time shortens you have to be more selective. There's only so much you can get done, so it had better be the stuff you really want. It focuses the mind. I thought it was a bit morbid but I do understand. I've been given a second chance . . . actually two if you count my fainting episode . . . because I didn't listen the first time.'

'I only needed one wake-up call,' Étienne said. 'Cara taught me not to waste a moment.'

Lily's heart squeezed with emotion that was almost too much to bear. She put her arm around him.

They were silent for half a minute, watching the twins running around the castle tower, squealing with glee while they fought off invaders with driftwood swords. The sky was impossibly blue and the channel a palette of greens and blues shimmering over russet rocks.

'Étienne, I've realised something else too . . . I think I already had, even before you told me about Cara last night.'

He turned to look at her yet stayed silent so she could speak.

'It's easy to make up a narrative that justifies what you wanted to do in the first place but I didn't come here looking for excuses to give up working. On the contrary, I came here hoping to tick a box, fend off the people wanting me to take a break – maybe get some sleep.'

He laughed softly.

'Yet I've reached a different conclusion. I can honour Cara's life not by killing myself to succeed at all costs, but by being a person I'm happy with. By allowing myself to be imperfect and flawed. By letting myself experience other riches in life – freedom, peace . . .' The next word formed in her head but dried in her throat. She was still too afraid to say it.

'And perhaps love?' he said, keeping his eyes on the horizon. 'Since I spoke to you, I've been thinking that maybe it's time I looked to the future too. Opened my own heart . . .'

'Oh, Étienne.' Lily felt tears sting the back of her eyes and the brief brush of his fingers against her forearm.

'You must tell Sam how you feel,' he said, an urgency in his voice that she couldn't ignore.

'He wouldn't listen. No, that's not true. He'd listen but not believe me.'

'Then you must *show* him.'

'What about my other life?' she said. 'My *real* life. I'm afraid that this is a dream I'm going to wake up from.' She waved her arm at the castle, the blue sky, the sailing boats, the kids wheeling around like gulls. 'It's so idyllic, it might be heaven.'

'It's not the place you're afraid of, it's having your heart broken.'

'Yes, and I don't need *that* on top of everything else. I've a big decision to make about the business that's been weighing on me.'

His brow creased in concern. 'You're not in trouble?'

'No, not trouble. The opposite, in fact. You don't need to

know the details and I think I already know my answer. Only it would affect everyone at the company.'

'Separate it off. That's work. This is about *you*.' He flattened his palm over the centre of his chest. 'Look after your heart. The rest will follow.'

Suddenly, like a murmuration of starlings, the children stopped whirling, changed direction and streaked back to them. They spoke as one: 'Can we go to the Hangman's Rock?'

Étienne's eyes widened. '*What* rock?'

'Hangman's Rock,' Tania said. 'Where they extinguished the pirates. Morven told us about it.'

'*Extinguished* the pirates?' Étienne echoed. 'I'd like to have seen that.'

Lily had to hold her hand over her mouth.

Amelie nodded solemnly. 'Yes, that's what Morven said.'

Lily caught her breath. 'Morven says a lot of things. You can't land on *that* rock these days but you can go to the Rock pub or the café for an ice cream. How does that sound?'

It sounded perfect, judging by the squeals of delight. Even Étienne did a little dance, much to Lily's amusement.

Twenty minutes later, back at Tresco harbour, Sam was adding a large polystyrene container to several others on the *Hydra*. Sweat glistened on his biceps in the hot June sun. Lily thought back to her first impression of him at the heliport: ruggedly handsome but rather reserved. Now her heart skipped a beat every time she looked at him.

Tania greeted him from the quayside above. 'Do you like ice cream?'

'Who doesn't?' he called back.

Lily jogged down the steps and onto the boat. 'Can we pop into the café for some? It's a more appealing option than trying to climb up Hangman's Rock ... Morven's been giving the twins a history lesson.'

'Has she? Wow. Well, I can't land on the rock,' he said, adding loudly, 'so I think it had better be ice cream.'

Everyone had some, and the adults had cold beers before they returned to Stark. Sam took them to explore the island before they massed on the beach around a fire to make scallop kebabs with samphire they'd found by the ruined cottage beach. The sun began its slow descent to the horizon, time was ticking by ...

The adults chatted about the islands, about living and working there in the winter. Sam asked Étienne about his job in London and Lily told them about the email she'd received from Penny, thanking her for going to the craft fair and saying what a boost it had been. She kept her plans for Lily Loves Scilly to herself. She hadn't yet worked out the right way to approach the makers without patronising them. Most of all, she wanted to run it by Richie and the team so the decision was a shared one.

Amelie and Tania snuggled between Étienne and Lily, wrapped in blankets as damp from the sand seeped into the air. Tania gave a huge yawn.

'Right. That's our cue.' Étienne rose to his feet, pulling his daughters up with him. 'Come on, sleepy heads. Time for bed.'

Amelie protested wearily.

'We all have a long journey tomorrow and I have to be on the late shift.'

'Will Lily read to us?' Tania asked.

'She has to help Sam clear up.'

'I don't mind,' Lily said.

'No, you stay here.' Étienne's tone meant business and she was grateful to him, for giving her permission to have this final time alone with Sam.

'I'll look in when I come to bed,' she said, but she knew they'd be asleep.

That was it, then. Just the two of them alone, drinking beers. Their final evening together. Time was precious, she'd learned that much, but could she summon the courage to do what she'd promised and make the most of it?

Chapter Thirty-Three

Much as he'd loved spending time with her family – the girls were sweethearts and Étienne was great company – Sam had been both longing for, and fearing, this moment.

Now it had come, he was so afraid of wasting his longed for gift. He'd rejected Lily the other evening – or had she rejected him? He still couldn't decide.

'I'll stoke the fire,' he said, stalling for time.

Abandoning his beer, he piled on a couple of sticks and some dry lichen. He didn't want it to die down because that would leave them in the dark and cold. He didn't want the evening to end.

Lily broke the silence. 'Thank you for making it such a wonderful weekend. The girls have had a fantastic time.'

'I've loved meeting them. I'm knackered but I've loved it.'

'They're livewires, that's for sure.'

'And Étienne is a great guy. I'm glad he's enjoyed the break. He deserves it after what he's been through.'

'They've all fallen in love with the islands, especially Stark. They want to come back . . .' He noticed she fell short of adding that she did.

He hid his disappointment with a joke. 'So, I might not be getting rubbish reviews after all?'

'You know you won't.' She winced. 'I'm sorry I was so rude about the retreat when I first arrived. I can hardly believe it was only a couple of weeks ago.'

A couple of weeks that had changed her life? They'd certainly changed his.

'Anyway,' she said, 'you'd never get rubbish reviews.' She smiled and her eyes were lit by the glow of the fire – or was it an inner glow that had come out during her stay on the islands? Sam smiled to himself, dismissing his romantic notions yet wanting to give in to them too.

'Étienne gave me a lecture last night.'

'Did he? What about?'

'It was about going after your dreams. Not wasting time. I think he feels that he might be ready to move on – romantically, I mean.'

Despite the warmth of the fire, Sam had goosebumps. He sensed Lily was heading along a new path yet hardly dared to hope where it might lead.

'How do you feel about that?' he said softly, adding a stick to the fire, hoping to fan the flames of this new and fragile intimacy between them.

'I was shocked at first. It's weird – a bit upsetting – to imagine him with anyone but Cara, or the girls with a different mum. Yet I also want him to be happy.' She looked at Sam. 'How could I ever wish for anything different?'

He thought back to when Rhiannon had left: how he

hadn't wanted her to be happy; he'd only wanted her to change her mind and come back to him. He didn't feel that way now ... in fact, he hadn't thought about her for the whole weekend.

He'd only thought about the woman at his side.

Realising this fact made him daring. Possibilities unfurled ahead of him that he hadn't dared to believe existed. 'You say you want Étienne to be happy with someone new but what about you?' he asked. 'You persuaded me to tell you about Rhiannon but you never mention anyone special.'

'Oh, I had flings when I was young before Lily Loves was so successful. All of a sudden, I was thirty with a tiger by the tail – Lily Loves took off so fast, I could hardly cope and then there really was no time for love. No time for anything.'

'Has staying here changed that?'

'Yes. In so many ways,' Lily said, watching the fire compete with the fiery ball sliding towards the horizon. The last daylight in the country. The final few hours. 'Time is so short, like Étienne said.'

'Étienne is a very wise man,' Sam said, treading warily, hoping yet fearing her response. 'Doesn't that mean we should make the most of the moment that's in front of us now? And,' he added softly, 'take a chance and leave no regrets?'

She looked up into his eyes, her lips parted slightly. He heard her breathing. 'You're right. I'd never have done the things I have without taking chances. We should live for now, and not worry about afterwards.'

Her face was lit by the flickering flames – and desire? His pulse quickened when she got to her feet and said, 'Shall we go for a walk?'

As he stood up, his whole body thrummed with need for her. 'I'd love that. Where to?'

'To the ruined cottages. On the far side of the island. Away from it all.'

His heart ached with a painful pleasure. Was she saying what he thought she was? Could this be happening?

She met his gaze, and he knew the answer. He picked up the blankets from the beach and took her hand in his.

'You have got to be kidding!' Lily said when she saw him pull off his T-shirt on the sand. The waves broke softly on the beach but further out, there was a swell that rolled in.

'It's now or never.'

'I've been in the sea already once this holiday and it's not an experience I'd like to repeat!'

'This will be different,' he said, unzipping his jeans. 'It's our choice this time.'

She shook her head. 'You're mad.' Then she tugged her T-shirt over her head. 'And so am I.'

Seconds later they stood on the beach, Lily in her bra and knickers, Sam in his boxers. She scrunched sand under toe-nails painted a pearly pink.

'We'll get wet,' she said.

'We'll dry. That's why I brought the blankets.'

Lily stared at him, then at the sea, and heaved a huge sigh. 'Oh, sod it. You only live once!'

Seconds later, they were hand in hand, running towards the foamy waves, their clothes abandoned on the beach.

'Oh! Oh!' She swore extravagantly and loudly because no one could hear. 'Arghh!' A wave broke at thigh-height. It was enough to make her stumble.

Sam scooped her up in his arms. 'I've got you!'

She shrieked.

'And I'll never let you go – whoops!'

He tossed her from his arms. Her scream of thrilled horror was cut off instantly by the shock of the water. She went under but bobbed up immediately, spluttering and cursing him before he pulled her into his arms again.

He was standing, holding her up, her legs wrapped around his waist and her arms around his neck. Sam was frozen yet exhilarated. In holding Lily, he felt he'd finally let go of the past.

'Lily,' he said, as the swell lifted him off his feet, 'I think I might be falling in . . .'

Suddenly, her eyes widened in horror. 'Look out!'

He turned to see the foamy crest rolling in behind them. The wave should have knocked them over but somehow he kept his balance and pulled her even tighter.

'I think that's enough,' he said and she nodded, unable to speak because her teeth were chattering. Feet sinking in sand, he carried her back to the beach and set her down.

'That was—'

'Absolutely nuts!' Lily danced up and down, shaking off water droplets. He loved the way her bottom was dusted with sand and wanted to tell her. She drew a blanket around her. 'It's freezing.'

Still wrapped in the blanket, she came up to him and stood on tiptoes, covering his mouth with a soft kiss. He put his arms around her and kissed her back and soon they were devouring each other like ravenous creatures. The blanket slipped from her shoulders and, in no time at all, they weren't cold any longer.

Sam gazed upwards, feeling the warmth of Lily's body next to him. They'd pulled the other blanket over them to look up into the sky. It wasn't dark and wouldn't be. This midsummer twilight would last a few hours until the earth turned its face to the sun again.

All too quickly.

'You realise we'll have to sneak back to the retreat.' She spoke to the stars. 'Although the girls will be asleep. Probably Étienne too.'

'Does it matter if they know?' He rested his fingers on hers under the blanket, feeling their warmth.

'There might be questions that I don't have the answers to.'

Finally, he turned to look at her, wondering if these magical times were only a blip in the grand scheme of her life.

She sat up and reached for her top. 'I suppose we ought to go back to the retreat,' she said regretfully. 'We've an early start tomorrow.'

With a sinking heart, he sat up too and pulled on his T-shirt. 'We both do.'

Although he'd urged her not to have any regrets, he could not dismiss the niggle in his mind. Had he been a temporary escape, a therapy she'd needed and would soon learn to do without?

On the walk back to the retreat, Lily too was lost in thought and Sam had a feeling that if he said anything, it might provoke an answer he didn't want to hear. For all the talk about being honest, about seizing the moment, they were both unable to say how they felt.

He because he felt too much.

Lily because she didn't want to commit herself or didn't feel the same way? Sam was thrown back into a maelstrom of uncertainty once more. What he'd feared – that he'd fall in love again with a woman who didn't feel the same way – seemed perilously close to coming true.

At the hub, he stood still. Lily tilted her head skywards and let out a deep sigh. 'I'll miss this,' she said and her voice held genuine regret that heartened him.

Sam saw the stars too. The same ones he could look on every day of his life though they would never shine as bright without Lily by his side. 'We're not that far apart, you know,' he said, though fearing she might as well be light years away. 'You can come back any time you like. You'll always be welcome at Hell Bay House.' In his bed, in his *life*, he ached to add.

'I know.' She looked at him. 'Of course I'll keep in touch.'

She smiled. 'I'll have to come and see the place when it's finished for one thing.'

And for another?

She left the phrase hanging like a loose thread. 'I'll see you in the morning. Goodnight, Sam, and thank you.' She kissed him and added, 'For everything.'

Chapter Thirty-Four

'Morning.'

Lily walked in on Sam as he was placing a basket of pastries on the table. He stiffened the moment he saw her.

'Morning.' He managed a quick smile. 'Coffee?'

'Thanks. Let me help.'

'It's your last morning. I'll do it. You won't have someone to wait on you after this.'

'No. That's true.' Lily slid into a chair, selecting a pain au chocolat from the basket. She ought to wait for the others but she wanted something, anything, to distract her from looking at him. To think that last night they'd been naked together and had made love on the beach. To think that she had almost told him she was in love with him.

She broke a piece off the pastry and nibbled at it though it was dry in her throat. Despite the previous evening's activity, her appetite was almost non-existent. Was it too big a risk to tell him she was in love with him after just a couple of weeks? She'd never made such a rash and risky decision in her life before, but love hadn't played by the rules: it had borne her on like a wave, lifted her up and down, swept her along in its path. She'd decided to let go of the helm of her business, to take time for herself, spend more of it with her family . . . but loving Sam?

That was totally out of her control and it terrified her.

He returned with a cafetière and a jug of orange juice. The smile on his face was strained. 'Would Étienne prefer tea? Or is that a stupid question?'

'I think you know the answer,' Lily said with a forced smile of her own.

He put the cafetière and jug down next to her. She caught his hand before he could move away.

'Sam.'

He looked up sharply.

'Last night . . . was wonderful and I *will* keep in touch.'

The conversation was terminated by the arrival of two mini whirlwinds, with their father close behind.

Sam withdrew his fingers. 'I have to get the rest of the breakfast.'

'Helllooooooo!' the girls said and ran up to the table. Tania started trying to pour the juice.

'Hold on, let me help,' Sam said, rescuing the heavy jug and half-filling her glass.

Étienne clapped his hands together and inhaled. 'Is that the smell of pains au chocolat?'

'It is!' Lily said.

'Did you sleep well?' Étienne asked when Sam went in the kitchen. The girls were crunching on cereal and giggling over some shared in-joke.

Lily wasn't fooled by his innocent tone. 'Yes. I was tired out after our day sightseeing.'

PHILLIPA ASHLEY

'Me too,' Étienne said. 'Even these two didn't wake me in the night, though I had the devil of a job to get them to pack. We seem to have acquired extra stuff. Tania had a bag of pebbles in her case and Amelie had a dried dogfish egg case!'

'It was a mermaid's purse, Daddy. Sam explained all that and you should have paid attention,' Amelie said sadly, as if Étienne was a clueless first-year medical student.

'Whatever it is, it stinks and it isn't coming home with us.'

'Why can't I take all my pebbles?' Tania piped up accusingly.

'We have stones in London,' Étienne said. 'And I said you could take a *few* of your favourites with Amelie's shells.'

Sam came back in.

'Can we come back and get some more?' Tania said.

Étienne exchanged a glance with Lily.

'Of course we can come back. It's not long until the school holidays.'

'Can we stay here?' Amelie asked.

'If Sam has room. The cottages might be booked.'

Tania shook her head and pouted. 'He would let us stay anyway. He would make other people move out.'

'I don't think he could do that, sweetheart,' Étienne said.

Sam smiled. 'I'd find room for you somehow. Whenever you decide to come back.' He shared a glance with Lily and she felt like crying.

Perhaps sensing the tension between them, Étienne stepped in. 'Girls, please finish your breakfast because we have a plane to catch and they won't wait for us.'

'Can I get you anything else?' Sam said, back in host mode.

'No, thanks,' Lily and Étienne said in unison.

'In that case, I'll load your luggage onto the boat.' He held up his hands to forestall any argument. 'Please stay here and enjoy breakfast. I'll get everything ready so we can get away as soon as you've finished.'

After that, there was no chance to speak alone with him. Time galloped by and soon they were stepping onto the *Hydra*, mooring at Tresco then trundling in the golf buggy to the heliport.

'Stay by me!' Étienne ordered, taking his daughters by the hand as the helicopter landed.

'I don't want to go home!' Tania wailed.

'I want to see Laura!' Amelie said, referring to their nanny. 'She can come with us next time.'

'Laura's gone to Ibiza with her boyfriend,' Étienne said. 'I'm sure she's enjoyed her holiday too. Oh, look, there's a red squirrel on the field.'

'Will it jump on the helicopter?'

Lily didn't hear what Étienne replied to Tania. She took her chance to speak to Sam.

I need time was a cop-out so she shifted into a mode she was more comfortable with: business. 'How long do you think you need to finish the retreat?'

'A month? Maybe less if we push it.'

She nodded. 'Do you have any takers for the housekeeper and chef's jobs?'

'The chef said yes. I've had a couple of possibles for the housekeeper. One can start straightaway.' He frowned. 'Lily, why are you asking this now?'

'Because I'm going to come back to visit you in four weeks' time and help you throw an official opening bash for the Stark Retreat.'

'If you say so.' He gave a wry smile that was tinged with sadness and doubt.

'I can see you don't believe me but I will. The Lily who arrived isn't the one who's leaving.'

'The one who arrived was just fine. More than fine; she'd just lost her way.' The gentleness with which he said it, the sincerity in his eyes, almost made her wobble and say that she would stay. Instead, she pulled back just in time.

'I never make promises I can't keep. You do understand?'

Sam said, 'I do, and I'd never ask you to make a promise apart from this: promise me you won't change your life for me.'

The rotor noise increased. Lily ignored it. 'What do you mean?' She was practically shouting.

'Auntie Lily!' Tania and Amelie tugged on her hands and dragged her away from Sam. 'Daddy says we have to go now or you'll be left behind.'

Étienne strode over.

'You should go,' Sam said.

'We'll miss you,' the girls shouted.

'I'll miss you. I'll miss you all.' Then he turned away and Lily was ushered towards the helicopter.

The islands fell away, like water through her hands. Soon they were mere shapes on a map, their ragged edges surrounded by aquamarine sea. In minutes they were memories and only the ocean was visible, flecked with frothy white caps and dotted with ships.

Across the aisle, the girls were pointing and chattering but Lily couldn't hear the words. A lighthouse came into view, then tall cliffs and a castle off the coast – St Michael's Mount – and, weirdly, a large retail park. The helicopter skimmed perilously close to a Sainsbury's before landing neatly on a yellow circle.

Lily said a silent prayer and sank back in the seat.

'It's OK. We're alive.' Étienne's hand was on her arm when she opened her eyes. He was smiling at her as the rotors slowed to a halt. He pointed out of the window. 'And look, I could pop to those shops for a lawn mower and some baked beans.'

'You don't have a lawn,' Lily said.

Étienne smiled at her. She knew he was trying to lighten the mood.

Tania fiddled with her safety belt. 'That was awesome!'

'Stay in your seats, please!' Étienne ordered.

A few minutes later, they'd collected their bags and clambered into Étienne's car. Lily rested her head against the seat, grateful she didn't have to make the long journey back to London by train on her own. The chatter of the children would distract her from the fact that every mile took her further from Scilly and from Sam.

Already the land seemed so big, so built-up, compared to the islands. Too many cars, too many people, too many questions – too many decisions to make.

The girls wore headphones and were playing on their tablets in the rear of the car.

'Missing it?' Étienne said. 'Missing him?'

Lily's heart shrank a little more. 'What do you think?'

'I think you've left a piece of your soul behind.'

She saw Sam turn his back again, heard his desperate plea: 'promise me you won't change your life for me.' What had he meant by that? Don't make an effort? Don't come back? Don't fall in love with me?

'Not my soul,' Lily murmured.

'Your heart, then?'

She chose not to answer. 'I said I'd go back for the launch of the retreat in four weeks' time.'

'He'll have all the cottages finished by then?'

'He agreed to my deadline.'

'He'll meet it.'

Étienne kept his eyes on the road, now thick with cars and caravans. 'Of course, you'll keep your side of the bargain too and go back.'

'I don't think Sam thinks so.' She wasn't sure he even wanted her back.

'Then you'll feel even more smug when you prove him wrong.'

'I don't want to feel smug. It's not a competition.' She sighed. 'Sorry, I don't mean to be snarky. I've a lot on my mind.' Every mile seemed to make her burden heavier: her business, Sam. Did he really not want her even to try and make their relationship work? Or was he simply protecting himself?

'Is there a plan? You always have a plan. It's what makes you so extraordinary.'

She laughed. 'I am anything *but* extraordinary. The past few weeks have made me realise that I'm as fallible as anyone else. I can crumble, I can fail, I can change everything I believed about my life.'

'Change can be the scariest thing of all,' he said.

'Terrifying . . . and I might have a plan for the business but I've so little experience in – love.' There. She'd said the momentous word out loud. 'I feel horribly out of my depth! It scares me to feel the way I do.'

'Daddy, I need a wee.'

'And me!'

Étienne glanced in the mirror. 'OK, we'll stop at that farm shop I saw on the sign.'

'The one with the baby llamas?' Tania piped up.

In the mirror, Lily saw the girls grin at each other. The llamas had also been on the sign.

Étienne sighed and said to Lily, 'Prepare yourself. I don't think it will be a quick stop.'

Chapter Thirty-Five

'Surprise!'

Lily almost had a heart attack when she walked into the office. Streamers fell into the air and party poppers exploded. A banner saying 'Welcome Home' had been hung across one wall and there was bunting looped along the other.

Momentarily, she was struck dumb and the grins on the faces of her team tugged at her heartstrings.

'Welcome home!' Richie said. 'We thought we'd surprise you after your ordeal!'

'You have,' Lily said, feeling like crying. She made an effort to give her broadest smile. 'It's good to be back. I've missed you and it's lovely to feel wanted.'

'You're welcome, hun.' Richie hugged her. 'I love the sun-kissed hair . . . and brighter colours suit you so well.'

Lily smiled, pleased he'd noticed her new outfit. She'd never have worn an orange dress to work previously, but it cheered her up and she *did* run a craft company – not a merchant bank.

The rest of the team came up to greet her.

Lando, deputy head of HR, brought out a tray of coffee and pastries. 'We thought we'd make your first day back a special one. We've missed you too. It's not the same here without you.'

There was a sincerity to his words that touched Lily deeply, yet also filled her with guilt about the decision she'd been wrestling with.

'How's it really been?' she asked Richie on the quiet, while helping herself to a pastry. A London pastry, she thought, bought in from a nearby café, and not quite as nice as one baked fresh by Sam – yet served with kindness and that was what mattered.

'We've survived. We've coped. We've not gone bust or caused any lawsuits or encountered any major PR issues.'

'Apart from my obituary.'

Richie flapped his hands. 'Thank God that wasn't real.'

Once again, a wave of gratitude and melancholy threatened to overwhelm her. It had resurfaced the previous evening when she'd called her parents to arrange to visit them the following weekend. It had almost bubbled up when she'd phoned two old friends from her Pilates class and accepted an invitation to their joint birthday party.

She'd hoped it might subside once she was inside the office yet it was sticking around stubbornly.

'Anyway,' Richie was saying, oblivious to the crumbs stuck in his goatee, 'we can run through our reports at the meeting. Shall I call everyone to order?'

'Yes,' Lily said. 'And I'll also have something to report.'

Richie's lower lip wobbled. 'That sounds ominous. Should we be worried?'

'No.' She smiled. 'But wait until you hear.'

Lily sat through their reports. Digital, marketing, PR, sales, HR and finance all gave their updates, and then it was her turn to speak.

'You've all managed very well. I should have stayed on retreat longer. Seriously, thank you for the way you all stepped in while I was away and during the period when reports of my – er – *death* had been greatly exaggerated.'

Everyone laughed. Lily hesitated for only a fraction of a second. She'd rehearsed this moment so many times.

'Ultimately someone has to be in charge, but in trying to micromanage everything myself and assuming only I could possibly do everything, I've lost sight of all the amazing things my team – all of you – can bring to the business. That's going to change.'

Richie's mouth gaped and the others gawped at her, eyes wide in disbelief. Though saddened by the reaction, it wasn't unexpected and she was resolute.

'And in case you're worried that this new Lily is a post-holiday version that won't last beyond a week, I'm going to start the changes right now.' She paused for breath. 'What none of you know is that a month before I left for Stark, I received an approach from a large supermarket chain. They want to put the Lily Loves brand on a range of giftware to be sold in their stores.'

Gasps all around.

'Wow,' Richie muttered. 'I'll go to the foot of our stairs.'

'Indeed.'

Amina, head of marketing, let out a whistle. 'That sounds amazing.'

The others looked at each other, smiling and shaking their heads.

'It is an amazing offer,' Lily said, 'but like all amazing offers, it comes with strings attached. While it would mean more revenue and growth for the brand and business, there's a downside.'

All eyes were intent on her.

'The retailer wants to put the Lily Loves brand on gifts that aren't handmade. They would need to be mass produced. I – we – would be able to curate them to a degree but to sell in the volume they want, they would have to be factory-produced, mostly outside the UK.'

'Oh . . .' Murmurs of concern rippled through the team.

'Yes, I'm afraid so. They need an answer very soon and I'll have to reach a decision, but not without your input. I've borne the burden too long. I want to know how you feel about things. It's time I ran the business more collaboratively and made more of the strengths and skills of my team.'

They exchanged glances. Lando and Richie mimed applause.

'Thank you for being frank with us,' Amina said.

'And also sharing the burden with you, you mean?' Lily gave a wry smile. 'I am the person ultimately responsible for what happens. There are so many pros and cons to deciding either way and I've gone through them all over the past weeks. When a choice is presented to us, well, it isn't always the dream we've longed for. Be careful what you wish for, eh? I won't ask for a show of hands now. You can come and see me privately and tell me what you think.'

Amina eyed her sharply. 'What do *you* think, Lily?'

'Me?' Lily smiled. 'I do have an opinion. But let's just say it's changed over the past couple of weeks. More than anything, I want to hear your views. Just ask Richie to make a time for you to come and see me.'

The meeting broke up and Lily escaped to her office. She checked her phone, hoping to see a message from Sam, but there was nothing. He had asked her to let him know she was safely home in London so she did. She had a text in reply: Good. Don't worry if you don't hear from me. Am living on Stark to get cottages finished. Sam x

Was that a pre-emptive strike? An excuse not to be in touch?

There was a knock and Richie poked his head round the door. 'Boss?'

'Yes?'

He came in, clutching some paperwork. 'I don't need time to decide. This might not be the answer you're looking for but I don't think this is the right way to go. Even if it means more money or security for the company and for us. Lily Loves lives and dies on its brand integrity.'

'Which has been tarnished of late.'

'Not so much as you think. Hun, you're already yesterday's news. The haters will find someone else to torment. Our brand will last and so I don't think we should accept the offer. Somehow, we'll find another way to strengthen our position and grow.'

'Oh, Richie. I have missed you.'

'Really?'

'Yes.' She gestured to the chair and he sat down. 'And I agree. If growing means selling our souls,' she said, 'I'd rather go back to the market stall any time. But you can't breathe a word of my opinion to the others. Let them make their own minds up.'

He zipped his lips. 'My lips are sealed, bab.'

She shook her head.

'Aren't you going to tell me not to call you bab?' he said with a cheeky grin, getting out of his seat.

'I've been called a lot worse. Oh, and while you're here, there's something else I want to discuss.'

With a grimace, he sat down again. 'Here we go.'

'Don't look so terrified. I'm seriously impressed with how you've managed the team while I've been away. You're more than a PA and I've known that for a long time. I simply haven't acknowledged or recognised it. I should have delegated more to you.'

'You should?'

'Totally. I don't think the place would have run as smoothly as it has without you. Behind every good CEO is an even better second-in-command.'

His eyes widened. 'Second-in-command?'

'Yes, I'm offering you the role of operational director. You'll be my deputy when – if – I'm not here. If I take a break.'

'A break?'

'Yes, when I'm on holiday.'

'*Holiday?*'

Her office had turned into an echo chamber, but Lily was well into her stride.

'Before you ask, I realise that more responsibility means you'd need your own assistant and a salary that reflects your new role. If you're interested, that is,' she added, as he gripped the arms of the chair in shock. 'I don't want to pressure you. Things can stay as they are if you like, but whatever you decide, I realise you still need more support. That means you'll be able to appoint your own PA.'

'My own PA?' he blurted out. 'No way! I mean, yes, I do need support and I *am* enjoying making decisions without you – I mean, not that I didn't *miss* you. We all missed you terribly and we want you to have a rest but I am *very* interested in talking about a new role.'

Lily laughed. 'Great. I'm so happy for you, for me and the team. It's a weight off my mind to know I can count on someone as capable and loyal as you.'

'Operational director? My own PA? I can't wait to share this news.'

'With Jakob?'

'No – well, yes – but first of all with my nanna. She will *not* believe this.'

'Good. Have a think overnight – discuss it with your nanna if you want – and then we'll draw up a contract.' She stood up. 'Shall we have a professional hug?'

He hugged her and almost danced with glee. 'I think I'll make it mandatory every morning for the whole team.'

'Er, I'd give that one some further thought,' Lily said, slightly dismayed.

He heaved a sigh of relief. 'Well, this conversation has gone a lot better than I expected. For one horrible moment, I thought you were going to tell me you'd decided to jack it all in and live on Stark.' He laughed and almost waltzed out of the office. 'See you later.'

When Richie had gone, Lily sat back in her chair. She curved her fingers around the mouse and scrolled through the first few of hundreds of emails she still hadn't replied to. Most didn't need a response, some needed a few words. Others were too complicated to deal with – or could be passed on to the team.

Richie brought her a decaf latte and she tried hard to focus but soon she had to get away from the screen. Coffee in hand, she walked to the window, gazing out over the rooftops and streets where red buses queued with black cabs, vans and cars. In the distance, spires and skyscrapers broke the skyline, shimmering in the city haze.

Outside her cocoon in the main office, she could hear the click of fingers on keyboards, phones ringing, low chatter and the occasional burst of laughter. Actually, not that occasional. She was sure there was more laughter than before she'd left, or was she only noticing now she wasn't trapped inside her own bubble?

She answered more emails and diarised meetings with her digital manager and marketing director to discuss their views on the supermarket deal. At lunchtime, she took her sandwiches into the nearby park and called her mother who was so surprised to hear from her in the middle of the working day that she answered the phone with: 'Lily! Oh my God, what's happened now?'

'Nothing. It's just a call to say – to say I love you. Dad too.'

'Oh. Oh, I love you too. We both do and we'll see you at the weekend. Are you sure you're OK, sweetheart?'

'Fine. Like I said, it's a social call and to tell you how much I'm looking forward to seeing you both.'

Sweetheart. Lily's mum hadn't called her that in a long time. Or if she had, Lily hadn't heard it ... perhaps she hadn't been listening, just like she hadn't heard the laughter in the office before.

She shook her head. Next thing you knew, she'd be taking off her shoes and walking barefoot on the grass, communing with nature. Or perhaps not, with all the duck poo around ...

Laughter bubbled up and out, causing a young boy on a scooter to stare and give her a wide berth.

While she was on a roll, she'd had a better idea: she could call Sam via the café.

As she dialled, she gave silent thanks for one city benefit: the luxury of – mostly – a strong mobile signal everywhere. Excitement and nerves bubbled; what if, by some chance, he happened to be in the café and Elspeth would put her through and she would hear that gorgeous deep Scilly accent again.

The phone rang and rang.

Lily grew twitchy. Was this such a good idea? She was about to cut the call when someone finally picked up.

'Oh, hello, Elspeth!' she said in relief.

'This is Barney,' the speaker said in a New Zealand accent. 'Who's this?'

'It's Lily. I was hoping to speak to Elspeth.'

'Elspeth's really busy in the kitchen right now. Load of Germans just arrived off a cruise ship and they all want bloody cream teas. Can I take a message?'

'No. It's fine,' Lily said. 'I'll call b—'

The phone went dead.

Wondering whether to have a word with Elspeth about Barney's customer service skills, Lily called Hell Bay House where the phone was answered after two rings.

'Yeah?'

'Morven, it's Lily. I was wondering if Sam was at home.'

Morven sounded bored, but at least she wasn't hostile. 'No, sorry, he's been working on Stark for the past couple of nights.'

'Oh. Of course he is.' Lily felt silly for even trying Hell Bay House when she might have known he wouldn't be there.

'If it's urgent, I could get him on the radio?' Morven offered.

'No, it's not urgent. No need for that, but thanks.'

'No problem. Shall I tell him you called?'

'Yeah, but it's no biggie. I'll catch up with him some time.'

Lily and Morven chatted a little longer – Lily was able to

ascertain that Morven was OK and had sold several more collages since the craft fair and had 'convinced' (Morven's word) Sam to commission some fish collages for the cottages.

'I'll have to go,' Morven said. 'A bunch of us are going swimming at Rushy Bay.'

Images of the endless skies, white sand and twin hills of Stark flooded Lily's mind. 'Sounds lovely. Have a good time.'

'We will.'

Lily ended the call. It was time to go back to work.

Stark felt a world and another time away. Everyone had their place there, their jobs, busy lives, worries and plans. They were too busy to talk to the demoralised CEO of a handmade gift company who was now not quite sure where her place lay.

She loved London, she loved her job, and *yet* . . . Richie's words kept coming back to her.

For one horrible moment, I thought you were going to tell me you'd decided to jack it all in and live on Stark.

Chapter Thirty-Six

'OK. I think that will do for today, bar the tidying up.'

Aaron swiped the back of his hand over his forehead and admired his handiwork on the bathroom tiling in cottage number four. Sam grabbed a can of Coke from the cooler and handed it over. A week after Lily had gone, with the help of Aaron and the plumber, Starfish was ready for letting and Sea Holly was well underway. Sam had been staying on Stark since Lily had left, working all hours to get the work done.

'Thanks for helping,' he said as Aaron knocked back the Coke.

'You're welcome. Soon be done.'

Mentally, Sam crossed his fingers. He hadn't told his friend about the deadline that Lily had set him. He didn't want to give Aaron the slightest excuse to quiz him on that subject. He was finding it impossible to avoid thinking about it – or her – and whether he'd done the right thing in letting her go so easily.

It had been the right thing for Lily, even if it meant he suffered.

Sam threw himself into the grind of clearing the site with

renewed vigour, trying to ease his aching heart with aching muscles.

After an hour, Aaron stopped working and glared at him. 'Sam, for God's sake. Why don't you slow down a bit?'

'I want to get the site fully cleared up by tonight,' he replied. 'Don't want to be starting on it again in the morning. It might rain tomorrow anyway, and I want my own bed tonight and to spend a bit of time at home with Morven.'

'You must be tracking a different forecast but whatever,' Aaron said, tossing broken tiles into the barrow with a clatter.

Sam was ready to drop by the time they'd made numerous trips with the rubbish down to the *Hydra* at the quay and then unloaded it on Bryher in the early-evening sunlight. It had been a hard day and the back of his neck felt gritty. He really needed his own bed – a concept he immediately regretted when he thought of Lily in it.

'You look done for. Tell me you're not going back. Take a break.'

'I'm staying at Hell Bay House tonight. Elspeth has been keeping an eye on Morven while I've been working and I think they'll both go mad if I don't come home.' Morven had actually been a big help, adding some of her creations to the existing cottages and bringing over more artwork, pots and textiles from her arty friends. Lily had also suggested a few items from local makers, which he'd had delivered to Bryher.

'Is Nate coming back soon?' Aaron asked.

'Three weeks' time. He's booked the flight and showed Morven the online ticket so she believes him.'

'Do you think he'll stay?'

'I don't know.' Sam sighed. 'They're now talking every few days so that's a big step forward. I can't decide for them. It's their futures.'

Aaron nodded. 'You can tell me it's none of my business, but what about your future? Are you and Lily going to see each other again?'

Sam had exchanged a few messages with her. Though short, each had taken a stupid amount of time to compose. He'd been so careful to get the tone right – light and cheerful – because he was afraid of letting her know how much he missed her and how much he longed for them to be together, however impossible that seemed.

'Have you even heard from her?' Aaron said.

'Yeah. She said she's coming back to help me officially launch the retreat in a few weeks.'

'Aha! So that's why you've been working all hours.'

Sam rolled his eyes. 'I need the revenue. I've taken bookings.'

'Sure you do.' Aaron eyed him shrewdly. 'Do you think she will come back? She's a busy woman.'

'Maybe. I don't know. I want to see her again, I won't deny I like her.'

Aaron snorted. '"Like". Oh, mate, listen to yourself. You were so busy trying not to look at her that night in the pub, it was painful.'

'Was it that obvious?'

'Only to someone who knows you very well. Fathoming you out can be almost impossible.'

'I almost *don't* want her to come back because it would never work between us. We're a million miles apart and I don't just mean the physical distance, though that's a problem too. You know what it's like living here, expecting someone to fit in. Our lives are so different. I'd rather not prolong the agony. Better to get it over with before it's begun.'

'Strikes me it's gone way past the beginning between you two.' Aaron sighed and slapped Sam on the back. 'I'm not enjoying watching you torment yourself.'

'I'm not enjoying it, either!' he said morosely.

'I can't tell you what to do. Same as you can't solve Nate's problems. Sorry, I'm a shit mate, aren't I?' Aaron grinned.

Sam had to smile. 'I wouldn't say that.'

'We can talk about it if you like – over a pint tomorrow night, maybe. I'd have said tonight but we're having a barbecue. My sister-in-law and the kids are staying. Seven of us in a two-bed bungalow. Should be fun.'

'Enjoy yourself.'

He pulled a face. 'I'll try!'

Aaron jumped into his red RIB and Sam untied for him.

Aaron's hand was on the throttle. 'Oh, and *radical* idea, but you could call Lily. On the actual telephone thingy that lets you speak to people.'

'Ha ha!' Sam said as Aaron gave a salute and fired the engine to motor the short distance over the channel to Tresco.

Sam made sure the *Hydra* was secure before heading home in the Land Rover. In the distance he imagined he could glimpse Land's End. He pictured Lily still in her

London office – what would she decide to do about the supermarket offer?

She'd probably be working late or heading off to a business meeting at a smart restaurant. One thing he was sure of: she wouldn't be looking out over the ocean and mooning about him.

He took Aaron's advice and sneaked out after dinner with Morven and Elspeth to call Lily. There was no way he was using video; he looked too scruffy.

His call had gone straight to her voicemail. 'Er . . . it's me. Sam.'

Shit, she knew that.

'Just wanted to say that Starfish is finished and Sea Holly is well on schedule . . . Morven has been helping to style Samphire with her creations and the pieces you suggested from the local makers. Um . . . hope you're OK. Speak soon. Bye.'

He ended the call with a groan. Why had he even called to leave such a stupid message?

Better he hadn't called at all.

He gazed out at Stark, slumbering in the evening sun.

By six a.m. the next morning he was back, checking on his tiling efforts from the day before. Stark was shrouded in a sea fret but a bit of murk wasn't going to stop him from working. He'd been looking forward to a night in his own bed but he'd spent too much of it thumping the pillow and staring into the darkness.

At least the mist seemed to be clearing. The fine droplets

had clung to his skin and soaked through his clothes. He'd soon dry when the fog finally burned off.

He made a coffee and took it down to the ruined cottages at Tean Porth, meaning to make some notes on what might need doing to restore them. Lily had suggested turning them into a private complex that could be rented by family groups or a corporate retreat.

All Sam could think of was the evening they'd skinny dipped in the sea, Lily trembling with cold and exhilaration, the sand on her bottom as she'd fled out of the water. He smiled to himself then heaved a sigh. It wasn't going to be easy to get any work done if he kept thinking like this.

Walking past the pest house, he sat on a broken granite lintel, paying a silent tribute to his ancestors and thanking them for their legacy. At least the Teagues had no need to forage for limpets now and if he made a success of the retreat, they would have a future.

He'd allowed himself to think that he and Lily might too, but the doubts were creeping up on him. They seemed so far apart, physically, what if she changed her mind and didn't come back for the launch at all?

After a morning of work, he locked up and headed back to the quay and on to Hell Bay House, to find Morven in the kitchen in the middle of the afternoon.

She was leaning over a pot that smelled a lot better than it looked. She resembled a witch stirring her cauldron and he smiled to himself at the thought, one of the few moments of light-heartedness he'd felt all day.

'Smells good. What is it?' he said.

'Spicy lentil casserole. Damon's recipe.'

'OK . . .'

'Don't sound so enthusiastic,' Morven grumbled.

'I'm starving. I'd be enthusiastic about anything.'

'Thanks! I'm making it in advance so we can have it for dinner. It'll taste better than it sounds.'

'I'm sure it will,' he said, amused, then headed upstairs, trying not to think about the night Lily had slept in the room down the hall. So close and yet so far . . .

When he came downstairs, Morven met him in the hallway. 'Oh, I forgot. There's a letter for you.'

'OK. Probably a bill.'

'No, it's not. It's an actual letter with handwriting on the front. Looks like a card to me.' Morven shrugged. 'I need to rescue the jacket potatoes from the oven.'

Sam picked the letter up from the hall table. It wasn't a bill. It was a card, but it couldn't possibly be a birthday card because the sender knew exactly when his birthday was. He'd recognise Rhiannon's writing anywhere.

Chapter Thirty-Seven

Lily slung her rucksack over her shoulders and stepped off the tourist ferry onto the quay at Bryher. A week, she'd been away, almost a whole week – and yet it felt like a year.

Over the weekend she'd managed to book a last-minute flight to Newquay from London City Airport and connected to an afternoon shuttle to Scilly. A car to the harbour, the passenger ferry to Bryher, and now she was here in the sunshine, the blue waters shimmering.

With her hair under a baseball cap, wearing shorts and a hoodie, she hoped she'd be taken for any other holiday-maker out for a day's walking. Not a deranged woman embarking on the biggest gamble of her life.

She set off along the path to Hell Bay House, stopping at the top to catch her breath.

The house shimmered in the sunshine, with the bay stretching ahead in front of it. The tide was out as far as she'd ever seen it: the sandbanks lying like stepping stones. If Sam was on Stark, she could almost walk across. Elspeth had told her it was possible once in a blue moon.

A glint of light drew her eye. The Land Rover was parked on the driveway . . . which meant he was at home.

Her stomach knotted and then tightened.

This was a huge risk. Leaving the business – again – and telling Richie she was off sick with a bug. She'd never done such a thing before and wouldn't have been impressed if an employee had. Yet these were extraordinary times, so she forgave herself this once.

The rucksack on her back felt comfortingly normal and she set off down the hill on the path that led to the rear of the house. Even with her eyes closed, the scent of honeysuckle drifting on the breeze would have told her she was in the garden. The flowers seemed brighter than ever: crimson geraniums, mauve agapanthus, yellow daisies nodding their heads in the breeze.

Familiar memories and anticipation made her heart beat faster.

She half-expected to see Sam or Morven in the kitchen window as she went straight up to the back door. It was open slightly, which reinforced her idea that someone was in. She might be seconds away from Sam: moments from explaining why she'd left work and travelled here on a mad impulse . . .

'Hello!' she called. 'Sam?'

There was no answer but the kitchen door was open a sliver, so she pushed it and stepped inside.

'Sam? It's Lily,' she said, walking into the kitchen. Yet while there were coffee mugs on the table by an open cook-book and some mail, there was no answer. She listened hard but heard only the wind rustling the shrubs outside.

Onwards through the kitchen she went, calling: 'Anyone home? Sam? Morven?'

Still, thick silence, not even the tell-tale creak of a floor-board upstairs.

She poked her head around the sitting-room door but by this point had surmised there was no one in. Someone must have left the kitchen door open so they couldn't have gone far, but then again, this was Scilly – a place where people did leave doors unlocked.

She shrugged off her backpack and sat on the sofa, calming herself.

What to do now?

She could hardly hunt all over Bryher for Sam. Suddenly she felt incredibly foolish and her bravado dropped off a cliff. Why had she thought it was a good idea simply to head down here unannounced? The sensible thing would be to call him and find out where he was, so she took her phone from her pocket and dialled his number.

It went straight to voicemail. Lily left a message: 'Hi, Sam. Lily here. Can you call me as soon as you get this, please?'

If he was on Stark he might not answer at all and, whatever else occurred, she wasn't going to be able to get back to the mainland today. She'd need a place to stay.

How had she not given that a thought until now? If it wasn't to be Stark or Hell Bay, she'd have to find accommodation – or stay with Elspeth, which would be excruciating if her gamble had failed and it turned out Sam didn't want her there.

She'd been so bound up in her determination to surprise him that she hadn't thought through the practicalities.

Thinking on the hoof, she decided the only thing to do

would be to head to the Quayside Café and find Elspeth to see if she knew where Sam was.

'Oh!'

Lily almost jumped off the sofa. A loud bang had come from the kitchen, the sound of a door slamming.

'Sam?'

She hurried through the hall to find the heavy oak door between it and the kitchen had slammed shut in the wind.

'Hello?'

The kitchen was empty, the back door wide open and the curtains fluttering. Papers and leaflets were scattered over the tiles so she went to pick them up. There were a couple of utility bills, a leaflet about mini-diggers and a card that had fallen open.

She put the junk mail on the table but kept the card in her fingers. It was too late to unsee it, with its painting of a beautiful bay, the message in neat handwriting and the signature at the bottom.

Dear Sam,

I bet you're surprised to hear from me after so long and by snail mail too, but I saw this card in a gallery and it reminded me of happier times. Do you remember when we took the Hydra over to Tresco and had a picnic in Apple Tree Bay? How could either of us forget . . .

Anyway, I've taken a month's leave from work and I'm staying with my parents in Penzance for a few days.

I know it's been a while, and that we haven't kept in touch, but I keep thinking of that 28 miles of sea between us – such a tiny distance after the 10,000 that have separated us for the past couple of years.

There was so much left unsaid when we parted. I think it would be good for both of us to set things straight, don't you?

It's a long shot and short notice but if you're on the mainland, maybe we can meet up in the next couple of days? I had thought of coming over to Bryher but it seemed a step too far to land on you without a warning after all this time.

Anyway, it would be <u>really</u> lovely to see you again.
Rhiannon x

Lily held the card in her fingertips. It was dated a couple of days previously and had been left on the table before it had blown onto the floor. Sam had made no attempt to hide it. In fact, if it had been blown off the table, had it been up on display? Had he decided, upon reading it, to take Rhiannon up on her offer to meet?

The note sounded very nostalgic, regretful even – was it a veiled plea to rekindle their old relationship? Rhiannon must have regrets if she'd broken her silence to ask to meet him, and Lily knew Sam had been devastated when they'd split up. How could he resist a request like that?

Her stomach turned over.

How stupid she felt for turning up unannounced at his home like this!

Her fingers weren't quite steady as she replaced the card on the table and hurried out by the front door.

Feeling more dejected by the second, she was about to take the path back to the quay when she spotted two figures heading towards the house from Hell Bay.

She jogged over to meet Morven and Damon carrying fold-up easels and kids' buckets.

Morven looked her up and down. 'What the hell are you doing here?'

The typical greeting was momentarily comforting. 'I was looking for Sam but he's not at home.'

'That's because he's gone to St Mary's to get a flight to the mainland.'

Lily's legs buckled slightly. All her worst fears were confirmed.

'Did he say why?' she asked, already knowing and dreading the answer.

Morven shrugged. 'Nope.'

Lily almost screamed. Only Morven could be so lacking in curiosity.

'Nothing at all?'

'He just said he was going to the mainland and to tell Elspeth when I saw her, he'd explain the rest later. He was in a rush. It wasn't that long ago. He might still be at the airport.' Morven wrinkled her nose in puzzlement. 'Anyway, you still haven't said why you're here out of the blue. Thought you weren't coming back until the launch of the retreat?'

'I took a few days off,' Lily said, not exactly lying. 'I was hoping to see Sam but if he's already at the airport, I'll have missed him. I'll never get there in time.' Despair washed over her.

'If you got a move on, you might catch him,' Morven said. 'And if you've come all this way, it must be important?' She gave Lily a smug smile, clearly wanting to provoke a response.

'It is. I really wanted to talk to him . . . but it's too late.' *In every way*, Lily thought.

'Not if we take you.' She glanced at the silent Damon. 'In your brother's boat.'

Damon finally spoke. 'It's got a new outboard. I've been dying to try it.'

'What will your brother say?'

'Nothing. He's in Gran Canaria with his girlfriend.' His eyes gleamed with excitement but Lily was torn.

'Do you want to go or not?' Morven said.

No matter how hurtful the news, Lily had to know where she stood with Sam, and now was the time to be honest and not to shrink away from hard truths. It was time to take her courage in her hands.

'Yes. I do.'

'Come on, then!' Morven said and hared off towards the quay.

Lily tried to call Sam as they jogged along but her calls went straight to voicemail. How had she ever thought it was a good idea to get a lift with two mad teenagers in a tiny RIB with an overpowered engine?

She clung to the straps of the boat for dear life as the craft smacked over the swell with Damon at the helm. Morven was laughing and speaking to him, though Lily couldn't hear a word above the roar of the outboard and the slap of waves against the hull every few seconds. Within minutes she was soaked through, but being wet was the least of her worries. Staying alive was the priority, with Damon whizzing past razor-sharp rock pinnacles. She didn't dare try to call Sam again.

Somehow they survived, and Morven tied up at the pontoon at St Mary's while Damon ushered Lily onto the back of his brother's quad bike and set off along the main street and up the hill towards the airport.

He dropped her off outside the terminal, sodden and shaken to bits. 'I'll park the bike and hang around in case you need a lift.'

Lily ran inside to find the terminal almost deserted and a plane taxiing along the runway.

'Is that the flight to Land's End?' she said to a uniformed man at the check-in desk.

'It is.'

'I've missed it!'

The plane hurtled towards the end of the runway.

'It was fully booked anyway,' the man said.

Lily's heart sank into her soggy trainers as the plane soared off over the cliff. 'I was looking for Sam Teague. You don't know if he was on board?'

He sucked in a breath. 'Sorry, I can't give out information about passengers.'

Although ready to burst into tears, Lily restrained herself. 'I understand that.'

'Uncle Jack!'

The check-in man grinned. 'What you doing here, Damon?'

'I gave Lily a lift.'

Lily looked from one to the other. 'This is your uncle?'

'Yeah,' Damon replied as if she should have telepathically known that.

'You didn't say you were with Damon,' Uncle Jack said with an eye roll, 'or I'd have told you Sam was on board straightaway.'

Finally defeated, Lily collapsed onto a seat.

'I'm sorry you've missed him,' Jack said, sympathetic now.

Lily nodded. 'Is there another flight to Cornwall this afternoon?'

'Nothing off the islands from here today.'

'Helicopter?' she said hopefully.

'One, but you'll never get to Tresco in time for it.'

Lily felt drained. 'OK, thanks.'

Damon sat next to her. 'We could try going to Penzance in the RIB,' he said. 'But it would take ages and I'm not sure the tank holds enough fuel.'

'God, no!' Lily cried, at the thought of a deep-sea crossing over the world's busiest shipping lane in a rubber dinghy. 'I mean, thank you for the offer but I wouldn't put you in danger.'

'Could be pretty awesome, though,' he said, his eyes lit with zeal. 'I could take some spare cans of fuel.'

'I don't think that would be a good idea,' she insisted. 'I'll try to call Sam when he lands. He'll be there in ten minutes.'

'Oh. OK.' Damon subsided like a sunken cake. 'Suppose I should wait here?'

'No, thanks. You go back to Morven. I'll take a taxi to the port if I need to.'

'We'll hang about down there in case you need a boat back.'

'Thanks.'

Damon slouched off, leaving Lily battling her emotions. It was excruciating to think she'd dropped everything to see Sam when he was clearly travelling to see another woman. She felt foolish for thinking her feelings for him were recip-rocated. But she also felt confused because she was normally a good judge of character, and she had never thought Sam would do something like this after the life-changing experi-ence they had shared on Stark. She owed it to him to give him an opportunity to at least explain before she made her way back to London.

The next twenty minutes were agony. Finally, her phone lit up.

As Lily answered, Sam launched a barrage of questions: Are you OK? What's happened? Where are you? I've a ton of missed calls and messages from you. I had to turn off my phone during the flight.'

'At the airport on St Mary's.'

Silence. 'St Mary's? What are you doing there?'

'Looking for you,' Lily said. 'I've not long landed at

Land's End airport. I thought you'd gone to Penzance ...' she said, regretting the words as soon as they left her mouth.

'I *am* going to Penzance.' He sounded completely confused. 'How do you know that?'

Lily sank into complete misery. 'I saw a card from Rhiannon in your house.'

'You read it?'

'Yes. And I'm sorry. I don't know what to say ...'

There was a long pause during which Lily could almost hear the beating of her heart, before he spoke again. 'Stay exactly where you are. I'm coming home. We need to talk.'

Chapter Thirty-Eight

Lily decided to do as he'd asked, sitting in the airport, staring through the windows, willing the little plane to appear. Jack had gone home from the check-in counter and the café had closed. The airport was empty apart from a man in Lycra cycling gear and a woman with a yappy pug, presumably waiting for the incoming flight like Lily was.

Only a few ground crew remained outside, standing by chocks and chatting with each other until suddenly they started to look more animated.

Lily jumped up, crossing to the windows overlooking the runway. The pug yapped as if it could sense something was happening. The cyclist checked his watch and spoke to the dog owner.

Then she saw it: the tiny Islander, wings wobbling on its approach to the cliff edge at the end of the short runway. Suddenly, it dropped to the ground with a rumble and a screech of brakes. Lily half-feared it might plough into the terminal but nobody else seemed bothered. The pug sniffed at the cyclist's shoes, while its owner chattered away.

The minutes stretched out agonisingly before the plane door opened and the passengers descended. Last of all, carrying a rucksack in one hand, was Sam.

The pug owner and cyclist had sauntered off to the side of the terminal, presumably where the passengers would arrive.

Lily followed them, her heart pounding fit to burst.

Then Sam was striding towards her, his mouth set in a line.

'Lily. What are you doing here?'

'I came back to surprise you because I couldn't wait until the launch, but now . . . why were you off to Penzance? Was it to meet Rhiannon?'

'No! I mean, yes, to the first part. I *was* on my way to Penzance. I'd already ordered a cab from Land's End airport but only to take me to the station, so I could get a train to London to see *you*.'

'But I – *why*?'

'Why do you think? I was going to turn up at your office or flat to tell you that I can't wait until I've finished the bloody retreat. I pushed you away because I could never make you choose between me and your life in London and thought I'd make it easy for you by acting as if I didn't care. But it was killing me. It seems completely crazy now.'

'No crazier than me coming all the way here without telling you and accidentally breaking into Hell Bay House. I'm sorry but the wind blew the card onto the floor – *really* – and I couldn't help but see it. I know I should never have read a personal message to you, and I'm sorry, only I saw her name, and then, well, I didn't know what I thought apart from that you might have gone to meet her.'

'No, I decided not to. It's been too long. And most of all,' he put his hands on Lily's arms, 'that card made me realise that I can't live my life looking backwards. I don't *want* to. It made me realise that I want to look to the future, and that that future is with *you*.'

Lily was speechless momentarily but then walked into his arms and held him as tightly as he held her. 'I feel the same,' she said. 'Back in London – without you – I knew I'd left a piece of me behind. I couldn't wait another moment to be with you. When I make up my mind, I go for it.'

His eyes lit with joy.

Lily threw her arms around him and planted a kiss on his lips that went on and on until finally she had to break away to breathe.

'Wow . . .' Sam said, drawing in air, his eyes full of happiness. 'You really do go for it!'

'Oh, I do! When there's something I want so much. I'm so happy I rushed down here even if we did almost miss each other!'

'We didn't and that's what matters,' he said, holding her tightly. 'We both came to our senses and realised the incredible thing we had within our grasp.' With a gentle touch he pushed a strand of hair off her face. 'You're an amazing person, Lily Harper, I worked that out fast. What it took me longer to work out was that I could have feelings for and find happiness with someone like you – someone I thought was so different to me. Once I did realise how I felt about you, I didn't want to risk getting hurt because I couldn't see how we could ever make it work.'

'We *will* make it work somehow. I've been thinking about

that. We both want to be together and that's all that matters.'

'It is. Rhiannon's card made me realise how much my new life means to me. How much you mean to me. I'd learned to live alone, expecting nothing, until you walked into my life.'

She laughed. 'You didn't seem too happy about it!'

'Neither did you.' His eyes lit with fresh pleasure.

'I said I'd come back, Sam. Why did you doubt it?'

'I was too *afraid* to believe. Terrified of getting hurt again and I'd no idea how we could build a future together when we exist in such different worlds.' He hesitated. 'I – I could come and live in London, if you want? In your place. Or we can get a new one?' He looked down at the floor, as if he was afraid to hear what came next.

'You can't run Stark from London but I can run Lily Loves from Stark – at least for part of the time. I'm going to refuse the supermarket deal and all my team are in agreement. I knew it was wrong: the stress, the hours – selling our souls. Better opportunities will come along.'

Sam looked skywards and let out a huge sigh of relief, then he took her face in his hands and kissed her so tenderly, she wanted the moment to last forever.

Finally, their kiss ended and they were joyfully looking into each other's faces.

'Shall we go home?' he said, still holding her.

'Ah, but whose home?'

'From now on, home is wherever you are.'

*

Morven was at Hell Bay when they returned, walking in hand in hand.

She rolled her eyes. 'Does this mean you two are official?'

'Official?' Lily said.

'If you mean, are we seeing each other, then yeah, I guess it's official.'

'About time,' said Morven. 'Right, now that's sorted, I'm going round to Rowan's for a sleepover.' She slung her backpack on her shoulder and waved goodbye. 'See you tomorrow.'

Elspeth walked in and spotted Sam holding Lily's hand. 'It's true, then?'

'Yes, it's true,' Lily said.

Elspeth sat down heavily on the sofa. 'Bugger me. When you turned up at the quay that filthy afternoon, I would have said it was the last thing I'd ever have expected.'

Lily exchanged a glance with Sam. 'Us too,' she said. 'I think it was loathing at first sight.'

Sam laughed.

'Well, there you go. You never know how life is going to turn out.' Elspeth shook her head. 'I'm happy for you both. Now, are you staying here tonight or going over to Stark?'

Sam turned to her. 'Lily?'

'I think I've had enough boat journeys for one day.'

'We'll stay here then.'

'And I'll get off to Zumba,' said Elspeth, getting up off the sofa. 'Enjoy your evening – though I warn you, this will probably be the talk of the islands before too long.'

'I'm used to being gossiped about,' Lily said, and gave Elspeth a warm hug. 'Thank you for making me welcome, even though you had so many misgivings.'

'Yes, well, you two aren't the only people who can change their minds. I'll see you tomorrow.'

'Yes, I'll come by the café. I need to talk to you about a more permanent office arrangement.'

'Great. I shall up my rates!'

'I'd do the same, if I were you.'

Chuckling to herself, after a farewell wave, Elspeth left them alone.

'I'm glad you chose to stay here,' Sam said when silence returned to the house again. He closed and locked the French doors with a firmness that sent a delicious shiver up Lily's spine.

'Why's that then?' she said.

He walked towards her, the fire of desire in his eyes. 'Because I don't think I can wait a moment longer to take you to bed.'

Lily smiled back, almost trembling. 'Why else do you think I wanted to stay here?'

She took his hand and let him lead her up the stairs to their bedroom.

Epilogue

Three months later

'Oh my God. You are not frigging going to believe this!' Morven burst through the door of Lily's new office, waving her phone in the air.

Fortunately, Lily had just finished a Zoom meeting with her new client Cockahoop – otherwise Morven would have played a starring role.

'You're in the news again!' she declared, standing behind the laptop and blocking Lily's view of Cromwell's Castle.

Lily let out a resigned breath. 'Oh, God, what have I done this time?'

Morven was unwilling to surrender her phone for a nanosecond. 'I've sent you the link.'

Lily pushed aside her brownie plate and returned to her laptop screen. She had needed a base on Scilly and had found the perfect spot: a room above a net loft next to the café.

The neglected space had been used by Elspeth for storing junk but was now a bright and cosy office with an upgraded WiFi package and Lily's own dedicated landline. It might not have a view over the London skyline, but the vista over the sparkling channel to Tresco more than made up for that.

Morven moved, hovering behind Lily's shoulder while she opened the page of a Cornish newspaper site. The headline read: SCILLY LOVES LILY? Under it were several grainy shots of her and Sam on Tean Porth. She was in a bikini and he was in board shorts. One showed her emerging from the sea, pulling a face; another showed Sam lifting her into the air above a wave. Lily groaned. The worst was a shot of them locked in a passionate embrace.

'Ewww,' Morven said, holding her phone away from her in case she might be infected by a deadly disease. 'That's disgusting.'

'Thanks,' Lily muttered, more worried about the gurning expression captured on her face when she'd run out of the sea. 'How do they get these shots? And why? Who really cares?'

'It's clickbait,' Morven said. 'It makes people look at the gross ads.'

Lily sighed, scrolling past banners for revolting diets, miracle cures for wrinkles and fake pictures of celebs looking like wizened goblins. The online world was as hideous as ever.

'You're on a few other sites too,' Morven declared with relish.

'I don't think I can take any more,' Lily sighed. Sam was on Stark, looking after a full house of visitors with the help of the chef and housekeeper. Lily was going over to stay with him in the flat that evening.

'I guess Sam has no idea about this?' she said to Morven.

'No way. He doesn't look online unless he's searching for something specific for work. Shall I get on the radio and tell him?' Morven's voice lifted hopefully as she scented a chance to ramp up the drama.

'No! No, don't bother him. He'll have his hands full with the guests. I'll break it to him later when I go over. Thanks for letting me know.'

Morven grinned. 'You're welcome!'

She skipped down the stairs that led to the courtyard between the café and her annexe. It was a challenge for Lily, shuttling between the islands and London, but gradually she was working towards a balance of spending one week in London and three on the islands.

Whether that was sustainable in the long term was an unknown, but Sam couldn't leave Stark just yet.

As the season drew towards its close, the cottages were almost fully booked for the two Crafty Scilly weeks with local makers – helped by a special guest appearance from Lily herself. With classes in watercolour and creative writing already scheduled, and wellness breaks planned for the following spring, there would be enough to tempt new visitors and keep old ones returning.

Lily was also going to speak at The Natural Balance, a four-day break where corporate executives could come to de-stress, enjoy nature, lean in to being 'unplugged' and learn about new techniques for promoting work–life balance – for their employees as well as themselves.

Together, their efforts were enough to have guaranteed

bookings in place for the quieter times of year. Over the bleakest part of the winter, when transport to the isles became more difficult, Sam was going to take an extended break in London with Lily. That was only a month away and she couldn't wait.

No one ever said it was going to be easy, but Lily loved a challenge and her reward was to be blissfully happy in a way she'd never thought possible.

Sam had called Rhiannon and said he wasn't going to visit her, but they'd had a brief conversation and he'd told Lily that she seemed happy and had accepted a promotion to another hospital in Australia. Lily would never know what she had really wanted by sending the letter but she was happy that Rhiannon, like Lily and Sam, had a fresh start to look forward to.

With a sigh, she closed down the latest gossip site and started a Zoom with Richie.

His face appeared and instead of being greeted with his trademark grin, he seemed twitchy, fiddling with his pen and looking anxious.

'Is everything OK?' she asked.

'Yes. Yes . . . I have some news.'

'Oh?' A horrible thought struck her. 'Don't say you've been offered another job?'

'No! Oh God, no, I'll never leave you.' He let out a breath and a smile crept onto his face. 'Let's just say, you're going to need a hat, bab.'

'What?' Lily processed the meaning of his words. 'No! You're getting married? Oh, I am so happy for you.'

Lily's eyes stung with unshed tears. Richie was glowing with happiness.

'I've wanted to ask him for ages but I was scared of him saying no. When I got the promotion, it gave me the push I needed. So I popped the question after we'd been to a Harry Styles concert and the gorgeous man said yes!'

'Of course he said yes. He's lucky to have you.' Lily sighed with happiness. 'I wish I could give you a hug through the screen.' She held out her hands.

Richie held out his and blew her an air kiss. 'You can when you get back.'

'What does your nanna have to say about it all?'

'I had to make sure my mum was there in case she had a funny turn. She was speechless and, believe me, that's not a family trait!'

Lily arched an eyebrow. 'You don't say?'

He grinned. 'We're so happy – I want everyone to be happy. Oh, I keep going around the office with a huge smile on my face. Now I've told you, I can share it with everyone else.'

After a few more minutes hearing about the proposal, Lily ended the Zoom. She was meeting up later with Penny and a number of the makers and artists from the craft fair who'd expressed an interest in being part of the Lily Loves Scilly collection that she wanted to sell from her website.

Cockahoop were also very interested in stocking it but Lily knew the key was to take things slowly, make sure everyone was happy with the set-up. She didn't want anyone to feel they were compromising their independence and individuality.

She got up, deciding that after Richie's momentous news, she needed a coffee – and possibly some cake – to help her recover before she went back to work.

In the sunshine, a few customers were sitting at the tables enjoying their food, when Morven emerged with a tray to clear away.

Lily was about to go into the café when Morven shrieked and the tray fell onto the terrace with a clatter that made one man spill his cappuccino over his lap.

'Dad!'

Morven ran towards a pony-tailed man who was wheeling a suitcase down the path from the quay. Even if Lily hadn't known who Nathan Teague was, she'd instantly have guessed he was related to Sam.

'Hello, sweetheart.' Nate folded her in his arms.

Elspeth walked onto the terrace, her hands dusty with flour. 'Nathan! It's so good to see you! Come inside.'

Morven broke away from Nate, still holding his hand. 'This is my dad!' she announced to Lily. 'You were in London when he came back before so you have to come and meet him now.'

'Pleased to meet you,' Lily said, deeply touched that Morven was so keen for them to meet. Sam had told her that when Nate had come home as promised, earlier in the summer, he'd finally reached a decision.

'Hi there. You're the famous Lily,' he said, giving her a warm handshake.

'Dad's back for good this time,' Morven said.

After Nate's previous visit, he'd gone back to LA, given

his notice and packed up his life there. Grady wasn't part of the plan any longer, much to everyone's relief. He'd told his daughter – and Sam – that it wasn't working out with his girl-friend and never would because anyone who wasn't willing to accept the most important person in his life wasn't for him.

This had raised him several notches in Lily's estimation and must have delighted Morven.

Nate put his arm around his daughter. 'I am and I've got a lot to catch up on. Morven's told me about your offer of a bursary, Lily?'

'Yes, and I'm so happy she's accepted it and that she's applying to Falmouth.'

'It's very generous of you,' he said, still with his arm around Morven. 'Isn't it?'

'Yes,' Morven said, shyly.

'She's so talented,' Elspeth said proudly.

'And she'll be the pioneer for what I hope will be an annual Lily Loves student bursary,' Lily added. 'A real trailblazer.'

'I always knew it!' Elspeth declared and Nate smiled at Lily.

Morven's cheeks went suspiciously pink. 'Shall we go inside, Dad?' she said, a little desperately.

'I'll see you in a while.' Lily was keen for the three of them to have a private catch-up. She watched them all walk into the café and decided to leave her coffee. It was the second time that morning that she'd had to bite back tears. But that was OK. It was OK to be human, to feel happiness – the whole spectrum of emotions.

She'd finally heeded the message that she should be kinder to herself by not always trying to be perfect.

Nate and Morven emerged from the café after a while and rejoined Lily before they all headed to Stark to see Sam. Morven took the helm, guided by Nate, who knew the waters almost as well as his brother.

Sam was waiting at the jetty and Lily spotted several guests were lounging in front of their cottages or wandering along the paths.

'We'll have to be quiet, though,' he said, possibly for Morven's benefit. 'The guests are relaxing.'

'I still can't believe what you've achieved here,' said Nate. 'I should have been here.'

'I didn't do it on my own. Aaron and the lads were incredible – and Lily, of course.' Sam winked at her. 'Morven's added her own creative touch and has been helping with the changeovers when she can.'

Morven grinned. 'I'll be too busy when I'm at uni next year,' she said.

'I know I've been no use until now, but I'll be here to lend a hand if I can,' Nate said. 'I've just negotiated a freelance contract with my old company in Exeter. They're doing well and with my US experience, I can charge them more. I could invest in the retreat, if you like, but it's your baby.'

'It's still ours jointly,' Sam said, fair-minded as always.

'Only in name. You put in all the work, took on all the responsibility, just as you always have. I'll never be able to repay you for looking after Morven and I want you to reap the rewards from Stark.'

'We'll talk about it some more,' Sam said, looking embarrassed. 'Another time.'

'Bro, I don't want anything from it. I'm doing pretty well myself.' Nate sounded resolute, so Sam nodded.

After Nate had taken Morven back to Hell Bay, Lily helped Sam with the dinner and bar service.

It was almost midnight by the time they got to bed but Lily wasn't tired.

Finally, she decided to tell Sam about their appearance on the local news site.

'Someone must have seen us on the beach yesterday and taken some photos. Look.'

He rolled his eyes. 'They don't waste much time. I can't believe people can be bothered to take so many photos of two ordinary people. Shall we go for a walk and unwind? Today's been a pretty big one and I don't feel like sleeping yet.'

'To Tean Porth?'

'Great idea.'

They collected blankets and walked down the hill, hand in hand, towards the beach. The full moon made a torch unnecessary and the night was mild and balmy.

They sat on the beach, watching the moon paint a shimmering path over the ocean. Sam's arm tightened comfortingly around her back. Life could not get much better than this, thought Lily.

'It's a good job we found each other,' he said. 'If you hadn't been forced to stay at my half-built retreat, I might have stayed in my miserable hole forever, always regretting what I'd lost instead of embracing happiness again.'

'Wow.' Lily stared at him in mock-horror. 'That sounds dangerously like Sam saying he's glad he decided to reach out to someone and accept help.'

'I am glad I did. I've learned that – and I hate to use a cliché – we all need to accept help.' He took her hand. 'And be brave enough to let someone else into our lives.'

She brushed his lips with hers. 'I was as much an island as you were, repelling all invaders.' That drew a smile from him. 'I didn't dare hand over control of any tiny part of my life in case it fell apart completely. I'm so glad I came to Stark, however much I hated it at first. It's scary to think it took nearly dying to change my life.'

She shivered again, but Sam folded her in his arms. 'Don't look back. Look forward. And, you know . . .' He hesitated, looking so intently at Lily that she felt a delicious thrill run through her from head to toe. 'If you want to, we could give those gossip sites something *really* big to write about . . .'

Now it was Lily's turn to search his face. 'What – what do you mean?'

Sam closed his warm hand around hers. 'We could give them the story they want: the happy ending.'

She held her breath for a moment, hardly daring to believe what he was saying.

But then he started speaking again, making the impossible breathtakingly real by getting down on one knee and gazing up into her face.

'Lily,' he said, 'Will you marry me?'

'*Marry* you?'

'Well, I don't see anyone else here,' he said, finally rising to his feet. 'What do you think? Is it too soon? Or should we seize this moment?'

For the third time that day, Lily felt tears prickling the back of her eyes and this time she didn't try to stop them.

'I think – I think . . . that is the best idea I've ever heard, and I might have to kiss you.'

She closed her eyes and their mouths met in one unforgettable moment when Lily thought she might actually take off into the sky. Still kissing Sam, she opened her eyes briefly and, high in the night sky, she saw a streak of light – a shooting star that might just be Cara telling her it was OK to be happy again.

Acknowledgements

Second Chance Summer marks a fresh start for me as much as for the characters.

Last year my husband surprised me with an Easter trip to the Isles of Scilly. I was mulling over the idea for this novel, when I glimpsed the now uninhabited isle of Samson.

It seemed the perfect inspiration for my first book with Penguin/Century and I'd like to say thank you to Katie Loughnane, Jess Muscio, Sarah Ridley, Issie Levin, Lynn Curtis and the fantastic Century team at Penguin Random House for their support – and for the cream tea, which I'm hoping will be an annual event. Just make sure it's jam first . . .

Talking of Scilly, while I have used *some* real place names, all the characters, businesses and Stark Island itself come completely from my imagination. I've also tried to give a realistic idea of getting to and fro around the islands; however these days you *can* reach Scilly on a Sunday from the mainland.

Before I finish, there are some other important people I want to thank. What would I do without the support of the Friday Floras, the Coffee Crew and the Party People who are always there for me? Thank you, all. Special thanks also go to my best mate and ace bookseller, Janice Hume, and to my agent, Broo Doherty.

As always, all my love goes to my parents, Charlotte, James and John for supporting me throughout my writing and publishing journey, no matter what. Love you. xx

Loved

Second Chance Summer?

Pre-order

Escape for Christmas

Coming November 2024

Sign up to

Phillipa Ashley's

newsletter for all the latest news, exclusives and giveaways!

www.penguin.co.uk/authors/298314/phillipa-ashley